The
GIVER
of
STARS

ALSO BY JOJO MOYES

★

Still Me

Paris for One and Other Stories

After You

One Plus One

The Girl You Left Behind

Me Before You

The Last Letter from Your Lover

The Horse Dancer

Silver Bay

The Ship of Brides

The Peacock Emporium

The
GIVER
of
STARS

JOJO MOYES

PAMELA DORMAN BOOKS · VIKING

VIKING
An imprint of Penguin Random House LLC
penguinrandomhouse.com

Grateful acknowledgment is made to the following for permission to
reprint previously published material:

Excerpt from the September/October 1937 issue of *The Furrow* used with
permission of John Deere's *The Furrow* magazine. All worldwide rights reserved.

Excerpt from "Introduction" by John C. Hennen, copyright © 2008
by John C. Hennen. Originally published in *Harlan Miner Speaks: Report on Terrorism
in the Kentucky Coal Fields* by the University Press of Kentucky. Reprinted with
permission of the University Press of Kentucky.

Excerpt from "'To Have, Hold, Develop, and Defend': Natural Rights and
the Movement to Abolish Strip Mining in Eastern Kentucky" as published in the
Journal of Appalachian Studies Vol. 11, No. 1/2 by Chad Montrie,
(https://www.jstor.org/stable/41446655). Used with permission of the author.

Excerpts from the *WPA Guide to Kentucky* edited by F. Kevin Simon copyright © 1939
by the University of Kentucky, reprinted with permission of University Press of Kentucky.

A Pamela Dorman Book/Viking

LIBRARY OF CONGRESS CATALOGING-IN-PUBLICATION DATA

Names: Moyes, Jojo, 1969– author.
Title: The giver of stars / Jojo Moyes.
Description: [New York] : Pamela Dorman Books/Viking, [2019]
Identifiers: LCCN 2019030049 (print) | LCCN 2019030050 (ebook) |
ISBN 9780399562488 (hardcover) | ISBN 9780399562501 (ebook) |
ISBN 9781984879394 (export edition)
Subjects: GSAFD: Love stories.
Classification: LCC PR6113.O94 G59 2019 (print) |
LCC PR6113.O94 (ebook) | DDC 823/.92—dc23
LC record available at https://lccn.loc.gov/2019030049
LC ebook record available at https://lccn.loc.gov/2019030050

Printed in the United States of America
5   7   9   10   8   6   4

Designed by Amanda Dewey

This is a work of fiction based on actual events.

To Barbara Napier,
who gave me stars when I needed them.

And to librarians everywhere.

The
GIVER
of
STARS

PROLOGUE

December 20, 1937

Listen. Three miles deep in the forest just below Arnott's Ridge, and you're in silence so dense it's like you're wading through it. There's no birdsong past dawn, not even in high summer, and especially not now, with the chill air so thick with moisture that it stills those few leaves clinging gamely to the branches. Among the oak and hickory nothing stirs: wild animals are deep underground, soft pelts intertwined in narrow caves or hollowed-out trunks. The snow is so deep the mule's legs disappear up to his hocks, and every few strides he staggers and snorts suspiciously, checking for loose flints and holes under the endless white. Only the narrow creek below moves confidently, its clear water murmuring and bubbling over the stony bed, headed down toward an endpoint nobody around here has ever seen.

Margery O'Hare tests her toes inside her boots, but feeling went a long time back and she winces at the thought of how they're going to hurt when they warm up again. Three pairs of wool stockings, and in this weather you might as well go bare-legged. She strokes the big mule's neck, brushing off the crystals forming on his dense coat with her heavy men's gloves.

"Extra food for you tonight, Charley boy," she says, and watches as his huge ears flick back. She shifts, adjusting the saddlebags, making sure the mule is balanced as they pick their way down toward the creek. "Hot molasses in your supper. Might even have some myself."

Four more miles, she thinks, wishing she had eaten more breakfast. Past the Indian escarpment, up the yellow pine track, two more hollers, and old Nancy will appear, singing hymns as she always does, her clear, strong voice echoing through the forest as she walks, arms swinging like a child's, to meet her.

"You don't have to walk five miles to meet me," she tells the woman, every fortnight. "That's our job. That's why we're on horseback."

"Oh, you girls do enough."

She knows the real reason. Nancy, like her bedbound sister, Jean, back in the tiny log cabin at Red Lick, cannot countenance even a chance that she will miss the next tranche of stories. She's sixty-four years old with three good teeth and a sucker for a handsome cowboy: "That Mack McGuire, he makes my heart flutter like a clean sheet on a long line." She clasps her hands and lifts her eyes to Heaven. "The way Archer writes him, well, it's like he steps right out of the pages in that book and swings me onto his horse with him." She leans forward conspiratorially. "Ain't just that horse I'd be happy riding. My husband said I had quite the seat when I was a girl!"

"I don't doubt it, Nancy," she responds, every time, and the woman bursts out laughing, slapping her thighs like this is the first time she's said it.

A twig cracks and Charley's ears flick. Ears that size, he can probably hear halfway to Louisville. "This way, boy," she says, guiding him away from a rocky outcrop. "You'll hear her in a minute."

"Goin' somewhere?"

Margery's head snaps around.

He is staggering slightly, but his gaze is level and direct. His rifle, she sees, is cocked, and he carries it, like a fool, with his finger on the trigger. "So you'll look at me now, will ya, Margery?"

She keeps her voice steady, her mind racing. "I see you, Clem McCullough."

"*I see you, Clem McCullough.*" He spits as he repeats it, like a nasty child in a schoolyard. His hair stands up on one side, like he's slept on it. "You see me while you're lookin' down that nose of yours. You see me like you see dirt on your shoe. Like you're somethin' special."

She has never been afraid of much, but she's familiar enough with these mountain men to know not to pick a fight with a drunk. Especially one bearing a loaded gun.

She conducts a swift mental list of people she may have offended—Lord knows there seem to be a few—but McCullough? Aside from the obvious, she can find nothing.

"Any beef your family had with my daddy, that's buried with him. It's only me left, and I ain't interested in blood feuds."

McCullough is directly in her path now, his legs braced in the snow, his finger still on the trigger. His skin has the purple-blue mottle of someone too drunk to realize how cold he is. Probably too drunk to hit straight, but it's not a chance she wants to take.

She adjusts her weight, slowing the mule; her gaze slides sideways. The banks of the creek are too steep, too dense with trees for her to get past. She would have to persuade him to move or ride right over him, and the temptation to do the latter is strong.

The mule's ears flick back. In the silence she can hear her own heartbeat, an insistent thump in her ears. She thinks absently that she's not sure she's ever heard it this loud before. "Just doing my job, Mr. McCullough. I'd be obliged if you'd let me pass."

He frowns, hears the potential insult in her too-polite use of his name, and as he shifts his gun she realizes her error.

"Your *job* . . . Think you're so high and mighty. You know what you need?"

He spits noisily, waiting for her answer. "I said, do you know what you need, girl?"

"Suspect my version of what that might be is going to differ a mile or two from yours."

"Oh, you got all the answers. You think we don't know what you all have been doing? You think we don't know what you've been spreading among decent God-fearing women? We know what you're up to. You got the devil in you, Margery O'Hare, and there's only one way to get the devil out of a girl like you."

"Well, I'd sure love to stop and find out, but I'm busy with my rounds, so maybe we can continue this—"

"Shut up!"

McCullough raises his gun. "Shut that damn mouth of yours."

She clamps it shut.

He takes two steps closer, his legs spread and braced. "Git off the mule."

Charley shifts uneasily. Her heart is an ice pebble in her mouth. If she turns and flees, he'll shoot her. The only route here follows the creek; the forest floor is hardscrabble flint, the trees too dense to find a way forward. There's nobody for miles, she realizes, nobody except old Nancy making her way slowly across the mountaintop.

She's on her own, and he knows it.

His voice lowers. "I said git down, *now*." He takes two steps closer, his footsteps crunching in the snow.

And there is the bare truth of it, for her and all the women around here. Doesn't matter how smart you are, how clever, how self-reliant—you can always be bettered by a stupid man with a gun. The barrel of his rifle is so close now that she finds herself gazing down two infinite black holes. With a grunt he drops it abruptly, letting it swing behind him on its strap and grabs at her reins. The mule wheels, so that she lurches forward clumsily onto his neck. She feels McCullough claw at her thigh as he reaches back for his gun with his other hand. His breath is sour with drink, and his hand is scaled with dirt; every cell of her body recoils at the feel of it.

And then she hears it, Nancy's voice in the distance.

Oh, what peace we often forfeit!
Oh, what needless pain we bear—

His head lifts. She hears a *No!*, and some distant part of her recognizes with surprise that it has emerged from her own mouth. His fingers grab and pull at her, one arm reaching for her waist, throwing her off-balance; in his determined grip, his rank breath, she feels her future morphing into something black and awful. But the cold has made him clumsy. He fumbles as he reaches for his gun again, his back to her, and at that moment she sees her chance. She reaches behind into her saddlebag with her left hand, and as he turns his head she drops the reins, grabs the other corner with her right fist, and swings the heavy book as hard as she can, *smack*, into his face. His gun goes off, the sound a three-dimensional *crack!* ricocheting off the trees, and she hears the singing briefly silenced, the birds rising into the sky—a shimmering black cloud of flapping wings. As McCullough drops, the mule bucks and lurches forward in fright, stumbling over him, so that she gasps and has to grab the horn of the saddle to stay on.

And then she is off along the creek bed, her breath tight in her throat, her heart pounding, trusting the mule's sure feet to find a hold in the splashing icy water, not daring to look back to see if McCullough has made it to his feet to come after her.

ONE

Three months earlier

It was, everyone agreed, fanning themselves outside the store or passing in the shade of the eucalyptus trees, unseasonably warm for September. The meeting hall at Baileyville was thick with the smells of lye soap and stale perfume, bodies wedged together in good poplin dresses and summer suits. The heat had permeated even the clapboard walls so that the wood creaked and sighed in protest. Pressed tight behind Bennett as he shuffled his way along the row of packed seats, apologizing as each person rose from their chair with a barely suppressed sigh, Alice swore that she felt the warmth of each body leach into her own as it leaned backward to let them pass.

So sorry. So sorry.

Bennett finally reached two empty seats and Alice, her cheeks glowing with embarrassment, sat down, ignoring the sideways glances of the people around them. Bennett looked down at his lapel, brushing at non-existent lint, then spotted her skirt. "You didn't change?" he murmured.

"You said we were late."

"I didn't mean for you to come out with your house clothes on."

She had been trying to make cottage pie, to encourage Annie to put something other than Southern food on the table. But the potatoes had gone green, she hadn't been able to gauge the heat of the range, and the grease had spattered all over her when she dropped the meat onto the griddle. And when Bennett came in looking for her (she had, of course, lost track of time) he could not for the life of him see why she wouldn't just leave culinary matters to the housekeeper when an important meeting was about to take place.

Alice placed her hand over the largest grease mark on her skirt and resolved to keep it there for the next hour. Because it would be an hour. Or two. Or—Lord help her—three.

Church and meetings. Meetings and church. Sometimes Alice Van Cleve felt as if she had merely swapped one tedious daily pastime for another. That very morning in church Pastor McIntosh had spent almost two hours declaiming the sinners who were apparently plotting ungodly dominance around the little town, and was now fanning himself and looking disturbingly ready to speak again.

"Put your shoes back on," Bennett murmured. "Someone might see you."

"It's this heat," she said. "They're English feet. They're not used to these temperatures." She felt, rather than saw, her husband's weary disapproval. But she was too hot and tired to care, and the speaker's voice had a narcoleptic quality so that she caught only every third word or so—*germinating . . . pods . . . chaff . . . paper bags*—and found it hard to care much about the rest.

Married life, she had been told, would be an adventure. Travel to a new land! She had married an American, after all. New food! A new culture! New experiences! She had pictured herself in New York, neat in a two-piece suit in bustling restaurants and on crowded sidewalks. She would write home, boasting of her new experiences. *Oh, Alice Wright? Wasn't she the one who married the gorgeous American? Yes, I had a postcard from her—she was at the Metropolitan Opera, or Carnegie Hall . . .*

Nobody had warned that it would involve so much small-talk over good china with elderly aunts, so much pointless mending and quilting or, even worse, so many deathly dull sermons. Endless, decades-long sermons and meetings. Oh, but these men did love the sound of their own voices! She felt as if she were being scolded for hours, four times a week.

The Van Cleves had stopped at no fewer than thirteen churches on their way back here, and the only sermon that Alice enjoyed had taken place in Charleston, where the preacher had gone on so long his congregation had lost patience and decided, as one, to "sing him down"—to drown him out with song until he got the message and rather crossly closed his religious shop for the day. His vain attempts to speak over them, as their voices rose and swelled determinedly, had made her giggle.

The congregations of Baileyville, Kentucky, she had observed, seemed disappointingly rapt.

"Just put them back on, Alice. Please."

She caught the eye of Mrs. Schmidt, in whose parlor she had taken tea two weeks previously, and looked to the front again, trying not to appear *too* friendly in case she invited her a second time.

"Well, thank you, Hank, for that advice on seed storage. I'm sure you've given us a lot to think about."

As Alice slid her feet into her shoes, the pastor added, "Oh, no, don't get up, ladies and gentlemen. Mrs. Brady has asked for a moment of your time."

Alice, now wise to this phrase, slid off her shoes again. A short middle-aged woman moved to the front—the kind her father would have described as "well upholstered," with the firm padding and solid curves one associated with a quality sofa.

"It's about the mobile library," she said, wafting her neck with a white fan and adjusting her hat. "There have been *developments* that I would like to bring to your attention.

"We are all aware of the—uh—*devastating* effects the Depression has had on this great country. So much attention has been focused on survival that many other elements of our lives have had to take a backseat. Some of you may be aware of President and Mrs. Roosevelt's *formidable* efforts to restore attention to literacy and learning. Well, earlier this week I was privileged to attend a tea with Mrs. Lena Nof-cier, chairman of the Library Service for the Kentucky PTA, and she told us that, as part of it, the Works Progress Administration has insti-tuted a system of mobile libraries in several states—and even a couple here in Kentucky. Some of you may have heard about the library they set up over in Harlan County. Yes? Well, it has proven *immensely* suc-cessful. Under the auspices of Mrs. Roosevelt herself and the WPA—"

"She's an Episcopalian."

"What?"

"Roosevelt. She's an Episcopalian."

Mrs. Brady's cheek twitched. "Well, we won't hold that against her. She's our First Lady and she is minding to do great things for our country."

"She should be minding to know her place, not stirring things up everywhere." A jowly man in a pale linen suit shook his head and gazed around him, seeking agreement.

Across the way, Peggy Foreman leaned forward to adjust her skirt at precisely the moment Alice noticed her, which made it seem that Alice had been staring at her. Peggy scowled and lifted her tiny nose into the air, then muttered something to the girl beside her, who leaned forward to give Alice the same unfriendly look. Alice sat back in her seat, trying to quell the color rising in her cheeks.

Alice, you're not going to settle in unless you make some friends, Bennett kept telling her, as if she could sway Peggy Foreman and her crew of sour faces.

"Your sweetheart is casting spells in my direction again," Alice murmured.

"She's not my sweetheart."

"Well, she thought she was."

"I told you. We were just kids. I met you, and . . . well, that's all history."

"I wish you'd tell her that."

He leaned toward her. "Alice, the way you keep hanging back, people are starting to think you're kind of—stand-offish . . . "

"I'm English, Bennett. We're not built to be . . . *hospitable*."

"I just think the more you get involved, the better it is for both of us. Pop thinks so, too."

"Oh. He does, does he?"

"Don't be like that."

Mrs. Brady shot them a look. "As I was saying, due to the success of such endeavors in neighboring states, the WPA has released funds to enable us to create our own traveling library here in Lee County."

Alice stifled a yawn.

On the credenza at home there was a photograph of Bennett in his baseball uniform. He had just hit a home run, and his face held a look of peculiar intensity and joy, as if at that moment he were experiencing something transcendent. She wished he would look at her like that again.

But when she allowed herself to think about it, Alice Van Cleve realized her marriage had been the culmination of a series of random events, starting with a broken china dog when she and Jenny Fitzwalter had played a game of indoor badminton (it had been raining—what else were they supposed to do?), escalating with the loss of her place at secretarial school due to persistent lateness, and finally her apparently unseemly outburst at her father's boss during Christmas drinks. ("But he put his hand on my bottom while I was handing around the vol-au-vents!" Alice protested. "Don't be vulgar, Alice," her mother said, shuddering.) These three events—with an incident involving her brother Gideon's friends, too much rum punch, and a ruined carpet (she hadn't realized the punch contained alcohol! Nobody said!)—had caused her parents to suggest what they called a "period of reflection," which had amounted to "keeping Alice indoors." She had heard them talking in the kitchen: "She's always been that way. She's like your aunt Harriet," Father had said dismissively, and Mother had not spoken to him for two whole days, as if the idea of Alice being the product of her genetic line had been so unbearably offensive.

And so, over the long winter, as Gideon went to endless balls and cocktail parties, disappeared for long weekends at friends' houses, or partied in London, she gradually fell off her friends' invitation lists, and sat at home, working half-heartedly at scrappy embroidery, her only outings accompanying her mother on visits to elderly relatives or to Women's Institute gatherings, where the subjects for discussion tended to be cake, flower-arranging and *Lives of the Saints*—it was as if they were literally trying to *bore* her to death. She stopped asking Gideon for details after a while as they made her feel worse. Instead she sulked her way through canasta, cheated grumpily at Monopoly, and sat at the kitchen table with her face resting on her forearms as she listened to the wireless, which promised a world far beyond the stifling concerns of her own.

So two months later, when Bennett Van Cleve turned up unexpectedly one Sunday afternoon at the minister's spring festival—with his American accent, his square jaw and blond hair, carrying with him the scents of a world a million miles from Surrey—frankly he could have been the Hunchback of Notre Dame and she would have agreed that moving into a clanging bell-tower was a very fine idea indeed, thank you.

Men tended to stare at Alice, and Bennett was immediately smitten by the elegant young Englishwoman with huge eyes and waved, bobbed blonde hair, whose clear, clipped voice was like nothing he'd ever heard back in Lexington, and who, his father remarked, might as well be a British princess for her exquisite manners and refined way of lifting a teacup. When Alice's mother revealed that they could claim a duchess in the family through marriage two generations back, the older Van Cleve almost expired with joy. "A duchess? A royal duchess? Oh, Bennett, wouldn't that have tickled your dear mother?"

Father and son were visiting Europe with an outreach mission of the Combined Ministry of East Kentucky Under God, observing how the faithful worshipped outside America. Mr. Van Cleve had funded several of the attendees, in honor of his late wife, Dolores, as he was prone to announcing during lulls in conversation. He might be a businessman, but it meant nothing, *nothing*, if it was not done under the auspices of the Lord. Alice thought he seemed a little dismayed by the small and rather un-fervent expressions of religious fervor at St. Mary's on the Common—and the congregation had certainly been taken aback by Pastor McIntosh's ebullient roaring about fire and brimstone (poor Mrs. Arbuthnot had had to be escorted through a side door for air). But what the British lacked in piety, Mr. Van Cleve observed, they more than made up for with their churches, their cathedrals and all their *history. And wasn't that a spiritual experience in itself?*

Alice and Bennett, meanwhile, were busy with their own, slightly less holy experience. They parted with clutched hands and ardent expressions of affection, the kind heightened by the prospect of imminent separation. They exchanged letters during his stops at Rheims, Barcelona and Madrid. Their exchanges reached a particularly feverish pitch when he reached Rome, and on the way back it was a surprise only to the most disengaged members of the household that Bennett proposed, and Alice, with the alacrity of a bird seeing its cage door swing open, hesitated a whole half-second before she said yes, she would, to her now lovelorn—and rather deliciously tanned—American. Who wouldn't say yes to a handsome, square-jawed man, who looked at her as if she were made of spun silk? Everyone else had spent the past months looking at her as if she were contaminated.

"Why, you are just perfect," Bennett would tell her, holding his thumb and forefinger around her narrow wrist as they sat on the swing seat in her parents' garden, collars up against the breeze and their fathers watched indulgently from the library window, both, for their own reasons, privately relieved about the match. "You're so delicate and refined. Like a Thoroughbred." He pronounced it *"refahnd."*

"And you're ridiculously handsome. Like a movie star."

"Mother would have loved you." He ran a finger down her cheek. "You're like a china doll."

Six months on, Alice was pretty sure he didn't think of her as a china doll any more.

They had married swiftly, explaining the haste as Mr. Van Cleve's need to return to his business. Alice felt as if her whole world had flipped; she was as happy and giddy as she had been despondent through the long winter. Her mother packed her trunk with the same faintly indecent delight with which she had told everyone in her circle about Alice's lovely American husband and his rich industrialist father. It might have been nice if she'd looked a tiny bit mournful at the thought of her only daughter moving to a part of America nobody she knew had ever visited. But, then, Alice had probably been equally eager to go. Only her brother was openly sad, and she was pretty sure he would recover with his next weekend away. "I'll come and see you, of course," Gideon said. They both knew he wouldn't.

Bennett and Alice's honeymoon consisted of a five-day voyage back to the United States, then onward by road from New York to Kentucky. (She had looked Kentucky up in the encyclopedia and been quite taken with all the horse-racing. It sounded like a year-long Derby Day.) She squealed with excitement at everything: their huge car, the size of the enormous ocean liner, the diamond pendant Bennett bought her as a gift from a store in London's Burlington Arcade. She didn't mind Mr. Van Cleve accompanying them the entire journey. It would, after all, have been rude to leave the older man alone, and she was too overcome with excitement at the idea of leaving Surrey, with its silent Sunday drawing rooms and permanent atmosphere of disapproval, to mind.

If Alice felt a vague dissatisfaction with the way Mr. Van Cleve stuck to them like a limpet, she smothered it, doing her best to be the delightful version of herself that the two men seemed to expect. On the liner between Southampton and New York she and Bennett at least managed to stroll the decks alone in the hours after supper while his father was working on his business papers or talking to the elders at the captain's table. Bennett's strong arm would pull her close, and she would hold up her left hand with its shiny new gold band, and wonder at the fact that she, Alice, was *a married woman*. And when they were back in Kentucky, she told herself, she would be *properly* married, as the three of them would no longer have to share a cabin, curtained off as it was.

"It's not quite the trousseau I had in mind," she whispered, in her undershirt and pajama bottoms. She didn't feel comfortable in less, after Mr. Van Cleve senior had, in his half-asleep state one night, confused the curtain of their double bunk with that of the bathroom door.

Bennett kissed her forehead. "It wouldn't feel right with Father so close by, anyway," he whispered back. He placed the long bolster between them ("Else I might not be able to control myself") and they lay side by side, hands held chastely in the dark, breathing audibly as the huge ship vibrated beneath them.

When she looked back, the long trip was suffused with her suppressed longing, with furtive kisses behind lifeboats, her imagination racing as the sea rose and fell beneath them. "You're so pretty. It will all be different when we get home," he would murmur into her ear, and she would gaze at his beautiful sculpted face and bury her face in his sweet-smelling neck, wondering how much longer she could bear it.

And then, after the endless car journey, and the stopovers with this minister and that pastor the whole way from New York to Kentucky, Bennett had announced that they would not be living in Lexington, as she had assumed, but in a small town some way further south. They drove past the city and kept going until the roads narrowed and grew dusty, and the buildings sat sparsely in random groupings, overshadowed by vast tree-covered mountains. It was fine, she assured him, hiding her disappointment at the sight of Baileyville's main street, with its handful of brick buildings and narrow roads that stretched to nowhere. She was quite fond of the countryside. And they could take trips to town, like her mother did to Simpson's in the Strand, couldn't they? She struggled to be equally sanguine at the discovery that, for the first year at least, they would be living with Mr. Van Cleve ("I can't leave Father alone while he's grieving Mother. Not just yet, anyway. Don't look so dismayed, sweetheart. It's the second largest house in town. And we'll have our own room.") And then once they were finally in that room, of course, things had gone awry in a way she wasn't sure she even had the words to explain.

. . .

With the same gritting of teeth with which she had endured board-
ing school and Pony Club, Alice attempted to adjust to life in the
small Kentucky town. It was *quite* the cultural shift. She could detect,
if she tried hard, a certain rugged beauty in the landscape, with its
huge skies, its empty roads and shifting light, its mountains among
whose thousands of trees wandered actual wild bears, and whose treetops were skimmed by eagles. She was awed at the size of everything,
the vast distances that felt ever-present, as if she had had to adjust her
whole perspective. But, in truth, she wrote, in her weekly letters to
Gideon, everything else was pretty much impossible.

She found life in the big white house stifling, although Annie, the
near silent housekeeper, relieved her of most household duties. It was
indeed one of the largest in town but was stuffed with heavy antique
furniture, every surface covered with the late Mrs. Van Cleve's photographs or ornaments or a variety of unblinking porcelain dolls that
each man would remark was "Mother's favorite," should Alice attempt
to move them an inch. Mrs. Van Cleve's exacting, pious influence
hung over the house like a shroud.

Mother wouldn't have liked the bolsters positioned like that, would she,
Bennett?

Oh, no. Mother had very strong opinions on soft furnishings.

Mother did love her embroidered psalms. Why, didn't Pastor McIntosh
say he didn't know a woman in the whole of Kentucky whose blanket stitch
was finer?

She found Mr. Van Cleve's constant presence overbearing; he decided what they did, what they ate, the very routines of their day. He
couldn't stand to be away from whatever was going on, even if it was
just she and Bennett playing the gramophone in their room and would
burst in unannounced: "Is it music we're having now, huh? Oh, you
should put on some Bill Monroe. You can't beat ole Bill. Go on, boy,
take off that racket and put some ole Bill on."

If he'd had a glass or two of bourbon, those pronouncements would come thick and fast, and Annie would find reasons to lurk in the kitchen before he could rile himself and find fault with dinner. He was just grieving, Bennett would murmur. You couldn't blame a man for not wanting to be alone in his head.

Bennett, she discovered swiftly, never disagreed with his father. On the few occasions she had spoken up and said, calmly, that no, actually, she'd never been a great fan of pork chops—or that she personally found jazz music rather thrilling—the two men would drop their forks and stare at her with the same shocked disapproval as if she had removed all her clothes and danced a jig on the dining table. "Why'd you have to be so contrary, Alice?" Bennett would whisper, as his father left to shout orders at Annie. She realized swiftly it was safer not to express an opinion at all.

Outside the house was little better; among the townspeople of Baileyville she was observed with the same assessing eye they turned on anything "foreign." Most people in the town were farmers; they seemed to spend their whole lives within a radius of a few miles and knew everything about one another. There were foreigners, apparently, up at Hoffman Mining, which housed some five hundred mining families from all over the globe, overseen by Mr. Van Cleve. But as most of the miners lived in the company-provided homes there, used the company-owned store, school and doctor, and were too poor to own either vehicles or horses, few ever crossed into Baileyville.

Every morning Mr. Van Cleve and Bennett would head off in Mr. Van Cleve's motor-car to the mine and return shortly after six. In between, Alice would find herself whiling away the hours in a house that wasn't hers. She tried to make friends with Annie, but the woman had let her know, through a combination of silence and overly brisk housekeeping, that she didn't intend to make conversation. Alice had offered to cook, but Annie had informed her that Mr. Van Cleve was *particular* about his diet and liked only Southern food, guessing correctly that Alice knew nothing about it.

Most households grew their own fruit and vegetables, and there were few that didn't have a pig or two or a flock of hens. There was one general store, huge sacks of flour and sugar lining the doorway, and its shelves thick with cans. And there was just the one restaurant: the Nice 'N' Quick with its green door, firm instruction that patrons *must wear shoes*, and which served things she'd never heard of, like fried green tomatoes and collard greens and things they called biscuits that were actually a cross between a dumpling and a scone. She once attempted to make some, but they emerged from the temperamental range not soft and spongy like Annie's but solid enough to clatter when dropped onto a plate (she swore Annie had jinxed them).

She had been invited to tea several times by local ladies and tried to make conversation but found she had little to say, being hopeless at quilting, which seemed to be the local preoccupation, and knowing nothing about the names they bandied around in gossip. Every tea after the first seemed obliged to begin with the story of how Alice had offered "biscuits" with her tea instead of "cookies" (the other women had found this hysterical).

In the end it was easier just to sit on the bed in her and Bennett's room and read again the few magazines she had brought from England or write Gideon yet another letter in which she tried not to reveal how unhappy she was.

She had, she realized gradually, simply traded one domestic prison for another. Some days she couldn't face another night watching Bennett's father reading scripture from the squeaking rocking chair on the porch (*God's word should be all the mental stimulation we require, wasn't that what Mother said?*), while she sat breathing in the oil-soaked rags they burned to keep the mosquitoes away and mending the worn patches in his clothes (*God hates waste—why, those pants were only four years old, Alice. Plenty of life left in them*). Alice grumbled inwardly that if God had had to sit in the near dark stitching up someone else's trousers He would probably have bought Himself a nice new pair from Arthur J. Harmon's Gentleman's Store in Lexington, but she smiled a tight smile and squinted harder at the stitches. Bennett, meanwhile, frequently wore the expression of someone who had been duped into something and couldn't quite work out what and how it had happened.

So, what the Sam Hill is a traveling library, anyway?" Alice was startled out of her reverie with a sharp nudge from Bennett's elbow.

"They got one in Mississippi, using boats," called a voice near the back of the hall.

"You won't get no boats up and down our creeks. Too shallow."

"I believe the plan is to use horses," said Mrs. Brady.

"They're gonna take horses up and down the river? Crazy talk."

The first delivery of books had come from Chicago, Mrs. Brady continued, and more were en route. There would be a wide selection of fiction, from Mark Twain to Shakespeare, and practical books containing recipes, domestic tips and help with child-rearing. There would even be comic books—a revelation that made some of the children squeal with excitement.

Alice checked her wristwatch, wondering when she would get her shaved ice. The one good thing about these meetings was that they weren't stuck in the house all evening. She was already dreading what the winters would be like, when it would be harder for them to find reasons to escape.

"What man has time to go riding? We need to be working, not paying social calls with the latest edition of *Ladies' Home Journal*." There was a low ripple of laughter.

"Tom Faraday likes to look at the ladies' undergarments in the Sears catalog, though. I heard he spends hours at a time in the outhouse reading that!"

"Mr. Porteous!"

"It's not men; it's women," came a voice.

There was a brief silence.

Alice turned to look. A woman was leaning against the back doors in a dark blue cotton coat, her sleeves rolled up. She wore leather breeches, and her boots were unpolished. She might have been in her late thirties or early forties, her face handsome and her long dark hair tied back in a cursory knot.

"It's women doing the riding. Delivering the books."

"Women?"

"By themselves?" came a man's voice.

"Last time I looked, God gave 'em two arms and two legs, just like the men."

A brief murmur rippled through the audience. Alice peered more closely, intrigued.

"Thank you, Margery. Over at Harlan County they've got six women and a whole system up and running. And, as I say, we'll be getting something similar going here. We have two librarians already, and Mr. Guisler has very kindly lent us a couple of his horses. I'd like to take this opportunity to thank him for his generosity."

Mrs. Brady motioned the younger woman forward. "Many of you will also know Miss O'Hare—"

"Oh, we know the O'Hares all right."

"Then you will be aware that she has been working these last weeks to help set things up. We also have Beth Pinker—stand up, Beth—" a freckled girl with a snub nose and dark blonde hair stood awkwardly and sat straight back down again "—who is working with Miss O'Hare. One of the many reasons I called this meeting is that we need more ladies who understand the rudiments of literature and its organization so that we can move forward with this most worthy of civic projects."

Mr. Guisler, the horse dealer, lifted a hand. He stood up and after hesitating a moment, he spoke with a quiet certainty: "Well, I think it's a fine idea. My own mother was a great reader of books, and I've offered up my old milk barn for the library. I believe all right-minded people here should be supporting it. Thank you." He sat down again.

Margery O'Hare leaned her backside against the desk at the front and gazed steadily out at the sea of faces. Alice noted a murmur of vague discontent moving around the room, and it seemed to be directed at her. She also noted that Margery O'Hare seemed supremely untroubled by it.

"We have a large county to cover," Mrs. Brady added. "We can't do it with just two girls."

A woman at the front of the hall called: "So, what would it mean? This horseback-librarian thing?"

"Well, it would involve riding to some of our more remote dwellings, and providing reading materials to those who might not otherwise be able to travel to the county libraries, due to, say, ill-health, frailty or lack of transportation." She lowered her head so that she could see over her half-moon spectacles. "I would add that this is to aid the spread of education, to help bring knowledge to those places where it might currently be sadly lacking. Our president and his wife believe this project can bring knowledge and learning back to the foreground of rural lives."

"I ain't letting my lady ride up in no mountain," came a call from the back.

"You just afraid she won't come back again, Henry Porteous?"

"You can have mine. I'd be more'n happy if she rode off and never come home!"

A burst of laughter traveled across the room.

Mrs. Brady's voice lifted in frustration. "Gentlemen. Please. I am asking for some of our ladies to contribute to our civic good and sign up. The WPA will provide the horse and the books, and you would simply be required to commit to at least four days a week delivering them. There will be early starts and long days, given the topography of our beautiful county, but I believe there will be huge rewards."

"So why don't you do it?" came a voice from the back.

"I would volunteer, but as many of you know I am a martyr to my hips. Dr. Garnett has warned me that to ride such distances would be too great a physical challenge. Ideally we are looking for volunteers among our younger ladies."

"It ain't safe for a young lady by herself. I'm agin it."

"'Tain't proper. Women should be looking after the home. What's next? Women down the mines? Driving lumber trucks?"

"Mr. Simmonds, if you can't see there's a world of difference between a lumber truck and a copy of *Twelfth Night*, then Lord help Kentucky's economy, for I don't know where we'll be headed."

"Families should be reading the Bible. Nothing else. Who's going to keep an eye on what they're putting out there, anyhow? You know what they're like up north. They might spread all kinds of crazy notions."

"It's books, Mr. Simmonds. The same you learned with when you were a boy. But, then, I seem to remember you were more keen on tweaking girls' pigtails than you were on reading."

Another burst of laughter.

Nobody moved. A woman looked at her husband, but he gave a small shake of his head.

Mrs. Brady raised a hand. "Oh, I forgot to mention. It is a *paid* opportunity. Remuneration will be in the region of twenty-eight dollars a month. So, who would like to sign up?"

There was a brief murmur.

"I can't," said a woman with extravagantly pinned red hair. "Not with four babies under five."

"I just don't see why our government is wasting hard-earned tax dollars dishing out books to people who can't even read," said Jowly Man. "Why, half of 'em don't even go to church."

Mrs. Brady's voice had taken on a slightly desperate note. "A month's trial. Come on, ladies. I can't go back and tell Mrs. Nofcier that not one person in Baileyville would volunteer. What kind of place would she think we were?"

Nobody spoke. The silence stretched. To Alice's left, a bee bumped lazily against the window. People began to shift in their seats.

Mrs. Brady, undaunted, eyed the assembly. "C'mon. Let's not have another incident like the Orphans Fundraiser."

There were apparently many pairs of shoes that suddenly required close attention.

"Not a one? Really? Well . . . Izzy will be the first, then."

A small, almost perfectly spherical girl, half hidden among the packed audience, raised her hands to her mouth. Alice saw rather than heard the girl's mouth form the protest. "Mother!"

"That's one volunteer. My little girl will not be afraid to do her duty for our country, will you, Izzy? Any more?"

Nobody spoke.

"Not one of you? You don't think learning is important? You don't think encouraging our less fortunate families to a position of education is imperative?" She glared out at the meeting. "Well. This is not the response that I anticipated."

"I'll do it," said Alice, into the silence.

Mrs. Brady squinted, raising her hand above her eyes. "Is that Mrs. Van Cleve?"

"Yes, it is. Alice."

"You can't sign up," Bennett whispered urgently.

Alice leaned forward. "My husband was just telling me that he believes strongly in the importance of civic duty, just as his dear mother did, so I would be happy to volunteer." Her skin prickled as the eyes of the audience slid toward her.

Mrs. Brady fanned herself a little more vigorously. "But . . . you don't know your way around these parts, dear. I don't think that would be very sensible."

"Yes," Bennett hissed, "you don't know your way around, Alice."

"I'll show her." Margery O'Hare nodded to Alice. "I'll ride the routes with her for a week or two. We can keep her close to town till she's got a nose for it."

"Alice, I—" Bennett whispered. He seemed flustered and glanced up at his father.

"Can you ride?"

"Since I was four years old."

Mrs. Brady rocked back on her heels in satisfaction. "Well, there you are, Miss O'Hare. You have another two librarians already."

"It's a start."

Margery O'Hare smiled at Alice, and Alice smiled back almost before she realized what she was doing.

"Well, I do not think this is a wise idea at all," said George Simmonds. "And I shall be writing to Governor Hatch tomorrow to tell him as much. I believe sending young women out by themselves is a recipe for disaster. And I can see nothing but the foment of ungodly thoughts and bad behavior from this ill-conceived idea, First Lady or not. Good day, Mrs. Brady."

"Good day, Mr. Simmonds."

The gathering began to rise heavily from its seats.

"I'll see you at the library on Monday morning," said Margery O'Hare, as they walked out into the sunlight. She thrust out a hand and shook Alice's. "You can call me Marge." She glanced up at the sky, wedged a wide-brimmed leather hat onto her head, and strode off toward a large mule, which she greeted with the same enthusiastic surprise as if it were an old friend she had just bumped into on the street.

Bennett watched her go. "Mrs. Van Cleve, I have no idea what you think you're doing."

He'd said it twice before she remembered that this, in fact, was now her name.

TWO

Baileyville was unremarkable among the towns of southern Appalachia. Nestled between two ridges, it comprised two main roads of a stuttering mixture of brick and timber buildings, linked in a V, off which sprouted a multitude of winding lanes and paths that led at the lower level to distant hollers, as the small valleys were known, and at the higher, to a scattering of mountain houses across the tree-covered ridges. Those houses near the upper reaches of the creek traditionally housed the wealthier and more respectable families—it being easier to make a legitimate living on the flatter lands, and easier to hide a liquor still in the wilder, higher parts—but as the century had crept forward, the influx of miners and supervisors, the subtle changes in the demographics of the little town and its county, had meant that it was no longer possible to judge who was who simply by which leg of the road they lived on.

The Baileyville WPA Packhorse Library was to be based in the last wooden cabin up Split Creek, a turning on the right off Main Street and a road that contained white-collar workers, shopkeepers and those who made a living mostly by trading what they grew. It was squat on the ground, unlike many of the lower buildings, which were set on stilts to protect them from the spring floods. Cast into part-shadow by an oversized oak to its left, the building measured approximately fifteen strides by twelve. From the front it was entered by a small flight of rickety wooden stairs and from the back by a wooden door that had once been wide enough for cows.

"It'll be a way for me to get to know everyone around town," she had told the two men over breakfast, as Bennett yet again questioned his wife's wisdom in taking the job. "Which is what you wanted, isn't it? And I won't be under Annie's feet all day."

She had discovered that if she exaggerated her English accent, they found it harder to disagree with her. In recent weeks she had begun to sound positively regal. "And, of course, I will be able to observe who is in need of religious sustenance."

"She has a point," said Mr. Van Cleve, removing a piece of bacon gristle from the side of his mouth and placing it carefully on the side of his plate. "She could do it just till the babbies come along."

Alice and her husband had studiously avoided looking at each other.

Now Alice approached the single-story building, her boots kicking up loose dirt in the road. She put her hand to her brow and squinted. A newly painted sign proclaimed "USA PACKHORSE LIBRARY, WPA" and the sound of hammering emerged in staccato bursts from inside. Mr. Van Cleve had indulged a little too freely the previous evening and had awoken determined to find fault with whatever anyone happened to do in his house. Including breathing. She had crept around, wrenched her way into her breeches, then found herself singing softly on the half-mile walk to the library, just for the joy of having somewhere else to be.

She stood back a couple of paces, trying to peer in, and as she did, she became aware of the low hum of an approaching motor, along with another, more erratic sound she couldn't quite distinguish. She turned to see the truck, noticing the shocked expression on the driver's face. *"Whoa! Look out!"*

Alice spun around just as a riderless horse came galloping down the narrow road toward her, its stirrups flapping, reins tangled in its spindly legs. As the truck swerved to avoid it, the horse shied and stumbled, sending Alice sprawling into the dust.

She was dimly aware of a pair of overalls leaping past her, the blare of a horn and a clatter of hoofs. *Whoa . . . whoa there. Whoa, fella . . .*

"Ow." She rubbed her elbow, her head ringing with the impact. When she finally sat up she saw that a few yards away a man was holding the horse's bridle and running a hand down its neck, trying to settle it. Its eyes rolled white, and veins popped on its neck, like a relief map.

"That fool!" A young woman was jogging down the road toward them. "Old man Vance tooted his horn on purpose and he bucked me off in the road."

"You okay? You took quite a spill there." A hand reached out and helped Alice to her feet. She stood, blinking, and regarded its owner: a tall man in overalls and a checked shirt, his eyes softening in sympathy. A nail still protruded from the corner of his mouth. He spat it into his palm and shoved it into his pocket before offering a handshake. "Frederick Guisler."

"Alice Van Cleve."

"The English bride." His palm was rough.

Beth Pinker appeared, panting, between them and snatched the reins from Frederick Guisler with a growl.

"Scooter, you ain't got the damn brains you was born with."

The man turned to her. "Told you, Beth. You can't run a Thoroughbred out of here at a gallop. It gets him wound up like a spring. Take the first twenty minutes at a walk and he'll be good for the day."

"Who has time to walk? I got to get to Paint Lick by midday. Shoot, he's put a hole in my best breeches." Beth tugged the horse over to the mounting block, still muttering under her breath, then turned abruptly. "Oh. You the new girl? Marge said to tell you she's coming."

"Thank you." Alice lifted a palm, before picking at the selection of small stones embedded in it. As they watched, Beth checked her saddlebags, cursed again, wheeled the horse round, and set off back up the road at a sideways canter.

Frederick Guisler turned back to Alice, shaking his head. "You sure you're okay? I can fetch you some water."

27

Alice tried to look nonchalant, as if her elbow wasn't throbbing and she hadn't just realized that a fine layer of grit was decorating her upper lip. "I'm fine. I'll just . . . sit here on the step."

"The stoop?" He grinned.

"Yes, that too," she said.

Frederick Guisler left her to it. He was lining the walls of the library with rough pine shelves, beneath which stood boxes of waiting books. One wall was already filled with a variety of titles, neatly labeled, and a pile in the corner suggested some had already been returned. Unlike the Van Cleve house, the little building held an air of purpose, the sense that it was about to become something useful.

As she sat rubbing dirt from her clothes, two young women walked past on the other side of the road, both in long seersucker skirts and wide-brimmed hats to keep off the worst of the sun. They glanced across the road at her, then put their heads together, conferring. Alice smiled and lifted a hand tentatively in greeting, but they scowled and turned away. Alice realized with a sigh that they were probably friends with Peggy Foreman. Sometimes she thought she might just make a sign and hang it around her neck: *No, I didn't know he had a sweetheart.*

"Fred says you took a fall before you even got on the horse. Takes some doing."

Alice glanced up to find Margery O'Hare looking down at her. She was atop a large, ugly-looking horse with excessively long ears, and leading a smaller brown and white pony.

"Um—well, I—"

"You ever rode a mule?"

"Is that a mule?"

"Sure is. But don't tell him. He thinks he's a stallion from Araby." Margery squinted at her from under her wide-brimmed hat. "You can try this little paint, Spirit. She's feisty but she's sure-footed as Charley here, and she don't stop at nothing. The other girl ain't coming."

Alice stood up and stroked the little mare's white nose. The horse half closed her eyes. Her lashes were half white and half brown and she gave off a sweet, meadow-grass scent. Alice was immediately taken back to summers spent riding around her grandmother's estate in Sussex, when she was fourteen and free to escape for whole days at a time, rather than constantly being told how she should behave.

Alice, you are too impulsive.

She leaned forward and sniffed the baby-soft hair at the mare's ears.

"So you going to make love to her? Or you going to get on and ride?"

"Now?" said Alice.

"You waiting for permission from Mrs. Roosevelt? C'mon, we got ground to cover."

Without waiting, she wheeled the mule around and Alice had to scramble aboard as the little paint horse took off after her.

For the first half-hour Margery O'Hare said little, and Alice rode silently behind, struggling to adjust to the very different style of riding. Margery wasn't stiff-backed, heels down and chin up, like the girls she had ridden with in England. She was loose-limbed, swayed like a sapling as she steered the mule around and up and down slopes, absorbing every movement. She talked to him more often than she spoke to Alice, scolding or singing to him, occasionally turning 180 degrees in her saddle to shout behind, as if she had just remembered she had company: "You okay back there?"

"Fine!" Alice would call, trying not to wobble as the mare tried again to turn and bolt back toward the town.

"Oh, she's just testing you," said Margery, after Alice let out a yelp. "Once you let her know you're in charge, she'll be sweet as molasses."

Alice, feeling the little mare bunch crossly under her, wasn't convinced, but she didn't want to complain in case Margery decided she was not up to the job. They rode through the small town, past lush fenced gardens swollen with corn, tomatoes, greens, Margery tipping her hat to those few people who passed on foot. The horse and the mule snorted and backed up briefly as a huge truck bearing timber came past, but then abruptly they were out of town and headed up a steep, narrow track. Margery pulled back a little as the track widened, so they could travel side by side.

"So you're the girl from England." She pronounced it Eng-er-land.

"Yes." Alice stooped to avoid a low-hanging branch. "Have you been?"

Margery kept her face forward, so Alice struggled to hear her. "Never been further east than Lewisburg. That's where my sister used to live."

"Oh, did she move?"

"She died." Margery reached up to break a switch from a branch and peeled the leaves from it, dropping the reins loose on the mule's neck.

"I'm so sorry. Do you have other family?"

"Had. One sister and five brothers. 'Cept there's just me now."

"Do you live in Baileyville?"

"Just a lick away. Same house I was born in."

"You've only ever lived in one place?"

"Yup."

"You're not curious?"

"'Bout what?"

Alice shrugged. "I don't know. What it would be like to go somewhere else?"

"Why? Is it better where you come from?"

Alice thought of the crushing silence of her parents' front room, the low squeak of the front gate, her father polishing his motor-car, whistling tunelessly through his teeth every Saturday morning, the minute rearrangements of fish forks and spoons on a carefully ironed Sunday tablecloth. She looked out at the endless green pastures, the huge mountains that rose up on either side of them. Above her a hawk wheeled and cried into the empty blue skies. "Possibly not."

Margery slowed so that Alice could draw level with her. "Got everything I need here. I suit myself, and people generally leave me be." She leaned forward and stroked the mule's neck. "That's how I like it."

Alice heard the faint barrier in her words, and was quiet. They walked the next couple of miles in silence, Alice conscious of the way the saddle was already rubbing the inside of her knees, the heat of the day settling on her bare head. Margery signaled that they would turn left through a clearing in the trees.

"We're going to pick up a little here. You'd best take a grip, case she spins round again."

Alice felt the little horse shoot forward under her and they were cantering up a long flint track that gradually became more shadowed until they were in the mountains, the horses' necks extending, their noses lowering with the effort of picking their way up the steep stony pathways between the trees. Alice breathed in the cooler air, the sweet damp scents of the forest, the path dappling with broken light in front of them, and the trees creating a cathedral canopy high above, from which birdsong trickled down. Alice leaned over the horse's neck as they surged forward, and felt suddenly, unexpectedly happy. As they slowed she realized she was smiling broadly, without thinking about it. It was a striking sensation, like someone suddenly able to exercise a lost limb.

"This is the northeast route. Thought it would be wise if we divided them into eight."

"Goodness, it's so beautiful," Alice said. She stared at the huge sand-colored rocks that seemed to loom out of nowhere, forming natural shelters. All around her the boulders emerged almost horizontally from the side of the mountain in thick layers, or formed natural stone arches, weathered by centuries of wind and rain. Up here she was separated from the town, from Bennett and his father, by more than geography. She felt as if she had landed on a different planet entirely, where gravity didn't work in the same way. She was acutely aware of the crickets in the grass, the silent slow glide of the birds overhead, the lazy swish of the horses' tails as they swept flies from their flanks.

Margery walked the mule under an overhang, and beckoned to Alice to follow. "See in there? That hole? That there's a hominy hole. You know a hominy hole?"

Alice shook her head.

"Where the Indians ground their corn. If you look over there you'll see two worn patches in the stone where the ol' chief used to rest his backside while the women worked."

Alice felt her cheeks glow and stifled a smile. She gazed up at the trees, her relaxed mood evaporating. "Are they . . . are they still around?"

Margery peered at her from under her wide-brimmed hat for a moment. "I think you're safe, Mrs. Van Cleve. They tend to go to lunch about now."

They stopped to eat their sandwiches under the shelter of a railroad bridge, then rode through the mountains all afternoon, the paths winding and doubling back so that Alice couldn't be sure of where they had been or where they were headed. It was hard to gauge north when the treetops spanned high above their heads, obscuring sun and shadow. She asked Margery where they might stop to relieve themselves, and Margery waved a hand. "Any tree you like, take your pick."

Her new companion's conversation was infrequent, pithy and mostly seemed to revolve around who was and wasn't dead. She herself, she said, had Cherokee blood from way back. "My great-granddaddy married a Cherokee. I got Cherokee hair, and a good straight nose. We was all a little dark-skinned in our family, though my cousin was born white albino."

"What does she look like?"

"She didn't live past two. Got bit by a copperhead. Everyone thought she was just cranky till they saw the bite. Course, by then it was too late. Oh, you'll need to watch out for snakes. You know about snakes?"

Alice shook her head.

Margery blinked, as if it were unthinkable that someone might not know about snakes. "Well, the poisonous ones tend to have heads shaped like a spade, you know?"

"Got it." Alice waited a moment. "One of the square ones? Or the digging ones with the pointy ends? My father even has a drain spade, which—"

Margery sighed. "Maybe just stay clear of all snakes for now."

As they rose up, away from the creek, Margery would jump down periodically and tie a piece of red twine around a tree trunk, using a penknife to slice through it, or biting it and spitting out the ends. This, she said, would show Alice how to find her way back to the open track.

"You see old man Muller's house on the left there? See the wood smoke? That's him and his wife and four children. She can't read but the eldest can and he'll teach her. Muller don't much like the idea of them learning but he's down the mine from dawn till dusk so I've been bringing them books anyway."

"He won't mind?"

"He won't know. He'll come in, wash off the dust, eat what food she's made and be asleep by sundown. It's hard down there and they come back weary. Besides, she keeps the books in her dress trunk. He don't look in there."

Margery, it emerged, had been running a skeleton library single-handed for several weeks already. They passed neat little houses on stilts, tiny derelict shingle-roofed cabins that looked like a stiff breeze might blow them down, shacks with ramshackle stands of fruit and vegetables for sale outside, and at each one Margery pointed and ex-plained who lived there, whether they could read, how best to get the material to them, and which houses to steer clear of. Moonshiners, mostly. Illegal liquor that they brewed in hidden stills in the woods. There were those who made it and would shoot you for seeing it, and those who drank it and weren't safe to be around. She seemed to know everything about everyone, and delivered each nugget of information in the same easy, laconic way. This was Bob Gillman's—he lost an arm in one of the machines at a factory in Detroit and had come back to live with his father. That was Mrs. Coghlan's house—her husband had beat her something awful, until he came home boss-eyed and she sewed him up in his bed sheet and went after him with a switch until he swore he'd never do it again. This was where two moonshine stills had exploded with a bang you could hear across two counties. The

Campbells still blamed the Mackenzies and would occasionally come past shooting the house up if they got drunk enough.

"Do you ever get frightened?" Alice asked.

"Frightened?"

"Up here, by yourself. You make it sound like anything could happen."

Margery looked as if the thought had never occurred to her. "Been riding these mountains since before I could walk. I stay out of trouble."

Alice must have seemed skeptical.

"It ain't hard. You know when you have a bunch of animals gathering at a waterhole?"

"Um, not really, no. Surrey isn't big on watering holes."

"You go to Africa, you got the elephant drinking next to the lion, and he's drinking next to a hippo, and the hippo's drinking next to a gazelle. And none of them is bothering each other, right? You know why?"

"No."

"Because they're reading each other. And that old gazelle sees that the lion is all relaxed, and that he just wants to take a drink. And the hippo is all easy, and so they all live and let live. But you put them on a plain at dusk, and that same old lion is prowling around with a glint in his eye—well, those gazelles know to git, and git fast."

"There are lions as well as snakes?"

"You read people, Alice. You see someone in the distance and it's some miner on his way home and you can tell from his gait he's tired and all he wants is to get back to his place, fill his belly and put his feet up. You see that same miner outside a honky-tonk, half a bottle of bourbon down on a Friday and giving you the stink-eye? You know to get out of the way, right?"

They rode in silence for a bit.

"So . . . Margery?"

"Yup."

"If you've never been further east than—where was it, Lewis-burg?—how is it you know so much about animals in Africa?"

Margery pulled her mule to a halt and turned to face her. "Are you seriously asking me that question?"

Alice stared at her.

"And you want me to make you a librarian?"

It was the first time she had seen Margery laugh. She hooted like a barn owl, and was still laughing halfway back down to Salt Lick.

So how was it today?"

"It was fine, thank you."

She didn't want to talk about how her backside and thighs ached so badly that she had nearly cried lowering herself onto the seat of the lavatory. Or the tiny cabins they had passed, where she could see the inside walls were papered with sheets of newspaper, which Margery told her were "to keep the drafts out in winter." She needed time to process the scale of the land she had navigated, the feeling, as they had picked a horizontal path through a vertical landscape, of being truly in the wild for the first time in her life, the huge birds, the skittering deer, the tiny blue skink lizards. She thought she might not mention the toothless man, who had sworn at them on the road, or the exhausted young mother with four small children running around outside, naked as the day they were born. But mostly the day had been so extraordinary, so precious, that she really didn't want to share any of it with the two men.

"Did I hear you was riding out with Margery O'Hare?" Mr. Van Cleve took a swig of his drink.

"I was. And Isabelle Brady." She didn't mention that Isabelle had failed to turn up.

"You want to steer clear of that O'Hare girl. She's trouble."

"How is she trouble?"

She caught Bennett's flashed look: *don't say anything.*

Mr. Van Cleve pointed his fork at her. "You mind my words, Alice. Margery O'Hare comes from a bad family. Frank O'Hare was the biggest 'shiner between here and Tennessee. You're too new to understand what that means. Oh, she might dress herself up in books and fancy words, these days, but underneath she's still the same, just like the no-good rest of 'em. I tell you, there's no decent ladies around here would take tea with her."

Alice tried to imagine Margery O'Hare giving a flying fig about taking tea with any ladies. She took the plate of cornbread from Annie and put a slice on her plate before passing it on. She realized she was ravenously hungry, despite the heat. "Please don't worry. She's just showing me where to deliver the books."

"I'm just saying. Mind you don't hang around her too much. You don't want her ways rubbing off on you." He took two slices of corn-bread and put half a slice straight into his mouth and chewed for a minute, his mouth open. Alice winced and looked away. "What kind of books are these, anyway?"

Alice shrugged. "Just . . . books. There's Mark Twain and Louisa May Alcott, some cowboy stories and books to help around the home, recipes and suchlike."

Mr. Van Cleve shook his head. "Half those mountain people can't read a word. Old Henry Porteous thinks it's a waste of time and tax dollars, and I have to say I'm minded to agree. And, like I said, any scheme with Margery O'Hare mixed up in it has to be a bad thing."

Alice was about to speak up in Margery's defense but a firm pressure from her husband's hand under the table warned her off.

"I don't know." Mr. Van Cleve wiped away some gravy at the side of his mouth. "I'm pretty sure my wife would not have approved of a scheme like this."

"But she did believe in charitable acts, Bennett tells me," said Alice.

Mr. Van Cleve looked across the table. "She did, yes. She was a most godly woman."

"Well," Alice said, after a moment, "I do believe that if we can encourage godless families to read, we can encourage them to turn to scripture, and the Bible, and that can only be good for everyone." Her smile was sweet and wide. She leaned forward over the table. "Can you imagine all those families, Mr. Van Cleve, finally able to truly grasp the word of God through a proper reading of the Bible? Wouldn't that be a marvelous thing? I'm sure your wife would have had nothing but encouragement for something like that."

There was a long silence.

"Well, yes," said Mr. Van Cleve. "You could have a point." He nodded, to suggest that that was the end of the matter, for now at least. Alice saw her husband deflate slightly with relief and wished she didn't hate him for it.

Three days in, bad family or not, Alice had swiftly realized that she would rather be around Margery O'Hare than almost anyone else in Kentucky. Margery didn't speak much. She was utterly uninterested in the slivers of gossip, veiled or otherwise, that seemed to fuel the women at the endless teas and quilting sessions Alice had sat in on up to now. She was uninterested in Alice's appearance, her thoughts or her history. Margery went where she liked, and said what she thought, hiding nothing behind the polite courtly euphemisms that everyone else found so useful.

Oh, is that the English fashion? How very interesting.

And Mr. Van Cleve Junior is happy for his wife to ride alone in the mountains, is he? Goodness.

Well, perhaps you're persuading him of the English ways of doing things. How . . . novel.

Margery behaved, Alice realized with a jolt, *like a man.*

This was such an extraordinary thought that she found herself studying the other woman at a distance, trying to work out how she had come to this astonishing state of liberation. But she wasn't yet brave enough—or perhaps still too English—to ask.

Alice would arrive at the library shortly after seven in the morning, the dew still thick on the grass, waving aside Bennett's offer to drive her in the motor-car and leaving him to breakfast with his father. She would exchange a greeting with Frederick Guisler, who was often to be found talking to a horse, like Margery, and then walk around the back where Spirit and the mule were tethered, their breath sending steam rising into the cool dawn air. The library shelves were almost finished now, stacked with donated books from as far away as New York and Seattle. (The WPA had put out a call to libraries to donate, and brown-paper parcels arrived twice a week.) Mr. Guisler had mended an old table donated by a school in Berea so that they had somewhere to lay the huge leather-bound ledger that listed books in and out. The pages were filling quickly: Alice discovered that Beth Pinker left at 5 a.m., and that before she met Margery each day, Margery had already done two hours' riding, dropping books at remote homesteads in the mountains. She would scan the list to see where she and Beth had been.

Wednesday 15th

The Farley children, Crystal—four comic books

Mrs. Petunia Grant, The Schoolmaster's House at Yellow Rock—two editions Ladies' Home Journal *(Feb, April 1937), one edition* Black Beauty *by Anna Sewell (ink marks on pages 34 and 35)*

Mr. F. Homer, Wind Cave—one edition Folk Medicine *by D. C. Jarvis*

The Sisters Fritz, The End Barn, White Ash—one edition Cimarron *by Edna Ferber,* Magnificent Obsession *by Lloyd C. Douglas (note: three back pages missing, cover water-damaged)*

The books were rarely new, and were often missing pages or covers, she discovered, while helping Frederick Guisler to shelve them. He was a wiry, weather-beaten man in his late thirties, who had inherited eight hundred acres from his father and who, like him, bred and broke horses, including Spirit, the little mare Alice had been riding. "She's got opinions, that one," he said, stroking the little horse's neck. "Mind you, never met a decent mare that didn't." His smile was slow and conspiratorial, as if he wasn't really talking about horses at all.

Every day that first week Margery would map out the route they would take, and they would head out into the still morning, Alice breathing in the mountain air in heady gulps after the stifling fug of the Van Cleve house. In direct sun, as the day wore on, the heat would rise in shimmering waves from the ground, and it was a relief to climb into the mountains, where the flies and biting creatures didn't buzz relentlessly around her face. On the more remote routes Margery would dismount to tie string to every fourth tree so that Alice could find her way back once she was working alone, pointing out landmarks and notable rock formations to help her. "If you can't work it out, Spirit will find the way back for you," she said. "She's smart as a tack."

Alice was getting used to the little brown and white horse now. She knew exactly where Spirit would try to spin, and where she liked to speed up, and she no longer yelped but leaned forward into it, stroking the horse's neck so that her neat little ears flicked back and forth. She had a rough idea now of which trails went where, and had drawn maps for each, which she tucked into her breeches, hoping she could find her way to each house on her own. Mostly she had just begun to relish the time in the mountains, the unexpected hush of the vast landscape, the sight of Margery ahead of her, stooping to avoid low branches, pointing out the remote cabins that rose up like organic growths amid clearings in the trees.

"Look outwards, Alice," Margery would say, her voice carrying on the breeze. "Not much point worrying what the town thinks about you—nothing you can do about that anyway. But when you look outwards, why, there's a whole world of beautiful things."

For the first time in almost a year, Alice felt herself unobserved. There was nobody to pass comment on how she wore her clothes or held herself, nobody shooting her curious glances, or hovering to hear the way she spoke. She had started to understand Margery's determination to have people "let her be." She was pulled from her thoughts as Margery slid to a stop.

"Here we go, Alice." She jumped off by a rickety gate, where chickens scratched in a desultory way in the dust by the house and a large hog snuffled by a tree. "Time to meet the neighbors."

Alice followed her lead, dismounting and throwing the reins over the post by the front gate. The horses immediately lowered their heads and began to graze and Margery lifted one of her bags from the saddle and motioned to Alice to follow. The house was ramshackle, the weatherboarding drooping out of place like a wonky smile. The windows were thick with dirt, obscuring the interior, and an iron wash kettle sat outside over the embers of a fire. It was hard to believe anybody lived there.

"Good morning!" Margery walked halfway toward the door. "Hello?"

There was no sound, then the creak of a board, and a man appeared in the doorway, a rifle cocked on his shoulder. He wore overalls that had not troubled a washtub in some time, and a clay pipe emerged from under a bushy mustache. Behind him two young girls appeared, their heads tilted as they tried to peer at the visitors. He gazed out suspiciously.

"How you doing, Jim Horner?" Margery walked into the little fenced-off enclosure (it could barely be called a garden) and closed the gate behind them. She appeared not to notice the gun or, if she did, she ignored it. Alice felt her heart race a little, but followed obediently.

"Who's this?" The man nodded at Alice.

"This is Alice. She's helping me with the traveling library. I wondered if we could talk to you about what we got."

"I don't want to buy nothing."

"Well, that suits me fine, because we ain't sellin' nothing. I'll take just five minutes of your time. Could you spare a cup of water, though? Sure is warm out here." Margery, a study in calm, removed her hat and fanned her head with it. Alice was about to protest that they had just drunk a pitcher of water between them not half a mile back, but stopped. Horner gazed at her for a moment.

"Wait out here," he said eventually, motioning to a long bench at the front of the house. He murmured to one of the girls, a skinny child with her hair in plaits, who disappeared into the dark house, emerging with a bucket, her brow furrowed with her task. "She'll get you water."

"Would you be kind enough to bring some for my friend here, too, please, Mae?" Margery nodded at the girl.

"That would be very kind, thank you," said Alice, and the man startled at her accent.

Margery tipped her head toward her. "Oh, she's the one from Engerland. The one married Van Cleve's boy?"

His gaze switched impassively between them. The gun stayed at his shoulder. Alice sat gingerly on the bench as Margery continued to talk, her voice a low, relaxed sing-song. The same way she spoke to Charley the mule when he became, as she called it, "ornery."

"So I'm not sure if you've heard from town but we got a book library going. It's for those who like stories, or to help your children get educated a little, especially if they don't go to the mountain school. And I came by because I wondered if you'd like to try some books for yours."

"I told you they don't read."

"Yes, you did. So I brought some easy ones, just to get 'em going. These ones here have got pictures and all the letters so they can learn by themselves. Don't even have to go to school to do it. They can do it right here in your home."

She handed him one of the picture books. He lowered his gun and took the book gingerly, as if she were handing him something explosive, and flicked through the pages.

"I need the girls to help with the picking and canning."

"Sure you do. Busy time of year."

"I don't want them distracted."

"I understand. Can't have nothing slowing the canning. I have to say it looks like the corn is going to be fine this year. Not like last year, huh?" Margery smiled as the girl arrived in front of them, lopsided with the weight of the half-filled bucket. "Why, thank you, sweetheart." She held out a hand as the girl filled an old tin cup. She drank thirstily, then handed the cup to Alice. "Good and cold. Thank you most kindly."

Jim Horner pushed the book toward her. "They want money for those things."

"Well, that's the beauty of it, Jim. No money, no signing up, no nothing. Library just exists so people can try a bit of reading. Maybe learn a little if they find they have a liking for it."

Jim Horner stared at the cover of the book. Alice had never heard Margery talk so much in one sitting.

"I tell you what? How about I leave these here, just for the week? You don't have to read 'em, but you can take a look if you like. We'll come by next Monday and pick them up again. If you like them, you get the kids to tell me and I'll bring you some more. You don't like 'em, just leave them on a crate by the fence post there and we'll say no more. How does that sound?"

Alice glanced behind her. A second small face vanished immediately into the gloom of the building.

"I don't think so."

"Tell you the truth, you'd do me a favor. Would mean I don't have to carry the darn things all the way back down the mountain. Boy, our bags are heavy today! Alice, you finished your water, there? We don't want to take up any more of this gentleman's time. Good to see you, Jim. And thank you, Mae. Haven't you grown like a string bean since I last saw you!"

As they reached the gate Jim Horner's voice lifted and hardened. "I don't want nobody else comin' up here botherin' us. I don't want to be bothered and I don't want my children bothered. They got enough to deal with."

Margery didn't even turn around. She lifted a hand. "I hear you, Jim."

"And we don't need no charity. I don't want anyone from town just coming by. I don't know why you even came here."

"Headed to all the houses between here and Berea. But I hear you." Margery's voice carried across the hillside as they reached the horses.

Alice glanced behind her to see that he had raised his gun to his shoulder again. Her heart thumped in her ears as she picked up her pace. She was afraid to look back again. As Margery swung herself onto the mule, she took the reins, mounted Spirit with trembling legs, and it was only when she calculated that they were too far away for Jim Horner to take a shot at them that she allowed herself to exhale. She kicked the mare forward so that she was level with Margery.

"Oh, my goodness. Are they all that awful?" Her legs, she realized, were now entirely liquid.

"Awful? Alice, that went great."

Alice wasn't sure she'd heard her correctly.

"Last time I rode up to Red Creek Jim Horner shot my hat clean off." Margery turned toward her and tilted her hat so that Alice could see the tiny hole that scorched straight through the top of it. She rammed it back onto her head. "Come on, let's kick on a little. I want to take you to meet Nancy before we break for lunch."

THREE

★

*. . . and best of all, the wilderness of books, in which
she could wander, where she liked, made the library a
region of bliss to her.*

· LOUISA MAY ALCOTT, *Little Women*

Two purple bruises on her knees, one on her left ankle and blisters
in places she didn't know blisters could exist, a cluster of infected
bites behind her right ear, four broken nails (slightly grubby, she
had to admit) and sunburn on her neck and nose. A two-inch-long
graze on her right shoulder from being scraped against a tree, and a
mark on her left elbow where Spirit had bitten her when she'd tried to
slap a horsefly. Alice peered at her grimy face in the mirror, wondering what people back in England would make of the scabby cowgirl
staring back at her.

It had been more than a fortnight and nobody had mentioned that
Isabelle Brady had still not arrived to join the little team of packhorse
librarians, so Alice didn't feel able to ask. Frederick didn't say much
other than to offer her coffee and help her with Spirit, Beth—the middle child of eight brothers—would march in and out with a brisk
boyish energy, nodding a cheerful hello, dumping her saddle on the
floor, exclaiming when she couldn't find her *goddamn saddlebags*, and
Isabelle's name simply failed to appear on the little cards on the wall

with which they signed themselves in and out of shifts. Occasionally a large dark green motor-car would sweep by with Mrs. Brady in the front, and Margery would nod, but no words passed between them. Alice began to think that putting her daughter's name out there had been a way for Mrs. Brady to encourage other young women to come forward.

So, it was something of a surprise when the motor-car pulled up on Thursday afternoon, its huge wheels sending a spray of sand and grit up the steps as it stopped. Mrs. Brady was an enthusiastic, if easily distracted driver, prone to sending locals scattering as she turned her head to wave at some passerby, or swerved extravagantly to avoid a cat in the road.

"Who is that?" Margery didn't look up. She was working her way through two piles of returned books, trying to decide which were too damaged to go out again. There was little point sending out a book in which the last page was missing, as had already happened once. *Waste of my time*, had been the response from the sharecropper who had been given *The Good Earth* by Pearl S. Buck. *I won't be reading a book again.*

"Think it might be Mrs. Brady." Alice, who had been treating a blister on her heel, peered out of the window, trying to remain inconspicuous. She watched as Mrs. Brady closed the driver's door and paused to wave at somebody across the street. And then she saw a younger woman emerge from the passenger side, red hair pulled back and pinned into neat curls. Isabelle Brady.

"It's both of them," Alice said quietly. She tugged her sock back on, wincing.

"I'm surprised."

"Why?" said Alice.

Isabelle made her way around the side of the car until she was level with her mother. It was then that Alice saw she walked with a pronounced limp, and that her lower left leg was encased in a leather and metal brace, the shoe at the end built up so that it resembled a small black brick. She didn't use a stick, but rolled slightly as she moved, and concentration—or possibly discomfort—was writ large on her freckled features.

Alice pulled back, not wanting to be seen to be watching as they made their way slowly up the steps. She heard a murmured conversation and then the door opened.

"Miss O'Hare!"

"Good afternoon, Mrs. Brady, Isabelle."

"I'm so sorry for the delay in getting Izzy started. She had . . . some things to attend to first."

"Just glad to have you. We're about ready to send Mrs. Van Cleve out on her own, so the more the merrier. I'll have to get you sorted out with a horse, though, Miss Brady. I wasn't sure when you were coming."

"I'm no good at riding," said Izzy, quietly.

"Wondered as much. Never seen you on a horse. So Mr. Guisler is going to lend you his old companion horse, Patch. He's a little heavy but sweet as anything, won't scare you none. He knows what he's doing and he'll go at your pace."

"I can't ride," Izzy said, an edge to her voice. She looked mutinously at her mother.

"That's only because you won't try, dear," her mother said, not looking at her. She clasped her hands together. "So what time shall we come by tomorrow? Izzy, we'll have to take you to Lexington to get you some new breeches. You've eaten your way right out of your old ones."

"Well, Alice here saddles up at seven, so why don't you come then? We may start a little earlier as we divide up our routes."

"You're not listening to me—" Izzy began.

"We'll see you tomorrow." Mrs. Brady looked around her at the little cabin. "It's good to see what a start you've made already. I hear from Pastor Willoughby that the McArthur girls read their way through their Bible samplers without so much as a prompt from him last Sunday, thanks to the books you've brought them. Wonderful. Good afternoon, Mrs. Van Cleve, Miss O'Hare. I'm much obliged to the pair of you."

Mrs. Brady nodded and the two women turned and made their

way out of the library. They heard the roar of the car's engine as it started up, then a skidding sound and a startled shout as Mrs. Brady pulled out onto the road.

Alice looked at Margery, who shrugged. They sat in silence until the sound of the engine died away.

"Bennett." Alice skipped up to the stoop, where her husband was sitting with a glass of iced tea. She glanced at the rocker, which was unusually empty. "Where's your father?"

"Having dinner with the Lowes."

"Is that the one who never stops talking? Goodness, he'll be there all night. I'm amazed Mrs. Lowe can draw breath long enough to eat!" She pushed her hair back from her brow. "Oh, I have had the most extraordinary day. We went to a house in the middle of absolutely nowhere and I swear this man wanted to shoot us. He didn't, of course—"

She slowed, noting the way his eyes had dropped to her dirty boots. Alice looked down at them and the mud on her breeches. "Oh. That. Yes. Misjudged where I should have been going through a creek and my horse stumbled and threw me straight over her head. It was actually very funny. I thought at one point Margery was going to pass out from laughing. Luckily I dried off in a wink, although just *wait* until you see my bruises. I am positively purple." She jogged up the steps to him and stooped to kiss him but he turned his face away.

"You smell awfully of horse, these days," he said. "Maybe you should wash that off. It does tend to . . . linger."

She was sure he hadn't meant it to sting, but it did. She sniffed at her shoulder. "You're right," she said, forcing a smile. "I smell like a cowboy! I tell you what, how about I freshen up and put on something pretty and then perhaps we could take a drive to the river. I could make us a little picnic of nice things. Didn't Annie leave some of that molasses cake? And I know we still have the side of ham. Say yes, darling. Just you and me. We haven't had a proper outing together for weeks."

Bennett rose from his chair. "Actually, I'm—uh—going to meet some of the fellas for a game. I was just waiting for you to come home so I could tell you." He stood in front of her and she realized he was wearing the white trousers he used for sport. "We're headed to the playing field over at Johnson."

"Oh. Fine, then. I'll come and watch. I promise I won't take a minute to scrub up."

He rubbed his palm over the top of his head. "It's kind of a guy thing. The wives don't really come."

"I wouldn't say anything, Bennett darling, or bother you."

"That's not really the point—"

"I just would love to see you play. You look so . . . *joyful* when you play."

The way his gaze flickered toward her and away told her she had said too much. They stood in silence for a moment.

"Like I said. It's a guy thing."

Alice swallowed. "I see. Another time, then."

"Sure!" Released, he looked suddenly happy. "A picnic would be great. Maybe we can get some of the other fellows to come too. Pete Schrager? You liked his wife, didn't you? Patsy's fun. You and she will become real friends, I know it."

"Oh. Yes. I suppose so."

They stood awkwardly in front of each other for a moment longer. Then Bennett reached out a hand, and leaned forward as if to kiss her. But this time it was Alice who stepped back. "It's okay, you really don't have to. Goodness, I do reek! Awful! How can you bear it?"

She backed away, then turned and ran up the steps two at a time so that he couldn't see her eyes had filled with tears.

Alice's days had settled into something of a routine since she had started work. She would rise at 5:30 a.m., wash and dress in the little bathroom along the hall (she was grateful for it, as she had swiftly become aware that half the homes in Baileyville still had "outhouses"—or worse).

Bennett slept like someone dead, barely stirring as she pulled on her boots, and she would lean over and kiss his cheek lightly, then tiptoe downstairs. In the kitchen she would retrieve the sandwiches she had made the evening before, grab a couple of the "biscuits" that Annie left out on the sideboard, wrap them in a napkin, and eat them as she walked the half-mile to the library. Some of the faces she passed on her walk had become familiar: farmers on their horse-drawn buggies, lumber lorries making their way toward the huge yards, and the odd miner who had overslept, his lunch pail in his hand. She had begun to nod to the people she recognized—people in Kentucky were so much more civil than they were in England, where you were likely to be viewed with suspicion if you greeted a stranger in too friendly a manner. A couple had started to call out across the road to her: *How's that library going?* And she would respond: *Oh, quite well, thank you.* They always smiled, though sometimes she suspected they spoke to her because they were amused by her accent. Either way it was nice to feel she was becoming part of something.

Occasionally she would pass Annie walking briskly, head down, on her way to the house—to her shame, she wasn't sure where the house-keeper lived—and she would wave cheerily, but Annie would simply nod, unsmiling, as if Alice had transgressed some unspoken rule in the employer-employee handbook. Bennett, she knew, would rise only after Annie arrived at the house, woken with coffee on a tray, Annie having already taken the same to Mr. Van Cleve. By the time the two men were dressed, the bacon, eggs and grits would be waiting for them on the dining table, the cutlery set just so. At a quarter to eight they would head off in Mr. Van Cleve's burgundy Ford convertible sedan, to Hoffman Mining.

Alice tried not to think too hard about the previous evening. She had once been told by her favorite aunt that the best way to get through life was not to dwell on things so she packed those events into a suit-case, and shoved it to the back of a mental cupboard, just as she had done with numerous suitcases before. There was no point lingering on the fact that Bennett had plainly gone drinking long after his baseball game had ended, returning to pass out on the daybed in the dressing room, from where she heard his convulsive snores until dawn. There was no point thinking too hard about the fact that it had now been more than six months, long enough for her to have to acknowledge that this might not be normal newlywed behavior. Like there was no point in thinking too hard that it was obvious neither of them had a clue how to discuss what was going on. Especially as she wasn't even sure *what* was going on. Nothing in her life up to now had given her the vocabulary or the experience. And there was nobody in whom she could confide. Her mother thought conversation about any bodily matters—even the filing of nails—was *vulgar*.

Alice took a breath. No. Better to focus on the road ahead, the long, arduous day, with its books and its ledger entries, its horses and its lush green forests. Better not to think too hard about anything, but to ride long and hard, to focus diligently on her new task, on memorizing routes, jotting down addresses and names and sorting books so that by the time she returned home it was all she could do to stay awake long enough to eat dinner, take a long soak in the tub and, finally, fall fast asleep.

It was a routine, she acknowledged, that seemed to suit them both.

"She's here," said Frederick Guisler, passing her on her way in. He tipped his hat, his eyes crinkling.

"Who?" She put down her lunch pail, and peered toward the window at the back.

"Miss Isabelle." He picked up his jacket and headed for the door. "Lord knows, I doubt she'll be riding the Kentucky Derby any time soon. There's coffee brewing out back, Mrs. Van Cleve. I brought you some cream, given that's how you seem to prefer it."

"That's very kind of you, Mr. Guisler. I have to say I can't drink it stewed black, like Margery. She can pretty much stand a spoon in hers."

"Call me Fred. And, well, Margery does things her own way, as you know." He nodded as he closed the door.

Alice tied a handkerchief around her neck to protect it from the sun and poured a mug of coffee, then walked around to the back where the horses were tethered in a small paddock. There she could see Margery bent double, holding Isabelle Brady's knee as the younger girl clutched the saddle of a solid-looking bay horse. He stood immobile, his jaw working in a leisurely manner around a clump of grass, as if he had been there for some time.

"You've got to spring a little, Miss Isabelle," Margery was saying, through gritted teeth. "If you can't put your shoe in the stirrup then you're going to have to bounce your way up. Just one, two, three, and hup!"

Nothing moved.

"Bounce!"

"I don't bounce," said Isabelle, crossly. "I'm not made of India rubber."

"Just lean into me, then one, two, three, and spring your leg over. Come on. I've got you."

Margery had a firm grip on Isabelle's braced leg. But the girl seemed incapable of springing. Margery glanced up and noticed Alice. Her expression was deliberately blank.

"It's no good," the girl said, straightening. "I can't do it. And it's pointless to keep trying."

"Well, it's a heck of a long walk up those mountains, so you're gonna have to work out how to get on him somehow." Surreptitiously, Margery rubbed at the small of her back.

"I told Mother this was a bad idea. But she wouldn't listen." Isabelle saw Alice and that seemed to make her even crosser. She flushed, and the horse shifted. She yelped as it nearly stood on her foot, and stumbled in her effort to get out of the way. "Oh, you stupid animal!"

"Well, that's a little rude," Margery said. "Don't listen, Patch."

"I can't get up. I don't have the strength. This whole thing is ridiculous. I don't know why my mother won't listen to me. Why can't I just stay in the cabin?"

"Because we need you out there delivering books."

It was then that Alice noticed the tears in the corners of Isabelle Brady's eyes, as if this were not just a tantrum but something that sprang from real anguish. The girl turned away, brushing at her face with a pale hand. Margery had seen them too—they exchanged a brief, awkward look. Margery rubbed at her elbows to get the dust from her shirt. Alice sipped her coffee. The sound of Patch's chewing, regular and oblivious, was the only thing that broke the silence.

"Isabelle? Can I ask you a question?" said Alice, after a moment. "If you're sitting, or only walking short distances, do you need to wear the brace?"

There was a sudden silence, as if the word had been *verboten*.

"What do you mean?"

Oh, I've done it again, thought Alice. But she was too far in now. "That leg brace. I mean, if we took it off, and your boots, you could wear—um—normal riding boots. You could mount on the other side of Patch here, using the other leg. And maybe just drop the books by the gates instead of climbing on and off, like we do. Or maybe if the walk isn't too far it wouldn't matter?"

Isabelle frowned. "But I—I don't take off the brace. I'm supposed to wear it all day."

Margery frowned, thinking. "You ain't gonna be standing, though, right?"

"Well. No," Isabelle said.

"You want me to see if we got some other boots?" Margery asked.

"You want me to wear another person's boots?" said Isabelle, dubiously.

"Only till your ma buys you a fancy pair from Lexington."

"What size are you? I have a spare pair," said Alice.

"But even if I get on, my . . . Well, one leg is . . . It's shorter. I won't be balanced," said Isabelle.

Margery grinned. "That's why we got adjustable stirrup leathers. Most people round here ride half crooked anyway, drunk or no."

Perhaps it was because Alice was British and had addressed Isabelle in the same clipped tones that she addressed the Van Cleves when she wanted something, or perhaps it was the novelty of being told she didn't have to wear a brace, but an hour later Isabelle Brady sat astride Patch, her knuckles white as she gripped the reins, her body rigid with fear. "You're not going to go fast, are you?" she said, her voice tremulous. "I really don't want to go fast."

"You coming, Alice? Reckon this is a good day for us to head round the town, schoolhouse and all. Long as we can keep Patch here from falling asleep we'll have a fine day. You okay, girls? Off we go."

Isabelle said almost nothing for the first hour of their ride. Alice, who rode behind her, heard the occasional squeal as Patch coughed, or moved his head. Margery would lean back in her saddle and call something encouraging. But it took a good four miles before Alice could see that Isabelle had allowed herself to breathe normally, and even then she looked furious and unhappy, her eyes glittering with tears, even though they barely broke out of a slumberous walk.

For all they had achieved in getting her onto a horse, Alice could not see how on earth this was going to work. The girl didn't want to be there. She couldn't walk without a brace. She clearly didn't like horses. For all they knew she didn't even like books. Alice wondered whether she would turn up the following day, and when she occasionally met Margery's eye, she knew she was wondering the same. She missed the way they normally rode together, the easy silences, the way she felt as if she were learning something with Margery's every casual utterance. She missed the exhilarating gallops up the flatter tracks, yelling encouragement at each other on wheeling horses as they worked out ways to traverse rivers, fences, and the satisfaction as they jumped a flint-strewn gap. Perhaps it would be easier if the girl weren't so sullen: her mood seemed to cast a pall over the morning, and even the glorious sunshine and soft breeze couldn't alleviate it. *In all likelihood we'll be back to normal tomorrow*, Alice told herself, and was reassured by the thought.

It was almost nine thirty by the time they stopped at the school, a small weather-boarded one-room building not unlike the library. Outside there was a small grassy area worn half bare from constant use, and a bench underneath a tree. Some children sat outside cross-legged, bent over slates, while inside others were repeating times tables in a frayed chorus.

"I'll wait out here," Isabelle said.

"No, you won't," Margery said. "You come on into the yard. You don't have to get off the horse if you don't want to. Mrs. Beidecker? You in there?"

A woman appeared at the open door, followed by a clamor of children.

As Isabelle, her face mutinous, followed them into the yard, Margery dismounted and introduced the two of them to the schoolteacher, a young woman with neatly coiled blonde hair and a German accent, who, Margery explained afterward, was the daughter of one of the overseers at the mine. "They got people from all over the world up there," she said. "Every tongue you can imagine. Mrs. Beidecker here speaks four languages."

The teacher, who professed herself delighted to see them, brought the entire class of forty-odd children out to say hello to the women, pet the horses and ask questions. Margery pulled from her saddlebag a selection of children's books that had arrived earlier that week, explaining the plot of each as she handed them out. The children jostled for them, their heads bent low as they sat to examine them in groups on the grass. One, apparently unafraid of the mule, stepped into Margery's stirrup and peered into her empty bag in case she might have missed one.

"Miss? Miss? Do you have more of the books?" A gap-toothed girl, her hair in twin plaits, gazed up at Alice.

"Not this week," she said. "But I promise we'll bring more next week."

"Can you bring me a comic book? My sister read a comic book and it was awful good. It had pirates and a princess and everything."

"I'll do my best," said Alice.

"You talk like a princess," the girl said shyly.

"Well, you look like a princess," said Alice, and the girl giggled and ran away.

Two boys, around eight years old, sauntered past Alice to Isabelle, who was waiting near the gate. They asked her name, which she gave them, unsmiling, in a one-word answer.

"He your horse, Miss?"

"No," said Isabelle.

"You got a horse?"

"No. I don't much care for them." She scowled, but the boys didn't appear to notice.

"What's his name?"

Isabelle hesitated. "Patch," she said eventually, casting a glance behind her as if bracing herself to be told she was wrong.

One boy told the other animatedly about his uncle's horse that could apparently leap a fire truck without breaking a sweat, and the other said he had once ridden a real-life unicorn at the County Fair, and it had had a horn and everything. Then, having stroked Patch's whiskery nose for a few minutes, they appeared to lose interest, and with a wave at Isabelle, they wandered off to where their classmates were looking at books.

"Isn't this lovely, children?" Mrs. Beidecker called. "These fine ladies will be bringing us new books every week! So we have to make sure we look after them, don't bend the spines and, William Bryant, that we do not throw them at our sisters. Even if they do poke us in the eye. We will see you next week, ladies! Much obliged to you!"

The children waved cheerfully, their voices rising in a crescendo of good-byes, and when Alice looked back some minutes later, there were still a few pale faces peering out, waving enthusiastically through the windows. Alice watched as Isabelle gazed after them and noted that the girl was half smiling; it was a slow, wistful thing, and hardly joyful, but it was a smile nonetheless.

. . .

They rode away in silence, into the mountains, following the narrow trails that bordered the creek and staying in single file, Margery deliberately keeping the pace steady in front. Occasionally she would call and point at landmarks, perhaps in the hope that Isabelle would be distracted or finally express some enthusiasm.

"Yes, yes," said Isabelle, dismissively. "That's Handmaiden's Rock. I know."

Margery twisted in her saddle. "You know Handmaiden's Rock?"

"Father used to make me walk with him in the mountains when I first recovered from the polio. Hours every day. He reckoned that if I used my legs enough I would level up."

They stopped in a clearing. Margery dismounted, pulling a water bottle and some apples from her saddle pack, passing them out, then taking a swig from the bottle. "It didn't work then," she said, nodding toward Isabelle's leg. "The walking thing."

Isabelle's eyes widened. "Nothing is going to work," she said. "I'm a cripple."

"Nah. You ain't." Margery rubbed an apple on her jacket. "If you were, you couldn't walk and you couldn't ride. You can clearly do both, even if you are a little one-ways." Margery offered the water to Alice, who drank thirstily, then passed it to Isabelle, who shook her head.

"You must be thirsty," Alice protested.

Isabelle's mouth tightened. Margery regarded her steadily. Finally, she reached out with a handkerchief, rubbed the neck of the water bottle, then handed it to Isabelle, with only the faintest eye-roll at Alice.

Isabelle raised it to her lips, closing her eyes as she drank. She handed back the bottle, pulled a small lace handkerchief from her pocket and wiped her forehead. "It is awfully warm today," she conceded.

"Yup. And no place on earth better than the cool of the mountains." Margery strode down to the creek and refilled her bottle, screwing the lid back on tightly. "Give me and Patch two weeks, Miss Brady, and I promise you, legs or no, you won't want to be anywhere else in Kentucky."

Isabelle looked unconvinced. The women ate their apples in silence, fed the horses and Charley the cores, then mounted again. This time, Alice noted, Isabelle scrambled up by herself without complaint. She rode behind her for a while, watching.

"You liked the children." Alice rode up next to her as they started on the track to the side of a long green field. Margery was some distance ahead, singing to herself, or perhaps to the mule—it was often hard to tell.

"I'm sorry?"

"You looked happier. At the school." Alice smiled tentatively. "I thought you might have enjoyed that part of today."

Isabelle's face clouded. She gathered up her reins and half turned away.

"I'm sorry, Miss Brady," said Alice, after a moment. "My husband tells me I speak without thinking. I've obviously done it again. I didn't mean to be . . . intrusive or rude. Forgive me."

She pulled her horse back so that she was once again behind Isabelle Brady. She cursed herself silently, wondering whether she would ever be able to find the right balance with these people. Isabelle plainly didn't want to communicate at all. She thought of Peggy's clique of young women, most of whom she only recognized in town because they scowled at her. She thought of Annie, who, half the time, looked at her as if she'd stolen something. Margery was the only one who didn't make her feel like an alien. And she, to be fair, was a little odd herself.

They had gone another half-mile when Isabelle turned her head so that she was looking over her shoulder. "It's Izzy," she said.

"Izzy?"

"My name. People I like call me Izzy."

Alice barely had time to digest this when the girl spoke again. "And I smiled because . . . it was the first time."

Alice leaned forward, trying to make out the words. The girl spoke so quietly.

"First time for what? Riding in the mountains?"

"No." Izzy straightened up a little. "The first time I've been in a school and nobody was laughing at me for my leg."

Y ou think she'll come back?"

Margery and Alice sat on the top step of the stoop, batting away flies and watching heat rise off the shimmering road. The horses had been washed and set loose in the pasture and the two women were drinking coffee, stretching creaking limbs and trying to summon the energy to check and enter the days' books in the ledger.

"Hard to say. She don't seem to like it much."

Alice had to admit she was probably right. She watched as a panting dog walked along the road, then lowered itself wearily into the shade of a nearby log store.

"Not like you."

Alice looked up at her. "Me?"

"You're like a prisoner sprung from jail most mornings." Margery sipped her coffee and gazed out at the road. "I sometimes think you love these mountains as much as I do."

Alice kicked at a pebble with her heel. "I think I might like them better than anywhere on earth. I just feel . . . more myself up here."

Margery glanced at her and smiled conspiratorially. "This is what people don't see, wrapped up in their cities, with the noise and the smoke, and their tiny boxes for houses. Up there you can breathe. You can't hear the town talking and talking. No eyes on you, 'cept God's. It's just you and the trees and the birds and the river and the sky and freedom . . . Out there, it's good for the soul."

A prisoner sprung from jail. Sometimes Alice wondered if Margery knew more about her life with the Van Cleves than she let on. She was dragged from her thoughts by a blaring horn. Bennett was driving his father's motor-car toward the library. He shuddered to an abrupt halt, so that the dog leaped up, its tail between its legs. He was waving at her, his smile wide and uncomplicated. She couldn't help but smile back: he was as handsome as a movie star on a cigarette card.

"Alice! . . . Miss O'Hare," he said, catching sight of her.

"Mr. Van Cleve," Margery answered.

"Came to fetch you home. Thought we might take that picnic you were talking about."

Alice blinked. "Really?"

"Got a couple of problems with the coal tipple that won't be fixed until tomorrow and Pa's in the office trying to sort it out. So I flew home and got Annie to do us a picnic. Thought I'd race you back in the car and you can get changed and we'll head straight out while it's still light. Pa says we can have this old girl all evening."

Alice stood up, delighted. Then her face fell. "Oh, Bennett, I can't. We haven't entered the books or sorted them and we're so behind. We've only just finished the horses."

"You go," said Margery.

"But that's not fair on you. Not with Beth gone and Izzy disappearing as soon as we got back."

Margery waved a hand.

"But—"

"Go on now. I'll see you tomorrow."

Alice glanced at her to check that she meant it, then gathered up her things and whooped as she raced down the steps. "I probably smell like a cowboy again," she warned, as she climbed into the passenger side and kissed her husband's cheek.

He grinned. "Why do you think I've got the top open?" He reversed into a speedy three-point turn, causing the dust to fly up in the road, and Alice squealed as they roared toward home.

He was not a mule prone to exaggerated shows of temper or high emotion, but Margery rode Charley home at a slow walk. He had worked hard and she was in no hurry. She sighed, thinking of the day.

A flighty Englishwoman who knew nothing of the area, whom the mountain people might not trust, and would probably be pulled away by that braying blowhard Mr. Van Cleve, and a girl who could barely walk, couldn't ride and didn't want to be there. Beth worked when she could but her family would need her for the harvest during much of September. Hardly the most auspicious start to a traveling library. She wasn't sure how long any of them would last.

They reached the broken-down barn where the trail split and she dropped her reins onto his narrow neck, knowing the mule would find his own way home. As she did, her dog, a young blue-eyed speckled hound, bolted toward her, his tail clamped between his legs and his tongue lolling in his delight to see her. "What in heck are you doing out here, Bluey boy? Huh? Why aren't you in the yard?"

She reached the small paddock gate and dismounted, noting that the ache in her lower back and shoulders probably owed more to hoisting Izzy Brady on and off a horse than any real distance she had traveled. The dog bounded around her, only settling when she ruffled his neck between her hands and confirmed that *yes, he was a good boy, yes, he was*, at which point he raced back into the house. She released the mule, watching as Charley dropped to the ground, folding his knees under him, then rocking backward and forward in the dirt with a satisfied groan.

She didn't blame him: her own feet were heavy as she made her way up the steps. She reached for the door, then stopped. The latch was off. She stared at it for a moment, thinking, then walked quietly to the empty barrel at the side of the barn where she kept her spare rifle under a piece of sacking. Alert now, she lifted the safety catch and raised it to her shoulder. Then she tiptoed back up the steps, took a breath, and quietly hooked the door open with the toe of her boot.

"Who's there?"

Directly across the room, Sven Gustavsson sat on her rocker, his feet up on the low table and a copy of *Robinson Crusoe* in his hands. He didn't flinch, but waited a moment for her to lower the gun. He put the book carefully on the table, and rose to his feet slowly, placing his hands with almost exaggerated courtesy behind his back. She stared at him for a moment, then propped her gun against the table. "I wondered why the dog didn't bark."

"Yeah, well. Me and him. You know how it is."

Bluey, that squirming traitor, was nestling under Sven's arm now, pushing at him with his long nose, begging to be petted.

Margery took off her hat and hung it on the hook, then pushed the sweaty hair from her forehead. "Wasn't expecting to see you."

"You weren't looking."

Without meeting his eye, she moved past him to the table, where she pulled the lace cover from a jug of water and poured herself a cup.

"You not going to offer me some?"

"Never knew you to drink water before."

"And you won't offer me anything stronger?"

She put the cup down. "What are you doing here, Sven?"

He looked at her steadily. He was wearing a clean checked shirt and he gave off a smell of coal-tar soap and something uniquely his, something that spoke of the sulfurous smell of the mine and smoke and maleness. "I missed you."

She felt something give a little in her, and brought the cup to her lips to hide it. She swallowed. "Seems to me you're doing just fine without me."

"You and I both know I can do just fine without you. But here's the thing: I don't want to."

"We've been through this."

"And I still don't get it. I told you if we marry I won't try to pin you down. I won't control you. I'll let you live exactly as you live now except you and I—"

"You'll *let* me, will you?"

"Goddamn it, Marge, you know what I mean." His jaw tightened. "I'll let you be. We can be exactly as we are now."

"Then what's the point in us going through with a wedding?"

"The point is that we'll be married in the eyes of God, not sneaking around like a pair of goddamn kids. You think I like this? You think I want to hide from my own brother, from the rest of the town, the fact that I love the bones of you?"

"I won't marry you, Sven. I always told you I wouldn't marry anybody. And every time you go on about it I swear my head feels like it's going to explode just like the dynamite in one of your tunnels. I won't talk to you if you're just going to keep coming here and going over the same thing again and again."

"You won't talk to me anyways. So what in hell am I supposed to do?"

"Leave me alone. Like we decided."

"Like you decided."

She turned away from him and walked to the bowl in the corner, where she had covered some beans she had picked early that morning. She began stringing them, one by one, snapping off the ends and throwing them into a pan, waiting for the blood to stop thumping in her ears.

She felt him before she saw him. He walked quietly across the room and stood directly behind her so that she could feel his breath on her bare neck. She knew without looking that her skin flushed where it touched her.

"I'm not like your father, Margery," he murmured. "If you don't know that about me by now then there's no telling you."

She kept her hands busy. Snap. Snap. Snap. *Keep the beans. Discard the string.* The floorboards creaked under her feet.

"Tell me you don't miss me."

Ten gone. Strip off that leaf. Snap. And another. He was so close now that she could feel his chest against her as he spoke.

His voice lowered. "Tell me you don't miss me and I'll head out of here right now. I won't bother you again. I promise."

She closed her eyes. She let the knife fall, and put her hands on the work surface, palms down, her head dipping. He waited a moment,

then placed his own over them gently, so that hers were entirely covered. She opened her eyes and regarded them: strong hands, knuckles
covered with raised burn scars. Hands she had loved for the best part
of a decade.

"Tell me," he said quietly, into her ear.

She turned then, swiftly taking his face between her hands and
kissing him, hard. Oh, but she had missed the feel of his lips on hers,
his skin against hers. Heat rose between them, her breath quickened,
and everything she had told herself, the logic, the arguments she had
rehearsed in her head in the long dark hours, melted away as his arm
slid around her, pulling her into him. She kissed him and she kissed
him and she kissed him, his body familiar and newly unfamiliar to
her, reason leaching away with the aches and pains and frustrations of
the day. She heard a clatter as the bowl fell to the floor, then it was
only his breath, his lips, his skin upon hers and Margery O'Hare, who
would be owned by nobody, and told by nobody, let herself soften and
give, her body lowering inch by inch until it was pinned against the
wooden sideboard by the weight of his own.

W hat kind of bird is that? Look at the color of it. It's so beautiful."
Bennett lay on his back on the rug as Alice pointed above
them to the branches of the tree. Around them sat the remains of their
picnic.

"Darling? Do you know what bird that is? I've never seen anything
as red as that. Look! Even its beak is red."

"I'm not much for reading up on birds and such, sweetheart." She
saw that Bennett's eyes were closed. He slapped at a bug on the side of
his cheek, and held out his hand for another ginger beer.

Margery knew all the different birds, Alice thought, as she reached
across to the hamper. She resolved to ask her the following morning. As
they rode, Margery talked to Alice of milkweed and goldenrod, pointing out Jack-in-the-pulpit and the tiny fragile flowers of touch-me-nots,

so that once where Alice had just seen a sea of green, she had pulled back a veil to reveal a whole new dimension.

Below them the creek trickled peacefully; the same creek, Margery had warned her, that would become a destructive torrent during the spring. It seemed so unlikely. For now the earth was dry, the grass a soft thatch under their heads, the crickets a steady hum across the meadow. Alice handed her husband the bottle and waited as he lifted himself on one elbow to take a swig from it, half hoping that he would just lean over her and scoop her up. When he lowered himself down she tucked herself into his arm and placed her hand on his shirt.

"Well, I could just stay like this all day," he said peaceably.

She reached her arm across him. Her husband smelled better than any man she'd ever met. It was as if he carried the sweetness of the Kentucky grass with him. Other men sweated and grew sour and grubby. Bennett always returned from the mine settlement as if he had just walked out of a magazine advertisement. She gazed at his face, at the strong contours of his chin, the way his honey-colored hair was clipped short just around his ears.

"Do you think I'm pretty, Bennett?"

"You know I think you're pretty." His voice was sleepy.

"Are you happy we got married?"

"Of course I am."

Alice trailed a finger around his shirt button. "Then why—"

"Let's not get all serious, Alice, huh? No need to go on about things, is there? Can't we just have a nice time?"

Alice lifted her hand from his shirt. She twisted and lowered herself down onto the rug so that only their shoulders were touching. "Sure."

They lay in the grass, side by side, looking up at the sky, in silence. When he spoke again, his voice was soft. "Alice?"

She glanced at him. She swallowed, her heart thumping against her ribcage. She placed her hand on his, trying to convey to him her tacit encouragement, to tell him without words that she would be a support, that it would be okay, whatever he said. She was his wife, after all.

She waited a moment. "Yes?"

"It's a cardinal," he said. "The red one. I'm pretty sure it's a cardinal."

FOUR

★

*. . . marriage, they say, halves one's rights and
doubles one's duties.*

· Louisa May Alcott, *Little Women*

The first memory Margery O'Hare had was of sitting under her
mother's kitchen table and watching through her fingers as her
father slugged her fourteen-year-old brother Jack across the room,
knocking two teeth clean out of his jaw when he tried to stop him
beating her mother. Her mother, who took a fair number of beatings
but would not tolerate that fate for her children, promptly threw a
kitchen chair at her husband's head, leaving him with a jagged scar on
his forehead that remained until he died. He hit her back with its
smashed leg, of course, once he was able to stand straight, and the fight
had only stopped when Papaw O'Hare had staggered round from next
door with his rifle at his shoulder and murder in his eyes and threatened
to blow Frank O'Hare's damn head clean off his damn shoulders if he
didn't stop. It wasn't that Grandpa believed his son beating his wife was
inherently wrong, Margery discovered some time later, but Memaw
had been trying to listen to the wireless and half the holler couldn't
hear past the screaming. There was a hole in the pinewood wall that
Margery could put her whole fist into for the rest of her childhood.

Jack left for good that day, a wad of bloodied cotton in his mouth and his one good shirt in his kit bag, and the next time Margery heard his name (leaving was considered such an act of family disloyalty he was effectively disappeared from family history) was eight years later when they received a wire to say that Jack had died after being hit by a railroad car in Missouri. Her mother had cried salty, heartbroken tears into her apron, but her father had hurled a book at her and told her to pull her damn self together before he really gave her something to cry about and disappeared to his stills. The book was *Black Beauty* and Margery never forgave him for having ripped off the back cover while doing so and somehow her love for her lost brother and her desire to escape into the world of books became melded together into something fierce and obstinate in that one broken-backed copy.

Don't you marry one of these fools, her mother would whisper to her and her sister, as she tucked them into the big hay bed in the back room. *You make sure you two get as far from this damn mountain as you can. As soon as you can. You promise me.*

The girls had nodded solemnly.

Virginia had got away all right, got as far as Lewisburg, only to marry a man who turned out to be just as handy with his fists as their father had been. Her mother, thank goodness, was not alive to see it, having caught pneumonia six months after the wedding and died within three days; the same strain that took three of Margery's brothers. Their graves were marked with small stones on a hill overlooking the holler.

When her father died, killed in a drunken gunfight with Bill McCullough—the latest sorry episode in a clan feud that had lasted generations—the residents of Baileyville noted that Margery O'Hare didn't shed so much as a tear. "Why would I?" she said, when Pastor McIntosh asked her if she was quite all right. "I'm glad he's dead. Can't do no more harm to no one." The fact that Frank O'Hare was reviled in town, and that everyone knew she was right, didn't stop them deciding that the surviving O'Hare girl was as odd as the rest of them and that, frankly, the fewer of that bloodline still around, the better.

"Can I ask you about your family?" Alice had said, as they saddled up the horses, shortly after dawn.

Margery, her thoughts still lost somewhere in Sven's strong, hard body, had had to be spoken to twice before she realized what Alice was saying. "Ask what you want." She glanced over. "Let me guess. Someone tell you you shouldn't be around me because of my daddy?"

"Well, yes," said Alice, after a pause. Mr. Van Cleve had given her a lecture on that exact subject the previous evening, accompanied by much spluttering and finger-pointing. Alice had wielded the good name of Mrs. Brady as a shield but it had been an uncomfortable exchange.

Margery nodded, as if this was no surprise. She swung her saddle onto the rail and ran her fingers over Charley's back, checking him for bumps and sores. "Frank O'Hare supplied moonshine to half the county. Shot up anyone who tried to take over his patch. Shot 'em if he reckoned they'd even thought about it. Killed more people than I know of, and left scars on everyone he was close to."

"Everyone?"

Margery hesitated a moment, then took a couple of steps toward Alice. She rolled up her shirt-sleeve, tugging it above the elbow, revealing a waxy, coin-shaped scar on her upper arm. "Shot me with his hunting rifle when I was eleven years old because I sassed him. If my brother hadn't pushed me out of the way he would have killed me."

Alice took a moment to speak. "Didn't the police do anything?"

"Police?" She said it *poh-lice.* "Up here people take care of things their own way. When Memaw found out what he'd done she took a horsewhip to him. Only two people he was ever scared of, his own mom and pop."

Margery put her head down so that her thick dark hair fell forward. She ran her fingers nimbly over her scalp until she found what she was looking for and pulled her hair to one side, revealing an inch-wide gap of bare skin. "That was where he pulled me up two flights of stairs by my hair three days after Memaw died. Pulled a handful of it clean out. They say he still had half my scalp attached to it when he dropped it."

"You don't remember?"

"Nope. He'd knocked me out before he did it."

Alice stood in stunned silence. Margery's voice was as level as always. "I'm so sorry," she faltered.

"Don't be. When he died there were two people in this whole town came to his funeral and one of those only did cos they felt sorry for me. You know how much this town loves to meet up? You imagine how much they hated him not even to show up at a man's funeral."

"You . . . don't miss him, then."

"Hah! Round here, Alice, you get a lot of what you call sundowners. They're good old boys in daylight hours, but come nightfall when they get to drinking, they're basically a pair of fists looking for a target."

Alice thought of Mr. Van Cleve's bourbon-fueled rants and shivered, despite the heat.

"Well, my daddy wasn't even a sundowner. He didn't need drink. Cold as ice. Don't have a single good memory of him."

"Not a single one?"

Margery thought for a moment. "Oh, no, you're right. There was one."

Alice waited.

"Yup. The day the sheriff stopped by to tell me he was dead."

Margery turned from the mule and the two women finished up in silence.

Alice felt completely out of her depth. Anyone else, she would have commiserated. Margery seemed to need less sympathy than anyone she'd ever met.

Perhaps Margery detected some of these mental gymnastics, or perhaps she felt she'd been a little harsh, because she turned to Alice and smiled suddenly. Alice was struck by the fact that she was actually quite beautiful. "You asked me a while back if I was ever frightened, up there in the mountains, on my own."

Alice's hand stilled on the girth buckle.

"Well, I'll tell you something. I've been afraid of nothing since the day my daddy passed. See that there?" She pointed toward the mountains that loomed in the distance. "That's what I dreamed of as a child.

Me and Charley, up there, that's my heaven, Alice. I get to live my heaven every day."

She let out a long breath, and as Alice was still digesting the softening of her face, the strange luminosity of her smile, she turned and slapped the back of her saddle. "Right. You all set? Big day for you. Big day for us all."

It was the first week that the four women had split up and ridden their own routes. They planned to meet at the library at the beginning and end of each week, to debrief, try to keep the books in order, and check the condition of those returned. Margery and Beth rode the longer routes, often leaving their books at a second base, a schoolhouse ten miles away and bringing those back fortnightly, while Alice and Izzy did the routes closer to home. Izzy had grown in confidence now, and several times Alice had arrived as she was already riding out, her polished new boots from Lexington gleaming, her humming audible the whole way down Main Street. "Good morning, Alice," she would call, her wave a little tentative, as if she were still not quite sure of the response she was going to get.

Alice didn't want to admit how nervous she felt. It wasn't just her fear of getting lost, or of making a fool of herself, but the conversation she had overheard between Beth and Mrs. Brady the week before, as she had unsaddled Spirit outside.

Oh, you all are just marvelous. But I confess I am a little anxious about the English girl.

She's doing fine, Mrs. Brady. Marge says she knows most of the routes pretty well.

It's not the routes, Beth dear. The whole point of using local girls to do the job was that the people you visit know you. They trust you not to look down at them, or to give their families anything unsuitable to read. If we have some strange girl going in talking with an accent and acting like the Queen of England, well, they're going to be on their guard. I'm afraid it's going to damage the whole scheme.

Spirit had snorted and they had quieted abruptly, as if realizing someone might be outside. Alice, ducking back behind the window, had felt a spasm of anxiety. If local people wouldn't take her books, she realized, they wouldn't let her have the job. She imagined herself suddenly back inside the Van Cleve house, heavy with silence, Annie's beady, suspicious gaze on her and a decade stretching ahead of her at every hour. She thought of Bennett, and the wall of his sleeping back, his refusal to try to talk about what was going on. She thought of Mr. Van Cleve's irritation that they had not yet provided him with a "little grandbabby."

If I lose this job, she thought, and something solid and heavy settled in her stomach, *I will have nothing.*

"Good mornin'!"

The whole way up the mountain Alice had been practicing. She had murmured, "Well, good morning! And how are you this fine day?" to Spirit over and over, rolling her mouth around the vowels, trying to stop herself sounding so clipped and English.

A young woman, probably not much older than Alice, emerged from a cabin and peered at her, shading her eyes. In the sunlit, grassy patch in front of the house, two children looked up at her. They resumed their desultory fight over a stick while a dog watched intently. A bowl of unshucked sweetcorn had been left, as if awaiting transport, and a pile of laundry lay on a sheet on the ground. Some pulled weeds were thrown in a pile by the vegetable patch, the earth still on their roots. The house appeared surrounded by such half-finished tasks. From inside Alice could hear a baby crying, a furious, disconsolate wail.

"Mrs. Bligh?"

"Can I help you?"

Alice took a breath. "Good maoahning! Ah'm from the traveling laahbrurry," she said carefully. "Ah wuz wondering if yew would lahk some bewks, fer you and the young'uns. Fer to do some book learnin'."

The woman's smile faded.

"It's okay. They don't cawst nuffink," Alice added, smiling. She pulled a book from her saddlebag. "Yew kin borreh four and ah'll jest come pick 'em up next week."

The woman was silent. She narrowed her eyes, pursed her lips and looked down at her shoes. Then she brushed her hands on her apron and looked up again.

"Miss, are you mocking me?"

Alice's eyes widened.

"You're the English one, right? Married to Van Cleve's boy? Because if you're after mocking me you can head straight off back down that mountain."

"I'm not mocking you," Alice said quickly.

"Then you got somethin' wrong with your jaw?"

Alice swallowed. The woman was frowning at her. "I'm so sorry," she said. "I was told people wouldn't trust me enough to take books from me if I sounded too English. I was just . . ." Her voice trailed away.

"You was trying to sound like you was from round here?" The woman's chin pulled into her neck.

"I know. Said like that it sounds rather—I—" Alice closed her eyes and groaned inwardly.

The woman snorted with laughter. Alice's eyes snapped open. The woman started to laugh again, bent over her apron. "You tried to sound like you was from round here. Garrett? You hear that?"

"I heard," came a man's voice, followed by a burst of coughing.

Mrs. Bligh clutched her sides and laughed until she had to wipe the corners of her eyes. The children, watching her, began to chuckle too, with the hopeful, bemused faces of those who weren't quite sure what they were laughing at.

"Oh, my. Oh, Miss, I ain't laughed like that since as long as I can remember. You come on in now. I'd take books off you if you was from the other side of the world. I'm Kathleen. C'mon in. You need some water? It's hot enough to fry a snake out here."

Alice tied Spirit to the nearest tree and pulled a selection of books out of her pack. She followed the young woman up to the cabin, noting that there was no glass in the windows, just wooden shutters, and wondered absently what it must be like in the winter. She waited in the doorway, as her eyes acclimatized to the darkness, and gradually the interior revealed itself. The cabin appeared to be divided into two rooms. The walls of the front one were lined with newspaper, and on the far side stood a large wood-burning stove, beside which stood a stack of logs. Above the fireplace hung a string of tied candles, and a large hunting rifle on the wall. A table and four chairs stood in the corner, and a baby lay in a large crate beside it, its little fists pummeled the air as it cried. The woman stooped and picked it up with a vague air of exhaustion and the crying stopped.

It was then that Alice noticed the man in the bed across the room. The quilted covers pulled up to his chest, he was young and handsome, but his skin had the waxy pallor of the chronically ill. The air was still and stale around him, despite the open windows, and every thirty seconds or so he coughed.

"Good morning," she said, when she saw he was looking at her.

"Morning," he said, his voice weak and raspy. "Garrett Bligh. Sorry I can't stand just now to—"

She shook her head, as if it was of no matter.

"Have you got any of those *Woman's Home Companion* magazines?" said the young woman. "This baby is just a devil to settle right now and I was wondering if they had anything would help? I can read good enough, can't I, Garrett? Miss O'Hare brought me some a while back and they had advice on all sorts. I think it's his teeth but he don't want to chew on nothin'."

Alice startled, pulled back into action. She began flicking through the books and magazines, eventually pulling out two that she handed over. "Would the children like something?"

"You got any of those picture books? Pauly's got his alphabet but his sister just looks at the pictures. She loves them, though."

"Of course." Alice found two primers and handed them over.

Kathleen smiled, placing them reverently on the table, and handed Alice a cup of water. "I got some recipes. Got one for honey apple cake handed down from my mama. If you want it, I'd be happy to write it out and give it to you."

Mountain people, Margery had instructed her, were proud. Many of them didn't feel comfortable receiving without giving something back. "I'd love that. Thank you so much." Alice drank the water and handed back her cup. She made to leave, muttering about time getting on, when she realized that Kathleen and her husband were exchanging a look. She stood, wondering if she had missed something. They looked back at her, and the woman smiled brightly. Neither said a word.

Alice waited a moment, until it became awkward.

"Well, it's lovely to meet you all. I'll see you in a week and I'll make sure to look out for more articles about teething babies. Anything you want, I'll be happy to search it out. We have new books and magazines coming in by the week." She gathered up the remaining books.

"I'll see you next time, then."

"Much obliged to you," came the whispering voice from the bed, and then the words were lost in another bout of coughing.

The outside seemed impossibly bright after the gloom of the cabin. Alice found herself squinting as she waved good-bye to the children and made her way back across the grass to Spirit. She hadn't realized how high up they were here: she could see halfway across the county. She stopped for a minute, reveling in the view.

"Miss?"

She turned. Kathleen Bligh was running toward her. She stopped a few feet from Alice, then compressed her lips briefly as if she were afraid to speak.

"Is there something else?"

"Miss, my husband, he loves to read but his eyes ain't too good in the dark and, to be honest, he struggles to focus because of the black lung. He's in some pain most days. Could you read to him a little?"

"Read to him?"

"It takes his mind away. I can't do it because I got the house to mind and the baby, and kindling to chop. I wouldn't ask but Margery

74

did it the other week, and if you could spare a half-hour just to read him a chapter of something, well . . . it would mean the world to both of us."

Kathleen's face, away from her husband, had collapsed into exhaustion and strain, as if she dared not show what she felt in front of him. Her eyes glittered. She lifted her chin abruptly, as if she were embarrassed to be asking for anything. "Of course if you're too busy—"

Alice reached out and put a hand on her arm. "Why don't you tell me a little of what he likes? I have a new book of short stories here that sounds like it might be just the ticket. What do you think?"

Forty minutes later Alice picked her way down the mountain. Garrett Bligh had closed his eyes while she read and, sure enough, twenty minutes into the story—a stirring tale of a sailor shipwrecked on high seas—she had glanced from her stool beside the bed and observed that the muscles of his face, which had been taut with discomfort, had indeed relaxed as if he had taken himself somewhere else entirely. She kept her voice low, murmuring, and even the baby seemed to settle at the sound. Outside, Kathleen was a pale blur, chopping kindling, fetching, picking and carrying, alternately calming arguments and scolding. By the time the story finished, Garrett was asleep, his breath rasping in his chest.

"Thank you," Kathleen said, as Alice loaded her saddlebags. She held out two large apples and a piece of paper on which she had carefully written a recipe. "That's what I was telling you about. These apples are good for baking because they don't go all to a mush. Just don't overcook them." Her face had brightened again, her former resolve apparently restored.

"That's very kind of you. Thank you," said Alice, and tucked them carefully into her pockets. Kathleen nodded, as if a debt had been repaid, and Alice mounted her horse. She thanked her again and set off.

"Mrs. Van Cleve?" Kathleen called, when Alice had gone some twenty yards down the track.

Alice turned in her saddle. "Yes?"

Kathleen folded her arms across her chest and lifted her chin. "I think your voice sounds real fine just like it is."

The sun was fierce and the no-see-ums, the biting midges, were relentless. Through the long afternoon Alice, slapping at her neck and cursing, was grateful for the canvas-brimmed hat Margery had lent her. She managed to press an embroidery primer onto twin sisters who lived down by the creek and seemed to view even that with suspicion, was chased from a large house by a mean-looking dog, and gave a Bible reader to a family of eleven in the smallest house she had ever seen, where a series of hay mattresses lay on the porch. "Children of mine read nothin' but the Good Book," the mother had said, from behind a half-closed door, and set her jaw, as if braced for contradiction.

"Then I'll look out for some more Bible stories for you next week," Alice said, and tried to make her smile brighter than it felt as the door closed.

After the small victory at the Bligh house, she had begun to feel dispirited. She wasn't sure if it was the books people were viewing with suspicion or her. She kept hearing Mrs. Brady's voice, her reservations about whether Alice could do the job, given her *foreignness*. She was so distracted by this that it was some time before she realized she had stopped registering Margery's red threads on the trees and was now lost. She stopped in a clearing, trying to gauge from her hand-drawn maps where she was meant to be, struggling to see the position of the sun through the dark green canopy above. Spirit stood stock still, her head drooping in the mid-afternoon heat that managed to penetrate the branches.

"Aren't you meant to be finding your way home?" said Alice, grumpily.

She was forced to conclude she had no clue where she was. She would have to retrace her steps until she found her way back to a landmark. She turned the horse and wearily made her way up the side of the mountain.

It was a full half-hour before she recognized anything. She had tamped down her rising sense of panic at the creeping realization that she could quite easily end up on the mountainside at night, in the dark, with snakes and mountain lions and goodness knew what all around, or, just as worrying, at one of the addresses she was on no account to make a stop at: *Beever, on Frog Creek (crazy like a fox), the McCullough House (moonshiners, mostly drunk, not sure about the girls as no one ever sees 'em), the Garside brothers (drunk, ornery with it).* She wasn't sure whether she was more afraid of the prospect of being shot for trespass, or of Mrs. Brady's response when it emerged that the English-woman had not, after all, known what on earth she was doing.

Around her the landscape seemed to have stretched, revealing its vastness and her own ignorance at her place within it. Why hadn't she paid more attention to Margery's instructions? She squinted at the shadows, trying to work out where she might be according to their direction, then cursed when the clouds or the movement of the branches made them vanish. She was so relieved when she spied the red knot on the tree trunk that it took her a moment to grasp the identity of the house she was now approaching.

Alice rode past the front gate with her eyes lowered and her head down. The weather-boarded house was silent. The iron kettle sat outside in a cold pile of ash, and a large ax lay abandoned in a chunk of tree stump. Two dirty glass windows eyed her blankly. And there they were, four books in a neat pile by the post, just where Margery had told Jim Horner to leave them if he decided he didn't want books in his house after all. She pulled Spirit up and climbed off, one eye warily on the window, remembering the bullet-sized hole in Margery's hat. The books appeared untouched. She picked them up under one arm, packed them carefully in her saddlebags, then checked the mare's girth. She had one foot in the stirrup, her heart beating uncomfortably fast, when she heard the man's voice echo out across the holler.

"Hey!"

She stopped.

"Hey—you!"

Alice closed her eyes.

"You that library girl stopped here before?"

"I wasn't bothering you, Mr. Horner," she called. "I just—I just came to pick up the books. I'll be gone before you know it. Nobody else will come by."

"You was lying?"

"What?" Alice took her foot out of the stirrup and spun round.

"You said you was going to bring us some more."

Alice blinked. He wasn't smiling, but he wasn't holding a gun either. He stood in the doorway, his hands loosely by his sides, and lifted one to point at the gatepost. "You want more books?"

"Said so, didn't I?"

"Oh, goodness. Of course. Um . . ." Nerves made her clumsy. She fumbled in the bag, pulling and rejecting what came to hand. "Yes. Well. I brought some Mark Twain and a book of recipes. Oh, and this magazine has some canning tips. You were all canning, weren't you? I can leave that if you like."

"I want a speller." He pointed loosely, as if that might summon it. "For the girls. I want one of them with just words and a picture each page. Nothing fancy."

"I think I have something like that . . . Hold on." Alice rummaged in her saddlebag and eventually pulled out a child's reading book. "Like this? This one has been very popular among—"

"Just leave them by the post."

"Done! There they are! . . . Lovely!" Alice stooped to place the books in a neat pile, then backed away and turned to spring onto her horse. "Right. I'm . . . I'm going now. Be sure to let me know if there's anything particular you want me to bring next week."

She lifted a hand. Jim Horner was standing in the doorway, two girls behind him, watching her. Although her heart was still beating wildly, when she reached the bottom of the dirt track she found she was smiling.

FIVE

*Each mine, or group of mines, became a social center with
no privately owned property except the mine, and no
public places or public highway except the bed of the creek,
which flowed between the mountain walls. These groups
of villages dot the mountain sides down the river valleys
and need only castles, draw-bridges, and donjon-keeps to
reproduce to the physical eye a view of feudal days.*

· **United States Coal Commission in 1923**

It pained Margery to admit it, but the little library on Split Creek
Road was growing chaotic and, faced with the ever-growing demand for books, not one of the four of them had time to do much
about it. Despite the initial suspicion of some inhabitants of Lee
County, word had spread about the book ladies, as they had become
known, and within a few short weeks it was more common for them
to be greeted by eager smiles than it was for doors to be rapidly closed
in their faces. Families clamored for reading material, from the *Woman's Home Companion* to *The Furrow* for men. Everything from Charles
Dickens to the *Dime Mystery Magazine* was ripped from their hands
almost as soon as they could pull it from their saddlebags. The comic
books, wildly popular among the county's children, suffered most,
being thumbed to death or their fragile pages ripped as siblings fought
over them. Magazines would occasionally be returned with a favorite

page quietly removed. And still the demand came: *Miss, have you got new books for us?*

When the librarians returned to their base at Frederick Guisler's cabin, instead of plucking rigorously organized books from his hand-made shelves, they were more often to be found on the floor, riffling through countless piles for the requested titles, yelling at each other when someone else turned out to be sitting on the one they needed.

"I guess we're victims of our own success," said Margery, glancing around at the stacks on the floor.

"Should we start sorting through them?" Beth was smoking a cigarette—her father would have whipped her if he'd seen it and Margery pretended she hadn't.

"No point. We'll barely touch the sides this morning and it'll be just as bad when we get back. No, I've been thinking we need someone here full time to sort it out."

Beth looked at Izzy. "You wanted to stay back here, didn't you? And she ain't the strongest of riders."

Izzy bristled. "I do not, thank you, Beth. My families know me. They wouldn't like it if someone else took over my routes."

She had a point. Despite Beth's sly digs, Izzy Brady, in six short weeks, had grown into a competent horsewoman, if not a great one, her balance compensating for her weaker leg, its difference now invisible in the dark mahogany leather boots that she kept polished to a high shine. She had taken to carrying her stick on the back of the saddle to aid her when she had to walk the last steps up to a house, and found it came in handy for whacking at branches, keeping mean dogs at bay, and shifting the occasional snake. Most families around Baileyville were a little in awe of Mrs. Brady, and Izzy, once she'd introduced herself, was usually welcomed.

"Besides, Beth," Izzy added, slyly producing her trump card, "you know if I stay here you'll have my mother fixin' and fussin' all the time. Only thing keeping her away now is thinking I'm out all day."

"Oh, I'd really rather not," said Alice, as Margery turned toward her. "My families are doing well, too. Jim Horner's eldest girl read the whole of *The American Girl* last week. He was so proud he even forgot to shout at me."

"I guess it's Beth, then," said Izzy.

Beth stubbed out her cigarette on the wood floor with the heel of her boot. "Don't look at me. I hate cleaning up. Do enough of it for my damn brothers."

"Do you have to curse?" Izzy sniffed.

"It's not just clearing up," Margery said, picking up a copy of *The Pickwick Papers*, from which the innards sagged in a weary spray. "These were ratty to start with and now they're falling apart. We need someone who can sew up the binders and maybe make scrapbooks out of all these loose pages. They're doing that over at Hindman and they're real popular. Got recipes and stories in them and everything."

"My sewing is atrocious," said Alice, quickly, and the others concurred loudly that they, too, were awful at it.

Margery pulled an exasperated face. "Well, I ain't doing it. Got paws for hands." She thought for a minute. "I got an idea, though." She got up from behind the table and reached for her hat.

"What?" said Alice.

"Where are you going?" said Beth.

"Hoffman. Beth, can you pick up some of my rounds? I'll see y'all later."

You could hear the ominous sounds of the Hoffman Mining Company a good couple of miles before you saw it: the rumble of the coal trucks, the distant *whumpf* of the explosions that vibrated through your feet, the clang of the mine bell. For Margery, Hoffman was a vision of Hell, its pits eating into the scarred and hollowed-out hillsides around Baileyville, like giant welts, its men, their eyes glowing white out of blackened faces, emerging from its bowels, and the low industrial hum of nature being stripped and ravaged. Around the settlement the taste of coal dust hung in the air, with an ever-present sense of foreboding, explosions covering the valley with a gray filter.

Even Charley balked at it. A certain kind of man looked at God's own land, she thought, as she drew closer, and instead of beauty and wonder, all he saw was dollar signs.

Hoffman was a town with its own rules. The price of a wage and a roof over your head was a creeping debt to the company store, and the never-ending fear of a misjudged measurement of dynamite, a lost limb from a runaway trolley, or worse: the end of it all, several hundred feet below, with little chance for your loved ones to recover a body to grieve over.

And, since a year back, all of this had become suffused in an air of mistrust as the union-busters arrived to beat back those who had the temerity to campaign for better conditions. The mine bosses didn't like change, and they had shown it not in argument and raised fists but with mobs, guns and, now, families in mourning.

"That you, Margery O'Hare?" The guard took two steps toward her as she rode up, his hand shielding his eyes from the sun.

"Sure is, Bob."

"You know Gustavsson's here?"

"Everything all right?" She felt the familiar metallic taste in her mouth whenever she heard Sven's name.

"Everyone accounted for. Think they're just having a bite to eat before they head off. Last saw them over by B Block."

She dismounted and tied up the mule, then walked through the gates, ignoring the glances from miners clocking off. She walked briskly past the commissary, its windows advertising various on-sale bargains that everyone knew to be no bargain at all. It stood on the hillside at the same level as the huge tipple. Above it were the generous, well-maintained houses of the mine bosses and their foremen, most with neat backyards. This was where Van Cleve would have lived, had Dolores not refused to leave her family home back in Baileyville. It was not one of the larger coal camps, like Lynch, where some ten thousand homes scattered the hillsides. Here a couple of hundred miners' shacks stretched along the tracks, their roofs covered with tar-paper, barely updated in the forty-odd years of their existence. A few children, mostly shoeless, played in the dirt beside a rootling pig. Car parts and washing pails were strewn outside front doors, and stray dogs trotted haphazard paths between them. Margery turned right, away from the residential roads, and walked briskly over the small bridge that led to the mines.

She spied his back first. He was sitting on an upturned crate, his helmet cradled between his feet as he ate a hunk of bread. She'd know him anywhere, she thought. The way his neck met his shoulders and his head tilted a little to the left when he spoke. His shirt was covered with smuts and the tabard that read "FIRE" on his back was slightly askew.

"Hey."

He turned at the sound of her voice, stood and lifted his hands as his workmates began a series of low whistles, as if he were trying to tamp down a fire. "Marge! What are you doing here?" He took her arm, steering her away from the catcalls as they walked around the corner.

She looked at Sven's blackened palms. "Everyone okay?"

His eyebrows lifted. "This time." He shot a look at the administrative offices that told her everything she needed to know.

She reached up and wiped a smudge from his face with her thumb. He stopped her and pressed her hand to his lips. It always made something flip inside her, even if she didn't let it show on her face.

"You missed me, then?"

"No."

"Liar."

They grinned at each other.

"I came to find William Kenworth. I need to speak to his sister."

"Colored William? He isn't here no more, Marge. He got injured out, oh, six, nine months back."

She looked startled.

"I thought I told you. Some powder monkey messed up his wires and he was in the way when they blasted that tunnel through Feller's Top. Boulder took his leg clean off."

"So where is he now?"

"No idea. I can find out, though."

She waited outside the administrative offices while Sven went in and sweet-talked Mrs. Pfeiffer, whose favorite word was "no" but she rarely used it on Sven. Everyone across the five coal patches of Lee County loved Sven. He had, along with solid shoulders and fists the size of hams, an air of quiet authority, a twinkle in his eye, which told men he was one of them, and women he liked them, not just in *that* way. He was good at his job, kind when he felt he needed to be, and he spoke to everyone with the same uncommon civility, whether it was a ragged-trousered kid from the next holler, or the big bosses at the mine. Most days she could reel off a whole list of the things she liked about Sven Gustavsson. Not that she'd tell him.

He came down the steps from the office holding a piece of paper. "He's over at Monarch Creek, at his late mother's place. Been pretty poorly by all accounts. Turns out they'd only treat him the first couple of months in the hospital here, then he was out."

"Good of them."

Sven knew well how little she regarded Hoffman. "What do you want him for, anyway?"

"I wanted to find his sister. But if he's sick, I don't know if I should be bothering him. Last I heard she was working in Louisville."

"Oh, no. Mrs. Pfeiffer just told me his sister's the one looking out for him. Chances are you head over there, you'll find her, too."

She took the piece of paper from him and looked up. His eyes were on her, and his face softened under the black. "So when will I see you?"

"Depends when you stop yammering on about getting married."

He glanced behind him, then pulled her around the corner, placing her back against the wall as he stood close, as close as he could get. "Okay, how's this? Margery O'Hare, I solemnly promise never to marry you."

"And?"

"And I won't talk about marrying you. Or sing songs about it. Or even think about marrying you."

"Better."

He glanced around him, then lowered his voice, placing his mouth beside her ear so that she squirmed a little. "But I will stop by and do sinful things to that fine body of yours. If you'll allow me."

"How sinful?" she whispered.

"Oh. Bad. Ungodly."

She slid her hand inside his overalls, feeling the faint sheen of sweat on his warm skin. For a moment it was just the two of them. The sounds and scents of the mine receded, and all she could feel was the thumping of her heart, the pulse of his skin against hers, the ever-present drumbeat of her need for him. "God loves a sinner, Sven." She reached up and kissed him, then delivered a swift bite to his lower lip. "But not as much as I do."

He burst out laughing and, to her surprise, as she walked back to the mule, the safety crew's catcalls still ringing out, her cheeks had gone quite, quite pink.

It had been a long day, and by the time she reached the little cabin at Monarch Creek, both she and the mule were weary. She dismounted and threw her reins over the post.

"Hello?"

Nobody emerged. A carefully tended vegetable patch lay to the left of the cabin, and a small lean-to skimmed it, with two baskets hanging from the porch. Unlike most of the houses around this holler, it was freshly painted, the grass trimmed and weeds beaten into submission. A red rocker sat by the door looking out across the water meadow.

"Hello?"

A woman's face appeared at the screen door. She glanced out, as if checking something, then turned away, speaking to someone inside. "That you, Miss Margery?"

"Hey, Miss Sophia. How you doing?"

The screen door opened and the woman stood back to let Margery in, her hands on her hips, thick dark coils of hair pinned to her scalp. She lifted her head as if surveying her carefully. "Well, now. I haven't seen you in—what—eight years?"

"Something like that. You haven't changed none, though."

"Get in here."

Her face, so thin and stern in repose, broke into a lovely smile, and Margery repaid it in full. For several years Margery had accompanied her father on his moonshine runs to Hoffman, one of his more lucrative routes. Frank O'Hare figured that nobody would look twice at a girl with her daddy making deliveries into the settlement and he figured right. But while he made his way around the residential section, trading jars and paying off security guards, she would make her way quietly to the colored block, where Miss Sophia would lend her books from her family's small collection.

Margery had not been allowed to go to school—Frank had seen to that. He didn't believe in book learning, no matter how hard her mother had pleaded. But Miss Sophia and her mother, Miss Ada, had fostered in her a love of reading that, many evenings, had taken her a million miles from the darkness and violence of her home. And it wasn't just the books: Miss Sophia and Miss Ada always looked immaculate, their nails perfectly filed, their hair rolled and braided with surgical precision. Miss Sophia was only a year older than Margery, but her family represented to her a kind of order, a suggestion that life could be conducted quite differently from the noise, chaos and fear of her own.

"You know, I used to think you were going to eat those books, you were so hungry for them. Never knew a girl read so many so fast."

They smiled at each other. And then Margery spied William. He was seated in a chair by the window and the left leg of his pants was pinned neatly under the stump where it ended. She tried not to let the shock of it show as even a flicker on her face.

"Good afternoon, Miss Margery."

"I'm real sorry to hear about your accident, William. Are you in much pain?"

"It's tolerable," he said. "Just don't like not being able to work, that's all."

"He's about as ornery as all get out," said Sophia, and rolled her eyes. "He hates being in the house more than he hates losing that leg. You sit down and I'll fetch you a drink."

"She tells me I make the place look untidy." William shrugged.

The Kenworth cabin was the neatest, Margery suspected, for twenty miles. There was not a speck of dust or an item out of place, testament to Sophia's fearsome organizational skills. Margery sat and drank a glass of sarsaparilla, and listened as William told her how the mine had laid him off after his accident. "Union tried to stand up for me but since the shootings, well, nobody wants to stick their neck out too far for a black fellow. You know what I'm saying?"

"They shot two more union men last month."

"I heard." William shook his head.

"The Stiller brothers shot the tires out of three trucks headed out from the tipple. Next time they went into the company store at Friars to organize some of the men, a bunch of thugs trapped them in there and a whole bunch had to come over from Hoffman's to get them out. He's sending a warning."

"Who?"

"Van Cleve. You know he's behind half of this."

"Everybody knows," said Sophia. "Everybody knows what goes on in that place but nobody wants to do nothing."

The three of them sat in silence for so long that Margery almost forgot why she had come. Finally she put her glass down. "This isn't just a social call," she said.

"You don't say," said Sophia.

"I don't know if you heard, but I've been setting up a library over at Baileyville. We got four of us librarians—just local girls—and a whole lot of donated books and journals, some on their last legs. Well, we need someone to organize us, and fix up the books, because it turns out you can't do fifteen hours a day in the saddle and keep the rest of it straight, too."

Sophia and William looked at each other.

"I'm not sure what this has to do with us," Sophia said.

"Well, I was wondering if you'd come and organize it for us. We have a budget for five librarians, and there's a decent wage. Paid for by the WPA, and the money's good for at least a year."

Sophia leaned back in her seat.

Margery persisted: "I know you loved working at the library at Louisville. And you could be back here in an hour each day. We'd be glad to have you."

"It's a colored library." Sophia's voice hardened. She folded her hands in her lap. "The library at Louisville. It's for colored folk. You must be aware of that, Miss Margery. I can't come work for a white person's library. Unless you're actually asking me to ride horses with you and I can sure as anything tell you I'm not going to be doing that."

"It's a traveling library. People don't come in and out borrowing stuff. We go to them."

"So?"

"So nobody even needs to know you're there. Look, Miss Sophia, we're desperate for your help. I need someone I can trust to mend the books, and get us straight, and you are, by anyone's standards, the finest librarian for three counties."

"I'm going to say it again. It's a white person's library."

"Things are changing."

"You tell the men in hoods that when they come knocking at our door."

"So what are you doing here?"

"I'm looking after my brother."

"I know that. I'm asking you what you're doing for money."

The two siblings exchanged a look.

"That's a mighty personal question. Even for you."

William sighed. "We ain't doing too good. We're living off what we got saved and what our mama left. But it ain't much."

"William!" Sophia scolded him.

"Well, it's the truth. We know Miss Margery. She knows us."

"So you want me to go get my head busted working in a white folks' library?"

"I won't let that happen," said Margery, calmly.

It was the first time Sophia did not answer. There were few advantages to being the offspring of Frank O'Hare, but people who had known him understood that if Margery promised something would happen, then in all likelihood, it would. If you had survived a childhood with Frank O'Hare, not much else was going to stand in your way.

"Oh, and it's twenty-eight dollars a month," said Margery. "Same wage as the rest of us."

Sophia looked at her brother, then down at her lap. Finally she lifted her head.

"We'll have to think about it."

"Okay."

Sophia pursed her lips. "You still as messy as you was?"

"Probably a little worse."

Sophia stood and straightened her skirt. "Like I said. We'll think about it."

William saw her out. He insisted, raising himself laboriously from his chair while Sophia handed him his crutch. He winced with the effort of shuffling to the door, and Margery tried not to let on that she saw it. They stood at the door and looked out at the relative peace of the creek.

"You know they're fixing to take a chunk out of the north side of the ridge?"

"What?"

"Big Cole told me. They're going to blow six holes straight through it. They reckon there's rich seams in there."

"But that part of the mountain is occupied. There's fourteen, fifteen families just down by the north side alone."

"We know that and they know that. But you think that's gonna stop them once they sniff paper money?"

"But—what'll happen to the families?"

"Same thing that happens every time." He rubbed his forehead. "Kentucky, huh? Most beautiful place on earth, and the most brutal. Sometimes I think God wanted to show us all His ways at once."

William leaned against the doorframe, adjusting his wooden crutch under his armpit while Margery digested this.

"It's good to see you, Miss Margery. You take care now."

"You too, William. And tell your sister to come work at our library."

He raised an eyebrow. "Huh! She's like you. No man going to tell her what to do."

She could hear him chuckling as he closed the screen door behind him.

SIX

—★—

My mother didn't hold with twenty-four-hour-old pies,
except mince. She would get up an hour earlier in order
to bake a pie before breakfast but she would not bake
any kind of custard or fruit pie, even pumpkin, the day
before it was to be used, and if she had my father
wouldn't have eaten it.

· DELLA T. LUTES, *Farm Journal*

In the first months after she had moved to Baileyville, Alice had almost enjoyed the weekly church dinners. Having a fourth or fifth
person at their table seemed to lift the atmosphere in the somber
house, and the food was mostly a cut above Annie's usual greasy fare.
Mr. Van Cleve tended to be on his best behavior, and Pastor McIntosh, their most frequent visitor, was essentially a kind man, if a little
repetitive. The most enjoyable element of Kentucky society, she observed, was the endless stories: the misfortunes of families, gossip
about neighbors—every anecdote served up beautifully formed and
with a punch-line that would leave the table rocking with laughter. If
there was more than one raconteur at the table it would swiftly become a competitive sport. But, more importantly, those animated tall
tales left Alice to eat her food largely unobserved and unbothered.

Or, at least, they had.

"So when are you two young 'uns going to bless my old friend here with a grandchild or two then, huh?"

"That's what I keep asking them." Mr. Van Cleve pointed his knife at Bennett and then Alice. "A house isn't a home without a babby running through it."

Maybe when our bedroom isn't so close to yours that I can hear you break wind, Alice responded silently, scooping mashed potato onto her plate. *Maybe when I'm free to walk to the bathroom without covering myself to the ankles. Maybe when I don't have to listen to this conversation at least twice a week.*

Pastor McIntosh's sister Pamela, visiting from Knoxville, observed, as someone invariably did, that her son had gotten his new wife with child on the very day of their wedding. "Nine months to the day the twins came. Can you believe that? Mind you, she has that house running like clockwork. You watch, she'll wean those two and the day after she'll be carrying again."

"Aren't you one of those packhorse librarians, Alice?" Pamela's husband eyed the world suspiciously from under two bushy brows.

"I am indeed."

"The girl's gone from the house all day!" Mr. Van Cleve exclaimed. "Some evenings she gets back so tired she can barely keep her eyes open."

"Strapping lad like you, Bennett. Young Alice there should be too tired to get on a horse in the first place!"

"She should be bow-legged like a cowboy, though!"

The two men roared with laughter. Alice forced a wan smile. She glanced at Bennett, who was steering black beans around his plate with intent focus. Then she looked at Annie, who was holding the sweet-potato dish and gazing at her with something that looked uncomfortably like satisfaction. Alice hardened her look until the other woman turned away.

"You got monthlies stains on your breeches," Annie had observed, as she brought Alice a pile of folded laundry the previous evening. "I couldn't get it all out so there's still a small mark." She had paused, and added, "Just like last month."

Alice had bristled at the idea of the woman monitoring her "month-lies." She had the sudden sensation of half the town discussing her apparent failure to fall pregnant. It couldn't be Bennett's fault, of course. Not their baseball champ. Not their golden boy.

"You know, my cousin—the one over at Berea—she couldn't fall pregnant for love nor money. I swear her husband was at her like a *dog*. She went to one of the snake-handling churches—Pastor, I know you disapprove but hear me out. They put a Green Garter around her neck and she was with child the very next week. My cousin said the baby has eyes as gold as a copperhead's. But then she always was the imagi-native type."

"My aunt Lola was the same. Her pastor had the whole congrega-tion praying for God to fill her womb. Took them a year, but they got five children now."

"Please don't feel obliged to do the same," said Alice.

"I think it's all this riding the girl is doing. It's no good for a woman to sit astride all day. Dr. Freeman says it jiggles up a lady's insides."

"Well, yes, I do believe I've read as much."

Mr. Van Cleve picked up his saltshaker and waggled it between his fingers. "It's like if you shake a jar of milk up too much, it turns sour. Curdles, if you like."

"My insides are not curdled, thank you," Alice said stiffly, then added, after a moment, "But I would be very interested to see the article."

"Article?" said Pastor McIntosh.

"That you mentioned. Where it says a woman shouldn't ride a horse. For fear of 'jiggling.' It's not a medical term I'm familiar with."

The two men looked at each other.

Alice dragged her knife across a piece of chicken, not looking up from her plate. "Knowledge is so important, don't you think? We all say at the library, without facts we really do have nothing. If I'm put-ting my health at risk by riding a horse, then I think it would be only responsible for me to read the article you're talking about. Perhaps you could bring it with you next Sunday, Pastor." She looked up and smiled brightly across the table.

"Well," said Pastor McIntosh, "I'm not sure I could lay my hands on it just like that."

"The pastor has a lot of papers," said Mr. Van Cleve.

"The funny thing is," Alice continued, waving a fork for emphasis, "in England, nearly all well-brought-up ladies ride. They go out hunting, jumping ditches, fences, all sorts. It's almost compulsory. And yet they pop out babies with extraordinary efficiency. Even the Royal Family. Pop, pop, pop! Like shelling peas! Do you know how many children Queen Victoria had? And she was *always* on a horse. They couldn't pull her off."

The table had grown quiet.

"Well . . ." said Pastor McIntosh ". . . that is . . . most interesting."

"It can't be good for you, though, dear," said the pastor's sister, kindly. "I mean, strenuous physical activity is not good for young women at the best of times."

"Goodness. You'd better tell some of the mountain girls I see every day. Those women are chopping firewood, hoeing vegetable patches, cleaning house for men who are too sick—or too lazy—to get out of bed. And, strangely, they too seem to have all those babies, one after another."

"Alice," said Bennett, quietly.

"I can't imagine too many of them are just floating around, flower-arranging and putting their feet up. Or perhaps they have a different biological makeup. That must be it. Perhaps there's a medical reason I haven't heard of for *that*, too."

"Alice," said Bennett, again.

"There is nothing wrong with me," she whispered angrily. She was furious to hear the tremor in her voice. It was what they had needed. The two older men exchanged kindly looks.

"Oh, don't you get yourself worked up now. We're not criticizing you, Alice dear," said Mr. Van Cleve, reaching across the table and placing his plump hand over hers.

"We understand it can be a disappointment when the Lord doesn't bless you straight off. But it's best not to get too *emotional* about it," said the pastor. "I'll say a little prayer for you both when you're next in church."

"That's most kind of you," said Mr. Van Cleve. "Sometimes a young lady doesn't always know what's in her own interests. That's what we're here for, Alice, to mind your best interests. Now, Annie, where's that sweet potato? My gravy's getting cold here."

What did you have to do that for?" Bennett sat beside her on the swing seat as the older men repaired to the parlor, finishing off a bottle of Mr. Van Cleve's best bourbon. Their voices rose and fell, punctuated by bursts of laughter.

Alice sat with her arms crossed. The evenings were growing cooler but she positioned herself at the far end of the swing seat, a good nine inches from the warmth of Bennett's body, a shawl around her shoulders. "Do what?"

"You know very well what. Pa was just trying to look out for you."

"Bennett, you know that riding horses has nothing to do with why I'm not getting pregnant."

He said nothing.

"I love my job. I truly love my job. I will not give it up because your father is under the impression that my insides are jiggling. Does anyone say you play too much baseball? No. Of course they don't. But your bits are jiggling all over the place three times a week."

"Keep your voice down!"

"Oh, I forgot. We can't say anything out loud, can we? Not about your *jiggling bits*. We can't talk about what's *really* going on. But I'm the one everyone's talking about. I'm the one they think is barren."

"Why do you mind what people think? You act like you don't care for half the people around here anyway."

"I mind because your family and your neighbors are harping on about it all the time! And they're going to keep on unless you explain what's going on! Or just . . . *do* something about it!"

She had gone too far. Bennett rose abruptly from the swing seat and strode off, slamming the screen door behind him. There was a sudden silence in the parlor. As the male voices slowly picked up again, Alice sat on the swing seat, listening to the crickets and wondering how she could be in a house full of people and also in the loneliest place on earth.

It had not been a good week at the library. The mountains turned from lush green to a fiery orange, the leaves forming a coppery carpet on the ground that muffled the horses' hoofs, the hollers filling with thick morning mists, and Margery observed that half her librarians were out of sorts. She watched Alice's uncharacteristically set jaw and shadowed eyes, and might perhaps have made an effort to sway her out of her mood, but she herself was antsy, still not having heard back from Sophia. Every evening she attempted to repair the more damaged books among their haul, but that pile had grown to a teetering height, and the thought of all the work, or all those wasted books, dismayed her even more. There was no time for her to do anything but get back on the mule and take another load out.

The appetite for books had become relentless. Children followed them down the street, begging for something to read. Families they saw fortnightly would beg for the same weekly allowance as those on the shorter routes, and the librarians would have to explain that there were only four of them and they were out all the hours of the day as it was. The horses were periodically lame from the long hours up hard, flinty tracks ("If I have to take Billy sideways up Fern Gully again I swear he's going to end up with two legs longer than the others"), and Patch developed girth sores so that he was off work for days.

It was never enough. And the strain was starting to show. As they returned on Friday evening, mud and fallen leaves treading in on their boots to add to the mess, Izzy snapped at Alice after she had tripped on Izzy's saddlebag and broken the strap. "Mind yourself!"

Alice stooped to pick it up as Beth peered at it. "Well, you shouldn't have left it on the floor, should you?"

"It was only there a minute. I was trying to put my books down and I needed my stick. What am I supposed to do now?"

"I don't know. Get your ma to buy you another?"

Izzy reeled as if she had been slapped and glared at Beth. "You take that back."

"Take what back? It's the damn truth."

"Izzy, I'm sorry," said Alice, after a moment. "It—it really was an accident. Look, I'll see if I can find someone to fix it over the weekend."

"You didn't need to be mean, Beth Pinker."

"Shoot. Your skin's thinner than a dragonfly's wing."

"Can you two stop bickering and enter your books? I'd like to be out of here by midnight."

"I can't enter mine because you haven't done yours, and if I bring my books over we're just going to get those mixed up with the ones by your feet."

"The books by my feet, Izzy Brady, are the ones you left yesterday because you couldn't be bothered to shelve them."

"I told you Mother had to pick me up early so she could get to her quilting circle!"

"Oh, well. We can't get in the way of a damn *quilting circle*, can we?"

Their voices had reached a pitch. Beth eyed Izzy from the corner of the room, where she had just emptied her own saddlebags, along with a lunch pail and an empty lemonade bottle.

"Ah, shucks. You know what we need?"

"What?" said Izzy, suspiciously.

"We need to let our hair down a little. We're all work and no play." She grinned. "I think we need to have us a meeting."

"We're having a meeting," said Margery.

"Not this kind of meeting." Beth strode past them, stepping neatly over the books. She opened the door and stepped outside, where her little brother was sitting on the steps, waiting. The women occasionally bought Bryn a poke of candies in return for running errands, and he looked up hopefully. "Bryn, go tell Mr. Van Cleve that Alice here has to stay late for a meeting on library policy and that we'll walk her home when we're done. Then head over to Mrs. Brady's and tell her the same—actually, don't tell her it's library policy. She'll be down here faster than you can say Mrs. Lena B. Nofcier. Tell her . . . tell her we're cleaning our saddles. Then you tell Mama the same thing, and I'll buy you a twist of Tootsie Rolls."

Margery narrowed her eyes. "This had better not be—"

"I'll be right back. And, hey—Bryn? Bryn! You tell Daddy I was smoking and I'll rip your damn ears off, one after the other. You hear me?"

"What is going on?" said Alice, as they heard Beth's footsteps disappear down the road.

"I could ask the same thing," said a voice.

Margery looked up to see Sophia standing in the doorway, her hands clasped together and her bag tucked under her arm. One eyebrow rose at the sight of the chaos. "Oh, my days. You said it was bad. You didn't tell me I was going to want to run screaming back to Louisville."

Alice and Izzy stared at the tall woman in the immaculate blue dress. Sophia looked back at them. "Well, I don't know why you all are just sitting there catching flies. You should be working!" Sophia put down her bag and untied her scarf. "I told William, and I'll tell you. I'll work the evenings, and I'll do it with the door bolted, so nobody's going to get aerated about me being here. Those are my terms. And I want the wage we discussed."

"Fine by me," said Margery.

The two younger women, bemused, turned and looked at Margery. Margery smiled. "Izzy, Alice, this is Miss Sophia. This is our fifth librarian."

Sophia Kenworth, Margery advised them as they began to get to grips with the stacks of books, had spent eight years at the colored library in Louisville, in a building so large that it had divided its books not just into sections but into whole floors. It served professors, lecturers from Kentucky State University, and had a system of professionally produced cards and stamps that would be used to leave date marks when anything came in and out. Sophia had undergone formal training, and an apprenticeship, and her job had only come to an end when her mother died and William had had his accident within three short months of each other, forcing her to leave Louisville to look after him.

"That's what we need here," Sophia said, as she sifted through the books, lifting each to examine its spine. "We need systems. You leave it with me."

An hour later the library doors were bolted, most of the books were off the floor and Sophia was whisking through the pages of the ledger, making soft sounds of disapproval. Beth, meanwhile, had returned and was now holding a large Mason jar of colored liquid under Alice's nose.

"I don't know . . ." Alice said.

"Just sip it. Go on. It's not going to kill you. It's Apple Pie moonshine."

Alice looked at Margery, who had already declined. Nobody seemed surprised that Margery didn't drink moonshine.

Alice raised the jar to her lips, hesitated, and lost her nerve again. "What's going to happen if I go home drunk?"

"Well, I guess you'll go home drunk," said Beth.

"I don't know . . . Can't someone else try it first?"

"Well, Izzy ain't going to, is she?"

"Says who?" said Izzy.

"Oh, boy. Here we go," said Beth, laughing. She took the jar from Alice's hands and passed it to Izzy. With an impish grin, Izzy took the jar in two hands and raised it to her mouth. She took a swig, coughing and spluttering, her eyes widening as she tried to hand the jar back. "You're not meant to be glugging it!" said Beth, and took a small sip. "You drink like that and you'll be blind by Tuesday."

"Give it here," said Alice. She looked down at the contents and took a breath.

You are too impulsive, Alice.

She took a sip, feeling the alcohol burn a mercury path down her throat. She clamped her eyes shut, waiting for them to stop watering. It was actually delicious.

"Good?" Beth's mischievous eyes were on her when she opened them again.

She nodded mutely, and swallowed. "Surprisingly," she croaked. "Yes. Let me have another."

Something shifted in Alice that evening. She was tired of the eyes of the town on her, sick of being monitored and talked about and judged. She was sick of being married to a man whom everyone else thought was the Good Lord Almighty and who could barely bring himself to look at her.

Alice had come halfway across the world to find that, yet again, she was considered wanting. Well, she thought, if that was what everyone thought, she might as well live up to it.

She took another sip, and then another, batting away Beth's hands when she shouted, "Steady now, girl." She felt, she told them, when she finally handed it back, *pleasantly squiffy.*

"Pleasantly squiffy!" Beth mimicked, and the girls fell about laughing. Margery smiled, despite herself.

"Well, I have no idea what kind of library this is," said Sophia, from the corner.

"They just need to let off steam, is all," said Margery. "They've been working hard."

"We have been working hard! And now we need music!" said Beth, holding up a hand. "Let's fetch Mr. Guisler's gramophone. He'll lend it to us."

Margery shook her head. "Leave Fred out of it. He doesn't need to see this."

"You mean he doesn't need to see Alice all inebriated," said Beth, slyly.

"What?" Alice looked up.

"Don't tease her," said Margery. "She's married, anyway."

"In theory," muttered Alice, who was having trouble focusing.

"Yeah. Just be like Margery and do what you want when you want." Beth looked sideways at her. "With who you want."

"You want me to be ashamed of how I live my life, Beth Pinker? Because you'll be waiting halfway to the heavens falling down."

"Hey," said Beth. "If I had a man as handsome as Sven Gustavsson come a-courting me, I'd have a ring on my finger so fast he wouldn't even know how he'd found himself at church. You want to take a bite out of the apple before you put it in the basket, that's up to you. Just make sure you keep hold of the basket."

"What if I don't want a basket?"

"Everyone wants a basket."

"Not me. Never have, never will. No basket."

"What *are* you all talking about?" said Alice, and started to giggle.

"They lost me at Mr. Guisler," said Izzy, and belched quietly. "Good Lord, I feel amazing. I don't think I've felt like this since I went on the Ferris wheel three times at Lexington County Fair. Except . . . No. That didn't end well."

Alice leaned in toward Izzy, and put a hand on her arm. "I really am sorry about your strap, Izzy. I didn't mean to break it."

"Oh, don't you worry. I'll just ask Mother to go get me another." For some reason they both found this hysterically funny.

Sophia looked at Margery and raised an eyebrow.

Margery lit the oil lamps that dotted the end of each shelf, trying not to smile. She wasn't really one for big groups, but she quite liked this, the jokes and the merriment, and the way that you could see actual friendships springing up around the room, like green shoots.

"Hey, girls?" said Alice, when she had got her giggles under control. "What would you do, if you could do anything you wanted?"

"Sort out this library," muttered Sophia.

"I'm serious. If you could do anything, be anything, what would you do?"

"I'd travel the world," said Beth, who had made herself a backrest of books, and was now making armrests to go with it. "I'd go to India and Africa and Europe and maybe Egypt and have me a little look around. I got no plans to stay around here my whole life. My brothers'll have me minding my pa till he's dribblin'. I want to see the Taj Mahal and the Great Wall of China and that place where they build little round huts out of ice blocks and a whole bunch of other places in the encyclopedias. I was going to say I'd go to England and meet the king and queen but we got Alice so we don't need to." The other women started to laugh.

"Izzy?"

"Oh, it's crazy."

"Crazier than Beth and her Taj Mahals?"

"Go on," said Alice, nudging her.

"I'd . . . well, I'd be a singer," said Izzy. "I'd sing on the wireless, or on a gramophone record. Like Dorothy Lamour or . . ." she glanced toward Sophia, who did a good job of not raising her eyebrows too far ". . . Billie Holiday."

"Surely your daddy could fix that for you. He knows everyone, don't he?" said Beth.

Izzy looked suddenly uncomfortable. "People like me don't become singers."

"Why?" said Margery. "You can't sing?"

"That'll do it," said Beth.

"You know what I mean."

Margery shrugged. "Last time I looked you didn't need your leg to sing."

"But people wouldn't listen. They'd be too busy staring at my brace."

"Oh, don't flatter yourself, Izzy girl. Enough people got leg braces and whatnot around here. Or just . . ." she paused ". . . wear a long dress."

"What do you sing, Miss Izzy?" said Sophia, who was arranging spines into alphabetical order.

Izzy had sobered. Her skin was a little flushed. "Oh, I like hymns, bluegrass, blues, anything, really. I even tried a little opera once."

"Well, you got to sing now," said Beth, lighting a cigarette and blowing on her fingers when the match burned too low. "Come on, girl, show us what you got."

"Oh, no," said Izzy. "I only really sing for myself."

"That's going to be some pretty empty concert hall, then," said Beth.

Izzy looked at them. Then she pushed herself up onto her feet. She took a shaky breath, and then she began:

My sweetheart's murmurs turned to dust
All tender kisses turned to rust
I'll hold him in my heart though he be far
And turn my love to a midnight star

Her eyes closed, her voice filled the little room, soft and mellifluous, as if it had been dipped in honey. Izzy, right in front of them, began to change into someone quite new, her torso extending, her mouth opening wider to reach the notes. She was somewhere quite distant now, somewhere beloved to her. Beth rocked gently and began to smile. It stretched across her face—pure, unclouded delight at this unexpected turn of events. She let out a "*Hell, yes!*" as if she couldn't contain it. And then, after a moment, Sophia, as if compelled by an impulse she could barely control, began to join in, her own voice deeper, tracing the path of Izzy's and complementing it. Izzy opened her eyes and the two women smiled at each other as they sang, their voices lifting, their bodies swaying in time with the beat, and the air in the little library lifted with them.

Its light is distant but it warms me still
I'm a million miles from heaven but I'll wait here till
My sweetheart comes again and the glow I feel
Is brighter than the stars above Kentucky hills

Alice watched, the moonshine coursing through her blood, the warmth and music making her nerves sing, and felt something give inside her, something she hadn't wanted to acknowledge to herself, something primal to do with love and loss and loneliness. She looked at Margery, whose expression had relaxed, lost in her own private reverie, and thought of Beth's comments about a man Margery never discussed. Perhaps conscious she was being watched, Margery turned to her and smiled, and Alice realized, with horror, that tears were sliding, unchecked down her cheeks.

Margery's raised eyebrows were a silent question.

Just a little homesick, Alice answered. It was the truth, she thought. She just wasn't sure she had yet been to the place she was homesick for.

Margery took her elbow and they stepped outside into the dusk, hopping down into the paddock where the horses grazed peacefully by the fence, oblivious to the noise inside.

Margery handed Alice her handkerchief. "You okay?"

Alice blew her nose. She had begun to sober immediately, out in the cool air. "Fine. Fine . . ." She looked up at the skies. "Actually, no. Not really."

"Can I help?"

"I don't think it's something anyone else can help with."

Margery leaned back against the wall, so that she was looking up at the mountains behind them. "There's not much I haven't seen and heard these thirty-eight years. I'm pretty sure whatever you have to say isn't going to knock me off my heels."

Alice closed her eyes. If she put it out there, it became real, a living, breathing thing that she would have to do something about. Her gaze flickered to Margery and away again.

"And if you think I'm the type to go talking, Alice Van Cleve, you really haven't worked me out at all."

"Mr. Van Cleve keeps going on about us not having any babies."

"Hell, that's just standard round here. The moment you put a ring on that finger they're all just counting down—"

"But that's just it. It's Bennett." Alice wrung her hands together. "It's been months and he just—he won't—"

Margery let the words settle. She waited, as if to check that she had heard right. "He won't . . . ?"

Alice took a deep breath. "It all started well enough. We'd been waiting so long, what with the journey and everything, and actually it was lovely and then just as things . . . were about to—well . . . Mr. Van Cleve shouted something through the wall—I think he thought he was being encouraging—and we were both a little startled, and then everything stopped and I opened my eyes and Bennett wasn't even looking at me and he seemed so cross and distant and when I asked him if everything was okay he told me I was . . ." she gulped ". . . unlady-like for asking."

Margery waited.

"So I lay back down and waited. And he . . . well, I thought it was going to happen. But then we could hear Mr. Van Cleve clomping around next door and . . . well . . . that was that. And I tried to whis-per something but he got cross and acted like it was my fault. But I don't really know. Because I've never . . . so I can't be sure whether it's something I'm doing wrong or he's doing wrong but, either way, his father is always next door and the walls are so thin and, well, Bennett, he just acts like I'm something he doesn't want to get too close to any more. And it's not like it's one of those things you can talk about." The words tumbled out, unchecked. She felt her face flood with color. "I want to be a good wife. I really do. It just feels . . . impossible."

"So . . . let me get this straight. You haven't . . ."

"I don't know! Because I don't know what it's supposed to be like!" She shook her head, then covered her face with her hands, as if horri-fied that she was even saying the words out loud.

Margery frowned at her boots. "Stay there," she said.

She disappeared into the cabin, where the singing had reached a new pitch. Alice listened anxiously, fearing the sudden cessation of voices that would suggest Margery had betrayed her. But instead the song lifted, and a little burst of applause met a musical flourish, and she heard Beth's muffled *whoop!* Then the door opened, allowing the voices to swell briefly, and Margery tripped back down the steps holding a small blue book, which she handed to Alice. "Okay, so this doesn't go in the ledger. This, we pass around to ladies who, perhaps, need a little help in some of the matters you've mentioned."

Alice stared at the leather-bound book.

"It's just facts. I've promised it to a woman over at Miller's Creek on my Monday route, but you can take a look over the weekend and see if there's anything in there might help."

Alice flicked through, startling at the words *sex, naked, womb.* She blushed. "*This* goes out with the library books?"

"Let's just say it's an unofficial part of our service, given it has a bit of a checkered history through our courts. It doesn't exist in the ledger, and it doesn't sit out on the shelves. We just keep it between ourselves."

"Have you read it?"

"Cover to cover and more than once. And I can tell you it has brought me a good deal of joy." She raised an eyebrow and smiled. "And not just me either."

Alice blinked. She couldn't imagine prizing joy out of her current situation, no matter how hard she tried.

"Good evening, ladies."

The two women turned to see Fred Guisler walking down the path toward them, an oil lamp in his hand. "Sounds like quite a party."

Alice hesitated, and thrust the book abruptly back at Margery. "I— I don't think so."

"It's just facts, Alice. Nothing more than that."

Alice walked briskly past her back to the library. "I can manage this by myself. Thank you." She half ran back up the steps, the door slamming as she entered.

Fred stopped when he reached Margery. She noted the faint disappointment in his expression. "Something I said?"

"Not even halfway close, Fred," she said, and placed a hand on his arm. "But why don't you come on in and join us? Aside from a few extra bristles on that chin of yours, you're pretty much an honorary librarian yourself."

She would have laid down money, said Beth afterward, that that was the finest librarians' meeting that had ever taken place in Lee County. Izzy and Sophia had sung their way through every song they could recall, teaching each other the ones they didn't know and making up a few on the spot, their voices wild and raucous as they grew in confidence, stamping and hollering, the girls clapping in time. Fred Guisler, who had indeed been happy to fetch his gramophone, had been persuaded to dance with each of them, his tall frame stooped to accommodate Izzy, disguising her limp with some well-timed swings so that she lost her awkwardness and laughed until tears leaked from her eyes. Alice smiled and tapped along but wouldn't meet Margery's eye, as if she were already mortified at having revealed so much, and Margery understood that she would simply have to say nothing and wait for the girl's feelings of exposure and humiliation, however unwarranted, to die down. And amid all this Sophia would sing out and sway her hips, as if even her rigor and reserve could not hold out against the music.

Fred, who had declined all offers of moonshine, had driven them home in the dark, all crammed into the backseat of his truck, taking Sophia first under cover of the rest, and they had heard her singing still as she tapped her way down the path to the neat little house at Monarch Creek. They had dropped Izzy next, the motor-car's tires spinning in the huge driveway, and had seen Mrs. Brady's amazement at her daughter's sweaty hair and grinning face. "I never had friends like you all before," Izzy had exclaimed, as they flew along the dark road, and they knew that it was only half moonshine talking. "Honestly, I never even thought I liked other girls till I became a librarian." She had hugged each of them with a child's giddy enthusiasm.

Alice had sobered completely by the time they dropped her off, and said little. The two Van Cleve men were seated on the porch, despite the chill in the air and the late hour, and Margery detected a distinct reluctance in her step as Alice made her way slowly up the path toward them. Neither rose from his seat. Nobody smiled under the flickering porch light, or leaned forward to greet her.

Margery and Fred drove the rest of the way to her cabin in silence, each lost in their own thoughts.

"Tell Sven I said hey," he said, as she opened the gate and Bluey came bounding down the slope to meet her.

"I will."

"He's a good man."

"As are you. You need to find yourself someone else, Fred. It's been long enough."

He opened his mouth as if to speak, then closed it again.

"You have a good rest of your evening," he said finally, and tipped his forehead, as if he were still wearing a hat, then turned the wheel and drove back down the road.

SEVEN

The prince told her she was the most beautiful girl he had ever seen, and then he asked if she would marry him. And they all lived happily ever after." Mae Horner brought the two sides of the book briskly together with a satisfying *slap*.

"That was really very good, Mae."

"I read it through four times yesterday after I collected the wood."

"Well, it shows. I do believe your reading is as good as any girl's in this county."

"She's smart all right."

Alice looked up to where Jim Horner stood in the doorway. "Like her mama. Her mama could read since she was three years old. Grew up in a houseful of books over near Paintsville."

"I can read too," said Millie, who had been sitting by Alice's feet.

"I know you can, Millie," said Alice. "And your reading is very good too. Honestly, Mr. Horner, I don't think I've ever met two children take to it like yours have."

He suppressed a smile. "Tell her what you did, Mae," he said.

The girl looked at him, just to check for her father's approval. "Go on."

"I made a pie."

"You made a pie? By yourself?"

"From a recipe. In that *Country Home* magazine you left us. A peach pie. I would offer you a slice but we ate it all."

Millie giggled. "Daddy ate three pieces."

"I was hunting up in North Ridge and she got the old range going and everything. And I walked in the door and there was a smell like . . ." He lifted his nose and closed his eyes, recalling the scent. His face briefly lost its habitual hardness. "I walked in and there she was, with it all laid out on the table. She had followed every one of those instructions to a T."

"I did burn the edges a little."

"Well, your mama always did the same."

The three of them sat in silence for a moment.

"A peach pie," said Alice. "I'm not sure we can keep up with you, young Mae. What can I leave you girls this week?"

"Did *Black Beauty* come in yet?"

"It did! And I remembered what you said about wanting it so I brought it with me. How about that? Now, the words in this one are a little longer, so you may find it a little harder. And it's sad in places."

Jim Horner's expression changed.

"I mean for the horses. There are some sad bits for the horses. The horses talk. It's not easy to explain."

"Maybe I can read to you, Daddy."

"My eyes ain't too good," he explained. "Can't seem to aim the way I used to. But we get by."

"I can see that." Alice sat in the center of the little cabin that had once spooked her so much. Mae, although only eleven, appeared to have taken charge of it, sweeping and organizing so that where it had once seemed bleak and dark, there was now a distinct homeliness, with a bowl of apples in the center of the table and a quilt across the chair. She packed up her books and confirmed that everyone was happy with what she had brought. Millie hugged her around her neck and she held her fiercely. It was some time since anybody had pulled her close and it provoked strange, conflicting feelings.

"It's a whole seven days till we see you again," the girl announced solemnly. Her hair smelled of woodsmoke and something sweet that existed only in the forest. Alice breathed it in.

"It certainly is. And I can't wait to see how much you've read in the meantime."

"Millie! This one's got drawings in it too!" Mae called, from the floor. Millie released Alice and hunkered down by her sister. Alice watched them for a moment, then made her way to the door, shrugging on her coat, a once fashionable tweed blazer that was now scuffed with moss and mud and sprouted messy threads where it had caught on bushes and branches. The mountain had grown distinctly colder these last days, as if winter were settling into its foundations.

"Miss Alice?"

"Yes?"

The girls were bent over *Black Beauty*, Millie's finger tracing the words as her sister read aloud.

Jim looked behind him, as if making sure their focus was elsewhere. "I wanted to apologize."

Alice, who had been tying her scarf, stopped.

"After my wife passed I was not myself for a while. Felt like the sky was falling in, you know? And I was not . . . *hospitable* when you first came by. But these last couple of months, seeing the girls stop crying for their mama, giving them something to look forward to every week, it's—it's . . . Well, I just wanted to say it's much appreciated."

Alice held her hands in front of her. "Mr. Horner, I can honestly tell you that I look forward to seeing your girls just as much as they look forward to my visits."

"Well, it's good for them to see a lady. I didn't realize till my Betsy was gone how much a child misses the more . . . feminine side of things." He scratched his head. "They talk about you, you know, how you speak and all. Mae there says she wants to be a librarian."

"She does?"

"Made me realize—I can't keep them close by me for ever. I want more for them than this, you know. Seeing as how smart they both are." He stood silent for a moment. Then he said: "Miss Alice, what do you think of that school? The one with the German lady?"

"Mrs. Beidecker? Mr. Horner, I think your girls would love her."

"She . . . doesn't take a switch to the children? You hear some things . . . Betsy got beat something awful at school so she never wanted the girls to go."

"I'd be happy to introduce you to her, Mr. Horner. She is a kind woman, and the students seem to love her. I cannot believe she would ever lay a hand on a child."

He considered this. "It's hard," he said, looking out at the mountain, "having to work all this stuff out. I thought I'd be just doing a man's job. My own daddy just brought home the food and put his feet up and let my mama do all the rest. And now I have to be mother as well as father. Make all these decisions."

"Look at those girls, Mr. Horner."

They glanced to where the girls, now lying on their stomachs, were exclaiming over something they had just read.

Alice smiled. "I think you're doing fine."

Finn Mayburg, Upper Pinch Me—one copy The Furrow, *dated May 1937*

Two copies Weird Tales *magazine, dated December 1936 and February 1937*

Ellen Prince—Eagles Top (end cabin)—Little Women *by Louisa May Alcott*

From Farm to Table *by Edna Roden*

Nancy and Phyllis Stone, Arnott's Ridge—Mack Maguire and the Indian Girl *by Amherst Archer*

Mack Maguire Takes a Fall *by Amherst Archer (note: they have read all current editions, ask if we can find out if there are any more)*

Margery flicked through the ledger, Sophia's elegant handwriting neatly transcribing date and routes at the top of each page. Beside it sat a pile of newly repaired books, their bindings stitched and the torn covers patched with pages from books that couldn't be salvaged. Beside that lay a new scrapbook—*The Baileyville Bonus*—this edition comprising four pages of recipes from spoiled copies of the *Woman's Home Companion*, a short story titled "What She Wouldn't Say," and a long feature about collecting ferns. The library was now immaculate, a system of labels marking the back of every shelved book so that it was easy for them to find their place, the books precisely ordered and categorized.

Sophia would come by at around 5 p.m. and would usually have done a couple of hours by the time the girls returned from their routes. The days were growing shorter now so they were having to return earlier because of the falling light. Sometimes they would all just sit and chat among themselves while unloading their bags and comparing their days before they headed off to their homes. Fred had been installing a woodburner in the corner in his free time, though it wasn't finished yet: the gap around the flue pipe was still stuffed with rags to stop the rain coming in. Despite this, all the women seemed to find reasons to hang around a little later each day and Margery suspected that once the stove started up she would have trouble persuading them to go home.

Mrs. Brady looked a little startled when Margery explained the identity of the newest member of their team but, having seen the altered state of the little building, to her credit she simply compressed her lips and raised her fingers to her temples. "Has anybody complained?"

"Nobody's seen her to complain. She comes in the back, by Mr. Guisler's house, and goes home the same way."

Mrs. Brady mulled this for a moment. "Are you familiar with what Mrs. Nofcier says? You know of Mrs. Nofcier, of course."

Margery smiled. They all knew of Mrs. Nofcier. Mrs. Brady would shoehorn her name into a conversation about horse liniment if she could.

"Well, I was recently lucky enough to attend an address for teachers and parents that the good lady gave where she said—hold on, I wrote this bit down." She riffled through her pocketbook: "'A library service should be provided for all people, rural as well as urban, colored as well as white.' There. 'Colored as well as white.' That was how she put it. I believe we have to be mindful of the importance of progress and equality just as Mrs. Nofcier is. So you'll have no objection from me about employing a colored woman here." She rubbed at a mark on the desk, then examined her finger. "Maybe . . . we won't actually *advertise* it just yet, though. There's no need to invite controversy, given we're such a fledgling venture. I'm sure you catch my drift."

"My feelings exactly, Mrs. Brady," Margery said. "I wouldn't want to bring trouble to Sophia's door."

"She does a beautiful job. I'll give her that." Mrs. Brady gazed around her. Sophia had stitched a sampler, which hung on the wall

beside the door—*To Seek Knowledge Is To Expand Your Own Universe*—
and Mrs. Brady patted it with some satisfaction. "I have to say, Miss
O'Hare, I am immensely proud of what you have achieved in just a
few short months. It has exceeded all our expectations. I have written
to Mrs. Nofcier to tell her as much several times and I am sure that at
some point she will be passing on those sentiments to Mrs. Roosevelt
herself . . . It is a profound shame not everyone in our town feels the
same way."

She glanced away, as if deciding not to say more. "But, as I said, I
do believe this is a true model of a packhorse library. And you girls
should be proud of yourselves."

Margery nodded. It was probably best not to tell Mrs. Brady about
the library's unofficial initiative: each day she sat down at the desk, in
the dark hours between her arrival and dawn, and she wrote out, according to her template, a half-dozen more of the letters that she had
been distributing to the inhabitants of North Ridge.

Dear Neighbor

It has come to our attention that the owners of Hoffman
are seeking to create new mines in your neighborhood. This
would involve the removal of hundreds of acres of timber,
the blasting of new pits and, in many cases, the loss of homes
and livelihoods.

I write to you in confidence, as the mines are known to
employ devious and harsh individuals in the interests of
getting their way, but I believe that it is both illegal and
immoral for them to do what they plan, that it would be the
cause of abject misery and destitution.

To that end, according to law books we have consulted,
there appears to be a precedent to stop such wholesale rape of
our landscape, and protect our homes, and I urge you to read
this extract provided below, or, if you have the resources, to
consult the legal representative at Baileyville's court offices
in order to put such obstructions in place as may be required

to prevent this destruction. In the meantime do not sign any
BROAD FORM DEEDS for these, despite the money and
assurances offered, will give the mine-owners the right to
mine under your very house.

If help is needed with the reading of such documents, the
packhorse librarians may be happy to assist, and will, of
course, do so with discretion.

In confidence,

A friend

She finished, folded them neatly, and placed one in each of the
saddlebags, except Alice's. She would deliver the extra one herself.
No point making things more complicated for the girl than they
already were.

The boy had finally stopped screaming, his voice now emerging as a
series of barely suppressed whimpers, as if he had remembered
himself to be among men. His clothes and skin were equally black
from where the coal had almost buried him, only the whites of his
eyes visible to betray his shock and pain. Sven watched as the stretcher-
bearers lifted him carefully, their job made harder by the low pitch of
the roof, and, stooping, began to shuffle out, shouting instructions at
each other as they went. Sven leaned back against the rough wall to let
them pass, then turned his light on those miners who were setting up
props where the roof had fallen, cursing as they struggled to wedge the
heavy timbers into place.

This was low-vein coal, the chambers of the mines so shallow in
places that men were barely able to rise onto their knees. It was the
worst kind of mining; Sven had friends who were crippled by the time
they were thirty, reliant on sticks just to stand straight. He hated these
rabbit warrens, where your mind would play tricks in the near dark to
tell you the damp, black expanse above your head was even now closing

in on you. He had seen too many sudden roof falls, and only a pair of boots left visible to judge where the body might be.

"Boss, you might want to take a look through here."

Sven looked round—itself a tricky maneuver—and followed Jim McNeil's beckoning glove. The underground chambers were connected, rather than reached through new shafts from the outside—not uncommon in a mine where the owner championed profit over safety. He made his way awkwardly along the passage to the next chamber and adjusted his helmet light. Some eight props stood in a shallow opening, each buckling visibly under the weight of the roof above it. He moved his head slowly, scanning the empty space, the black surface glittering around him as it was met by the carbide lamplight.

"Can you see how many they took out?"

"Looks like about half remaining."

Sven cursed. "Don't go any farther in," he said, and, twisting, turned to the men behind him. "No man is to go into Number Two. You hear me?"

"You tell Van Cleve that," said a voice behind him. "You got to cross Number Two to get to Number Eight."

"Then nobody is to go into Number Eight. Not till everything's shored up right."

"He ain't going to hear that."

"Oh, he'll hear it."

The air was thick with dust, and he spat behind him, his lower back already aching. He turned to the miners. "We need at least ten more props in Seven before anyone goes back in. And get your fire boss to check for methane before anyone starts work again."

There was a murmur of agreement—Gustavsson being one of the few authority figures a miner could trust to be on his side—and Sven motioned his team into the haulage-way and then outside, already grateful for the prospect of sunlight.

So what's the damage, Gustavsson?"

Sven stood in Van Cleve's office, his nostrils still filled with the smell of sulfur, his boots leaving a fine dusty outline on the thick red carpet, waiting for Van Cleve in his pale suit to look up from his paperwork. Across the room he could see young Bennett glance up from behind his desk, his blue-cotton shirtsleeves marked with a neat crease. The younger man never looked quite comfortable at the mine. He rarely stepped out of the administrative block, as if the dirt and unpredictable nature of it were anathema to him.

"Well, we got the boy out, though it was a close thing. His hip's pretty bust."

"That's excellent news. I'm much obliged to you all."

"I've had him taken to the company doctor."

"Yes. Yes. Very good."

Van Cleve appeared to believe that was the end of the conversation. He flashed a smile at Sven, holding it a moment too long, as if to question why he was still standing there—then shuffled his papers emphatically.

Sven waited a beat. "You might want to know what caused the roof fall."

"Oh. Yes. Of course."

"Looks like props holding up the roof have been moved from the mined-out area in Number Two to support the new chamber in Seven. It destabilized the whole area."

Van Cleve's expression, when he finally looked up again, betrayed exactly the manufactured surprise Sven had known it would. "Well, now. The men should not be reusing props. We have told them as much many a time. Haven't we, Bennett?"

Bennett, behind his desk, looked down, too cowardly even to tell a straight lie. Sven swallowed the words he wanted to say, and considered those that followed carefully. "Sir, I should also point out that the amount of coal dust on the ground is a hazard in every one of your mines. You need more non-combustible rock atop it. And better ventilation, if you want to avoid more incidents."

Van Cleve scribbled something on a piece of paper. He no longer appeared to be listening.

"Mr. Van Cleve, of all the mines our safety crew serves, I have to inform you that Hoffman's conditions are by some distance the least . . . satisfactory."

"Yes, yes. I have told the men as such. Goodness knows why they won't just get on and rectify matters. But let's not make too big of a deal of it, Gustavsson. It's a temporary oversight. Bennett will get the foreman up and we'll—uh—we'll sort it out. Won't you, Bennett?"

Sven might reasonably have pointed out that Van Cleve had said exactly this the last time the sirens had gone off some eighteen days previously because of an explosion in the entrance of Number Nine, caused by a young breaker who hadn't known not to go in with an open light. The boy had been lucky to escape with superficial burns. But workers came cheap, after all.

"Anyway, all's well, thank the Lord." Van Cleve lifted himself with a grunt from his chair and walked around his large mahogany desk toward the door, signifying that the meeting was over. "Thank you and your men for your service, as ever. Worth every cent our mine pays toward your team."

Sven didn't move.

Van Cleve opened the door. A long, painful moment passed.

Sven faced him. "Mr. Van Cleve. You know I'm not a political man. But you must understand that it's conditions like these here that give root to those agitating for union membership."

Van Cleve's face darkened. "I hope you're not suggesting—"

Sven lifted his palms. "I have no affiliation. I just want your workers to be safe. But I have to say it would be a shame if this mine were considered too dangerous for my men to come here. I'm sure that would not go down well in the locality."

The smile, half-hearted as it was, had now vanished completely. "Well, I'm sure I thank you for your advice, Gustavsson. And as I said,

I will get my men to attend to it. Now, if you don't mind, I have pressing matters to attend to. The foreman will fetch you and your crew any water you might need."

Van Cleve continued to hold the door. Sven nodded—then as he passed, thrust out a blackened hand so that the older man, after a moment's hesitation, was forced to take it. After clasping it firmly enough to be sure he would have left some kind of imprint at least, Sven released it and walked away down the corridor.

With the first frost in Baileyville came hog-slaughtering time. The mere words made Alice, who couldn't tread on a bug, feel a little faint, especially when Beth described, with relish, what happened in her own home each year: the stunning of the squealing pig, the slitting of its throat as the boys sat hard on it, its legs pumping furiously, the hot dark blood pouring out onto the scraping board. She mimed the men tipping scalding water over it, attacking the bristles with flat blades, reducing the animal to flesh and gristle and bone.

"My aunt Lina will be waiting there with her apron open, ready to catch the head. She makes the best souse—that's from the tongue, ears and feet—this side of the Cumberland Gap. But my favorite part of the whole day, since I was small, is when Daddy tips all the innards into a tub and we get to choose the best bit to roast. I'd elbow my brothers in the eye to get to that old liver. Put it on a stick and roast it in the fire. Oh, boy, nothing like it. Fresh roasted hog liver. Mmm-mm."

She laughed as Alice covered her mouth and shook her head mutely.

But, like Beth, the town seemed to greet the prospect with an almost unseemly relish, and everywhere they went the librarians were offered a lick of salt bacon or—on one occasion—hog brains scrambled with egg, a mountain delicacy. Alice's stomach still turned at the thought of that.

But it wasn't just the hog-slaughtering that was causing a frisson of anticipation to run through the town: Tex Lafayette was coming.

Posters of the white-clad cowboy clutching his bullwhip were all over town, tacked hastily onto posts, and scrutinized by small boys and lovelorn women alike. At every other settlement the name of the Singing Cowboy was spoken like a talisman, followed by—*Is it true? Are you going?*

Demand was so great that he was no longer booked to appear in the theater, as originally planned, but would perform in the town square, where a stage was already being constructed from old pallets and planks, and for days beforehand whooping boys would run across it, imitating playing a banjo, ducking their heads to avoid the flat hands of the irritated workmen as they passed.

"Can we finish early tonight? Not like anyone's going to be reading. Everyone for ten miles yonder's already headed to the square," said Beth, as she pulled her last book from her saddlebag. "Shoot. Look at what those Mackenzie boys have done to poor old *Treasure Island*." She stooped to pick up the scattered pages from the floor, cursing.

"Don't see why not," said Margery. "Sophia has it all under control, and it's dark already anyhow."

"Who is Tex Lafayette?" said Alice.

The four women turned and stared at her. "*Who is Tex Lafayette?*"

"Haven't you seen *Green Grows My Mountain*? Or *Corral My Heart*?"

"Oh, I love *Corral My Heart*. That song near the end just about broke me," said Izzy, and let out a huge, happy sigh.

You didn't have to trap me—
For I'm your willing prisoner

—broke in Sophia.

You didn't need a rope to corral my heart . . .

they sang in unison, each lost in a reverie.

Alice looked blank.

"You don't go to the picture house?" said Izzy. "Tex Lafayette has been in *everything*."

"He can bullwhip a lit cigarette out of a man's mouth and not leave a scratch on him."

"He is a grade-A *dreamboat*."

"I'm too tired to go out most evenings. Bennett goes sometimes."

In truth, Alice would have found it too strange to be beside her husband in the dark now. She suspected he felt the same way. For weeks they had taken care that their lives crossed as little as possible. She was gone long before breakfast, and he was often out for dinner, either on work errands for Mr. Van Cleve or playing baseball with his friends. He spent most nights on the daybed in their dressing room, so that even the shape of him had become unfamiliar to her. If Mr. Van Cleve thought there was anything odd about their behavior, he didn't say: he spent most of his evenings late at the mine, and seemed largely preoccupied with whatever was going on there. Alice now hated that house with a passion, its gloom, its stifling history. She was so grateful not to have to spend her evenings stuck in the dark little parlor with the two of them that she didn't care to question any of it.

"You're coming to Tex Lafayette, right?" Beth brushed her hair, and straightened her blouse in the mirror. Apparently she had a thing for a boy from the gas station but had shown him her affection by punching him twice on the arm, hard, and was now at a loss to work out what to do next.

"Oh, I don't think so. I don't really know anything about him."

"All work and no play, Alice. C'mon. The whole town is going. Izzy's going to meet us outside the store and her mama has given her a whole dollar for cotton candy. It's only fifty cents if you want a seat. Or you can stand back and watch for free. That's what we're doing."

"I don't know. Bennett's working late over at Hoffman. I should probably just go home."

Sophia and Izzy started to sing again, Izzy blushing, as she always did when she found herself singing to an audience.

Your smile's a rope around me
Has been since you found me
You didn't need to chase me to corral my heart . . .

Margery took the small mirror from Beth and checked her face for smudges, rubbing at her cheekbone with a moistened handkerchief until she was satisfied. "Well, Sven and I are going to be over by the Nice 'N' Quick. He's reserved us an upstairs table so we can get a good view. You'd be welcome to join us."

"I have things to do here," said Alice. "But thank you. I may join you later." She said it to mollify them and they knew it. Secretly she wanted just to sit in peace in the little library. She liked to be on her own there in the evenings, to read by herself, in the dim light of the oil lamp, escaping to the tropical white of Robinson Crusoe's island, or the fusty corridors of Mr. Chips's Brookfield School. If Sophia came while she was still there she tended to let Alice alone, interrupting only to ask if Alice might place her finger on this piece of fabric while she put in a couple of stitches, or whether she thought this repaired book cover looked acceptable. Sophia was not a woman who required an audience, but seemed to feel easier in company, so although they said little to each other, the arrangement had suited both of them for the past few weeks.

"Okay. We'll see you later, then!"

With a cheery wave, the two women clumped across the boards and out down the steps, still in their breeches and boots. As the door opened, a swell of anticipatory noise carried into the little room. The square was full already, a local group of musicians fiddling to keep the waiting crowds happy, the air thick with laughter and cat-calling.

"You not going, Sophia?" said Alice.

"I'll have a listen out the back later on," said Sophia. "Wind's carrying this way." She threaded a needle, lifted another damaged book, and added quietly, "I'm not crazy about places where there are crowds."

· · ·

Perhaps as a kind of concession, Sophia propped the back door open with a book and allowed the sound of the fiddle to creep in, her foot finding it impossible not to tap along occasionally. Alice sat on the chair in the corner, her writing paper on her lap, trying to compose a letter to Gideon, but her pen kept stilling in her hand. She had no idea what to tell him. Everyone in England believed she was enjoying an exciting cosmopolitan life in an America full of huge cars and high times. She didn't know how to convey to her brother the truth of her situation.

Behind her, Sophia, who seemed to know the tunes to everything, hummed along with the fiddle, sometimes allowing her voice to act as a descant, sometimes adding a few lyrics. Her voice was soft and velvety and soothing. Alice put down her pen and thought a little wistfully of how nice it would be to be out there with her husband of old, the one who had taken her in his arms and whispered lovely things in her ears and whose eyes had promised a future full of laughter and romance, instead of the one she caught looking at her occasionally with bemusement, as if he couldn't work out how she had got there.

"Good evening, ladies." The door closed gently behind Fred Guisler. He was wearing a neatly pressed blue shirt and suit trousers, and removed his hat at the sight of them. Alice startled slightly at the unexpected sight of him without his habitual checked shirt and overalls. "Saw the light was on, but I have to say I didn't expect to find you in here this evening. Not with our local entertainment and all."

"Oh, I'm not really a fan," said Alice, who folded away her writing pad.

"You can't be persuaded? Even if you don't enjoy cowboy tricks, Tex Lafayette has a heck of a voice. And it's a beautiful evening out there. Too beautiful to spend in here."

"That's very kind but I'm just fine here, thank you, Mr. Guisler."

Alice waited for him to ask the same of Sophia, then grasped, with a slightly sick feeling, that of course it was obvious to everyone but her why he wouldn't, why the others hadn't pressed her to go with them either. A square full of drunk and rowdy young white men would not be a safe place for Sophia. She realized suddenly that she wasn't entirely sure what was a safe place for Sophia.

"Well, I'm going to take a little stroll down to watch. But I'll stop by later and drive you home, Miss Sophia. There's a fair bit of liquor flying around that square tonight and I'm not sure it'll be a pleasant place for a lady come nine o'clock."

"Thank you, Mr. Guisler," said Sophia. "I appreciate it."

You should go," said Sophia, not looking up from her stitching, as the sound of Fred's footsteps faded down the dark road.

Alice shuffled some loose sheets of paper. "It's complicated."

"Life is complicated. Which is why finding a little joy where you can is important." She frowned at one of her stitches and unpicked it. "It's hard to be different from everyone around here. I understand that. I really do. I had a very different life in Louisville." She let out a sigh. "But those girls care about you. They are your friends. And you shutting yourself off from them ain't going to make things any easier."

Alice watched as a moth fluttered around the oil lamp. After a moment, unable to bear it, she cupped it carefully in her hands, walked to the partially open door and released it. "You'd be here by yourself."

"I'm a big girl. And Mr. Guisler is going to come back for me."

She could hear the music starting up in the square, the roar of approval that announced the Singing Cowboy had taken center stage. She looked at the window.

"You really think I should go?"

Sophia put down her stitching. "Lord, Alice, you need me to write a song about it? Hey," she called, as Alice made for the front door. "Let me fix up your hair before you go. Appearances are important."

Alice ran back and held up the little mirror. She rubbed at her face with her handkerchief as Sophia ran a comb through her hair, pinning and tutting as she worked with nimble fingers. When Sophia stood back Alice reached into her bag for her lipstick and drew coral pink over her lips, pursing them and rubbing them together. Satisfied, she looked down, brushing at her shirt and breeches. "Not much I can do about what I'm wearing."

"But the top half is pretty as a picture. And that's all anyone will notice."

Alice smiled. "Thank you, Sophia."

"You come back and tell me all about it." She sat back at the desk and resumed tapping her foot, half lost already in the distant music.

Alice was partway up the road when she glimpsed the creature. It scuttled across the shadowy road and her mind, already a quarter-mile ahead at the square, took a moment to register that something was in front of her. She slowed: a ground squirrel! She felt, oddly, as if the talk of all the murdered hogs had hung a sad fog over the week, adding to her vague sense of depression. For people who lived so deep in nature, the inhabitants of Baileyville seemed oblivious to the idea of respecting it. She stopped, waiting for the squirrel to cross in front of her. It was a large one, with a huge, thick tail. At that moment the moon emerged from a cloud, revealing to her that it wasn't a squirrel after all, but something darker, more solid, with a black and white stripe. She frowned at it, perplexed, and then, as she was about to take a step forward, it turned its back on her, raised its tail, and she felt her skin sprayed with moisture. It took a second for that sensation to be supplanted by the most noxious smell she had ever breathed. She gasped and gagged, covering her mouth and spluttering. But there was no escaping it: it was all over her hands, her shirt, in her hair. The creature scuttled off nonchalantly into the night, leaving Alice batting at her clothes, as if by waving her hands and yelling she could make it all go away.

The upper floor of the Nice 'N' Quick was thick with bodies pressed against the window, three deep, some yelling their appreciation for the white-suited cowboy below. Margery and Sven were the only ones left seated, the two in a booth beside each other, as they preferred. Between them were the dregs of two iced teas. Two weeks previously a local photographer had stopped by and persuaded the ladies onto their horses in front of the WPA Packhorse Library sign and all four, Izzy, Margery, Alice and Beth, had posed, shoulder to shoulder, on their mounts. A copy of that photograph now took pride of place on the wall of the diner, the women gazing out, decorated by a string of streamers, and Margery could not take her eyes off it. She wasn't sure she had ever been prouder of anything in her life.

"My brother's talking of buying some of that land up on North Ridge. Bore McCallister says he'll give him a good price. I was thinking I might go in with him. I can't work down those mines for ever."

She pulled her attention back to Sven. "How much land you talking about?"

"About four hundred acres. There's good hunting."

"You haven't heard, then."

"Heard what?"

Margery reached round and pulled the template letter out of her bag. Sven opened it carefully and read it, placing it back on the table in front of her. "Where'd you hear this?"

"Know anything about it?"

"Nope. Everywhere we go they're all about busting the United Mine Workers of America's influence just now."

"The two things go together, I worked it out. Daniel McGraw, Ed Siddly, the Bray brothers—all those union organizers—they all live on North Ridge. If the new mine shakes those men out of their homes, along with their families, it's that much harder for them to get organized. They don't want to end up like Harlan, with a damn war going on between the miners and their bosses."

Sven leaned back in his seat. He blew out his cheeks and studied Margery's expression. "I'm guessing the letter is you."

She smiled sweetly at him.

He ran a palm across his forehead. "Jeez, Marge. You know what

127

those thugs are like. Is trouble actually in your blood? . . . No, don't answer that."

"I can't stand by while they wreck these mountains, Sven. You know what they did over at Great White Gap?"

"Yes, I do."

"Blew the valley to pieces, polluted the water, and disappeared overnight when all the coal was gone. All those families left without jobs or homes. They won't do it over here."

He picked up the letter and read it again. "Anyone else know about this?"

"I got two families headed over to the legal offices already. I looked up legal books that say the mine-owners can't blow up land if the families didn't sign those broad form contracts that give the mines all the rights. Casey Campbell helped her daddy to read all the paperwork." She sighed with satisfaction, jabbing her finger onto the table. "Nothing more dangerous than a woman armed with a little knowledge. Even if she's twelve years old."

"If anyone at Hoffman finds out it's you, there's going to be trouble."

She shrugged, and took a swig of her drink.

"I'm serious. Be careful, Marge. I don't want nothing happening to you. Van Cleve has bad men on his payroll on the back of this union fight—guys from out of town. You've seen what's happened in Harlan. I—I couldn't bear it if anything happened to you."

She peered up at him. "You're not getting sentimental on me, are you, Gustavsson?"

"I mean it." He turned so that his face was inches from hers. "I love you, Marge."

She was about to joke, but there was an unfamiliar look to his face, something serious and vulnerable, and the words stilled on her lips. His eyes searched hers, and his fingers closed around her own, as if his hand might say what he wasn't able to. She held his gaze, and then, as a roar went up in the diner, she looked away. Below them Tex Lafayette struck up with "I Was Born in the Valley," to loud whoops of approval.

"Oh, boy, those girls are going to go hog wild now," she murmured.

"I think what you meant to say is 'I love you too,'" he said, after a minute.

"Those dynamite sticks have done something to your ears. I'm sure I said it ages ago," she said, and shaking his head, he pulled her toward him again and kissed her until she stopped grinning.

It didn't matter where they'd said they were going to meet, Alice thought, as she fought her way through the teeming town square: the place was so dark and dense with people that she had almost no chance of finding her friends. The air was thick with the smell of cordite from firecrackers, cigarette smoke, beer and the burned-sugar scent of cotton candy from the stalls that had sprung up for the evening, but she could make out almost none of it. Wherever she went, there was a brief, audible intake of breath and people would back away, frowning and clutching their noses. "Lady, you got sprayed by a skunk!" a freckled youth yelled, as she passed him.

"You don't say," she answered crossly.

"Oh, good Lord." Two girls pulled back, grimacing at Alice. "Is that Van Cleve's English wife?"

Alice felt the people part like waves around her as she drew closer to the stage.

It was a minute before she saw him. Bennett was standing over near the corner of the temporary bar, beaming, a Hudepohl beer in his hand. She stared at him, at his easy smile, his shoulders loose and relaxed in his good blue shirt. She observed, absently, that he seemed so much more at ease when he wasn't with her. Her surprise at his not being at work after all was slowly replaced by a kind of wistfulness, a remembrance of the man she had fallen in love with. As she watched, wondering whether to walk over and confide in him about her disastrous evening, a girl standing just to his left turned, and held up a bottle of cola. It was Peggy Foreman. She leaned in close and said something that made him laugh, and he nodded, his eyes still on Tex Lafayette, then he looked back at her, and his face creased into a goofy smile. She wanted to run up to him then, to push that girl out of the way. To take her place in the arms of her husband, have him smile tenderly at her as he had before they were married. But even as she stood, people were backing away from her, laughing or muttering: *Skunk.* She felt her eyes brim with tears and, head down, began to push her way back through the crowd.

"*Hey!*"

Alice's jaw jutted as she wound her way through the jostling bodies, ignoring the jeers and laughter that seemed to swell in bursts around her, the music fading into the distance. She was grateful that the dark meant barely anybody could see who it was as she wiped the tears away.

"Good Lord. Did you catch that smell?"

"Hey! . . . Alice!"

Her head spun round and she saw Fred Guisler pushing his way through the crowd toward her, his arm outstretched. "You okay?"

It took him a couple of seconds to register the smell; she saw shock flicker across his features—a silent *whoa*—and then, almost immediately, his determined attempt to hide it. He placed an arm around her shoulders, resolutely steering her through the crowd. "C'mon. Let's get you back to the library. Move over there, would you? Coming through."

It took them ten minutes to walk back up the dark road. As soon as they were out of the center of town, away from the crowds, Alice stepped out of the shelter of his arm and took herself to the side of the road. "You're very kind. But you really don't need to."

"It's fine. Got almost no sense of smell anyway. First horse I ever broke caught me in the nose with a back foot and I've never been the same since."

She knew he was lying, but it was kind and she shot him a rueful smile. "I couldn't see for sure, but I think it was a skunk. It just stopped in front of me and—"

"Oh, it was a skunk all right." He was trying not to laugh.

Alice stared at him, her cheeks flaming. She thought she might actually burst into tears, but something in his expression felled her and, to her surprise, she began to laugh instead.

"Worst thing ever, huh?"

"Truthfully? Not even close."

"Well, now I'm intrigued. So what was the worst?"

"I can't tell you."

"Two skunks?"

"You have to stop laughing at me, Mr. Guisler."

"I don't mean to hurt your feelings, Mrs. Van Cleve. It's just so unlikely—a girl like you, so pretty and refined and all . . . and that smell . . ."

"You're not really helping."

"I'm sorry. Look, come to my house before you go to the library. I can find you some fresh clothes so you can at least get home without causing a commotion."

They walked in silence the last hundred yards, peeling off the main road up the track to Fred Guisler's house, which, being behind the library and set back from the road, Alice realized she had barely registered until now. There was a light on in the porch and she followed him up the wooden steps, glancing left to where, a hundred yards away, the library light was still on, only visible from this side of the road through a tiny crack in the door. She pictured Sophia in there, hard at work stitching new books out of old, humming along to the music, and then he opened the door and stood back to let her in.

Men who lived alone around Baileyville, as far as she could make out, lived rough lives, their cabins functional and sparsely furnished, their habits basic and hygiene often questionable. Fred's house had sanded wood floors, waxed and burnished through years of use; a rocker sat in a corner, a blue rag rug in front of it, and a large brass lamp cast a soft glow over a shelf of books. Pictures lined the wall and an upholstered chair stood opposite, with a view out over the rear of the building and Fred's large barn full of horses. The gramophone was on a highly polished mahogany table and an intricate old quilt lay neatly folded to its side. "But this is beautiful!" she said, realizing as she did the insult in her words.

He didn't seem to catch it. "Not all my work," he said. "But I try to keep it nice. Hold on."

She felt bad, bringing this stench into his sweet-smelling, comfortable home. She crossed her arms and winced as he jogged upstairs, as if that could contain the odor. He was back in minutes, with two dresses across his arm. "One of these should fit."

She looked up at him. "You have dresses?"

"They were my wife's."

She blinked.

"Hand me your clothes out and I'll douse them in vinegar. That'll help. When you take them home get Annie to put some baking soda into the washtub with the soap. Oh, and there's a clean washcloth on the stand."

She turned and he gestured toward a bathroom, which she entered. She stripped down, pushed her clothes out through a gap in the door, then washed her face and hands, scrubbing at her skin with the washcloth and lye soap. The acrid smell refused to dissipate; in the confines of the warm little room, it almost made her gag and she scrubbed as hard as she could without actually removing a layer of skin. As an afterthought she poured a jug of water over her head, rubbing at her hair with soap and rinsing it, then rough drying it with a towel. Finally she slipped into the green dress. It was what her mother would have called a tea-dress, short-sleeved and floral with a white lace collar, a little loose around the waist, but at least it smelled clean. There was a bottle of scent on top of a cabinet. She sniffed it, then sprayed a little on her wet hair.

She emerged some minutes later to find Fred standing by the window looking down at the illuminated town square. He turned, his mind clearly lost elsewhere, and perhaps because of his wife's dress, he seemed suddenly shaken. He recovered himself swiftly and handed her a glass of iced tea. "Thought you might need this."

"Thank you, Mr. Guisler." She took a sip. "I feel rather silly."

"Fred. Please. And don't feel bad. Not for a minute. We've all been caught."

She stood for a moment, feeling suddenly awkward. She was in a strange man's home, wearing his dead wife's dress. She didn't know what to do with her limbs. A roar went up somewhere in town and she winced. "Oh, goodness. I haven't just made your lovely house smell awful but you've missed Tex Lafayette. I'm so sorry."

He shook his head. "It's nothing. I couldn't leave you, looking so . . ."

"Skunks, eh!" she said brightly, and his concerned expression didn't shift, as if he knew that the smell was not the thing that had so upset her.

"Still! You can probably catch the rest of it if we head back now," she said. She had started to gabble. "I mean, it looks like he'll be singing a while. You were quite right. He's *very* good. Not that I heard a huge amount, what with one thing and another, but I can see why he's so popular. The crowd does seem to love him."

"Alice—"

"Goodness. Look at the time. I'd better head back." She walked past him toward the door, her head down. "You should absolutely head back to the show. I'll walk home. It's no distance."

"I'll drive you."

"In case of more skunks?" Her laugh was high and brittle. Her voice didn't even sound like her own. "Honestly, Mr. Guisler—Fred—you've been so very kind already and I don't want to put you to more trouble. Really. I don't—"

"I'll take you," he said firmly. He took his jacket from the back of a chair, then removed a small blanket from another and placed it around her shoulders. "It's turned chilly out there."

They stepped onto the porch. Alice was suddenly acutely aware of Frederick Guisler, of the way he had of observing her, as if looking through whatever she said or did to assess its true purpose. It was oddly discomfiting. She half stumbled down the porch steps and he reached out a hand to steady her. She clutched at it, then immediately let go as if she'd been stung.

Please don't say anything else, she said silently. Her cheeks were aflame again, her thoughts a jumble. But when she glanced up he wasn't looking at her.

"Was that door like that when we came in?" He was staring at the back of the library. The door, which had been open a sliver to allow in the sound of the music, was now wide open. A series of distant, irregular thumps came from within. He stood very still, then turned to Alice, his ease of the previous minutes gone. "Stay there."

He strode swiftly back inside and then, a moment later, emerged from his house with a large double-barreled rifle. Alice stepped back as he passed, watching as he walked toward the library. Then, unable to stop herself, she followed a few paces behind, her feet silent on the grass as she tiptoed down the back path.

What seems to be the problem here, boys?"

Frederick Guisler stood in the doorway. Behind him Alice, her heart in her mouth, could just make out the scattered books on the floor, an overturned chair. There were two, no, three young men in the library, dressed in jeans and shirts. One held a beer bottle, and another an armful of books, which, as Fred stood there, he dropped with a kind of provocative deliberation. She could just make out Sophia standing, rigid, in the corner, her gaze fixed on some indeterminate point on the floor.

"You got a colored in your library." The boy's voice held a nasal whine and was slurred with drink.

"Yup. And I'm standing here trying to work out what business that is of yours."

"This is for white folks. She shouldn't be here."

"Yeah." The other two young men, emboldened by beer, jeered back at him.

"Do you run this library now?" Fred's voice was icy. It held a tone she had never heard before.

"I ain't—"

"I said, do you run this library, Chet Mitchell?"

The boy's eyes slid sideways, as if the sound of his own name had reminded him of the potential for consequences. "No."

"Then I suggest you leave. All three of you. Before this gun slips in my hand and I do something I regret."

"You threatening me over a *colored*?"

"I'm telling you what happens when a man finds three drunk fools on his property. And if you like, just as easy, I'll tell you what happens if a man finds they don't leave as soon as he tells them. Pretty sure you ain't going to like it, though."

"I don't see why you're sticking up for her. You got a thing fer Brownie here?"

Quick as a flash, Fred had the boy by the throat, pinned against the wall with a white-knuckled fist. Alice ducked backward, her breath in her throat. "Don't push me, Mitchell."

The boy swallowed, raised his palms. "It was just a joke," he choked. "Can't take a joke now, Mr. Guisler?"

"I don't see anyone else laughing. Now git." Fred dropped the boy, whose knees buckled. He rubbed at his throat, shot a nervous look at his friends and then, when Fred took a step forward, ducked out through the back door. Alice, her heart pounding, stepped back as the three stumbled out, adjusting their clothes with a mute bravado, then walked in silence back down the grit path. Their courage returned when they were out of easy range.

"You got a thing for Brownie, Frederick Guisler? That why your wife left?"

"You can't shoot for shit anyway. I seen you hunting!"

Alice thought she might be sick. She leaned on the back wall of the library, a fine sweat prickling on her back, her heart rate only easing when she could just make them out disappearing around the corner. She could hear Fred inside, picking up books and placing them on the table.

"I'm so sorry, Miss Sophia. I should have come back sooner."

"Not at all. It's my own fault for leaving the door open."

Alice made her way slowly up the steps. Sophia, on the surface, looked unperturbed. She stooped, picking up books and checking them for damage, dusting their surfaces and tutting at the torn labels. But when Fred turned away to adjust a shelf that had been shoved from its moorings, she saw Sophia's hand reach out to the desk for support, her knuckles tightening momentarily on its edge. Alice stepped in and, without a word, began tidying, too. The scrapbooks that Sophia had so carefully been putting together had been ripped to pieces in front of her. The carefully mended books were newly torn and hurled across the room, loose pages still fluttering around the interior.

"I'll stay late this week and help you fix them," Alice said. And then, when Sophia didn't respond, she added: "That is . . . if you're coming back?"

"You think a bunch of snot-nosed kids are going to keep me from my job? I'll be fine, Miss Alice." She paused, and gave her a tight smile. "But your help would be appreciated, thank you. We have ground to make up."

"I'll speak to the Mitchells," said Fred. "I'm not going to let this happen again." His voice softened and his body was easy as he moved around the little cabin. But Alice saw how every few minutes his focus would shift to the window, and that he only relaxed once he had the two women in his truck, ready to drive them home.

EIGHT

Before today, Jody had been a boy, dressed in overalls and a blue shirt—quieter than most, even suspected of being a little cowardly. And now he was different. Out of a thousand centuries they drew the ancient admiration . . . that a man on a horse is spiritually as well as physically bigger than a man on foot. They knew that Jody had been miraculously lifted out of equality with them, and had been placed over them.

· JOHN STEINBECK, *The Red Pony*

Given the speed at which news traveled through Baileyville, its snippets of gossip starting as a trickle, then pushing through its inhabitants in an unstoppable torrent, the stories of Sophia Kenworth's employment at the Packhorse Library and its trashing by three local men were swiftly deemed serious enough to warrant a town meeting.

Alice stood shoulder to shoulder with Margery, Beth and Izzy, in a corner at the back, while Mrs. Brady addressed the assembled gathering. Bennett sat two rows back beside his father. "You going to sit down, girl?" Mr. Van Cleve had said, looking her up and down as he entered.

"I'm fine right here, thank you," she had answered, and watched as his expression turned disapprovingly toward his son.

"We have always prided ourselves on being a pleasant, orderly town," Mrs. Brady was saying. "We do not want to become the kind of place where thuggish behavior becomes the norm. I have spoken to the parents of the young men concerned and made it clear that this will not be tolerated. A library is a sacred place—a sacred place of learning. It should not be considered fair game just because it is staffed by women."

"I'd like to add to that, Mrs. Brady." Fred stepped forward. Alice recalled the way he had looked at her on the night of Tex Lafayette's show, the strange intimacy of his bathroom, and felt her skin prickle with color, as if she had done something to be ashamed of. She had told Annie the green dress belonged to Beth. Annie's left eyebrow had lifted halfway to the heavens.

"That library is in my old shed," said Fred. "That means, in case anyone here is in any doubt, that it is on my property. I cannot be responsible for what happens to trespassers." He looked slowly around the hall. "Anyone who thinks they have business heading into that building without my permission, or that of any of these ladies, will have me to answer to."

He caught Alice's eye as he stood down, and she felt her cheeks color again.

"I understand you have strong feelings about your property, Fred." Henry Porteous stood. "But there are larger issues to discuss here. I, and a good number of our neighbors, am concerned about the impact this library is having on our little town. There are reports of wives no longer keeping house because they are too busy reading fancy magazines or cheap romances. There are children picking up disruptive ideas from comic books. We're struggling to control what influences are coming into our homes."

"They're just books, Henry Porteous! How do you think the great scholars of old learned?" Mrs. Brady's arms folded across her chest, forming a solid, unbridgeable shelf.

"I'd put a dollar to a dime the great scholars were not reading *The Amorous Sheik of Araby*, or whatever it was my daughter was wasting her time with the other day. Do we really want their minds polluted with this stuff? I don't want my daughter thinking she can run off with some *Egyptian*."

"Your daughter has about as much chance of having her head turned by a Sheik of Araby as I do of becoming Cleopatra."

"But you can't be *sure*."

"You want me to go through every book in this library to check for things that you might find fanciful, Henry Porteous? There are more challenging stories in the Bible than there are in the *Pictorial Review* and you know it."

"Well, now you sound as sacrilegious as they do."

Mrs. Beidecker stood. "May I speak? I would like to thank the book ladies. Our pupils have very much enjoyed the new books and learning materials, and the textbooks have proven very useful in helping them progress. I go through all the comic books before we hand them out, just to check what is inside, and I have found absolutely nothing to concern even the most sensitive of minds."

"But you're foreign!" Mr. Porteous interjected.

"Mrs. Beidecker came to our school with the highest of credentials," Mrs. Brady exclaimed. "And you know it, Henry Porteous. Why, doesn't your own niece attend her classes?"

"Well, maybe she shouldn't."

"Settle down! Settle down!" Pastor McIntosh climbed to his feet. "Now I understand feelings are running high. And yes, Mrs. Brady, there are some of us who do have reservations about the impact of this library on formative minds but—"

"But what?"

"There is clearly another issue here . . . the employment of a colored."

"What issue would that be, Pastor?"

"You may favor the progressive ways, Mrs. Brady, but many in this town do not believe that colored folks should be in our libraries."

"That's right," said Mr. Van Cleve. He stood, and surveyed the sea of white faces. "The 1933 Public Accommodations Law authorizes— and I quote here—'the establishment of *segregated libraries* for different

139

races.' The colored girl should not be in our library. You believe you're above the law now, Margery O'Hare?"

Alice's heart had lodged somewhere in her throat, but Margery, stepping forward, appeared supremely untroubled. "Nope."

"Nope?"

"No. Because Miss Sophia isn't *using* the library. She's just working there." She smiled at him sweetly. "We've told her *very* firmly she is under no circumstances to open any of our books and read them."

There was a low ripple of laughter.

Mr. Van Cleve's face darkened. "You can't employ a colored in a white library. It's against the law, and the laws of nature."

"You don't believe in employing them, huh?"

"It's not about me. It's about the *law*."

"I'm most surprised to hear you complaining, Mr. Van Cleve," she said.

"What do you mean by that?"

"Well, given the number of colored folk you got over there at your mine . . ."

There was an intake of breath.

"I do not."

"I know most of them by person, as do half the good people here. You listing them as mulatto on your books doesn't change the facts."

"Oh, boy," said Fred, under his breath. "She went there."

Margery leaned back against the table. "Times are changing and colored folk are being employed in all sorts of ways. Now, Miss Sophia is fully trained and is keeping published material in commission that wouldn't otherwise be able to stay on the shelves. Those *Baileyville Bonus* magazines? You all enjoy them, right? With the recipes and the stories and all?"

There was a low murmur of agreement.

"Well, those are all Miss Sophia's work. She takes books and magazines that have been spoiled and she stitches what she can save back together to create new books for you all." Margery leaned forward to flick something from her jacket. "Now, I can't stitch like that and neither can my girls, and as you know, volunteers have been hard to come by. Miss Sophia isn't riding out, visiting families or even choosing the books. She's just keeping house for us, so to speak. So until it's one rule for everyone, Mr. Van Cleve, you and your mines and me and my library, I will keep on employing her. I trust that's acceptable to y'all."

With a nod, Margery walked out through the center of the room, her gait unhurried and her head held high.

The screen door slammed behind them with a resounding *crash*. Alice had said nothing the whole journey back from the meeting hall, walking a way behind the two men, from where she could hear the kind of muttered expletives that suggested an imminent and volcanic explosion. She didn't have long to wait.

"Who the Sam Hill does that woman think she is? Trying to embarrass me in front of the whole town?"

"I don't think anyone felt you were—" Bennett began, but his father threw his hat on the table, cutting him off.

"She's been nothing but trouble her whole life! And that criminal daddy of hers before her. And now standing there trying to make me look a fool in front of my own people?"

Alice hovered in the doorway, wondering if she could sidle upstairs without anybody noticing. In her experience Mr. Van Cleve's tantrums rarely burned out quickly—he would fuel them with bourbon and continue shouting and declaiming until he passed out late in the evening.

"Nobody cares what that woman says, Pop," Bennett began again.

"Those coloreds are listed as mulatto at my mine because they're light-skinned. Light-skinned, I tell you!"

Alice pondered Sophia's dark skin, and wondered, if she was sister to a miner, how siblings could be completely different colors. But she said nothing. "I think I'll head upstairs," she said quietly.

"You can't stay there, Alice."

Oh, God, she thought. *Don't make me sit on the porch with you.*

"Then I'll come—"

"At that library. You ain't working there no more. Not with that girl."

"What?"

She felt his words close around her like a stranglehold.

"You'll hand in your notice. I'm not having my family aligned with Margery O'Hare's. I don't care what Patricia Brady thinks—she's lost her mind along with the rest of them." Van Cleve walked to the drinks cabinet and poured himself a large glass of bourbon. "And how the heck did that girl see who was on the mine's books, anyway? I wouldn't put it past her to be sneaking in. I'm going to put a ban on her coming anywhere near Hoffman."

There was a silence. And then Alice heard her voice.

"No."

Van Cleve looked up. "What?"

"No. I'm not leaving the library. I'm not married to you, and you don't tell me what I do."

"You'll do what I say! You live under my roof, young lady!"

She didn't blink.

Mr. Van Cleve glared at her, then turned to Bennett, and waved a hand. "Bennett? Sort your woman out."

"I'm not leaving the library."

Mr. Van Cleve turned puce. "Do you need a slap, girl?"

The air in the room seemed to disappear. She looked at her husband. *Don't you think of laying a hand on me*, she told him silently. Mr. Van Cleve's face was taut, his breath shallow in his chest. *Don't you even think about it.* Her mind raced, wondering suddenly what she would do if he actually lifted his hand to her. Should she hit back? Was there something she could use to protect herself? *What would Margery do?* She took in the knife on the breadboard, the poker by the range.

But Bennett looked down at his feet and swallowed. "She should stay at the library, Pa."

"What?"

"She likes it there. She's . . . doing a good job. Helping people and all."

Van Cleve stared at his son. His eyes bulged out of his beet-red face, as if someone had squeezed him from the neck. "Have you lost your damned mind as well?" He stared at them both, his cheeks blown out and his knuckles white, as if braced for an explosion that wouldn't come. Finally he threw the last of the bourbon down his throat, slammed down his glass and set off outside, the screen door bouncing on its hinges in his wake.

Bennett and Alice stood in the silent kitchen, listening to Mr. Van Cleve's Ford Sedan starting up and roaring into the distance.

"Thank you," she said.

He let out a long breath, and turned away. She wondered then whether something might shift. Whether the act of standing up to his father might alter whatever had gone so wrong between them. She thought of Kathleen Bligh and her husband, the way that, even as Alice read to him, Kathleen would stroke his head as she passed, or place her hand on his. The way, sick and frail as he was, Garrett would reach out for her, his hollowed face always finding even the faintest smile for his wife.

She took a step toward Bennett, wondering if she might take his hand. But, as if reading her mind, he thrust both into his pockets.

"Well, I appreciate it," she said quietly, stepping back again. And then, when he didn't speak, she fixed him a drink and went upstairs.

Garrett Bligh died two days later, after weeks of hovering in a strange, rasping hinterland while those who loved him tried to work out whether his lungs or his heart would give out first. The word went round the mountain, the bell tolled thirty-four times, so that everyone nearby could tell who had departed. After they had finished their day's work the neighboring men gathered at the Bligh household, carrying good clothes in case Kathleen had none, ready to lay out, wash and dress the body, as was the local custom. Others began to build the coffin that would be lined with cotton and silk.

Word reached the Packhorse Library a day later. Margery and Alice, by tacit agreement, shared out their routes between Beth and Izzy as best they could, then set out for the house together. There was a sharp wind that, instead of being blocked by the mountains, simply used them as a funnel, and Alice rode the whole way with her chin pressed into her collar, wondering what she could say when she reached the little house, and wishing she had an appropriate greetings card, or perhaps a posy to offer.

In England a house in mourning was a place of silence, of vaguely whispered conversation, shaded by a cloak of sadness, or awkwardness, depending on how well the deceased was known or loved. Alice, who often managed to say the wrong thing, found such hushed occasions oppressive, a trap that she would no doubt fall into.

When they reached the top of Hellmouth Ridge, though, there was little suggestion of silence: they passed cars and buggies dotted lower down the track, abandoned on the verge as the passing became impossible, and when they reached the house, strange horses' heads poked out of the barn, whickering at each other, and muffled singing came from inside. Alice looked over to a small bank of pine trees, where three men were digging in heavy coats, their picks sending clanging sounds into the air as they hit rock, their faces puce, and their breath pale gray clouds. "Is she going to bury him here?" she said to Margery.

"Yup. His whole family's up there." Alice could just make out a succession of stone slabs, some large, some heartbreakingly small, telling of a Bligh family history on the mountain stretching back generations.

Inside, the little cabin was full to bursting. Garrett Bligh's bed had been shoved to one side and covered with a quilt for people to sit on. Barely an inch of space remained that wasn't covered with small children, trays of food, or singing matriarchs, who nodded at Alice and Margery as they entered, without breaking off their song. The windows, which, Alice remembered, had contained no glass, were shuttered and carbide lamps and candles lit the gloom so that it was hard to tell inside if it was day or night. One of the Bligh children sat on the lap of a woman with a prominent chin and kind eyes, and the others nestled into Kathleen, as she closed her eyes and sang too, the only one of the group to be somewhere far from there. A trestle table had been set up on which lay a pine coffin, and Alice could just make out within it the body of Garrett Bligh, his face relaxed in death, so much so that, for a moment, she wondered whether it was him at all. His hollowed cheekbones had somehow softened, his brow now smooth under soft, dark hair. Only his face was visible, the rest of him covered with an intricate patchwork quilt and strewn with flowers and herbs that scented the air. She had never seen a dead body, but somehow here, surrounded by the songs and warmth of the people around him, it was hard to feel shock or discomfort at its proximity.

"I'm so sorry for your loss," Alice said. It was the only phrase she had been coached to say, and here it seemed sterile and useless. Kathleen opened her eyes and, taking a moment to register, smiled vaguely at Alice. Her eyes were rimmed pink and shadowed with exhaustion.

"He was a fine man, and a fine father," said Margery, sweeping in and holding her tightly. Alice wasn't sure she'd ever seen Margery hug someone before.

"He'd had enough," Kathleen murmured, and the child in her arms looked at her blankly, her thumb thrust deep into her mouth. "I couldn't wish him to stay any longer. He's with the Lord now."

The slack of her jaw and her sad eyes failed to mirror the conviction of her words.

"Did you know Garrett?" An older woman with two crocheted shawls around her shoulders tapped the four inches of bed-space beside her, so that Alice felt obliged to squeeze her way in too.

"Oh, a little. I—I'm just the librarian."

The woman peered at her, frowning.

"I only knew him from my visits." It came out apologetically, as if she knew she shouldn't really be there.

"You're the lady used to read to him?"

"Yes."

"Oh, child! That was such a comfort to my son." The woman reached out and pulled Alice to her. Alice stiffened, then gave in to her. "Kathleen told me many times how much Garrett looked forward to your visits. How they would take him quite out of himself."

"Your son? Oh, my goodness. I'm so sorry." She meant it. "He really did seem the nicest of men. And he and Kathleen were so very fond of each other."

"I'm much obliged to you, Miss . . ."

"Mrs. Van Cleve."

"My Garrett was a fine young man. Oh, you didn't see him before. He had the broadest shoulders this side of the Cumberland Gap, didn't he, Kathleen? When Kathleen married him there were a hundred crying girls between here and Berea."

The young widow smiled at the memory.

"I used to tell him I had no idea how he could even make his way into that mine with a build like his. Course, now I wish he hadn't. Still—" the older woman swallowed and lifted her chin, "—not for us to question God's plan. He's with his own father and he's with God the Father. We just have to get used to being down here without him, don't we, sweetheart?" She reached out and squeezed her daughter-in-law's hand.

"Amen," someone called.

Alice had assumed that they would pay their respects and leave, but as morning became afternoon and afternoon swiftly fell to dusk, the little cabin grew fuller, with miners arriving after their shift, their wives bringing pies and souse and fruit jellies, and as time slid and stalled in the dim light, more people piled in, and nobody left. Chicken appeared in front of Alice, then soft biscuits and gravy, fried potatoes and more chicken. Somebody shared some bourbon, and there were outbreaks of laughter, tears and singing, and the air in the tiny cabin grew warm, thick with the scents of roasted meats and sweet liquor. Someone produced a fiddle and played Scottish tunes that made Alice feel vaguely homesick. Margery occasionally shot her a look, as if checking she was okay, but Alice, surrounded by people who would clap her on the back and thank her for her service, as if she were a military man, not just an Englishwoman delivering books, was oddly glad just to sit and absorb it all.

So Alice Van Cleve gave herself to the strange rhythms of the evening. She sat a few feet from a dead man, ate the food, sipped a little of the drink, sang along to hymns she barely knew, clasped the hands of strangers, who no longer felt like strangers. And when night fell and Margery whispered in her ear that they really should get going now, because a hard frost would be setting in, Alice was surprised to find that she felt as if she was leaving home, not heading back to it, and this thought was so disconcerting that it pushed away all else for the whole of the slow, cold, lantern-lit ride back down the mountain.

NINE

*Many medical men now recognize that numerous
nervous and other diseases are associated with the lack
of physiological relief for natural or stimulated sex
feelings in women.*

· Dr. Marie Stopes, *Married Love*

According to the local midwives, there was a reason most babies came in summer, and that was because there wasn't a whole heap to do in Baileyville once the light had gone. The picture house tended to get its movies some months after they had been and gone elsewhere. Even when they came Mr. Rand, who ran it, loved his liquor, to the extent that you could never be sure that you'd see the end of the show before a reel crumpled and burned on screen, victim to one of his impromptu naps, prompting jeers and disappointment across the audience. Harvest festival and hog-slaughter had slid past and it was too early for Thanksgiving, which left a long month with nothing but darkening skies, the increasing smell of wood smoke in the air, and the encroaching cold to look forward to.

And yet. It was apparent to anybody who took notice of such things (and Baileyville's residents made whole careers out of taking notice) that this fall an inordinate number of local men seemed oddly cheerful. They raced home as soon as they could and whistled their way through their days bug-eyed with sleep deprivation but shorn of their usual short tempers. Jim Forrester, who drove for the Mathews lumber yard, was barely seen at the honky-tonks, where he usually spent his non-working hours. Sam Torrance and his wife had taken to walking around holding hands and smiling at each other. And Michael Murphy, whose mouth had been welded into a thin line of dissatisfaction for most of his thirty-odd years, had been seen singing—actually *singing*—to his wife on his porch.

These were not developments that the elders of the town felt able to complain about, exactly, but certainly added, they confided to each other with a vague feeling of discombobulation, to a sense that things were shifting in a way they were at a loss to understand.

The inhabitants of the Packhorse Library were not quite as perplexed. The little blue book—which had proven more popular and more useful than any number of bestsellers, and required almost constant repair—was dispatched and returned week after week, under piles of magazines, with quick, grateful smiles, accompanied by whispered murmurings of *My Joshua never even heard of such a thing, but he sure does seem to like it!* And *No baby this springtime for us. I cannot tell you the relief.* A honeymooner's blush would accompany many of these confidences, or a distinct twinkle in the eye. Only one woman returned it stony-faced, with the admonition that *she had never seen the devil's work cast into print before.* But even then Sophia noted that there were several pages where the corners had been carefully turned to keep their place.

Margery would slide the little book back into its home in the wooden chest where they kept cleaning materials, blister liniment and spare stirrup leathers, and a day or two later the word would be passed to another remote cabin, and the query would be made, tentatively, to another librarian: "Um . . . before you go, my cousin over at Chalk Hollow says you have a book that covers matters of . . . a certain delicacy . . ." and it would find itself on its way again.

"What are you girls doing?"

Izzy and Beth sprang back from the corner as Margery walked in, kicking mud from the heels of her boots in a way that would infuriate Sophia later. Beth was quite helpless with laughter, and Izzy's cheeks glowed pink. Alice was at the desk, entering her books into the ledger and pretending to ignore them.

"Are you girls looking at what I think you're looking at?"

Beth held up the book. "Is this true? That 'female animals may actually die if denied sexual union'?" Beth was open-mouthed. "Because I'm not hanging off no man and I don't look like I'm fit to drop, do I?"

"But what do you die of?" said Izzy, aghast.

"Maybe your hole closes up and then you can't breathe properly. Like one of them dolphins."

"Beth!" exclaimed Izzy.

"If that's where you're breathing out of, Beth Pinker, then lack of sexual congress isn't the thing we need to be worrying about," said Margery. "Anyway, you girls shouldn't be reading about that. You're not even married."

"Nor are you, and you've read it twice."

Margery pulled a face. The girl had a point.

"Jeez, what are the 'natural completions of a woman's sex-functions'?" Beth started to giggle again. "Oh, my, look here, this says that women who don't get satisfaction may suffer an actual *nervous breakdown*. Can you believe that? But if they do get satisfaction, 'every organ in their bodies is influenced and stimulated to play its part, while their spirits, after soaring in the dizzy heights of rapture, are wafted to oblivion.'"

"My organs are meant to be wafting?" said Izzy.

"Beth Pinker, will you just shut up for five minutes?" Alice slammed her book down on the desk. "Some of us are actually trying to work here."

There was a brief silence. The women exchanged sideways looks.

"I'm just joking with you."

"Well, some of us don't want to hear your horrible jokes. Can you just cut it out? It's not funny."

Beth frowned at Alice. She picked casually at a piece of cotton on her breeches. "I'm so sorry, Miss Alice. I hate that I might have caused you distress," she said, solemnly. A sly smile spread across her face. "You're not . . . you're not having a *nervous breakdown*, are you?"

Margery, who had lightning-quick reaction times, managed to get between them just before Alice's fist made contact. She raised her palms, pushing them apart, and gestured Beth toward the door. "Beth, why don't you check those horses have fresh water? Izzy, put that book back in the trunk and come and sweep up this mess. Miss Sophia gets back from her aunt's tomorrow and you know what she'll have to say about it all."

She looked at Alice, who had sat down again and was now staring with intense concentration at the ledger, her whole demeanor warning Margery not to say another thing. She would be there long after the rest of them had gone home, as she was every working night. And Margery knew she wasn't reading a word.

Alice waited until Margery and the others had left, raising her head to mutter good-bye. She knew they would talk about her when they were gone but she didn't care. Bennett wouldn't miss her: he would be out with friends. Mr. Van Cleve would be late at the mine, as he was most nights, and Annie would be tutting about three dinners gone dry and shriveled in the bottom of the range.

Despite the companionship of the other women, she felt so lonely she could weep with the weight of it. She spent most of her time alone in the mountains and some days she talked more to her horse than any other living being. Where once it had offered her a welcome sense of freedom, now the vast expanses seemed only to emphasize her sense of isolation. She would turn up her collar against the cold, wedge her fingers into her gloves, with miles of flinted track in front of her and only the ache in her muscles to distract her. Sometimes she felt as if her face was set in stone, apart from when she finally stopped to deliver her books. When Jim Horner's girls ran to her for hugs it was all she could do not to hold tight to them and let out an involuntary silent sob. She had never thought of herself as someone who needed physical contact, but night after night, yards away from Bennett's sleeping body, she felt herself slowly turning to marble.

"Still here, huh?"

She jumped.

Fred Guisler had put his head around the door. "Just came to bring a new coffee pot. Marge said the old one had sprung a leak."

Alice wiped at her eyes and gave him a bright smile. "Oh, yes! Go right ahead."

He hesitated on the threshold. "Am I . . . disturbing something?"

"Not at all!" Her voice was forced, too cheery.

"I won't be a minute." He walked over to the side, replacing the metal coffee pot and checking the tin for supplies. He kept the women in coffee every week without so much as mentioning it, and brought in logs to keep the fire burning so that they could get warm between rounds. "Frederick Guisler," Beth would announce every morning, smacking her lips at her first cup, "is a veritable saint."

"Brought you all some apples too, thought you could take a couple each to work. You'll be getting hungrier now the days are colder." He pulled a bag from inside his overcoat and put them on the side. He was still wearing his work clothes, his boots hemmed by a layer of mud around the sole. Sometimes she would hear him outside as she arrived, talking to his young horses with a *yip!* And a "C'mon, now, smarty-pants, you can do better than that," as if they were just as much his friends as the women in the cabin, or standing, arms crossed, beside some fancy horse-owner from Lexington, sucking his teeth as they discussed conformation and price. "These here are Rome Beauties. They ripen a little later than the rest." He shoved his hands into his pockets. "I always like . . . to have something to look forward to."

"That's very kind of you."

"It's nothing. You girls work hard . . . and don't always get the credit you deserve."

She thought he would leave then, but he hesitated in front of the desk, chewing the side of his lip. She lowered her book and waited.

"Alice? Are you . . . all right?" He spoke the words as if this was a question he had already rolled over in his head twenty, thirty times. "It's just, well, I hope you don't mind me mentioning, but you . . . you seem—well, you seem so much less happy than you did. I mean, when you first came."

She felt her cheeks color. She wanted to say *I'm fine* but her mouth had dried and nothing would come.

He studied her face for a moment and then he walked slowly across to the shelves to the left of the front door. He scanned them, a nod of satisfaction escaping him when he found what he was looking for. He pulled a book from the shelf and brought it to her. "She's a bit of a misfit, but I like the fire in her words. When I felt low, a few years back, I found some of these were . . . helpful." He took a scrap of paper, marking the page he had sought, and handed it to her. "I mean, you may not like them. Poetry is kind of a personal thing. I just thought . . ." He kicked at a loose nail on the floor. Then finally he looked up at her. "Anyways. I'll leave you to it." Then, as if compelled, he added, "Mrs. Van Cleve."

She didn't know what to say. He walked to the door, raising a hand in awkward salute. His clothes were scented with wood smoke.

"Mr. Guisler? . . . Fred?"

"Yes?"

She stood paralyzed, consumed with the sudden need to confide in another human being. To tell him of the nights that she felt something was being hollowed out at the very core of her, that nothing that had happened to her in her life up to now had left her feeling so leaden of heart, so lost, as if she had made a mistake that there was simply no coming back from. She wanted to tell him she feared the days she didn't work like she feared a fever, because outside the hills and the horses and the books, she often felt she had nothing at all.

"Thank you." She swallowed. "For the apples, I mean."

His response came a half-second too late. "My pleasure."

The door closed quietly behind him and she heard his footsteps heading up the path toward his house. He stopped halfway up and she found herself sitting very still, waiting for what, she wasn't even sure, and then the footsteps continued, fading into nothing.

She looked down at the little book of poetry and opened it.

The Giver of Stars *by Amy Lowell*

Hold your soul open for my welcoming.
Let the quiet of your spirit bathe me
With its clear and rippled coolness,
That, loose-limbed and weary, I find rest,
Outstretched upon your peace, as on a bed of ivory.

She stared at the words, her heart thumping in her ears, her skin prickling as they shaped and re-formed themselves in her imagination. She thought suddenly of Beth's astonished voice: *Is it true that some female animals will* die *if denied sexual union?*

Alice sat for a long time, gazing at the page in front of her. She wasn't sure how long she stayed like that. She thought about Garrett Bligh, his hand reaching blindly for his wife's, the way their eyes locked in mutual understanding even in his final days. Finally she stood up and walked to the wooden trunk. Glancing behind her, as if even then someone might see what she was doing, she rummaged through it until she pulled out the little blue book. She sat down at the desk and, opening it, began to read.

It was almost 9:45 p.m. by the time she returned home. The Ford was outside and Mr. Van Cleve was in his room, pulling open his drawers and ramming them shut with so much force that she could hear him from the hall. She closed the front door behind her and walked quietly upstairs, her mind humming, her fingers trailing lightly on the banister. She reached the bathroom, closed and bolted the door, allowed her clothes to fall around her ankles and used a washcloth to wipe away the day's grime so that her skin was once again soft and sweet-smelling.

Then she walked back into her room and reached into her trunk for her silk nightdress. The peach-colored fabric collapsed, soft and fluid, across her skin.

Bennett wasn't on the daybed. She saw only the broad back of him on their bed, lying, as he so often did, on his left side away from her. He had lost his summer tan and his skin was pale in the half-light, the outline of his muscles moving gently as he shifted. Bennett, she thought. Bennett, who had once kissed the inside of her wrist and told her she was the most beautiful thing he had ever seen. Who had promised a world in whispers. Who had told her he adored every last bit of her. She lifted the coverlet and climbed into the warm space inside, barely making a sound.

Bennett didn't stir, but his long, easy breaths told her he was deeply asleep.

Let the flickering flame of your soul play all about me
That into my limbs may come the keenness of fire . . .

She moved close, so close that she could feel her breath on his warm skin. She inhaled the scent of him, the soap mixed with something primal that even his military attempts at cleanliness couldn't erase. She reached out, hesitated just a moment, and then placed her arm over his body, finding his fingers and entwining them with her own. She waited, and felt his hand close around hers, and she let her cheek rest against his back, closing her eyes the better to absorb the rise and fall of his breath.

"Bennett," she whispered, "I'm sorry." Even as she was not entirely sure what she was sorry for.

He released her hand and, for a second, her heart stilled, but he shifted his weight, turning so that he was facing her, his eyes just visible and open. He gazed down at her, her eyes great sad pools, begging him to love her, and perhaps in that moment there was something in her expression that no sane man could refuse because with a sigh he placed an arm around her and allowed her to nestle into his chest. She placed her fingers lightly on his collarbone, her breath a little shallow now, her thoughts jumbling with desire and relief.

"I want to make you happy," she murmured, so quietly that she wasn't even sure he would hear her. "Really I do."

She looked up. His eyes searched hers, and then he lowered his mouth to hers and kissed her. Alice closed her eyes and let him, feeling the deep easing of something that had been wound so tightly that she had felt she could barely breathe. He kissed her and stroked her hair with his broad palm, and she wanted to just stay in that moment for ever, where it was like they used to be. Bennett and Alice, a love story at its beginning.

The life and joy of tongues of flame,
And, going out from you, tightly strung and in tune,
I may rouse the blear-eyed world, and pour into it—

She felt desire build in her swiftly, its fuse lit by the poetry and the unfamiliar words of the little blue book, which conjured images that her imagination yearned to make flesh. She yielded her lips to his, let her breath quicken, felt a bolt of electricity when he let out a low groan of pleasure. His weight was on her now, his muscular legs between hers. She moved against him, her thoughts now lost, her whole body sparking with new nerve endings. *Now*, she thought, and even that thought was misted with urgent pleasure.

Now. At last. Yes.

"What are you doing?"

It took her a moment to work out what he was saying.

"What are you doing?"

She pulled her hand back. Looked down. "I—I was just touching you?"

"*There?*"

"I . . . thought you'd like it."

He pulled back, dragging the cover over his groin, leaving her exposed. Some part of her was still flushed with need, and it made her bold. She lowered her voice and placed her hand on his cheek. "I read a book this evening, Bennett. It's about what love can be between a man and his wife. It's by a medical doctor. And it says that we should feel free to give each other pleasure in all sorts of—"

"You're reading *what*?" Bennett pushed himself upright. "What is *wrong* with you?"

"Bennett—it was about married people. It was designed to help couples to bring each other joy in the bedroom and . . . well, men apparently do love to be touched—"

"Stop! Why can't you just . . . be a lady?"

"What do you mean?"

"This *touching* and this reading of *smut*. What in hell is wrong with you, Alice? You—you make it *impossible*!"

Alice sprang back. "*I* make it impossible? Bennett, nothing has happened in almost a year! Nothing! And in our vows, we promised to love each other with our bodies, as in all ways! Those were vows we made before God! This book says it's perfectly normal for a husband and wife to touch each other wherever they like! We're *married*! That's what it says!"

"Shut up!"

She felt her eyes brim with tears. "Why are you being like this when all I am trying to do is make you happy? I just want you to love me! I'm your wife!"

"Stop talking! Why do you have to talk like a prostitute?"

"How do you know how a prostitute talks?"

"*Just shut up!*"

He hurled the lamp from the bedside table so that it shattered on the floor. "Shut up! Do you hear me, Alice? Will you ever just stop *talking*?"

Alice sat frozen. From next door they heard the sound of Mr. Van Cleve groaning his way out of bed, the springs shrieking a protest, and she dropped her face into her hands, braced for what would inevitably come next. Sure enough, a few short seconds later there was a loud rapping at their bedroom door.

"What's going on in there, Bennett? Bennett? What's all the noise? Did you break something?"

"Go away, Pa! Okay? Just leave me alone!"

Alice stared at her husband in shock. She waited for the sound of the fuse of Mr. Van Cleve's temper being lit again but—perhaps equally surprised by his son's uncharacteristic response—there was only silence. Mr. Van Cleve stood on the other side of the door for a moment, coughed twice, and then they heard him shuffle back to his room.

This time it was Alice who rose. She climbed off the bed, picking up the pieces of the lamp so that she didn't tread on them in bare feet, and placed them carefully on the bedside table. Then, without looking at her husband, she straightened her nightdress, pulled on her bed-jacket, and made her way next door into the dressing room. Her face once again returned to stone as she lay down on the daybed. She pulled a blanket over herself and waited for morning, or for the silence from the next room to stop weighing like a dead thing on her chest, whichever would come first, or would deign to come at all.

TEN

One of the most notorious feuds of the Kentucky
mountains began . . . in Hindman as a result of the
killing of Linvin Higgins. Dolph Drawn, a deputy
sheriff of Knott County, organized a posse and started
for Letcher County with warrants for the arrest of
William Wright and two other men accused of the
murder . . . In the fight that followed several men were
wounded and the sheriff's horse was killed. ("Devil
John" Wright, leader of the Wright faction, later paid
for the animal because he "regretted the killing of a fine
horse.") . . . This feud lasted several years and was
responsible for the death of more than 150 men.

· WPA, *The WPA Guide to Kentucky*

Winter had come hard to the mountain, and Margery wrapped
herself around Sven's torso in the dark, hooking her leg around
him for extra warmth, knowing that outside there would be
four inches of ice to hack out of the top of the well and a whole bunch
of animals waiting bad-temperedly to be fed and that these two facts,
every morning, made the last five minutes under the huge pile of
blankets all the sweeter.

"Is this your way of trying to persuade me to make the coffee?"

Sven murmured sleepily, lowering his lips to her forehead, and shifting, just so she could be assured of quite how sweet he found it too.

"Just saying good morning," she said, and let out a long, contented breath. His skin smelled so good. Sometimes when he wasn't there she would sleep wrapped in his shirt, just to feel him near her. She trailed her finger speculatively across his chest, a question he answered silently. The minutes crept by pleasurably until he spoke again.

"What's the time, Marge?"

"Um . . . a quarter to five."

He groaned. "You do realize that if you'd stay with me we could get up a whole half-hour later?"

"And it would be just as hard to do it. Plus Van Cleve would no more let me near his mine, these days, than he would ask me to take tea at his house."

Sven had to admit she had a point. The last time she had come to see him—bringing a lunch pail he had forgotten—Bob at the Hoffman gate had informed her regretfully that he had specific orders not to let her in. Van Cleve had no proof, of course, that Margery O'Hare had anything to do with the legal letters about blocking the strip mining of North Ridge, but there were few enough people who had either the resources—or the courage—to have been behind it. And her public crack about the colored miners had plainly stung.

"So I guess it'll be Christmas here, then," he said.

"All the relatives as usual. A packed house," she said, her lips an inch from his. "Me, you, um . . . Bluey over there. Down, Blue!" The dog, taking his name as a sign that food was imminent, had hurled himself onto the bed and across the coverlet, his bony legs scrabbling on top of their entwined bodies, licking their faces. "Ow! Jeez, dog! Oh, that's done it. Okay. I'll make the coffee." She sat up and pushed him away. She rubbed sleep from her eyes and detached regretfully the hand that had slid around her stomach.

"You saving me from myself, Bluey boy?" Sven said, and the dog rolled over between them, tongue lolling, for his belly to be tickled. "Both of you, huh?"

She grinned as she heard him fussing over the dog, the damn fool, and kept grinning the whole way into the kitchen, where she stooped, shivering, to light the range.

So, tell me something," Sven said, as they ate their eggs, their boots entwined under the table. "We spend nearly every night together. We eat together. We sleep together. I know how you like your eggs, the strength of your coffee, the fact that you don't like cream. I know how hot you run your bath, the way you brush your hair forty strokes, tie it back and then don't look at it a lick for the rest of the day. Hell, I know the names of all your animals, even that hen with the blunt beak. Minnie."

"Winnie."

"Okay. Nearly all your animals. So what is the difference between us living like this and doing it but just with a ring on your finger?"

Margery took a swig of her coffee. "You said we weren't going to do this any more." She tried to smile, but there was a warning underneath it.

"I'm not asking, I promise. I'm just curious. Because it seems to me there's not a whole heap of difference."

Margery put her knife and fork together on her plate. "Well, there is a difference. Because right now I can do what I like and there's not much anyone could do about it."

"I told you that wouldn't change. I'd hope you know after ten years that I'm a man of my word."

"I do. But it's not just freedom to act without having to ask permission, it's freedom in my head. The knowledge that I'm answerable to nobody. To go where I want. Do what I want. Say what I want. I love you, Sven, but I love you as a free woman." She leaned over and took his hand. "You don't think knowing that I'm here purely because I want to be—not because some ring says I have to be—is a greater kind of love?"

"I understand your reasoning."

"Then what?"

"I think." He pushed his plate away. "I guess I'm just . . . afraid."

"Of what?"

He sighed. Turned her hand over in his. "That one day you'll tell me to go."

How could she convey to him how wrong he was? How could she let him know that he was in all ways the finest man she had known and that the few months she had spent without him had made every day feel like the bleakest winter? How could she tell him that even now, ten years in, him simply resting a hand on her waist made something buck and spark inside her?

She got up from the table and placed her arms around his neck, her seat upon his lap. She rested her cheek against his, so that her words were murmured in his ear. "I will *never, ever* tell you to go. There is no chance of that happening, Mr. Gustavsson. I will be with you, day and night, for as long as you can stand me. And you know I never say anything I don't mean."

He was late to work, of course. He struggled to feel bad about it all day.

A holly wreath, a corn-husk doll, a pot of preserved fruit or a bracelet of polished stone; as Christmas drew closer, the girls would return each day with small thank-you gifts from the homes they visited. They pooled them at the library building, agreeing that something should be given to Fred Guisler for his support over the past six months but that bracelets and dollies were probably a little wide of the mark. Margery suspected there was only one gift that would make him happy, and that was something he was unlikely to put on his Christmas list.

Alice's life now seemed to revolve around the library. She was fiercely efficient, had memorized every route from Baileyville to Jeffersonville, never balking at any extra mileage that Margery threw her way. She was the first to arrive each morning, striding down the dark, frost-covered road, and the last to leave at night, determinedly stitching books that

Sophia would unpick and redo after she had gone. She had grown wiry, muscles newly visible in her arms, her skin weathered by long days exposed to the elements, and her face was set so that her lovely smile rarely lit her features, but flashed up only when it was required, and rarely stretched as far as her eyes.

"That girl is the saddest thing I ever saw," Sophia remarked, as Alice brought her saddle in and went straight back out into the dark to give Spirit a rub-down. "Something ain't right in that house." She shook her head as she sucked a piece of cotton, ready to rethread her needle.

"I used to think Bennett Van Cleve was the greatest catch in Baileyville," said Izzy. "But I watched him walking with Alice from church the other day and he acts like she's got chiggers. Wouldn't even take her arm."

"He's a pig," said Beth. "And that damn Peggy Foreman is always strolling past him in her finest, with her girls, trying to catch his eye."

"Ssh," said Margery, evenly. "No need for gossip. Alice is our friend."

"I meant it nicely," Izzy protested.

"Doesn't stop it being gossip," Margery said. She glanced at Fred, who was focused intently on framing three maps of the new routes they had taken on that week. He often stayed late, finding excuses to walk down and fix things that didn't really need fixing long after he had finished with his horses, stacking up logs for the burner, or blocking drafts with rags. It didn't take a genius to work out why.

How you doing, Kathleen?"

Kathleen Bligh wiped her forehead, and tried to raise a smile. "Oh, you know. Getting by."

There was a peculiar weighted quality to the silence left by Garrett Bligh's absence. On the table there was a selection of filled bowls and baskets, food gifts left by neighbors, and some mourning cards stood on the mantel; outside the back door two hens ruffled their feathers on a large stack of firewood that had arrived, unheralded, overnight. Further up the slope, the newly carved gravestone stood bleached white against its neighbors. People of the mountain, whatever anyone said about them, knew how to look after their own. So the cabin was warm, and food ready to be eaten, but the interior was still, motes floating in the undisturbed air, and the children lay motionless in the cot, their arms thrust across each other in afternoon sleep, as if the whole domestic tableau were suspended in time.

"I brought you some magazines. I know you couldn't face reading the last few, but I thought maybe some short stories? Or something for the children?"

"You're very kind," said Kathleen.

Alice stole a look at her. She didn't know what to do, faced with the enormity of the woman's loss. It was etched across Kathleen's face, in her downturned eyes and the new lines around her mouth, visible in the effort it seemed to take her just to move her hand across her brow. She looked almost unbearably weary, as if she just wanted to lie down and sleep for a million years.

"Did you want a drink?" Kathleen said abruptly, as if remembering herself. She glanced behind her. "I think I have some coffee. Should still be warm. I'm sure I made some this morning."

"I'm fine. Thank you."

They sat in the little room and Kathleen pulled her shawl around her. Outside, the mountain was silent, the trees bare, and the gray sky hung low over the spindly branches. A solitary crow broke the stillness, its harsh, abrasive cry rising above the mountaintop. Spirit, tied to the fence post, stamped a foot, steam rising from her nostrils.

Alice pulled the books from her saddlebag. "I know little Pete loves the rabbit stories and this one is new in from the publishing house itself. But I've earmarked some Bible readings in this one that you might take comfort in, if you really didn't want to read anything longer. And there's some poetry. Have you heard of George Herbert? Those can be good to dip into. I've been . . . reading quite a bit of poetry myself lately."

She placed the books neatly on the table. "And you can keep these until the New Year."

Kathleen regarded the little pile for a moment. She reached out a finger and traced the title of the book on the top. Then she withdrew it. "Miss Alice, you may as well take these back with you." She pushed her hair back from her face. "I wouldn't want to waste them. I know how desperate everyone is for reading. And that's a long wait for some."

"It's no trouble."

Kathleen's smile wavered. "In fact, I can't see how it's worth you wasting your time coming all the way up here just now. To tell you the truth, I can't hold a thought in my head and the children . . . Well, I don't seem to have much time or energy to read to them either."

"Don't you worry. There are plenty of books and magazines to go round. And I'll just leave picture books for the children. You won't need to do anything and they can—"

"I can't—I can't seem to fix on much. I can't do anything. I get up each day and I get through my chores and I feed the children and mind the animals but it all seems . . ." Her smile broke. Kathleen lowered her face into her hands and let out an audible shaky sigh. A moment passed. Her shoulders began to convulse silently and, just as Alice was wondering what to say, a low, broken howl emerged from somewhere deep within Kathleen, raw and animal. It was the most painful sound Alice had ever heard. It rose and fell on a tide of grief, and seemed to come from some place completely broken. "*I miss him.*" Kathleen wept, her hands pressed tightly to her face. "I just miss him. I miss him so much. I miss the feel of him and the touch of him and I miss his hair and I miss the way he used to say my name and I know he was sick for so long and that by the end he was barely a shell of himself but, oh, Lord, how am I meant to go on without him? Oh, God. Oh, God, I can't do it. I just can't. Oh, Miss Alice, I want my Garrett back. I just want him back."

It was doubly shocking because, outside anger, Alice had never seen any of the local families express greater emotion than either mild disapproval or amusement. Mountain people were stoic, not given to unexpected shows of vulnerability. Which made this somehow even more unbearable. Alice leaned forward and took Kathleen in her arms, the young woman's body racked with sobs so fierce that Alice's own body shook with them. She placed her arms tightly around her, pulled her close and let her cry, holding her so tightly that the sadness seeping out of Kathleen became an almost tangible thing, the grief she carried a weight that settled over them both. She pressed her head to Kathleen's, trying to lift a little of the sadness, to tell her silently that there was still beauty in this world, even if some days it took every bit of strength and obstinacy to find it. Eventually, like a wave crashing onto the shore, Kathleen's sobs slowed, and quieted into sniffs and hiccups, leaving her to shake her head with embarrassment, and wipe at her eyes.

"*I'm sorry I'm sorry I'm so sorry.*"

"Don't be," Alice whispered back. "Please don't be sorry." She took Kathleen's hands in her own. "It's wonderful that you got to love somebody that much."

Kathleen raised her head then, and her swollen, red-rimmed eyes searched Alice's. She squeezed Alice's hands. Both were roughened from work, thin and strong. "I'm sorry," she said again, and this time Alice understood that she meant something quite different. She held the woman's gaze, until Kathleen finally released her hand and swiped at her tears with her flat palm, glancing over at the still sleeping children.

"My goodness. You'd best be getting on," she said. "You got rounds to get through. Lord knows the weather's closing in. And I'd better wake those babies or they'll have me up half the night again."

Alice didn't move. "Kathleen?"

"Yes?" That desperate bright smile again, wavering, and yet determined. It seemed to take all the effort in the world.

Alice lifted the books onto her lap. "Would . . . would you like me to read to you?"

For everything there is a season, and a time for every matter under the heaven: a time to be born, and a time to die; a time to plant, and a time to pluck up that which is planted; a time to kill, and a time to heal; a time to break down, and a time to build up; a time to weep, and a time to laugh; a time to mourn, and a time to dance.

Two women sat in a tiny cabin on the side of a vast mountain as the sky slowly darkened, and inside the lamps sent out slivers of gold light through the gaps in the wide oak planks. One read, her voice quiet and precise, and the other sat, her stockinged feet tucked up under her on the chair, her head resting against her open palm, lost in her thoughts. Time passed slowly, and neither of them minded and the children, when they stirred awake, didn't cry but sat quietly and listened, even though they understood barely any of what was said. An hour later, the two women stood at the door and, almost on an impulse, hugged each other tightly.

They wished each other a happy Christmas, and both smiled wryly, knowing that for each this year it would simply have to be endured. "Better days," said Kathleen.

"Yes," Alice responded. "Better days." And with this thought she wrapped her scarf high around her neck so that it covered everything but her eyes, mounted the little brown and white horse and made her way back toward the town.

Perhaps it was boredom at being stuck in the house after years of long days spent in the camaraderie of other miners, but William liked Sophia to tell him what had been happening at the library each day. He knew all about Margery's anonymous letters to the families of North Ridge, who had asked for which books at the cabin, about Mr. Frederick's deepening crush on Miss Alice, and the way she herself seemed to be hardening, like ice creeping across water, as that fool

Bennett Van Cleve gave her the cold shoulder and killed her love for him, inch by frozen inch.

"You think he's one of *them*?" William asked. "Men that like . . . other men?"

"Who knows? Far as I can see that boy don't love nothin' but his own reflection. Wouldn't surprise me if he stands in front of the mirror and kisses the glass every day 'stead of his wife," she retorted, and enjoyed the rare sight of her brother bent double with laughter.

But she was darned if she could find much to tell him today. Alice had sat down heavily on the little cane chair in the corner and her shoulders had slumped like she was carrying the weight of the world.

Tiredness doesn't make you look like that. When they were physically tired the girls would pull off their boots and bitch and moan and rub at their eyes and laugh at each other. Alice just sat there, still as a stone, her thoughts somewhere far from the little cabin. Fred saw it. Sophia saw he was pretty much itching to walk over there, and comfort her, but instead he just went to his coffee jug and brewed her a fresh mug, placing it in front of her so gently that it took her a moment even to register that he had done it. Your heart would break to see how tender he looked at her.

"You okay, girl?" Sophia said quietly, when Fred had stepped out for more logs.

She didn't speak for a moment, then wiped at her eyes with the heel of her palms. "I'm fine, Sophia. Thank you." She looked over her shoulder at the door. "Plenty worse off than me, right?" She said it like it was something she'd repeated to herself many times. She said it like she was trying to convince herself of it.

"Ain't that always the truth," Sophia responded.

But then there was Margery. She'd blown in like a whirlwind as dusk fell, her eyes wild, her coat dusted with snow and a strange, brittle energy about her so that she forgot to close the door and Sophia had to scold her to remind her that it was still blizzarding outside, and was she actually born in a barn?

"Anyone been by here?" she said. The girl's face was as white as if she'd seen a haint.

"Who you expecting?"

"Nobody," she said quickly. Her hands were trembling, but it wasn't from cold.

Sophia put down her book. "You okay, Miss Margery? You don't seem yourself."

"I'm fine. I'm fine." She peered out of the door, like she was waiting for something.

Sophia eyed her bag. "You want to give me those books, so I can enter them?"

Margery didn't answer, her attention still fixed on the door, so Sophia got up and pulled them out herself, placing them on the desk one by one. "*Mack Maguire and the Indian Chief*? Weren't you taking this to the Stone sisters up at Arnott's Ridge?"

Margery's head spun round. "What? Oh. Yes. I'll . . . I'll take them tomorrow."

"Ridge not passable?"

"No."

"Then how you going to get up there tomorrow? It's still snowing."

Margery seemed temporarily lost for words. "I'll . . . I'll work it out."

"Where's *Little Women*? You signed that out too, remember?"

She was behaving real strange. And then, she told William, Mr. Frederick came in and it got really odd.

"Fred, you got any spare guns?"

He put a basket of logs down by the burner. "Guns? What you want guns for, Marge?"

"I just thought . . . I thought maybe it would be good for the girls to learn to shoot. To take a firearm on the remote routes. In case." She blinked twice. "Of snakes."

"In winter?"

"Bears, then."

"Hibernating. 'Sides, nobody's seen a bear in these mountains for five, ten years. You know that as well as I do."

Sophia looked incredulous. "You think Mrs. Brady's gonna let her little girl carry a gun? You're meant to be carrying books, Marge, not guns. You think some family who don't trust you girls anyways gonna trust you more if you turn up at their house with a hunting rifle strapped to your back?"

Fred was frowning at her. He and Sophia exchanged a bemused look.

Margery appeared to snap out of whatever weird funk she was in. "You're right. You're right. Don't know what I was thinking." She raised an unconvincing smile.

But here was the thing, Sophia told William, as they sat at the little table eating supper. Two days later when Margery returned, Sophia picked up her saddlebag to unpack it while Margery stepped out to use the water closet. The days were cold and hard and she liked to help the girls whichever way she could. She took out the last of the books, then nearly dropped the canvas bag in fright. At the bottom, neatly wrapped in a red handkerchief, she could just make out the bone grip of a Colt .45 pistol.

Bob told me you were waiting out here. I wondered why you canceled on me last night." Sven Gustavsson emerged from the gates of the mine still in his work overalls but with his thick flannel jacket over the top and his hands thrust deep into his pockets. He walked up to the mule and stroked his neck, letting Charley's soft nose nuzzle his pockets for treats. "Get a better offer, did you?" He smiled and placed his hand on Margery's leg. She flinched.

He removed it, his smile vanishing. "You okay?"

"Can you come to mine when you're done?"

He studied her face. "Sure. But I thought we weren't seeing each other till Friday."

"Please."

She never said please.

Despite the freezing temperatures he found her on the rocking chair on the stoop, her rifle across her legs in the dark, the light of the little oil lamp flickering across her face. She was rigid, her eyes trained on the horizon, her jaw set. Bluey sat at her feet, glancing up at her from minute to minute, as if her anxiety had rubbed off on him, and shaking in short bursts from the cold.

"What's going on, Marge?"

"I think Clem McCullough is coming after me."

Sven walked up to her. There was something absent and watchful in the way she spoke, as if she barely registered him being there. Her teeth chattered.

"Marge?" He went to place his hand on her knee, but remembering her reaction of earlier, he touched the back of her hand lightly instead. She was frozen. "Marge? It's too cold to sit out here. You got to come inside."

"I need to be ready for him."

"The dog will let us know if anyone's coming. C'mon. What happened?"

She stood finally and allowed him to steer her in. The cabin was freezing, and he wondered if she'd been inside at all. He lit the stove and brought in some more logs as she stood by the window looking out. Then he fed Bluey and boiled some water. "You stayed up all last night like that?"

"Didn't sleep a wink."

Finally he sat down beside her and handed her a bowl of soup. She looked at it as if she didn't want it, but then drank it in short, greedy bursts. And when she'd finished, she told him the story of her ride to Red Lick, her voice uncharacteristically halting, her knuckles white and trembling, as if even now she could feel McCullough's grip still on her, his hot breath on her skin. And Sven Gustavsson, a man renowned for his unusually level temperament in a town full of hotheads, a man who would break up a bar fight nineteen times out of twenty where another would be unable to resist the satisfaction of the hurled punch, found that he was possessed of an uncharacteristic rage, a red mist that descended and made him want to seek out McCullough and deliver some of his own brand of vengeance, a vengeance that involved blood and fists and busted teeth.

None of this showed in his face, or in the calm of his voice when he spoke again. "You're exhausted. Go to bed."

She looked up at him. "You not coming?"

"Nope. I'll be out here while you sleep."

Margery O'Hare was not a woman who liked to depend on anyone. It was a measure of how shaken she was, he realized, that she thanked him quietly, and took herself to bed without a word of protest.

ELEVEN

Fair Oaks was built about 1845 by Dr. Guildford D. Runyon, a Shaker who renounced his vow of celibacy and erected the house in anticipation of his marriage to Miss Kate Ferrel, who died before the house was completed. Dr. Runyon remained a bachelor until his death in 1873.

· **WPA,** *The WPA Guide to Kentucky*

There were fifteen dolls on the dresser. They sat shoulder to shoulder, like a mismatched family, their porcelain faces pale and rosy and their real hair (where had it come from? Alice shuddered) curled into immaculate glossy ringlets. They were the first thing Alice saw when she woke up in the morning on the little daybed, their blank faces watching her impassively, their cherry-colored lips curled into faint, disdainful smiles, frothy white pantalettes peeking out from under full Victorian skirts. Mrs. Van Cleve had loved her dolls. Like she had loved her little stuffed bears and her tiny china ornaments and her porcelain snuff boxes and her carefully embroidered psalms that hung around the house, each the result of hours of intricate needlecraft.

Every day Alice was reminded of a life that had been almost solely focused on the inside of these walls, on tiny, meaningless tasks, tasks Alice felt increasingly strongly that no adult woman should view as the sum total of her day's activities: dolls, embroidery, the dusting and precise rearranging of totems that no man noticed anyway. Until she had gone, after which they had become a shrine to a woman they now insisted they idolized.

She hated those dolls. Like she hated the heavy silence in the air, the endless stasis of a house in which nothing could move forward and nothing could change. She might as well be one of those dolls, she thought, as she walked through the bedroom. Smiling, immobile, decorative and silent.

She glanced down at the picture of Dolores Van Cleve that sat in a large gilt frame on Bennett's bedside table. The woman held a small wooden cross between two plump hands and an expression of pained disapproval, which to Alice seemed to settle on the two of them whenever they were alone together. "Perhaps we could move your mother a little further away? Just . . . at night?" she had ventured when she had first been shown their room. But Bennett had frowned, as disbelieving as if she had cheerfully suggested digging up his mother's grave.

She snapped out of her thoughts, gasping quietly as she splashed the icy water on her face and hurried into her many layers. The librarians were riding a half-day today, to allow them all some time for Christmas shopping, and a small part of her had to fight her disappointment at the prospect of time away from her routes.

She would see Jim Horner's girls this morning. That helped. The way they would wait at the window for the sight of Spirit making her way up the track, then bolt through the wooden door, bouncing on tiptoe until she climbed off the horse, their voices bubbling over each other as they clamored to find out what she had with her, where she had been, whether she would stay for a little while longer than the last time. The way they would hang casually around her neck while she read to them, little fingers stroking her hair or planting kisses on her cheeks as if, despite the slow recovery of the little family, they were both desperate for feminine contact in some way they could barely understand. And Jim, his expression no longer hard and suspicious, would place a mug of coffee at her side, then use the time she was there to chop wood or sometimes, now, just sit and watch, as if he took pleasure in the sight of his girls' happiness as they showed off what they had learned to read that week (and they were smart; their reading was way ahead of other children's, thanks to lessons with Mrs. Beidecker). No, the Horner girls were consolation indeed. It was just a shame that girls like them would have so little in the way of Christmas gifts.

Alice wrapped her scarf around her neck and pulled on her riding gloves, wondering briefly whether to put on an extra pair of socks for the ride up the mountain. All the librarians had chilblains now, their toes pink and swollen from the cold, their fingers frequently corpse-white from lack of blood. She looked out of the window at the chill gray sky. She no longer checked her reflection in the mirror.

She pulled the envelope from the side, where it had sat since the previous day, and tucked it into her bag. She would read it later, once she'd done her rounds. No point getting worked up when you had two silent hours on a horse facing you.

She looked at the dresser as she made to leave. The dolls were still staring at her.

"What?" she said.

But this time they seemed to be saying something quite different.

For us?" Millie's mouth had dropped so far open Alice could almost hear Sophia warning that bugs would fly straight in.

She handed the other doll to Mae, its petticoats rustling as it was pulled swiftly into the child's lap. "One each. We had a little chat this morning and they told me in confidence that they'd be much happier here with you than where they've been living."

The two girls gawped at the angelic porcelain faces, and then, in unison, their heads turned toward their father. Jim Horner's own expression was unreadable.

"They're not new, Mr. Horner," Alice said carefully. "But where they come from has no real use for them. It's . . . a house of men. It didn't seem right to have them sitting there."

She could see his indecision, the *I don't know . . .* forming on his lips. The air in the cabin seemed to still as the girls held their breath.

"Please, Pa?" Mae's voice emerged as a whisper. They sat cross-legged, and Millie's hand absently stroked the shiny chestnut curls, letting each one spring back into place, her gaze flickering from the painted face to her father's. The dolls, having for months seemed sinister, rebuking, were suddenly benign, joyful things. Because they were in the place they were meant to be.

"They're awful fancy," he said finally.

"Well, I believe all girls deserve something a little fancy in their lives, Mr. Horner."

He rubbed a rough hand over the top of his head and looked away. Mae's face lengthened, fearful of what he was about to say. He motioned toward the door. "Would you mind stepping outside with me a moment, Mrs. Van Cleve?"

She heard sighs of dismay from the girls as she followed him to the back of the cabin, her arms wrapped around her to keep out the cold, mentally running over the various arguments she would employ to try to change his mind.

All little girls need a doll.

They would likely be thrown away if the girls didn't take them.

Oh, for goodness' sake, why must your wretched pride get in the way of a—

"What do you think?"

Alice stopped in her tracks. Jim Horner lifted a piece of hessian sacking to reveal the head of a large, somewhat threadbare stag, its antlers thrusting into the air three feet to each side of it, its ears stitched haphazardly to its head. It was mounted on a roughly carved oak base, which had been painted with pitch.

She stifled the strangled noise that emerged unbidden from her throat.

"Shot him over at Rivett's Creek two months ago. Stuffed and mounted him myself. Got Mae to help me send off for them glass eyes on the mail order. They're pretty lifelike, don't you think?"

Alice gaped at the deer's glassy, overlarge eyes, the left of which had a definite squint. The stag looked faintly demented and sinister, a nightmare beast, conjured in fever dreams. "It's . . . very . . . imposing."

"It's my first go. Figured I might set up a trade in them. Do one every few weeks and sell them in town. Help keep us going through the winter months."

"That's an idea. Maybe you could do some smaller creatures too. A rabbit, or a ground squirrel."

He mulled this over, then nodded. "So. You'll take it?"

"I'm sorry?"

"For the dolls. A trade."

Alice lifted her palms. "Oh, Mr. Horner, you really don't need to—"

"Can't take 'em for nothing." He folded his arms firmly across his chest, and waited.

What the heck is *that?*" said Beth, as Alice dismounted wearily, pulling bits of foliage from the deer's antlers. It had caught on every second tree the whole way down the mountain, causing her almost to fall off several times, and now looked even more bedraggled and wonky than it had on the ridge, strung with a variety of stray twigs and leaves. She walked up the steps and placed it carefully against the wall, reminding herself, as she had now done a hundred times, of the joy on the girls' faces as they learned the dolls were truly theirs, the way they cradled and sang to them, their endless thanks and kisses. The softening of the planes on Jim Horner's face as he looked on.

"It's our new mascot."

"Our what?"

"Touch a hair on its head and I'll stuff you worse than Mr. Horner stuffed that deer."

"Shoot," said Beth to Izzy, as Alice strode back out to her horse. "Remember when Alice made out like she was a lady?"

. . .

Lunch service had nearly finished at the White Horse Hotel, Lexington, and the restaurant had started to thin out, leaving tables scattered with the detritus of napkins and empty glasses as, fortified, the guests wrapped themselves in scarves and hats. They were braced to venture back out onto sidewalks teeming with last-minute Christmas shoppers. Mr. Van Cleve, who had eaten well on a sirloin steak and fried potatoes, leaned back in his chair and stroked his stomach with both hands, a gesture that conveyed a satisfaction he seemed to feel less and less in other areas of his life.

The girl was giving him indigestion. In any other town, such misdemeanors might eventually be forgotten, but in Baileyville a grudge could last a century and still nurture a head of steam. The people of Baileyville were descended from Celts, from Scots and Irish families, who could hold on to resentment until it was dried out like beef jerky, and bearing no resemblance to its original self. And Mr. Van Cleve, although he was about as Celtic as the Cherokee sign on the outside of the gas station, had absorbed this trait thoroughly. More than that, he had his daddy's habit of fixing on one person, then training on them his grievances and blaming them for all that ailed him. That person was Margery O'Hare. He rose with a curse for her on his lips, and he went to sleep with images of her taunting him.

Beside him Bennett tapped intermittently on the side of the table with his fingers. He could tell the boy wanted to be elsewhere; in truth, he didn't seem to have the focus needed for business. The other day he had caught a gang of miners mimicking his obsession with cleanliness, pretending to rub at their blackened overalls as he passed. They straightened when they saw him watching, but the sight of his son being mocked pained him. At first he had been almost proud of Bennett's determination to marry the English girl. He had seemed to know his own mind, finally! Dolores had cosseted the boy so, fussing over him as if he were a girl. He had stood a little taller when he informed Van Cleve that he and Alice were to be married and, well, it was a shame about Peggy but that was just too bad. It was good to see him hold a firm opinion for once. Now he watched the boy gradually emasculated by the English girl and her sharp tongue, her odd ways, and he regretted the day he had ever been convinced to take that damn European tour. No good ever came from mixing. Not with coloreds and, it turned out, not with Europeans neither.

"You've left crumbs here, boy." He stabbed a fat finger on the table so that the waiter apologized and hurriedly combed them off onto a plate. "A bourbon, Governor Hatch? To round things off?"

"Well, if you're going to twist my arm, Geoff . . ."

"Bennett?"

"Not for me, Pa."

"Get me a couple of Boone County bourbons. Straight up. No ice."

"Yes, sir."

"Bennett. You want to head over to the tailor while the governor and I talk business? Ask him if he's got any more of those dress shirts, will you? I'll be there shortly."

He waited for his son to disappear from his table before he leaned forward and spoke again. "Now, Governor, I was hoping to discuss a matter of a certain sensitivity with you."

"Not more problems at the mine, Mr. Van Cleve? I hope you're not dealing with the same mess they're having down there in Harlan. You know they've got state troopers lined up to head in if they can't sort themselves out. There's machine-guns and all sorts heading back and forth across state lines."

"Oh, you know we work hard to keep a lid on that kind of thing at Hoffman. No good can come of the unions; we know that. We've been sure to take measures to protect our mine at the very whisper of trouble."

"Glad to hear it. Glad to hear it. So . . . uh . . . what seems to be the problem?"

Mr. Van Cleve leaned forward over the table. "It's this . . . *library* business."

The governor frowned.

"The women's library. Mrs. Roosevelt's initiative. These women taking books to rural families and the like."

"Ah, yes. Part of the WPA, I believe."

"The very one. Now, while I'm usually a great supporter of such enterprises, and I absolutely agree with our president and the First Lady that we should be doing what we can to educate our populace, I have to say that the women—well, certain women—in our county are causing problems."

"Problems?"

"This traveling library is fomenting unrest. It's encouraging all sorts of irregular behavior. For instance—Hoffman Mining was planning to explore new areas on the North Ridge. The kind of thing we've been doing entirely legitimately for decades. Now, I believe these librarians have been spreading rumors and falsehoods about it, because the next thing we've been hit with is a series of legal orders forbidding us our usual mining rights in the area. Not just one family but a great number of them have signed up to block our path."

"That's unfortunate." The governor lit a cigarette, offering Mr. Van Cleve the packet, which he refused.

"Indeed. If they do this with other families, we'll end up with nowhere to mine. And then what are we supposed to do? We are a major employer in this part of Kentucky. We provide a vital resource to our great nation."

"Well, Geoff, you know it doesn't take a lot to get folk up in arms about mining, these days. Do you have proof it was these librarians stirring things up?"

"Well, here's the thing. Half the families now blocking us through the courts couldn't read a word last year. Where would they have got information on legal matters if it wasn't for these library books?"

The bourbons arrived. The waiter lifted them from a silver tray and placed each one reverently in front of the two men.

"I don't know. From what I understand it's just a bunch of girls on horses taking recipe cards here and there. What harm are they really going to do? I think you may just have to chalk this one up to misfortune,

Geoff. The amount of trouble we have around the mines just now, why, it could have been anyone."

Mr. Van Cleve felt the governor's attention starting to slide. "It's not just the mines. They are changing the very *dynamics* of our society. They are fixing to alter the laws of nature."

"The laws of *nature*?"

When the governor looked disbelieving, he added: "There are reports of our women engaging in *unnatural practices*."

Now he had his attention. The governor leaned forward.

"My son, God bless him, my wife and I raised him according to godly principles, so I admit he is not entirely *worldly* in conjugal matters. But he tells me that his young bride—who has taken up work at this library—mentioned to him a book the women are passing among them. A book of *sexual* content."

"Sexual content!"

"Quite!"

The governor took a gulp of his drink. "And—uh—what would this 'sexual content' comprise exactly?"

"Well, I don't want to shock you, Governor. I won't go into details—"

"Oh, I can take it, Geoff. Go into all the—uh—details you like."

Mr. Van Cleve glanced behind him and lowered his voice. "He said his bride—who was, by all accounts, brought up like a princess—from a *very* good family, you understand—well, she was suggesting she do things to him in the bedroom that one might expect at a *French whorehouse*."

"*A French whorehouse*." The governor swallowed hard.

"At first I thought this was maybe an English thing. Due to their proximity to the European ways, you know. But Bennett told me she said it was definitely from the library. Spreading *filth*. Suggestions that would make a grown man blush. I mean, where will it end?"

"That's the, uh, pretty blonde? The one I met last year at dinner."

"The very one. Alice. Finer than frog hair. The shock of hearing salaciousness proposed by a girl like that . . . Well . . ."

The governor took another very long sip of his drink. His eyes had gone a little glassy. "Did he give, uh, details of the exact activities she was proposing? Just so, you know, I can be clear on the full picture."

Mr. Van Cleve shook his head. "Poor Bennett was so shook up it took him weeks even to confide in me. Hasn't felt able to lay a finger on her since. I mean it ain't right, Governor. Not for decent God-fearing wives to be suggesting such deviance."

The governor appeared to be deep in thought.

"Governor?"

"Filth . . . Right. Sorry, yes . . . I mean, no."

"Anyway. I would appreciate knowing whether other counties are having the same issues with their women and these so-called libraries. I can't believe this is a good thing, for our workforce or Christian families. My inclination would be to shut the scheme down altogether. Likewise with this mining-permissions business."

Mr. Van Cleve folded his napkin and laid it on the table. The governor was still apparently considering this very carefully.

"Or perhaps you think the best way forward would be just . . . to deal with the matter in whichever way we thought fit."

He wasn't sure, he told Bennett afterward, whether the governor's drink had actually gone to his head. He seemed markedly distracted toward the end of lunch.

"So what did he say?" said Bennett, who had cheered up with the purchase of some new corduroys and a striped sweater.

"I told him maybe I should deal with all these matters how I liked and he just said, 'hmm, yes, quite,' and then said he had to leave."

Dear Alice

I am sorry married life is not as you expected. I'm not sure what you think marriage should be about, and you have not given us details of what it is you find so dispiriting, but Daddy and I wonder if we haven't given you false expectations. You have a handsome husband, financially secure and able to offer you a good future. You have married

into a decent family with significant resources. I think you need to learn to count your chickens.

Life is not always about happiness. It is about duty, and taking satisfaction from doing the right thing. We were hoping you had learned to be less impulsive; well, you've made your bed, and you're just going to have to learn to stick things out. Perhaps if you have a baby it will give you a focus, so you don't dwell on things so.

If you do choose to return without your husband, I have to inform you that you will not be welcome to stay here.

Your loving mother

Alice had held off opening the letter, perhaps because she had known the words she was going to find within it. She felt her jaw tighten, then folded it carefully and placed it back in her bag, noting once more as she did so that her fingernails, once highly polished and filed, were now ragged or cut down to the quick, and some small part of her wondered, as she did daily, whether *that was the reason he didn't want to touch her?*

"Okay," said Margery, appearing at her shoulder. "I ordered two new girths and a saddle cloth from Crompton's and I thought maybe this for Fred as a thank-you. Think he'll like it?" She held up a dark green scarf. The department-store assistant, transfixed by Margery's beaten-up leather hat and breeches (she couldn't see the point in dressing up to come to Lexington, she had told Alice, as she'd only have to get changed again when she got back), had needed a second to remember to take it from her, ready to wrap in tissue. "We'll have to hide it from Fred on the ride back."

"Sure."

Margery squinted at her. "Did you even look at it? . . . What's going on, Alice?"

"Look at what? . . . Oh, Lord—Bennett. I have to find something for Bennett." Alice's hands flew to her face as she realized she no longer knew what her husband liked, let alone his collar size. She reached for a set of boxed handkerchiefs on the shelf, decorated with a sprig of holly. Were handkerchiefs too impersonal a gift for one's husband? How intimate could a gift be when you hadn't seen more than an inch of his bare skin for the best part of six weeks?

She startled as Margery took her arm, steering her toward a quiet part of the men's department. "Alice, are you okay? 'Cause you got a face on you most days like blinked milk."

"There are no complaints, are there?" Alice glanced down at the handkerchiefs. Would it be better if she had his initials embroidered on them? She tried to imagine Bennett opening them on Christmas morning. Somehow she couldn't picture him smiling. She couldn't imagine him smiling at anything she did any more. "Anyway," she said, her tone defensive, "you're a fine one to talk. You've barely said a word the last couple of days."

Margery seemed a little taken aback, and gave a shake of her head. "Just . . . just had a little upset on one of my rounds." She swallowed. "Rattled me a bit."

Alice thought of Kathleen Bligh, the way that the young widow's grief would cast a pall over her own day. "I understand. It's a tougher job than you think, sometimes, isn't it? Not really about delivering books at all. I'm sorry if I've been miserable. I'll pull myself together."

The truth was that the prospect of Christmas made Alice want to weep. The idea of sitting at that tense table, Mr. Van Cleve glowering across from her, Bennett silent and simmering at whatever she had supposedly done wrong now. The watchful Annie, who seemed to delight in the worsening atmosphere.

Derailed by this thought, it took Alice a minute to realize that Margery was regarding her closely.

"I'm not getting at you, Alice. I'm . . ." Margery shrugged, as if the words were unfamiliar to her. "I'm asking as a friend."

A friend.

"You know me. Been content my whole life to be on my own. But this last few months? I've . . . well, I've grown to enjoy your company. I like your sense of humor. You treat people with kindness and respect. So I'd like to think we're friends. All of us at the library, but you and I most of all. And you looking this sad every day is just about breaking my heart."

If they had been anywhere else Alice might have smiled. It was quite an admission from Margery, after all. But something had closed over these last months, and she didn't seem to feel things in the way she used to.

"You want to get a drink?" Margery said finally.

"You don't drink."

"Well, I won't tell no one if you don't." She held out an arm, and after a moment, Alice took it, and they headed out of the department store toward the nearest bar.

Bennett and I . . ." Alice said, over the noise of the music and the two men yelling at each other in the corner ". . . we have nothing in common. We don't understand each other. We don't talk to each other. We don't seem to make each other laugh, or long for each other, or count the hours when we're apart—"

"Sounds like marriage from where I'm sitting," Margery observed.

"And, of course, there is . . . the other thing." Alice looked awkward even saying the words.

"Still? Well, now, that is a problem." Margery recalled the comfort of Sven's body wrapped around hers just that morning. She felt stupid now for how afraid she'd been, asking him to stay, trembling like one of Fred's spooked Thoroughbreds. McCullough hadn't shown up. Sounded like he had been so drunk he couldn't hit the ground with his hat, Sven pointed out. He most likely wouldn't even remember what he'd done.

"I read that book. The one you recommended."

"You did?"

"But it . . . it only seemed to make things worse." Alice threw her hands up. "Oh, what is there to say? I hate being married. I hate living in that house—I'm not sure which of us is more miserable. But he's all

I have. I'm not going to have a baby, which might have made everyone happier, because . . . Well, you know why. And I'm not even sure I want one because then I wouldn't be able to ride out any more. Which is the only thing that brings me any happiness at all. So, I'm trapped."

Margery frowned. "You're not trapped."

"Easy for you to say. You have a house. You know how to get by on your own."

"You don't have to play by their rules, Alice. You don't have to play by anyone's rules. Hell, if you wanted you could pack up today and head home to England."

"I can't." Alice reached into her bag and pulled out the letter.

"Well, hello there, pretty ladies."

A man in a wide-shouldered suit, his mustache slick with wax, his eyes wrinkling with practiced bonhomie, planted himself against the bar plumb between the two of them. "You looked so deep in conversation I almost didn't want to disturb you. But then I thought, *Henry boy, those pretty ladies look like they could do with a drink.* And I could not forgive myself if I let you sit there thirsty. So what'll it be, huh?"

He slid an arm around Alice's shoulders, his eyes flickering over her chest.

"Let me guess your name, beautiful. It's one of my skills. One of my *many* special skills. Mary Beth. You look pretty enough to be a Mary Beth. Am I right?"

Alice stuttered a no. Margery stared at the two short inches between his fingers and Alice's breast, the proprietorial nature of his grip.

"No. That don't do you justice. Laura. No, Loretta. I once knew a very beautiful girl called Loretta. That must be it." He leaned in to Alice who turned her head, her smile uncertain as if she didn't want to offend him. "You gonna tell me I'm right? I'm right, ain't I?"

"Actually, I—"

"Henry, is it?" said Margery.

"Yes, it is. And you would be a . . . Let me guess!"

"Henry, can I tell you something?" Margery smiled sweetly.

"You can tell me anything, darling." He raised an eyebrow, his smile knowing. "Anything you like."

Margery leaned forward so that she was whispering in his ear. "The hand that's in my pocket? It's resting on my gun. And if you don't take your hands off my friend here by the time I'm done talking, I'm going to close my fingers around the trigger and blow your oily head halfway across this bar." She smiled sweetly, and then moved her lips closer to his ear. "And, Henry? I'm a *real* good shot . . ."

The man stumbled over the feet of the stool she was sitting on. He didn't say a word but walked briskly back to the other end of the bar, shooting glances behind him as he went.

"Oh, and it's real kind of you, but we're just fine for drinks!" Margery called, more loudly. "Thank you, though!"

"Whoa," said Alice, adjusting her blouse as she watched him go. "What did you say to him?"

"Just that . . . kind as his offer was, I didn't think it was gentlemanly to lay his hands on a lady without an invitation."

"That's a very good way of putting it," said Alice. "I can never think of the right words to say when I need them."

"Yeah. Well . . ." Margery took a slug of her drink ". . . I've had some practice lately."

They sat for a moment and let the bar chatter rise and fall around them. Margery asked the bartender for another bourbon, then changed her mind and canceled it. "Go on," she said. "With what you were saying."

"Oh. Just that I can't go home. That's what the letter said. My parents don't want me back."

"What? But why? You're their only daughter."

"I don't *fit*. I've always been something of an embarrassment to them. It's like . . . I don't know. How things look is more important to them than anything else. It's like . . . it's like we speak different languages. I honestly thought Bennett was the one person who just liked me as I was." She sighed. "And now I'm trapped."

They sat in silence for a moment. Henry was leaving, casting furious, anxious glances at them as he hauled at the door.

"I'm going to tell you one thing, Alice," said Margery, as the door closed behind him. She took Alice's arm and gripped it, uncharacteristically tightly. "There is always a way out of a situation. Might be ugly. Might leave you feeling like the earth has gone and shifted under your feet. But you are never trapped, Alice. You hear me? There is *always* a way around."

don't believe it."

"What?" Bennett was examining the creases in his new trousers. Mr. Van Cleve, who had been standing with his arms outstretched, being pinned for a new waistcoat, gestured abruptly toward the door, so that a pin caught him in his armpit and made him curse. "Goddamn it! Out there, Bennett!"

Bennett looked up and through the tailor's shop window. To his astonishment, there was Alice, arm in arm with Margery O'Hare, walking out of Todd's Bar, a spit and sawdust establishment that advertised "BUCKEYE BEER ON SALE HERE" on a rusty sign outside the door. They had their heads tilted together and were laughing fit to bust.

"O'Hare," said Van Cleve, shaking his head.

"She said she wanted to do some shopping, Pop," Bennett said wearily.

"Does that look like Christmas shopping to you? She's being corrupted by the O'Hare girl! Didn't I tell you she was made of the same stuff as her no-good daddy? Goodness knows what she's encouraging Alice to get up to. Take the pins out, Arthur. We'll fetch her home."

"No," said Bennett.

Van Cleve's head swiveled. "What? Your wife's been drinking in a goddamn honky-tonk! You have to start taking control of the situation, son!"

"Just leave her."

"*Has that girl ripped the damn balls off you?*" Van Cleve bellowed into the silent shop.

Bennett flashed a look at the tailor, whose expression betrayed the kind of nothing that would be discussed feverishly among his colleagues afterward. "I'll talk to her. Let's just . . . go home."

"That girl is causing chaos. You think it does this family's standing any good for her to be dragging your wife into a low-life bar? She needs sorting out, and if you won't do it, Bennett, I will."

Alice lay on the daybed in the dressing room, staring up at the ceiling, as Annie prepared the evening meal downstairs. She had long since given up offering to help, as whatever she had done—peeling, chopping, frying—had been met with barely concealed disapproval, and she was weary of Annie's sly comments.

Alice no longer cared that Annie knew she was sleeping in the dressing room and had no doubt told half of Baileyville, too. She no longer cared that it was obvious she still had her monthlies. What was the point in trying to pretend? Outside the library there were few people she cared about impressing anyway. She heard the sound of the men returning, the exuberant roar of Mr. Van Cleve's Ford as it ground to a halt in the gravel drive, the slamming of the screen door that he plainly felt unable to close quietly, and she let out a quiet sigh. She closed her eyes for a moment. Then she raised herself, and walked into the bathroom ready to make herself look nice for the evening meal.

They were already seated when Alice came downstairs, the two men opposite each other at the dining table, their plates and cutlery laid neatly in front of them. Small bursts of steam escaped through the swinging door, and inside the kitchen Annie's clattering pan lids suggested the imminence of food. Both men looked up as Alice entered the room, and the thought occurred to her that it might be because she had made a little extra effort: she was wearing the same dress she had worn when Bennett had proposed to her, her hair neatly brushed and pinned back. But their expressions were unfriendly.

"Is it true?"

"Is what true?" Her mind raced with all the things she might have got wrong today. *Drinking in bars. Talking to strange men. Discussing the Married Love book with Margery O'Hare. Writing to her mother to ask if she might come home.*

"Where is Miss Christina?"

She blinked. "Miss who?"

"Miss Christina!"

She looked at Bennett and back again at his father. "I—I have no idea what you are talking about."

Mr. Van Cleve shook his head, as if she were mentally deficient. "Miss *Christina*. And Miss Evangeline. My wife's dolls. Annie says they're missing."

Alice relaxed. She pulled out a seat, as nobody else was going to, and sat down at the table. "Oh. Those. I . . . took them."

"What do you mean you 'took' them? Where'd you take them?"

"There are two sweet little girls on my rounds who lost their mother not long back. They didn't have any gifts coming at Christmas and I knew that passing them on would make them happier than you can imagine."

"Passing them on?" Van Cleve's eyes bulged. "You gave away my dolls? To . . . *hillbillies?*"

Alice laid the napkin neatly on her lap. She glanced at Bennett, who was staring at his plate. "Only two. I didn't think anyone would mind. They were just sitting there doing nothing and there are plenty of dolls left. I didn't think you'd even notice, to be honest." She tried to raise a smile. "You are grown men after all."

"They were Dolores's dolls! My darling Dolores! She'd had Miss Christina since she was a child!"

"Then I'm sorry. I really didn't think it would matter."

"What has gotten into you, Alice?"

Alice let her gaze fix on a point of the tablecloth just past her spoon. Her voice, when it emerged, was tight. "I was being charitable. Like you always tell me Mrs. Van Cleve was. What were you going to do with two dolls, Mr. Van Cleve? You're a man. You don't care about dolls any more than you care about half the trinkets in this place. They're dead things! Meaningless!"

"They were heirlooms! They were for Bennett's children!"

Her mouth opened before she could stop it. "Well, Bennett isn't having any children, is he?"

She looked up and saw Annie in the doorway, her eyes wide with delight at this turn of events.

"What did you just say?"

"Bennett isn't going to have any wretched children. Because . . . we are not *involved* in that way."

"If you're not involved in that way, girl, it's because of your disgusting notions."

"I beg your pardon?"

Annie began to put the plates down. Her ears had gone quite pink.

Van Cleve leaned forward over the table, his jaw jutting. "Bennett told me."

"Pa—" Bennett's voice held a warning.

"Oh, yes. He's told me about your filthy book and the depraved things you tried to do to him."

Annie's plate dropped in front of Alice with a clatter. She skittered back to the kitchen.

Alice blanched. She turned to look at Bennett. "You talked to your father about what goes on in our *bed*?"

Bennett rubbed at his cheek. "You . . . I didn't know what to do, Alice. You . . . kinda shocked me."

Mr. Van Cleve threw his chair back from the table and stomped round to where Alice was sitting. She flinched involuntarily as he towered over her, spraying saliva as he spoke. "Oh, yes, I know all about that book and your so-called library. You know that book has been banned in this country? That's how degraded it is!"

"Yes, and I know that a federal judge overturned that same ban. I know just as much as you do, Mr. Van Cleve. I read the *facts*."

"You are a snake! You have been corrupted by Margery O'Hare and now you are trying to corrupt my son!"

"I was trying to be a wife to him! And there's more to being a wife than arranging dolls and stupid china birds!"

Annie peered around the doorway with the last plate, immobile.

"Don't you *dare* criticize my Dolores's precious things, you ungrateful wretch! You aren't fit to touch the heel of that woman's shoes! And tomorrow morning you're going to go up those mountains and fetch my dolls back."

"I will not. I'm not taking those dolls away from two motherless children."

Van Cleve raised a stubby finger and jabbed it at her face. "Then you're banned from that damned library from now on, you hear me?"

"No." She didn't blink.

"What do you mean, no?"

"I told you before. I'm a grown woman. You don't get to ban me from anything."

Afterward she remembered thinking distantly that old man Van Cleve's face had grown so crimson that she feared his heart might give out. But instead he lifted his arm, and before she realized what was happening a white-hot pain exploded at the side of her head, and she collapsed against the table, her knees buckling under her.

Everything went black. Her hands gripped the tablecloth, the plates collapsing toward her as her fingers closed around the white damask, pulling it down until her knees hit the floor.

"Pa!"

"I'm doing what you should have done a long time ago! Knocking some sense into this wife of yours!" Van Cleve roared, his fat fist banging down on the tablecloth so that everything in the room seemed to shudder. Then, before she could gather her thoughts, her hair was pulled back sharply, and another blow, this time her temple, so that her head bounced off the edge of the table, and as the room spun, she was dimly aware of movement, shouting, the clatter of plates hitting the floor. Alice lifted an arm, tried to shield herself, braced for the next. But from the corner of her eye, she glimpsed Bennett in front of his father, an exchange of voices she could barely make out over the ringing in her ears.

She climbed heavily to her feet, pain clouding her thoughts, and staggered. As the room bucked around her she was dimly aware of Annie's shocked face at the kitchen door. The taste of iron flooded the back of her throat.

She heard distant shouting, Bennett's "No . . . No, Pa!" Alice realized that her napkin was still balled in her fist. She looked down. It was spattered with blood. She stared at it, blinking, trying to register what she was seeing. She straightened up, took a moment for the room to stop spinning, then placed it neatly on the table.

And then, without stopping to pick up her coat, Alice walked unsteadily past the two men into the hallway, opened the front door, and continued walking all the way up the snow-covered drive.

An hour and twenty-five minutes later, Margery opened the door a crack, her eyes narrowed in the dark, and found not McCullough or one of his clan, but the thin figure of Alice Van Cleve, shivering in a pale blue dress, her stockings ripped and her shoes crusted with snow. Her teeth chattered and the side of her head was bloodied, her left eye pursed into a livid purple bruise. Blood leached rust and scarlet into the neckline of her dress, and what looked like gravy spattered her lap. They stared at each other as Bluey barked furiously at the window.

Alice's voice, when it came, was thick, as though her tongue was swollen.

"You . . . said we were friends?"

Margery un-cocked her rifle and placed it against the doorframe. She opened the door and took her friend's elbow. "Come on in. You come on in." She glanced around at the darkened mountainside, then closed and bolted the door behind her.

TWELVE

— ★ —

The woman of the mountains leads a difficult life, while the man is lord of the household. Whether he works, visits, or roams through the woods with dog and gun is nobody's business but his own. . . . He is entirely unable to understand any interference in his affairs by society; if he turns his corn into "likker," he is dealing with what is his.

— WPA, *The WPA Guide to Kentucky*

There were certain unspoken rules of society in Baileyville, and one lasting tenet was that you didn't interfere in the private business of a man and his wife. There were many who might have been aware of beatings in their holler, man to woman, and, occasionally, the other way around, but few inhabitants would have dreamed of intervening, unless it directly infringed upon their own lives in lost sleep or disturbed routines. It was just the way things were. Words were shouted, blows were delivered, and occasionally apologies were given, or not, bruises and cuts healed and things returned to normal.

Luckily for Alice, Margery had never paid much heed to how other people did things. She cleaned the blood from Alice's face and applied a comfrey paste to the bruises. She asked nothing, and Alice volunteered nothing, except to wince and tighten her jaw at the worst of it.

Then, when the girl finally went to bed, Margery spoke discreetly to Sven and they agreed to take it in turns to sit downstairs in the small hours before dawn so that should Van Cleve come by he would find that there were circumstances in which a man might not simply drag his wife—or his daughter-in-law—home again, no matter what public embarrassment that might apparently entail for him.

Predictably, for a man used to getting his own way, Van Cleve did come by shortly before dawn, though Alice would never know that, sleeping the sleep of the profoundly shocked in Margery's spare room. Margery's cabin was not accessible by road, and he was obliged to walk the last half-mile so that he arrived florid and sweaty despite the snow, a torch held up in front of him.

"O'Hare?" he roared. And then when no answer came: "*O'HARE!*"

"You going to answer him?" Sven, who was making coffee, lifted his head.

The dog barked furiously at the window, earning a muttered curse from outside. In the stables Charley kicked at his bucket.

"Don't really see why I should answer a man who won't give me the courtesy of a title, do you?"

"No, I don't believe you should," said Sven, calmly. He had sat playing solitaire for half the night, one eye on the door, a river of dark thoughts running through his head about men who beat women.

"*Margery O'Hare!*"

"Oh, Lord. You know he'll wake her if he carries on this loud."

Wordlessly, Sven handed Margery his gun and she walked to the screen door and opened it, the rifle held loosely in her left hand as she stepped out onto the stoop, making sure Van Cleve could see it. "Can I help you, Mr. Van Cleve?"

"Fetch Alice. I know she's in there."

"And how would you know that?"

"This has gone far enough. You bring her out and we'll say no more about it."

Margery stared at her boot, considering this. "I don't think so, Mr. Van Cleve. Good morning."

She turned to walk back in and his voice lifted. "What? Wait, you don't shut a door on me!"

Margery turned slowly until she was facing him. "And you don't beat up on a girl who answers you back. Not a second time."

"Alice did a foolish thing yesterday. I admit tempers were running high. She needs to come on home now so we can sort things out. In the family." He ran a hand over his face and his voice softened. "Be reasonable, Miss O'Hare. Alice is married. She can't stay here with you."

"The way I see it, she can do what she likes, Mr. Van Cleve. She's a grown woman. Not a dog, or a . . . a *doll*."

His eyes hardened.

"I'll ask her what she wants to do when she wakes. Now I have work to get to. So I'd be obliged if you'd leave me to wash up my breakfast dishes. Thank you."

He stared at her for a moment, his voice lowering. "You think you're mighty clever, don't you, girl? You think I don't know what you did with them letters over at North Ridge? You think I don't know about your filthy books and your immoral girls trying to steer good women into the path of sin?"

For a few seconds the air seemed to disappear around them. Even the dog fell quiet.

His voice, when he spoke again, was thick with menace. "You watch your back, Margery O'Hare."

"You have a nice day now, Mr. Van Cleve."

Margery turned and walked back inside the cabin. Her voice was calm and her gait steady, but she stopped by the curtain and watched from the side of the window until she was sure Van Cleve had disappeared.

Where the heck is *Little Women*? I swear I've been searching for that book for ages. Last time I saw it checked out was for old Peg down at the store, but she says she returned it and it's been signed off in the book."

Izzy was scanning the shelves, her finger tracing the spines of the books as she shook her head in frustration. "Albert, Alder, Allemagne . . . Did somebody steal it?"

"Maybe it got ripped and Sophia's fixing it."

"I asked. She says she ain't seen it. It's bugging me because I got two families asking and nobody seems to know where it's gone. And you know how ornery Sophia gets when books go missing." She adjusted her stick under her arm and moved to her right, peering closely at the titles.

The voices quieted as Margery walked through the back door, closely followed by Alice.

"You got *Little Women* tucked away in your bag somewhere, Margery? Izzy's bitching fit to bust and—*whoo-hoo*. Looks like someone took a beating."

"Fell off her horse," said Margery, in a tone of voice that brooked no discussion. Beth stared at Alice's swollen face, then her gaze slid to Izzy, who looked down at her feet.

There was a brief silence.

"Hope you—uh—didn't hurt yourself too bad, Alice," said Izzy, quietly.

"Is she wearing your breeches?" said Beth.

"You think I've got the only pair of leather breeches in the state of Kentucky, Beth Pinker? I've never known you so fixated on someone's appearance before. Anyone would think you'd got nothing better to do." Margery walked up to the ledger on the desk and began to flick through it.

Beth took the rebuke cheerfully. "Reckon they look better on her than you anyway. Lord, it's colder than a well-digger's backside out there. Anyone seen my gloves?"

Margery scanned the pages. "Now, Alice is a little sore so, Beth, you take the two routes over at Blue Stone Creek. Miss Eleanor is staying with her sister so she won't need new books this time round. And, Izzy, if you could take the MacArthurs? Would that work? You can cut across that forty-acre field to tie in with your usual routes. The one with the falling-down barn."

They agreed without complaint, sneaking glances at Alice, who said nothing, her attention fixed on some unidentified point three feet from her toes, her cheeks burning. As Izzy left she put out her hand and squeezed Alice's shoulder gently. Alice waited until they had packed their bags and mounted their horses, and then she sat, gingerly, on Sophia's chair.

"You all right?"

Alice nodded. They sat and listened to the sound of hoofs fading up the road.

"You know the worst thing about a man hitting you?" Margery said finally. "Ain't the hurt. It's that in that instant you realize the truth of what it is to be a woman. That it don't matter how smart you are, how much better at arguing, how much better than them, period. It's when you realize they can always just shut you up with a fist. Just like that."

Alice remembered how Margery's demeanor had changed when the man in the bar had placed himself between them, how her gaze had landed hard where the man touched Alice's shoulder.

Margery pulled the coffee pot from its stand and cursed as she discovered it was empty. She mulled over it for a moment, then straightened up, and flashed Alice a tight smile. "Course, you know that only happens till you learn to hit back harder."

Despite the daylight hours being now so short, the day ran lengthy and strange, the little library filled with a vague sense of suspense, as if Alice were not quite sure whether she should be waiting for someone or for something to happen. The blows hadn't hurt too much the night before. Now she grasped that was her body's reaction to shock. As the hours crept by, various parts of her had begun to swell and stiffen, a dull throb pushing at the parts of her head where it had made contact with Van Cleve's meaty fist or the unforgiving table-top.

Margery left, after Alice assured her that, yes, she was fine, and, no, she didn't want any more people missing out on their books, promising to bolt the door all the time she was gone. In truth, she needed time alone, time where she didn't have to worry about everybody else's reactions to her, as well as everything else.

And so, for a couple of hours, it was just Alice in the library, alone with her thoughts. Her head ached too much to read, and she didn't know what to look at anyway. Her thoughts were muddied, tangled. She found it hard to focus, while the questions of her future—where she would live, what to do, whether even to try to return to England—seemed so huge and intractable that eventually it seemed easier simply to concentrate on the small tasks. Tidy some books. Make some coffee. Step outside to use the outhouse, then return swiftly to bolt the door again.

At lunchtime there was a knock on the door and she froze. But it was Fred's voice that called, "It's only me, Alice," and she raised herself from the chair and slid back the bolt, stepping behind it as he came in.

"Brought you some soup," he said, placing a bowl with a cloth draped over its rim on the desk. "Thought you might be getting hungry."

It was then that he saw her face. She registered the shock, suppressed as quickly as it flared, to be supplanted by something darker, and angrier. He walked to the end of the room and stood there for a minute, his back to her, and it was as if he were suddenly made of something harder, as if his frame had turned to iron.

"Bennett Van Cleve is a fool," he said, and his jaw barely moved, as if he were having trouble containing himself.

"It wasn't Bennett."

It took him a moment to absorb this. "Well, damn." He walked back and stopped in front of her. She turned her head away from him, color rising in her cheeks, as if it were she who had done something to be ashamed of. "Please," she said, and she wasn't sure what she was asking of him.

"Let me see." He stood before her and lifted his fingertips to her face, studying it with a frown. She closed her eyes as they traced the line of her jaw, his fingers gentle. He was so close she could smell the warmth of his skin, the faint scent of horse he carried on his clothes. "You seen a doctor?"

She shook her head.

"Can you open your mouth?"

She obliged. Then closed it again with a wince. "Brushed my teeth this morning. Think a couple of them may have rattled a bit."

He didn't laugh. His fingertips moved up the sides of her face, so gently that she barely felt them, even across the cuts and bruises, the same way they moved softly across a young horse's spine, checking for misalignments. He frowned as they crossed her cheekbones and met at her forehead where he hesitated, then pushed aside a lock of hair. "I don't think anything's broken." His voice was a low murmur. "Doesn't make me want to hurt him any less, though."

It was always the kindness that would kill you. She felt a tear slide slowly down her cheek, and hoped he didn't see it.

He turned away. She could hear he was now by the desk, clattering a spoon onto it. "It's tomato. Make it myself with herbs and a little cream. Figured you wouldn't have brought anything. And it—uh—doesn't require chewing."

"I don't know many men who cook." Her voice emerged in a little sob.

"Yeah. Well. Would've gone pretty hungry by now if I didn't."

She opened her eyes and he was placing the spoon to the side of her bowl, laying a folded gingham napkin neatly beside it. For a moment she had a flashback of the place setting the previous evening, but shoved it down. This was Fred, not Van Cleve. And she was surprised to find that she was hungry.

Fred sat while she ate, his feet up in a chair as he read a book of poetry, apparently content to let her be.

She ate almost all the soup, wincing every time she opened her mouth, her tongue occasionally working back toward the two loose teeth. She didn't speak, because she didn't know what to say. A strange and unexpected sense of humiliation hung over her, as if she had somehow brought this on herself, as if the bruises on her face were emblematic of her failure. She found herself replaying and replaying the night's events. Should she have kept quiet? Should she simply have agreed? And yet to do those things would have left her—what? No better than one of those damned dolls.

Fred's voice interrupted her thoughts. "When I found out my wife was carrying on, I reckon every second man from here to Hoffman asked me why I hadn't given her a good hiding and brought her home again."

Alice moved her head stiffly to look at him, but he was studying his book, as if he were reading from the words within it.

"They said I should teach her a lesson. I never got it, not even in the first flush of anger, when I thought she had pretty much stomped all over my heart. You beat a horse and you can break it all right. You can make it submit. But it'll never forget. And it sure as hell won't care for you. So if I wouldn't do it to a horse, I could never work out why I should do it to a human."

Alice pushed the bowl away slowly as he continued.

"Selena wasn't happy with me. I knew it, though I didn't want to think about it. She wasn't made for out here, with the dust and the horses and the cold. She was a city girl, and I probably paid that too little mind. I was trying to build the business after my daddy died. Guess I thought she'd be like my ma, happy to forge her own path. Three years of it and no babies, I should have known the first sweet-talking salesman to promise her something different would turn her head. But, no, I never laid a hand on her. Not even when she was standing in front of me, suitcase in hand, telling me all the ways I had failed to be a man to her. And I reckon half this town still thinks I'm less of a man because of it."

Not me, she wanted to tell him, but the words somehow wouldn't emerge from her mouth.

They sat in silence a while longer, alone with their thoughts. Finally he stood and poured her some coffee, set it before her and walked to the door with the empty bowl. "I'll be working with Frank Neilsen's young colt at the near paddock this afternoon. He's a little unbalanced and prefers the level ground. Anything you're worried about, you just bang on that window. Okay?"

She didn't speak.

"I'll be right here, Alice."

"Thank you," she said.

She's my wife. I got a right to talk to her."

"You think I give a Sam Hill what you—"

Fred got to him first. She had been dozing in the chair—she felt exhausted to her bones—and woke to the sound of voices.

"It's okay, Fred," she called out. "Let him in."

She drew back the bolt and opened the door a sliver.

"Well, then, I'm coming in, too." Fred walked in behind Bennett so that the two men stood there for a moment, shaking snow from their boots and patting themselves down.

Bennett flinched when he saw her. She hadn't dared look at her face, but his expression told her much of what she needed to know. He took a breath and rubbed his palm over the back of his head. "You need to come home, Alice," he said, adding: "He won't do it again."

"Since when did you have any say over what your father does, Bennett?" she said.

"He's promised. He didn't mean to hit you that hard."

"Just the little bit. Oh, that's fine, then," said Fred.

Bennett shot him a look. "Tempers were high. Pa just . . . Well, he's not used to a woman sassing him."

"So what's he going to do next time Alice opens her mouth?"

Bennett turned and squared up to Fred. "Hey, Guisler, you want to butt out of this? Because, far as I can see, this ain't no business of yours."

"It's my business when I see a defenseless woman get beat to a pulp."

"And you'd be the expert on how to manage a wife, huh? Because we all know what happened to your wife—"

"That's enough," said Alice. She stood slowly—sudden movements

made her head throb—and turned to Fred. "Can you leave us a moment, Fred? . . . Please?"

His gaze darted from her to Bennett and back again. "I'll be right
outside," he muttered.

They stared at their feet until the door closed. She looked up first,
at the man she had married just over a year ago, a man, she now realized, who had symbolized an escape route rather than any genuine
meeting of minds or souls. What had they really known about each
other, after all? They had been exotic to one another, a suggestion of
a different world to two people who were each trapped, in their own
way, by the expectations of those around them. And then, slowly, her
difference had become repugnant to him.

"You coming on home, then?" he said.

Not *I'm sorry. We can fix this, talk it out. I love you and I've spent the
whole night worrying about you.*

"Alice?"

Not *We'll go somewhere by ourselves. We'll start again. I missed you, Alice.*

"No, Bennett, I'm not coming back."

It took him a moment to register what she had said. "What do you
mean?"

"I'm not coming back."

"Well . . . where will you go?"

"I'm not sure yet."

"You—you can't just *leave*. It doesn't work like that."

"Says who? Bennett—you don't love me. And I can't . . . I can't be
the wife you need me to be. We are making each other desperately
unhappy and there's nothing . . . nothing to suggest that is going to
change. So, no. There's no point in me coming back."

"This is Margery O'Hare's influence. Pa was right. That woman—"

"Oh, for goodness' sake. I know my own mind."

"But we're *married*."

She straightened up. "I'm not coming back to that house. And if
you and your father drag me out of here a hundred times, I will just
keep on leaving."

Bennett rubbed the back of his neck. He shook his head and turned a quarter away from her. "You know he won't accept this."

"*He* won't."

She watched his face, across which several emotions seemed to be competing with each other, and felt briefly overwhelmed by the sadness of it all, at the admission that this really was it, the end. But there was something else in there: something she hoped he could detect too. Relief.

"Alice?" he said.

And there it was again, this bizarre hope, irrepressible as a spring bud, that even at this late hour he might take her in his arms, swear that he couldn't live without her, that this was all a hideous mistake and that they would be together, like he had promised. The belief, engraved deep within her, that every love story held, at its heart, the potential for a happy ending.

She shook her head.

And, without another word, he left.

Christmas was a muted affair. Margery didn't celebrate Christmas traditionally, it being associated with not one good memory for her, but Sven insisted and bought a small turkey that he stuffed and cooked, and made cinnamon cookies from his mother's Swedish recipe. Margery had many skills, he told her, shaking his head, but if he relied on her to cook, he'd be the width of that broom handle.

They invited Fred, which for some reason made Alice self-conscious, and every time he looked across the table at her he managed to time it to the exact second she glanced up at him so that she blushed. He brought with him a Dundee cake, baked to his mother's recipe, and a bottle of French red wine, left in his cellar from before his father died, and they drank it and pronounced it interesting, although Sven and Fred agreed that you couldn't beat a cold beer. They didn't sing carols or play games, but there was something restful about the easy companionship of four people who felt warmly toward each other and were just grateful for good food and a day or two off work.

That being said, all day Alice feared the knock on the door, the inevitable confrontation. Mr. Van Cleve was a man used to getting his own way, after all, and there were few occasions more guaranteed to heat the blood than Christmas. And, indeed, the knock did come— though not as she had expected. Alice leaped up, peering out of the window, fighting for space with a giddy and frantically barking Bluey, but it was Annie who appeared on the stoop, as cross-looking as ever, though, given it was a holiday, Alice couldn't really blame her.

"Mr. Van Cleve asked me to bring this," she said, the words popping from her lips, like angry bubbles. She thrust an envelope at her.

Alice held onto Bluey, who wriggled to be free and jump up to greet this new visitor. He was the most hopeless of guard dogs, Margery would say fondly, all sound and no fury. The runt of the litter. Always stupidly glad to let everyone know how happy he was just to be alive.

Annie kept one wary eye on him as Alice took the envelope. "And he said to wish you a merry Christmas."

"Couldn't get up from the table to say it himself, though, huh?" called Sven, through the doorway. Annie scowled at him and Margery scolded him quietly.

"Annie, you'd be most welcome to stop for a bite to eat before you head out," she called. "It's a cold afternoon and we'd be happy to share."

"Thank you. But I have to get back." She seemed reluctant to stand close to Alice, as if by mere proximity she risked being infected by her predilection for *deviant sexual practices*.

"Well, thank you anyway for coming all the way out here," said Alice. Annie looked at her suspiciously, as if she were making fun at her expense. She turned away and increased her pace back down the hill.

Alice closed the door and released the dog, who immediately leaped up and started barking at the window, as if he had completely forgotten whom he had just seen. Alice stared at the envelope.

"What d'you get then?"

Margery sat down at the table. Alice caught the glance that passed between her and Fred as she opened the card, an elaborate fixing of glitter and bows.

"He'll be trying to win her back," said Sven, leaning back in his chair. "That's a fancy romantic thing. Bennett's trying to impress her."

But the card was not from Bennett. She read the words.

> **Alice, we need you back in the house. Enough's enough and my boy is pining. I know I did you a wrong and I'm prepared to make amends. Here's a little something for you to buy yourself some fineries in Lexington and sent with the hope that it improves your feelings about your swift return home. This was always a fruitful measure with my dear late Dolores and I trust you will view it equally favorably.**
>
> **We can all let bygones be bygones.**
> **Your father,**
> **Geoffrey Van Cleve**

She looked at the card, from which a crisp fifty-dollar bill slid onto the tablecloth. She stared at it where it lay.

"That what I think it is?" said Sven, leaning forward to examine it.

"He wants me to go out and buy a nice dress. And then come home." She placed the card on the table.

There was a long silence.

"You're not going," said Margery.

Alice lifted her head. "I wouldn't go if he paid me a thousand dollars." She swallowed, and stuffed the money back into the envelope. "I will try to find somewhere else to stay, though. I don't want to get under your feet."

"Are you kidding? You stay as long as you like. You're no trouble, Alice. Besides, Bluey's so taken with you it's nice not to have to fight the dog for Sven's attention."

Only Margery noticed Fred's sigh of relief.

"Right!" said Margery. "That's settled. Alice stays. Why don't I clear up? Then we can fetch Sven's cinnamon cookies. If we can't eat them, we can use them for target practice."

27 December 1937

Dear Mr. Van Cleve

You have made quite clear on more than one occasion that you think I am a whore. But, unlike a whore, I can't be bought.

I am therefore returning your money via Annie's safekeeping.

Please could you arrange to have my things sent to Margery O'Hare's home for the time being.

Sincerely

Alice

Van Cleve banged the letter down on his desk. Bennett glanced up from across the office and slumped a little, as if he had already guessed the contents.

"That's it," Van Cleve said, and screwed the letter into a ball. "That O'Hare girl has crossed the line."

Ten days later the flyers went round. Izzy spotted one first, blowing across the road down by the schoolhouse. She dismounted and picked it up, brushing the snow from it so she could read it better.

*Good citizens of Baileyville—please be
aware of the moral danger
posed by the Packhorse Library.
All right-minded citizens are
advised to decline its use.*

Meeting House, Tuesday 6 p.m.

*OUR TOWN'S MORAL RECTITUDE
IS AT STAKE.*

"Moral rectitude. From a man who smashed a girl's face halfway across his dining table." Margery shook her head.

"What are we going to do?"

"Go to the meeting, I guess. We're right-minded citizens after all." Margery looked sanguine. But Alice noted the way her hand closed around the leaflet, and a tendon ran tight along her neck. "And I'm not letting that old—"

The door flew open. It was Bryn, his cheeks pink and his breath heavy from running.

"Miss O'Hare? Miss O'Hare? Beth's took a fall on some ice and broke her arm up real bad."

They bolted from the library and followed him up the snow-covered road, where they were met by the bulky figure of Dan Meakins, the local blacksmith, carrying a whey-faced Beth across his chest. She was clutching her arm and there were vivid dark shadows under each eye, as if she hadn't slept for a week.

"Horse went down on a patch of ice just by the gravel pit," Dan Meakins said. "Checked him over and I think he's okay. But it looks like her arm took the full force of it."

Margery stepped closer to peer at Beth's arm and her heart sank. It was already swollen and dark red three inches above the wrist.

"You're making a fuss," said Beth, through clenched teeth.

"Alice, fetch Fred. We need to get her to the doctor at Chalk Ridge."

An hour later the three of them stood in the little treatment room at Dr. Garnett's as he carefully set the injured arm between two splints, humming quietly as he bound it. Beth sat with her eyes closed and her jaw tight, determined not to let the pain show, consistent with her upbringing as the sole girl in a family of brothers.

"I can still ride, though, right?" said Beth, when the doctor had finished. She held her arm in front of her as he looped the sling around her neck and tied it carefully.

"Absolutely not. Young lady, you need to spend at least six weeks resting it. No riding, no lifting things, no banging it against anything."

"But I have to ride. How else am I supposed to get the books out?"

"I don't know if you heard about our little library, Doctor—" Margery began.

"Oh, we've all heard about your library." He allowed himself a wry smile. "Miss Pinker, at the moment the fracture appears clean, and I'm confident it should mend well. But I cannot stress enough how important it is to protect it from further injury. If an infection were to set in, then we could face having to amputate."

"Amputate?"

Alice felt something wash over her, revulsion or fear, she wasn't sure. Beth was suddenly wide-eyed, her previous composure evaporated.

"We'll manage, Beth." Margery sounded more convincing than she felt. "You just listen to the doctor."

Fred drove as swiftly as he could but by the time they arrived back the meeting had already been going almost half an hour. Alice and Margery crept in at the back of the meeting hall, Alice tipping her hat low over her brow and pulling her hair loose around her face to try to hide the worst of the bruises. Fred followed just behind her, as he had done the whole day, like some kind of guard. The door closed softly behind them. Van Cleve was in such full flow that nobody even stopped to look when they entered.

"Don't get me wrong. I am *all* for books and learning. My own son Bennett here was valedictorian at the school, as some of you may remember. But there are good books and there are books that plant the wrong kinds of ideas, books that spread untruths and impure thoughts. Books that can, if left unmonitored, cause *divisions* in society. And I fear we may have been lax in letting such books loose in our community without applying sufficient *vigilance* to protect our young and most vulnerable minds."

Margery scanned the assembled heads, noting who was there, and who was nodding along. It was hard to tell from behind.

Van Cleve walked along the row of chairs at the front, shaking his head, as if the information he had to impart made him truly sorrowful. "Sometimes, neighbors, good neighbors, I wonder if the only book we should really be reading is the Good Book itself. Doesn't that have all the facts and learning we need?"

"So what are you proposing, Geoff?"

"Well, ain't it obvious? We have to shut this thing down."

Faces in the crowd met each other, some shocked and concerned, others nodding their approval.

"I appreciate that there has been some good work done with sharing recipes and teaching the kiddies to read and all. And I thank you for that, Mrs. Brady. But enough's enough. We need to take back control of our town. And we start with closing this so-called library. I will be putting this to our governor at the earliest opportunity, and I hope that as many of you as are right-minded citizens out here will be supporting me."

The crowd drained away half an hour later, uncharacteristically muted and hard to read, whispering to each other, a few casting curious glances at the women who stood together at the back. Van Cleve walked out deep in conversation with Pastor McIntosh and either failed to notice them, or had simply decided not to acknowledge that they were there.

But Mrs. Brady saw them. Still in the heavy fur hat she wore outside, she scanned the back of the crowd until she spied Margery and motioned to her to meet her over by the small stage. "Is it true? About the *Married Love* book?"

Margery held her gaze. "Yes."

Mrs. Brady exclaimed softly under her breath. "Do you realize what you've done, Margery O'Hare?"

"It's just facts, Mrs. Brady. Facts, to help women take control of their own bodies, their own lives. Nothing sinful about it. Hell, even our own federal court approved that book."

"Federal courts." Mrs. Brady sniffed. "You know as well as I do that down here we're a long way from federal courts, or indeed anyone who cares a lick about what they decide. You know our little corner of the world is highly conservative, especially when it comes to matters of the flesh." She folded her arms across her chest, and her words suddenly exploded out of her. "Darn it, Margery, I trusted you not to create a stir! You know how sensitive this project is. Now the whole town is alive with rumors about the kind of material you're distributing. And that old fool is stirring fit to bust to make sure he gets his own way and shuts us down."

"All I've done is be straight with people."

"Well, a wiser woman than you would have realized that sometimes you have to play a politician's game to get what you want. By doing what you've done, you've given him the very ammunition he was hoping for."

Margery shifted awkwardly. "Ah, come on, Mrs. Brady. Nobody pays any heed to Mr. Van Cleve."

"You think? Well, Izzy's father, for one, has put his foot down."

"What?"

"Mr. Brady has tonight insisted Izzy withdraw from the program."

Margery's jaw dropped. "You're kidding."

"I most certainly am not. This library relies on the goodwill of locals. It relies on the notion of the public good. Whatever it is you're doing, you have created a controversy and Mr. Brady does not want his only child dragged into it."

She raised a hand suddenly to her cheek. "Oh, my. Mrs. Nofcier will not be happy when she hears about this. She will not be happy at all."

"But—but Beth Pinker just broke her arm. We're already one librarian down. If we lose Izzy, too, the library won't be able to continue."

"Well, perhaps you should have thought about that before you started mixing things up with your . . . radical literature." It was then that she noticed Alice's face. She blinked hard, frowned at her, then shook her head as if this, too, were evidence of something going deeply wrong down at the

Packhorse Library. Then she swept out, Izzy throwing a despairing glance their way as she was pulled along by her sleeve toward the door.

W ell, that's torn it."

Margery and Alice stood on the stoop of the now empty meeting hall as the last of the buggies and murmuring couples disappeared. For the first time Margery seemed truly at a loss. She was still holding a crumpled leaflet in her fist and now threw it down, grinding it under her heel into the snow on the step.

"I'll ride tomorrow," said Alice. Her voice still emerged muffled from her swollen mouth, as if she were speaking through a pillow.

"You can't. You'd spook the horses, let alone the families." Margery rubbed at her eyes and took a deep breath. "I'll take what extra routes I can. But Lord knows the snow has pushed everything back already."

"He wants to destroy us, doesn't he?" said Alice, dully.

"Yes, he does."

"It's me. I told him where to put his fifty dollars. He's so mad he'll do anything to punish me."

"Alice, if you hadn't told him where to put his fifty dollars, I would have done it and in capital letters. Van Cleve's the kind of man can't bear to see a woman take any kind of place in the world. You can't go blaming yourself for a man like him."

Alice shoved her hands deep into her pockets. "Maybe Beth's arm will heal quicker than the doctor said."

Margery gave her a sideways look.

"You'll work something out," Alice added, as if she were confirming it to herself. "You always do."

Margery sighed. "C'mon. Let's head back."

Alice took two steps down and pulled Margery's jacket tight around her. She wondered whether Fred would come with her to pick up the last of her belongings. She was afraid of going by herself.

Then a voice broke into the silence. "Miss O'Hare?"

Kathleen Bligh appeared around the corner of the meeting hall, holding an oil lamp in front of her with one hand and the reins of a horse in the other. "Mrs. Van Cleve."

"Hey, Kathleen. How are you doing?"

"I was at the meeting." Her face was drawn under the harsh light. "I heard what your man there was saying about y'all."

"Yes. Well. Everyone has an opinion in this town. You don't want to believe everything you—"

"I'll ride for you."

Margery tilted her head, as if she wasn't sure she was hearing right.

"I'll ride. I heard what you was saying to Mrs. Brady. Garrett's ma will mind the babies for me. I'll ride with you. Until your girl's arm is mended."

When neither Margery nor Alice responded, she said: "I know my way around every holler for twenty miles yonder. Can ride a horse as well as anyone. Your library kept me going and I won't see some old fool shut it down."

The women stared at each other.

"So what time do I come by tomorrow?"

It was the first time Alice had seen Margery truly lost for words. She stuttered a little before she spoke again. "A little after five would be good. We got a lot of ground to cover. Course, if that's too difficult because of your bab—"

"Five it is. Got my own horse." She lifted her chin. "Garrett's horse."

"Then I'm obliged to you."

Kathleen nodded at them both, then mounted the big black horse, steered him round, and was lost in the darkness.

When she looked back afterward, Alice would remember January as the darkest of months. It wasn't just that the days were short and frozen, and that much of their riding was now done in the pitch black, collars high around their necks and their bodies swaddled in as many clothes as they could wear and still move. The families they visited were often blue with cold themselves, children and old people tucked up together in beds, some coughing or rheumy-eyed, huddled around half-hearted fires and all still desperate for the diversion and hope that a good story could bring. Getting books to them had become infinitely harder: routes were often impassable, the horses staggering through deep snow or sliding on ice on steep paths so that Alice would dismount and walk, haunted by the image of Beth's red and swollen arm.

True to her word, Kathleen would turn up at 5 a.m. four mornings a week on her husband's rangy black horse, collect two bags of books, and ride off wordlessly into the mountains. She rarely needed to double-check the routes, and the families she served met her with open doors, and expressions of pleasure and respect. Alice observed that leaving the house was good for Kathleen, despite the travails of the job and the long hours away from her children. Within weeks she carried a new air of, if not happiness, then quiet accomplishment, and even those families swayed by Mr. Van Cleve's emphatic takedown of the library were persuaded to stay with it, given Kathleen's insistence that the library was *a good thing, and she and Garrett had honest reasons for believing so.*

But it was hard all the same. Something like a quarter of the mountain families had dropped out, and a good number in the town, and the rumor mill had gone into overdrive so that those who had previously welcomed them now viewed them with wary eyes.

Mr. Leland says one of your librarians is with child out of wedlock after becoming crazed with lust from a romance novel.

I heard all five sisters over at Split Willow are refusing to help their parents in the house after having their heads turned by political texts slipped into their recipe books. One of them has grown hair on the back of her hands.

Is it true that your English girl is really a Communist?

Occasionally they even received insults and abuse from people they visited. They had started to avoid riding past the honky-tonks on Main Street as men would catcall obscenities from the doorways, or follow them down the street, mimicking what they claimed was in the reading material. They missed Izzy's presence, her songs and her cheerful, awkward enthusiasms, and while nobody spoke openly of it, the absence of Mrs. Brady's support felt like they had lost their backbone. Beth stopped by a few times but was so grumpy and despondent that she—and eventually they—found it easier for her not to be there at all. Sophia spent the hours she no longer had to fill with filing books by making up more scrapbooks. "Things can still change," she would tell the two younger women firmly. "Have faith."

Alice plucked up courage and made her way to the Van Cleve House, flanked by Margery and Fred. She felt weak with relief when Van Cleve wasn't there and it was Annie who silently handed her two neatly packed suitcases and closed the door with an all-too-emphatic slam. But once back in Margery's cabin, despite Margery's assurances that she could stay as long as she liked, Alice couldn't help feeling like an interloper, a refugee in a world whose rules she still didn't entirely understand.

Sven Gustavsson was solicitous; he was a kind man who never made Alice feel unwelcome, and took time to ask her during every visit about herself, her family back in England, what she had done with her day, as if she were a favored guest he was always quietly delighted to find there, not just a lost soul clogging up their living area.

He told her about what really went on at Van Cleve's mines: the brutality, the union-breakers, broken bodies and conditions she could barely stand to picture. He explained it all in a voice that suggested this was simply how it was, but she felt a deep shame that the comforts in which she had lived at the big house had been provided from its proceeds.

She would retreat to a far corner and read one of Margery's 122 books, or she would lie awake through the unlit hours, her thoughts periodically interrupted by the sounds emerging from Margery's bedroom and their frequency. Their uninhibited nature and unexpected joyfulness left her feeling first acute embarrassment then, after a week, curiosity tinged with sadness at how Margery and Sven's experience of love could be so different from her own.

But mostly she would sneak glances at the way he was around

Margery, the way he watched her move with quiet approval, the way his hand strayed to her whenever she was nearby, as if the touch of his skin on hers was as necessary to him as breathing. She marveled at how he discussed Margery's work with her, as if it were something he took pride in, offering suggestions or words of support. She noted that he pulled Margery to him without embarrassment or awkwardness, murmuring secrets into her ears and sharing smiles lit with unspoken intimacies, and it was then that something in Alice would hollow out, until she felt there was something cavernous inside her, a great gaping hole that grew and grew until it threatened to swallow her whole.

Focus on the library, she would tell herself, pulling the counterpane up to her chin and blocking her ears. *As long as you have that, you have something.*

THIRTEEN

*There is no religion without love, and people may talk
as much as*
        *they like about their religion, but if it does not
teach them to be good*
        and kind to man and beast, it is all a sham.

· ANNA SEWELL, *Black Beauty*

In the end they sent Pastor McIntosh, as if God's word might hold
sway where Van Cleve's could not. He knocked on the door of the
Packhorse Library on a Tuesday evening and found the women in a
circle, cleaning their saddles, a bucket of warm water between them,
chatting companionably as the log burner roared in the corner.

He removed his hat, folding it to his chest. "Ladies, I am sorry to
interrupt your work but I wondered if I might have a word with Mrs.
Van Cleve here."

"If it's Mr. Van Cleve sent you, Pastor McIntosh, I'll save your
breath and tell you exactly what I told him, and his son, and his house-
keeper, and anyone else who wants to know. I'm not going back."

"Lord, but that man is relentless," muttered Beth.

"Well, that's an understandable emotion, given the high feelings of
recent weeks. But you are married now, dear. You are subject to a
higher authority."

"Mr. Van Cleve's?"

"No. God's. *Those whom God has joined together, let no man put asunder.*"

"Good thing she's a lady, then," muttered Beth, and sniggered.

Pastor McIntosh's smile wavered. He sat heavily on the seat by the door, and leaned forward. "You were married under God, Alice, and it's your duty to return home. You just walking out like this is . . . well, it's causing ripples. You need to think about the wider effects of your behavior. Bennett's unhappy. His father is unhappy."

"And my happiness? I'm guessing that doesn't come into it."

"Dear girl—it is through domestic life that you will achieve true contentment. A woman's place is in the home. *Wives, submit yourselves unto your own husbands as unto the Lord. For the husband is the head of the wife, even as Christ is the head of the church, and he is the savior of the body.* Ephesians, Chapter five, Verse twenty-two."

Margery rubbed vigorous circles into the saddle soap without looking up. "Pastor, you know you're talking to a room full of happily unmarried women here, right?"

He acted like he couldn't hear. "Alice, I urge you to be guided by the Holy Bible, to hear the word of God. *I will therefore that the younger women marry, bear children, guide the house, give none occasion to the adversary to speak reproachfully*—that one is from the first epistle to Timothy, Chapter five, Verse fourteen. Do you understand what he is saying to you, dear?"

"Oh, I think I understand, thank you, Pastor."

"Alice, you don't have to sit here and—"

"I'm fine, Margery," Alice said, holding up a hand. "The pastor and I have always had interesting conversations. And I do think I understand what it is you're telling me, Pastor."

The other women exchanged silent looks. Beth gave a tiny shake of her head.

Alice scrubbed at a stubborn patch of dirt with a rag. She cocked her head, thinking. "I would be much obliged if you could advise me a little further, though."

The pastor steepled his fingers. "Why, yes, child. What is it you want to know?"

Alice compressed her mouth for a moment, as if choosing her words carefully. Then, without looking up, she started to speak. "What does God say about smashing your daughter-in-law's head repeatedly into a table because she had the audacity to give two old toys to some motherless girls? Do you have a verse for that one? Because I'd love to hear it."

"I'm sorry—what did you—"

"Perhaps you have one for when a woman's sight is still blurred in one eye because her father-in-law smacked her so hard in the face that she saw stars? Or what's the Bible verse for when a man tries to give you paper money to make you behave as he wants you to? Do you think Ephesians has a view on that? Fifty dollars is quite a sum, after all. Large enough to ignore all kinds of sinful behavior."

Beth's eyes widened. Margery thrust her head down.

"Alice, dear, this—uh—this is all a private ma—"

"Is that godly behavior, Pastor? Because I'm listening really hard and all I'm hearing is everyone telling me what *I'm* apparently doing wrong. When actually I think I may have been the godliest one in the Van Cleve household. I might not spend enough time in church, granted, but I actually do minister to the poor and sick and needy. Never looked at another man, or given my husband reason to doubt me. I give away what I can." She leaned forward over the saddle. "I'll tell you what I don't do. I don't call in men with machine-guns from across state lines to threaten my own workforce. I don't charge that same workforce four times the fair amount for groceries and sack them if they try to buy food anywhere but the company store, until they run up debts they'll die before they can pay back. I don't throw the sick out of their company homes when they can't work. I certainly don't beat up young women until they can't see, then send a servant over with money to smooth it over. So tell me, Pastor, who really is the ungodly one in all this? Just who needs a lecture on how to behave? Because I'm darned if I can work this one out."

The little library had fallen completely silent. The pastor, his mouth working up and down, regarded each of the women's faces: Beth and Sophia stooped innocently over their work, Margery's gaze flickering between the two of them, and Alice, her chin up, her face a blazing question.

He placed his hat on his head. "I—I can see you're busy, Mrs. Van Cleve. Perhaps I'll come back another time."

"Oh, please do, Pastor," she called, as he opened the door and hurried off into the dark. "I do so enjoy our Bible studies!"

With that final attempt by Pastor McIntosh—a man who could not accurately be described as the soul of discretion—word had finally traveled around the county that Alice Van Cleve really had left her husband and was not coming back. It had not improved Geoffrey Van Cleve's mood—already weighted down by those rabble-rousers at the mine—one jot. Emboldened by the anonymous letters, the same troublemakers who had tried to resurrect the unions were now rumored to be doing so again. This time, however, they were smarter about it. This time it had been done in quiet conversations, in casual talks down at Marvin's Bar or the Red Horse honky-tonk, and often mentioned so swiftly that by the time Van Cleve's men had arrived all there was to see was a few Hoffman men legitimately downing a cold beer after a long week's work and just a vague sense of disturbance in the air.

"Word is," said the governor, as they sat in the hotel bar, "you're losing your grip."

"My grip?"

"You've been obsessing about that damn library and not focusing on what's going on at your mine."

"Where did you hear such nonsense? I have the firmest of grips, Governor. Why, didn't we discover a whole bunch of those troublemakers from the UMWA just two months ago and shut that down? I got Jack Morrissey and his boys to see them off. Oh, yes."

The governor gazed into his drink.

"I got eyes and ears all over this county. I'm keeping track of these subversive elements. But we have sent a warning, if you like. And I have friends at the sheriff's office who are very understanding about such matters."

The governor raised the slightest of eyebrows.

"What?" said Van Cleve, after a pause.

"They say you can't even keep control of your own home."

Van Cleve's neck shot to the back of his collar.

"Is it true that your Bennett's wife ran off to a cabin in the woods and you ain't been able to get her home again?"

"The young 'uns may be having a few hiccups just now. She—she asked to stay with her friend. Bennett's letting her just till things simmer down." He ran a hand over his face. "The girl got very emotional, you know, about not being able to bear him a child . . ."

"Well, I'm sad to hear that, Geoff. But I have to tell you that's not how it's being parlayed."

"What?"

"They say the O'Hare girl's running rings around you."

"Frank O'Hare's daughter? Pfft. That little . . . hillbilly. She—she just hangs off Alice's coattails. Got some kind of fascination with her. You don't want to listen to anything anyone says about that girl. Hah! Last I heard, her so-called library was on its last legs anyway. Not that I'm much troubled by the library one way or another. Oh, no."

The governor nodded. But he didn't laugh and agree, slap Van Cleve on the back and offer him a whiskey. He just nodded, finished his drink, slid off his bar stool and left.

And when Van Cleve finally got up to leave the bar, several bourbons and a whole lot of brooding later, his face was the dark purple of the upholstery.

"You good, Mr. Van Cleve?" said the bartender.

"Why? You got an opinion as well as everyone else around here?" He sent the empty glass skidding and it was only the bartender's sharp reflexes that stopped it flying off the end of the bar.

ennett looked up as his father slammed the screen door. He had been listening to the wireless and reading a baseball magazine.

Now Van Cleve smacked it out of his hand. "I'm done with this. Go get your coat."

"What?"

"We're bringing Alice home. We'll pick her up and put her in the trunk if necessary."

"Pop, I told you a hundred times. She says she'll just keep leaving until we get the message."

"And you're going to take that from a little girl? Your own wife? You know what this is doing to my name?"

Bennett opened his magazine again, mumbling into his collar. "It's just folk talking. It'll die down soon enough."

"Meaning what?"

Bennett shrugged. "I don't know. Just . . . we should maybe leave her be."

Van Cleve squinted at his son, as if he might have been replaced by some alien he barely recognized. "Do you even *want* her to come home?"

Bennett shrugged again.

"What in hell does that mean?"

"I don't know."

"Oho . . . Is this because little Peggy Foreman's been hanging around you again? Oh, yes, I know all about that. I see you, son. I hear things. You think your mother and I didn't have our difficulties? You think there weren't times we didn't want to be around each other? But she was a woman who understood her responsibilities. You're *married*. Do you understand, son? Married in the eyes of God and in the eyes of the law and according to the laws of nature. If you want to be fooling around with Peggy you do it quietly and on the side of things, not so that everybody's looking and talking. You hear me?"

Van Cleve adjusted his jacket, checking his reflection in the mirror over the mantel. "You have to be a man now. I'm done with waiting around while some stuck-up English girl wrecks my family's reputation. The Van Cleve name means something around here. Get your damn coat."

"What are you going to do?"

"We're going to fetch her." Van Cleve looked up at the larger figure of his son, now standing in his way. "Are you blocking me, boy? My own son?"

"I won't be part of it, Pa. Some things are best . . . left."

The older man's mouth, clamped shut, worked like a trap. He shoved past him. "This is the thin end of the wedge. You might be too pussy to send that girl a message. But if you think I'm the kind of man to sit by and do nothing, then you really don't know your old pa at all."

Margery rode home deep in thought, nostalgic for times when all she had to think about was whether she had enough food for the next three days. As she often did, when her thoughts grew deep and cold, she murmured to herself under her breath. "It's not so bad. We're still here, aren't we, Charley boy? Books are still getting out there."

The mule's big ears flicked back and forth so that she swore he understood half her conversation. Sven laughed at the way she talked to her animals, and every time she would retort that they made more sense to her than half the humans around there. And then, of course, she would catch him murmuring to the damn dog like a baby when he thought she wasn't looking—*Who's a good boy then, huh? Who's the best dog?* Soft-hearted, for all his bluntness. Kind with it. Not many men would have been so welcoming of another woman in the house. Margery thought about the apple pie Alice had rustled up the night before, half of which was still sitting on the side. Seemed like the cabin was always chock full of people, these days, bustling around, making food, helping with chores. A year ago she would have bridled at it. Now returning to an empty house seemed like a strange thing, not the relief she might have imagined.

A little delirious with tiredness, Margery's thoughts meandered and splintered as the mule plodded up the dark track. She thought of Kathleen Bligh, returning to a home echoing with loss. Thanks to her, these last two weeks, despite the weather, they had managed to cover nearly all their rounds, and the loss of those families who had fallen out of the project due to Van Cleve's rumors meant they were pretty much up to date. If she had the budget she'd take Kathleen on for good. But Mrs. Brady wasn't much for talking about the future of the library just now. "I have held off writing to Mrs. Nofcier about our current troubles," she had told her the previous week, confirming that Mr. Brady was as yet unbending on the issue of Izzy's return. "I am hoping that we can win round enough townspeople that Mrs. Nofcier might never have to hear about this . . . misfortune."

Alice had started riding again, her bruises luminous yellow echoes of the injuries she had endured. She had taken the long route up to Patchett's Creek that day, supposedly to stretch Spirit out a little, but Margery knew it was so she, Margery, could have some time with Sven alone at the house. The families on the creek route liked Alice, made her speak English place names to them—*Beaulieu* and *Piccadilly* and *Leicester Square*—and fell about laughing at her accent. She never minded. She was slow to offend, that girl. It was one of the things Margery liked about her, she thought. While enough people round here would find a slight in the mildest of words, every compliment a secret barb aimed just at them, Alice still seemed primed to see the best in everyone she came across. Probably why she'd married that human beefsteak Bennett.

She yawned, wondering how long it was going to take Sven to come home. "What do you think, Charley boy? Have I got time to boil up some hot water and get this grime off me? Do you think he'll care a whit one way or the other?"

She pulled the mule to a halt at the large gate, dismounting to open it up. "The way I feel, I'll be lucky if I manage to stay awake long enough for him to get here."

It took her a minute after replacing the catch to realize what was missing.

"Bluey?"

She walked up the path, calling him, her boots crunching in the snow. She hooked the mule's reins over the pole by the porch, and lifted her hand to her brow. Where had the darn dog shot off to now? Two weeks ago he had made his way three miles across the creek to Henscher's place, just to play with the young dog there. Came home sheepish with his ears down, like he knew he'd done wrong, his face so full of guilt that she didn't have the heart to tell him off. Her voice echoed back across the holler. "Bluey?"

She took the porch steps two at a time. And then she saw him, at the far end by the rocker. A pale limp body, his ice-colored eyes staring blankly at the roof, his tongue lolling and his legs splayed, as if he had been stopped directly in the act of running. A clean dark red bullet hole ran straight through his skull.

"Oh, no. Oh, no."

Margery ran to him and dropped to her knees and a wail emerged from somewhere she hadn't known she possessed. "Oh, not my boy. No. No."

She cradled the dog's head, feeling the velvet-soft fur of his cheeks, stroking his muzzle, knowing even as she did that there was nothing to be done. "Oh, Bluey. My sweet baby." She pressed her face to his— *I'm sorry I'm so sorry I'm sorry*—her hands clutching him to her, her whole body mourning a stupid young hound that would never bounce onto her bed again.

It was like this that Alice found her, as she rode up on Spirit half an hour later, her legs aching and her feet numb with cold.

Margery O'Hare, a woman who had remained dry-eyed throughout her own father's funeral, who had bitten her lip until it bled as she buried her sister, a woman who had taken the best part of four years to confess her feelings to the man she loved most in the world, and still swore she had not a sentimental bone in her body, sat keening like a child on the porch, her back doubled over with grief and her dead dog's head cradled tenderly in her lap.

Alice saw Van Cleve's Ford before she saw him. For weeks she had backed into the shadows when he passed, had turned her face, her heart in her mouth, braced for another puce-faced demand that she come home right now and stop all this nonsense or she might just find herself regretting it. Even in company the sight of him made her tremble a little, as if some residual memory was lodged in her cells that still felt the impact of that blunt fist.

But now, propelled by a long night of grief that had been somehow so much more painful to witness than her own, she dug in her heels as she saw the burgundy car heading down the hill, sending Spirit wheeling hard across the road so that she was directly in front of him and he had to stamp on the brakes, screeching to a halt in front of the store, causing all passersby—a fair number, given that the store had a special deal on flour—to stop and observe the commotion. Van Cleve blinked at the girl on the horse through his windshield, unsure at first who it was. He wound down his window. "You properly lost your mind now, Alice?"

Alice glared at him. She dropped her reins and her voice carried, clear as cut glass, through the still air, glittering with anger. "You shot her *dog*?"

There was a brief silence.

"You shot Margery's *dog*?"

"I shot nothing."

She lifted her chin and looked steadily at him. "No, of course you didn't. You wouldn't get your own hands dirty, would you? You probably got your men to come out here just to shoot that puppy." She shook her head. "My God. What kind of man *are* you?"

She saw then from the questioning way Bennett swiveled to look at his father that he hadn't known, and some small part of her was glad.

Van Cleve, who had been open-mouthed, swiftly recovered his composure. "You're crazy. Living with that O'Hare girl has turned you crazy!" He glanced out of his window, noting the neighbors who had stopped to listen, murmuring to each other. This was rich meat indeed for a quiet town. *Van Cleve shot Margery O'Hare's dog.* "She's crazy! Look at her, riding her horse straight into my car! As if I'd shoot a dog!" He slapped his hands on the steering wheel. Alice didn't move. His voice rose a register. "Me! Shoot a damn dog!"

And finally, when nobody moved, and nobody spoke: "Come on, Bennett. We got work to do." He wrestled the wheel so that the car spun around her and accelerated briskly up the road, leaving Spirit to prance and shy as the gravel sprayed at her feet.

It shouldn't have been a surprise. Sven leaned over the rough wooden table with Fred and the two women and relayed the tales coming out of Harlan County, of men dynamited clean out of their beds because of the escalating union disputes, of thugs with machine-guns, of sheriffs turning the blindest of eyes. In the light of all this a dead dog shouldn't have been much of a surprise. But it seemed to knock the fight right out of Margery. She'd been sick twice with the shock of it, and she cast around for her hound reflexively when they were home, her palm pressed to her cheek, as if even now she half expected him to come bounding around the corner.

"Van Cleve's canny," muttered Sven, as she left the room to check on Charley, as she did repeatedly through each evening. "He knew Margery wouldn't bat an eyelid if someone looked at her down the barrel of a gun. But if he picked off the things she loves . . ."

Alice considered this. "Are . . . *you* worried, Sven?"

"For me? No. I'm a company man. And he needs a fire captain. I'm not unionized, but anything happens to me, all my boys go out. We're agreed on that. And if we walk, the mine shuts down. The sheriff might be in Van Cleve's pocket but there are limits to what the state will tolerate." He sniffed. "Besides, this one's about him and you two girls. And he won't want attention drawn to the fact that he's engaged in a fight with a pair of women. Oh, no."

He took a slug of bourbon. "He's just trying to spook you. But his men wouldn't hurt a woman. Even those thugs of his. They're bound by the code of the hills."

"What about the ones he's bringing in from out of state?" said Fred. "You sure they're bound by the code of the hills, too?"

Sven didn't seem to have an answer for that.

Fred taught her how to use a shotgun. He showed her how to balance the stock and pull the butt against her shoulder, how to factor in the hefty kick backward when she lined up her sights, reminding her not to hold her breath but to release the trigger as she breathed out slowly. The first time she pulled the trigger he was standing close behind her, his hands on hers, and she bounced so hard against him that her face stayed pink for an hour.

She was a natural, he told her, lining up cans on the fallen tree at the edge of Margery's land. Within days she could pick them off, like apples falling from a branch. At night, as she secured the new locks on the doors, Alice would run her hands along the barrel, lift it speculatively to her shoulder, firing imaginary rounds at unseen intruders coming up the track. She would pull the trigger for her friend; she had no doubt of that.

Because something else had changed too, something fundamental. Alice had discovered how, for a woman at least, it was much easier to feel anger on behalf of someone you cared about, to access that cold burn, to want to make someone suffer if they had hurt someone you loved.

Alice, it turned out, was no longer afraid.

FOURTEEN

Riding all winter, a librarian would wrap up so heavily it was hard to remember what she looked like underneath: two vests, a flannel shirt, a thick sweater and a jacket with maybe a scarf or two over the top—that was the daily uniform up in the mountains, perhaps with a pair of man's thick leather gloves over her own, a hat rammed low as she could get it, and another scarf pulled high over her nose, so that her breath might bounce back and warm her skin a little. At home, she'd strip off reluctantly, revealing only the swiftest slice of bare skin to the elements between shedding undergarments and sliding, shivering, under her blankets. Aside from cloth-washing, a woman working for the Packhorse Library could go for weeks without seeing her body much at all.

Alice was still locked into her own private battle with the Van Cleves although, thankfully, they seemed to have gone quiet for now. She could most often be found in the woods behind the cabin practicing with Fred's old gun, the *crack* and *zing* of bullets hitting tin cans echoing through the still air.

Izzy could be seen only in glimpses, trailing her mother miserably around town. And there were only intermittent appearances from Beth, the one person who could be relied on to notice these things, or joke about them, and she was mostly preoccupied with her arm and what she could and couldn't do. So nobody observed that Margery had put on a little weight, or thought to comment upon it. Sven, who knew Marge's body like he knew his own, understood the fluctuations that occurred in the female form and enjoyed all of them equally, and was a wise enough man not to say anything.

Margery herself had become accustomed to being bone-tired, trying to double up on routes, fighting every day to convince the disbelievers of the importance of stories, of facts, of knowledge. But this and the constant air of foreboding left her struggling each morning to lift her head from the pillow. The cold was etched into her after months of snow, and the long hours outside had left her permanently, ravenously hungry. So a woman could be excused for not noticing the things that other women might have picked up on faster, or if she did, for sweeping the thought away under the larger pile of things she had to worry about.

But there is always a point at which these things become impossible to ignore. One night in late February Margery told Sven not to stop by, adding with deceptive casualness that she had a few things to catch up on. She helped Sophia with the last of the books, waved Alice off into the snowy night and bolted the door behind her until it was just her alone in the little library. The log burner still glowed warm because Fred, God bless him, had packed it full of logs before he, too, disappeared to eat, his mind full of someone else entirely. She sat in the chair, her thoughts hanging low around her head in the darkness, until eventually she stood, pulled a heavy textbook from the shelf and flicked through the pages until she found what she was looking for. Brow furrowed, she scanned the information carefully. She absorbed it, then counted off her fingers: *one, two, three, four, five, five and a half.*

And then she did it a second time.

Despite what people might have thought around Lee County about Margery O'Hare's family, about the kind of woman she must surely be, given where she came from, she was not prone to cursing. Now, however, she cursed softly once, twice, and let her head sink silently into her hands.

FIFTEEN

> The small town bankers, grocers, editors and lawyers,
> the police, the sheriff, if not the government, were all
> apparently subservient to the money and corporate
> masters of the area. It was their compulsion, if possibly
> not always their desire, to stand well with these who
> had the power to cause them material or personal
> difficulties.
>
> · THEODORE DREISER, introduction to
> *Harlan Miners Speak*

hree families who wouldn't let me so much as hand over a book unless we read Bible stories, one slammed door up by those new houses near Hoffman, but Mrs. Cotter seems to have come back round now she understands we're not trying to tempt her into the ways of the flesh, and Doreen Abney says can she have the magazine with the recipe for the rabbit pie as she forgot to write it out two weeks ago." Kathleen's saddlebag landed with a thump on the desk. She turned to look at Alice and rubbed dirt from her hands.

"Oh, and Mr. Van Cleve stopped me in the street to tell me that we were an abomination and the sooner we were gone from this town the better."

"I'll show him abomination," said Beth, darkly.

By mid-March, Beth had returned to work full-time, but nobody had the heart to tell Kathleen she was no longer needed. Mrs. Brady, who was a fair woman if a little unbending, had declined to draw Izzy's wage since she had gone, and Margery simply handed the little brown paper packet directly to Kathleen. It was something of a relief, as she had been paying her out of her own pocket with the few savings she had hidden since her father's death. Twice Kathleen's mother-in-law had come by the library to bring her children and show them what their mama was engaged in, her voice filled with pride. The children were great favorites among the women, who showed them the newest books and let them sit on the mule, and there was something in Kathleen's slow smile, and the genuine warmth of her mother-in-law toward her, that made everyone feel a little better.

Realizing Alice would not be budged on the matter of returning to the house, Mr. Van Cleve had taken a new tack, insisting she leave town, that she wasn't wanted here, pulling alongside her in his car as she headed out on her early-morning rounds so that Spirit's eyes rolled white and she pranced sideways to get away from the man bellowing out of the driver's window.

"You got no way to support yourself. And that library's going to be finished in a matter of weeks. I've heard it from the governor's office himself. You ain't coming back to the house, then you'd best find somewhere else. Somewhere back in England."

She had learned to ride with her face fixed straight ahead, as if she couldn't hear him, and this would enrage him more so that he would invariably end up shouting halfway down the road, while Bennett slunk down in the passenger seat.

"*You ain't even all that pretty any more!*"

"Do you think Margery is really okay with me staying at the cabin?" she would ask Fred afterward. "I don't want to be in the way. But he's right. I don't have anywhere else to go."

Fred would bite his lip, as if he wanted to say something he couldn't.

"I think Margery likes having you around. Like all of us," he would answer carefully.

She had started to notice new things about Fred: the confident way his hands rested on horses, the fluidity in the way he moved, not like Bennett who, despite his athleticism, had always seemed uncomfortable, restrained by his own muscles, as if movement could only burst out of him sporadically. She found excuses to stay late in the cabin, helping Sophia, who kept her lips pursed. She knew. Oh, they all knew.

"You like him, don't you?" Sophia asked her outright, one night.

"Me? Fred? Oh, my. I—" she stammered.

"He's a good man." Sophia said it with the emphasis on *good*, as if she were comparing him to someone else.

"Were you ever married, Sophia?"

"Me, no." Sophia raised a thread to her teeth and bit it through neatly. And just at the point where Alice wondered if she had yet again been too direct, she added: "Loved a man once. Benjamin. A miner. He was best friends with William. We knew each other since we were children." She held her stitching up to the lamp. "But he's dead now."

"Did he . . . die in the mines?"

"No. Some men shot him. He was minding his business, just walking home from work."

"Oh Sophia. I'm so sorry."

Sophia's expression was unreadable, as if she had had years of practice of hiding what she felt. "I couldn't stay here for a long time. Took myself off to Louisville and put all my heart into working at the colored library there. Built something of a life, though I missed him every day. When I heard William had suffered his accident I prayed to God not to make me come back here. But you know, He has His ways."

"Is it still difficult?"

"It was at first. But . . ." she shrugged, "things change. Ben died fourteen years ago now. The world moves on."

"Do you think . . . you'll ever meet anyone else?"

"Oh no. That ship has sailed. Besides, I don't fit nowhere. Too educated for most of the men around here. My brother would say too opinionated." Sophia laughed.

"That sounds familiar," said Alice, and sighed.

"I got William for company. We get by. And I'm hopeful. Things are good." She smiled. "Got to count your blessings. I enjoy my job. I got friends here now."

"That's a little how I feel, too."

Almost on impulse, Sophia reached out a slim hand and squeezed Alice's. Alice squeezed back, struck by the unexpected comfort of a human touch. They held each other's grip tightly and then, almost reluctantly, released it.

"I do think he's kind," said Alice, after a moment. "And . . . quite handsome."

"Girl, all you'd have to do is say the word. That man's been pining after you like a dog after a bone since the day I got here."

"But I can't, can I?"

Sophia looked up.

"Half the town thinks this library is a hotbed of immorality, and me at the heart of it. Can you imagine what they'd say about us if I took up with a man? A man who wasn't my husband?"

She had a point, Sophia told William afterward. Just seemed a damn shame, two good people so glad to be in each other's company.

"Well," said William, "nobody ever said this world was going to be fair."

"Ain't that the truth," said Sophia, and returned to her stitching, briefly lost in the memory of a man with an easy laugh who had never failed to make her smile, and the long-lost weight of his arm around her waist.

She's a schoolmistress, old Spirit," Fred said, as they rode home in the encroaching dusk. He was wearing a heavy oilcloth jacket to keep off the thin rain, and the green scarf the librarians had bought him for Christmas was wrapped around his neck, as it had been every day since they'd given it to him. "You see it today? Every time this one spooked she gave him a look as if to say, 'You get a hold of yourself.' And when he didn't listen her ears went flat back. She's telling him, all right."

Alice watched the two horses walking side by side and marveled at the tiny differences Fred could distinguish. He could assess a horse's conformation, sucking his teeth at sloping shoulders or cow hocks or an underdeveloped top line, when all Alice saw was "nice horsey." He could assess their characters too—they were pretty much who they were from birth, as long as men didn't muck them up too much, he said. "Course, most couldn't help themselves." She was often left with the impression that when Fred said these things he was talking about something else entirely.

He had taken to meeting her along her routes on a young Thoroughbred with a scarred ear—Pirate. He said it was helpful to have the young horse work alongside Spirit's more level temperament, but she suspected he had other reasons for being there and she didn't mind. It was hard enough being alone with her thoughts most of the day.

"Did you finish the Hardy?"

Fred screwed up his face. "I did. Couldn't warm to that Angel character, though."

"No?"

"Found myself kind of wanting to give him a kick half the time. There she was, that poor girl, just wanting to love him. And him like some kind of preacher, judging her. Even though none of it was her fault. And then at the end he goes and marries her sister!"

Alice stifled a laugh. "I'd forgotten that bit."

They talked of books they had recommended to each other. She had quite enjoyed the Mark Twain, found the George Herbert poems unexpectedly moving. Lately it had seemed easier for them to talk about books than anything in real life.

"So . . . can I give you a ride home?" They had reached the library and turned the horses into Fred's barn for the night. "It's awful wet to be walking all the way up to Marge's. I could drive you as far as the big oak."

Oh, but it was tempting. The long walk in the dark was the worst part of the day, a point at which she was hungry and aching and her mind had nowhere good to settle. There was a time when she might have ridden Spirit and kept her there overnight, but they had an unspoken agreement not to keep any other animals at the cabin just now.

Fred had closed up the barn and was looking at her expectantly. She thought of the quiet pleasure of sitting alongside him, of watching his strong hands on the wheel, his smile as he told her things in small bursts, confidences offered up like shells in the palm of his hand. "I don't know, Fred. I can't really be seen—"

"Well, I was thinking . . ." He shifted on his feet a little. "I know you like to allow Margery and Sven a little space together . . . and right now more than most . . ."

Something odd was going on with Margery and Sven. It had taken her a week or two to notice, but the little cabin was no longer filled with the muffled cries of lovemaking. Sven was often gone before Alice rose in the morning, and when he was there, there were no whispered jokes or casual intimacies but stiff silences and loaded glances. Margery seemed preoccupied. Her face was set stern, and her manner short. The previous evening, though, when Alice had asked her if she would rather she left, the woman's face had softened. Then she had responded quite unexpectedly—not by telling her dismissively that she was fine, and not to fuss, but by saying quietly, *No. Please don't leave.* A lover's tiff? She would not betray her friend by talking about her private business but she felt utterly at a loss.

". . . so I was wondering if you would like to have some food with me? I'd be happy to cook. And I could—"

She dragged her attention back to the man in front of her.

"—have you back at the cabin by half past eight or thereabouts."

"Fred, I can't."

He closed his mouth abruptly over his words.

"I—It's not that I wouldn't like to. It's just . . . if I were seen—well, things are tricky just now. You know how this town talks."

He looked like he had half expected it.

"I can't risk making things worse for the library. Or . . . for myself. Perhaps when things have calmed down a little."

Even as she said the words she realized she wasn't sure how that would work. This town could polish a piece of gossip and preserve it like an insect in amber. It would still be rolling around whole centuries later.

"Sure," he said. "Well, just wanted you to know the offer's there. In case you get tired of Margery's cooking."

He tried to laugh and they stood facing each other, each a little awkward. He broke it, raised his hat in greeting, and trudged back up the wet path to his house. Alice stood watching, thinking of the warmth inside, the blue rag rug, the sweet smell of the polished wood. And then she sighed, pulled her scarf over her nose and began the long walk up the cold mountain to Margery's.

Sven knew that Margery was not a woman who would be pushed. But when she told him it would be best if he stayed at his own house for the third time that week, he could no longer ignore the feeling in his gut. Watching her unsaddle Charley, he found himself crossing his arms and observing her with cooler, assessing eyes until finally he uttered the words he'd been mulling over for weeks.

"Have I done something, Marge?"

"What?"

And there it was again. The way she would barely look at him when she spoke.

"Seems like the last few weeks you barely want me around."

"You're talking crazy."

"I can't seem to say nothing to please you. When we go to bed you're bundled up like a silkworm. Don't want me to touch you . . ." he stuttered, faltering uncharacteristically. "We've never been cold with each other, even when we were apart. Not in ten years. I just . . . want to know if I've done something to offend you."

Her shoulders slumped a little. She reached under the horse for his girth and flipped it over the saddle, the buckle jangling as it landed. There was something weary in the way she did it that reminded him of a mother dealing with ill-behaved children. She allowed a short silence before she spoke. "You've done nothing to offend me, Sven. I'm . . . just tired."

"So why don't you want me even to hold you?"

"Well, I don't always want to be held."

"You never used to mind."

Disliking the sound of his voice, he took the saddle from her and walked it over to the house. She turned Charley loose into his stall, rugged him, bolted the barn door, and followed in silence. They locked everything, these days, their eyes sharp for change, ears tuned to any strange sound around the holler. The track up from the road was strewn with a series of strings set with bells and tin cans to give her fair warning, and two loaded shotguns flanked the bed.

He placed the saddle on its stand and stood, thinking. Then he took a step toward her, lifted a hand, and touched the side of her face softly, an olive branch. She didn't look up. Before, she would have pressed his palm to her skin and kissed it. The fact of this made something plummet inside him.

"We've always been straight with each other, haven't we?"

"Sven—"

"I respect how you want to live. I accepted that you don't want to be tied. I haven't so much as mentioned it since—"

She rubbed at her forehead. "Can we not do this now?"

"What I mean is—we agreed. We agreed that . . . if you did decide you didn't want me any more, you would say."

"Are we on this again?" Margery sounded sad and exasperated. She turned away from him. "It's not you. I don't want you to go anywhere. I just—I just got a lot to think about."

"We've all got a lot to think about."

She shook her head.

"Margery."

And there she stood, mulish as Charley. Giving him nothing.

Sven Gustavsson was not a man possessed of a difficult temperament, but he was proud and he had his limits. "I can't keep doing this. I'm not going to keep bothering you." She raised her head as he turned. "You know where to find me when you're ready to see me again." He held up one hand as he walked off down the mountain. He didn't look back.

Sophia was off on Friday as it was William's birthday and, given they were up to date with the repairs (possibly due to Alice's spending so much extra time at the library), Margery had urged her to stay with her brother. Alice rode up Split Creek as dusk fell, noting that the light was still on, and wondered, given Sophia's absence, which of the librarians was still inside. Beth was always swift to finish, dumping her books and racing home to the farm (if she didn't get there quick enough her brothers would have eaten whatever food had been put by for her). Kathleen was equally keen to get home, to catch her children's last waking moments before bedtime. It was only she and Izzy who kept their horses at Fred's barn, and Izzy, it appeared, was gone from the project for good.

Alice unsaddled Spirit and stood for a minute in the warmth of the stall, then kissed the mare's sweet-smelling ears, pressing her face against her warm neck and finding treats for her when she nuzzled her pockets with her soft, inquisitive nose. She loved the animal now, knew her traits and strengths as well as she knew her own. The little horse was, she realized, the most constant relationship in her life. When she was sure the mare was comfortable, she headed for the back door of the library, from which she could still see a sliver of light through the unpapered gaps in the wood.

"Marge?" she called.

"Well, you sure do take your time."

Alice blinked at the sight of Fred, seated at a little table in the middle of the room, dressed in a clean flannel shirt and blue jeans.

"Took your point about not being seen with me in public. But I thought maybe we could have a meal together anyway."

Alice closed the door behind her, taking in the neatly laid table, with a little vase of coltsfoot, harbinger of spring, in the center, the two chairs, and the oil lamps flickering on the desks nearby, sending shadows over the spines of the books around them.

He seemed to take her shocked silence for reticence. "It's just pork and black bean stew. Nothing too fancy—I wasn't sure what time you'd make it back. The greens may have cooled a little. I didn't realize you'd be so thorough with that horse of mine." He lifted the lid off the heavy iron pot and the room was suddenly filled with the scent of slow-cooked meat. Beside her on the table sat a heavy pan of corn bread and a bowl of green beans.

Alice's stomach gurgled unexpectedly and loudly, and she pressed a hand to it, trying not to blush.

"Well, someone approves," Fred said evenly. He stood and walked over to pull out a chair for her.

She put her hat on the desk, and unwound her scarf. "Fred, I—"

"I know. But I enjoy your company, Alice. And being a man in these parts, I don't get to entertain someone like you too often." He leaned toward her to pour her a glass of wine. "So I'd be much obliged if you'd . . . indulge me?"

She opened her mouth to protest, then found she wasn't sure what she was protesting. When she looked up, he was watching her, waiting for a sign. "This all looks wonderful," she said.

He let out a little breath then, as if perhaps even up to that point he had not been sure whether she would cut and run. And then, as he began to serve the food, he smiled, a slow, broad smile that was so filled with satisfaction she couldn't help but smile back at him.

The Packhorse Library had become, in the months of its existence, a symbol of many things, and a focus for others, some controversial and some that would provoke unease in certain people however long it stayed around. But for one freezing damp evening in March, it became a tiny, glowing refuge. Two people locked safely inside, briefly released from their complicated histories and the weighty expectations of the town around them, ate good food and laughed and discussed poetry and stories, horses, and mistakes they had made, and while there was barely a touch between them, apart from the accidental brushing of skin against skin while passing bread or refilling a glass, Alice rediscovered a little part of her that she hadn't known she missed: the flirtatious young woman who liked to talk about things she had read, seen and thought about as much as she liked to ride a mountain track. In turn Fred enjoyed a woman's full attention, a ready laugh at his jokes and the challenge of an idea that might differ from his own. Time flew, and each ended the night full and happy, with the rare glow that comes from knowing your very being has been understood by somebody else, and that there might just be someone out there who will only ever see the best in you.

Fred lifted the table easily down the last of the steps, ready to move it back into his house, then turned back to double-lock the door. Alice stood beside him, wrapping her scarf around her face, her belly full and a smile on her lips. Both were shielded from view by the library and somehow found themselves standing just inches apart.

"You sure you won't let me drive you back up the mountain? It's cold, and dark, and that's a long walk."

She shook her head. "It'll feel like five minutes tonight."

He studied her in the half-light. "You ain't spooked by much these days, are you?"

"No."

"That'll be Margery's influence."

They smiled at each other and he looked briefly thoughtful. "Wait there."

He jogged up to the house and returned, a minute later, with a shotgun, which he handed to her. "Just in case," he said. "You might not be spooked, but it'll allow me to rest easy. Bring it back tomorrow."

She took it from him without protest, and there followed a strange, elongated couple of minutes, the kind in which two people know they have to part, and don't want to, and while neither can acknowledge it, each believes the other feels it too.

"Well," she said, at last, "it's getting late."

He rubbed his thumb speculatively across the table-top, his mouth closed over words he could not say.

"Thank you, Fred. It was honestly the nicest evening I've had. Probably since I came here. I—I really appreciate it."

A look passed between them that was a complicated mixture of things. An acknowledgment, of the kind that might normally make a heart sing, but cut with the knowledge that some things were impossible and that your heart could break a little knowing it.

And suddenly a little of the magic of the evening dissipated.

"Goodnight, then, Alice."

"Goodnight, Fred," she said. Then, placing the gun over her shoulder, she turned and strode up the road before he could say anything that would make more of a mess of things than they already were.

SIXTEEN

*That's the one trouble with this country: everything,
weather, all, hangs on too long. Like our rivers, our
land: opaque, slow, violent; shaping and creating the life
of man in its implacable and brooding image.*

· WILLIAM FAULKNER, *As I Lay Dying*

The rain came late into March, first turning the frozen sidewalks and stones into skating rinks, and then, through sheer relentlessness, obliterating the snow and ice on the lower ground in an endless gray sheet. There was limited pleasure to be found in the slight lifting of temperatures, the prospect of warmer days ahead. Because it didn't stop. After five days the rain had turned the unfinished roads to mud or, in some places, washed away the top layers completely, revealing sharp boulders and holes on the surface that would catch the unwary. Waiting horses stood tethered outside, their heads low and resigned, their tails clamped to their hindquarters, and cars bucked and growled along the slippery mountain roads. Farmers muttered in the feed store, while the shopkeepers observed that the Lord only knew why that much water was still hanging up there in the heavens.

Margery arrived back from her 5 a.m. round soaked to her socks, to find the librarians sitting with steepled fingers and fidgeting feet with Fred.

"Last time it rained like this, the Ohio burst its banks," said Beth, peering out of the open door, from where you could hear the gurgle of surface water as it made its way down the road. She took a last drag of her cigarette and ground it under the heel of her boot.

"Too wet to ride, that's for sure," said Margery. "I'm not taking Charley out again."

Fred had looked out first thing and warned Alice it was a bad idea, and though there was little that would normally stop her, she took him seriously. He had moved his own horses up onto high land, where they could just be seen in a slick, wet huddle.

"I'd put them in the barn," he had told her, as she helped him walk the last two up, "but they're safer up there." His father had once lost an entire locked barn of mares and foals when Fred was a boy: the river had flooded while the family was sleeping and by the time they woke only the hayloft was still above water. His father had wept in telling him, the only time Fred had ever seen that happen.

He told Alice of the great flood the previous year, how water had flipped whole houses and sent them downriver, of how many people died, and how they had found a cow wedged twenty-five feet up in a tree when the waters receded and had to shoot it to put it out of its misery—nobody could work out how to get it down.

The four of them sat in the library for an hour, nobody keen to leave, yet with nothing to be there for. They talked of misdeeds they'd performed as children, of the best bargains to be had in animal feed, of a man three of them knew who could whistle tunes through a missing tooth and add his voice to become a one-man orchestra. They talked about how if Izzy were here she would have sung them a song or two. But the rain grew heavier, and slowly the conversation ebbed away, and they were all left glancing at the door with a creeping sense of foreboding.

"What do you think, Fred?" Margery broke the silence.

"I don't like it."

"Me neither."

At that moment they heard the sound of horses' hoofs. Fred strode to the door, perhaps concerned it might be an escapee. But it was the mailman, water sluicing from the brim of his hat.

"The river's rising, and fast. We need to warn people on the creek beds but there's no one at the sheriff's office."

Margery turned to Beth and Alice.

"I'll get the bridles," said Beth.

Izzy was so deep in thought that she didn't notice when her mother took the embroidery off her lap and tutted loudly. "Oh, *Izzy*. I'm going to have to unpick all those stitches. That's nothing like the pattern whatsoever. What *have* you been doing?"

Mrs. Brady dragged a copy of *Woman's Home Companion* to her lap and flicked through until she found the pattern she was looking for. "Absolutely nothing like it. Why, you've done running stitch where it should be a chain stitch."

Izzy dragged her attention to the sampler. "I hate sewing."

"You never used to mind it. I don't know what's got into you lately." Izzy didn't rise to it, which made Mrs. Brady tut more loudly. "I've never met a girl more out of sorts."

"You know very well what's got into me. I'm bored and I'm stuck here, and I can't bear that you and Daddy have been swayed by an idiot like Geoffrey Van Cleve."

"That's no way to talk. Why don't you do some quilting? You used to enjoy it. I have some lovely old fabrics in my chest upstairs and—"

"I miss my horse."

"He was not your horse." Mrs. Brady closed her mouth and took a diplomatic moment before she opened it again. "But I was thinking we could perhaps buy you one if you think horseback riding is something you'd like to pursue."

"For what? To go around and around in circles? To make it look pretty, like a stupid doll? I miss my job, Mother, and I miss my friends. I had real friends for the first time in my life. I was happy at the library. Doesn't that mean anything to you?"

"Well, now you're just being dramatic." Mrs. Brady sighed, and sat down on the settle beside her daughter. "Look, dear, I know how you love singing. Why don't I talk to your father about some proper lessons? We could perhaps find out if there's anybody in Lexington who might help you work on your voice. Perhaps when Daddy hears how good you are he'll change his mind. Oh, Lord, though, we'll have to wait until this rain eases. Have you ever seen anything like it?"

Izzy didn't answer. She sat by the parlor window, gazing out at the blurred view.

"You know, I think I'm going to telephone your father. I'm anxious the river will flood. I lost good friends in the Louisville floods and I haven't felt the same about the river since. Why don't you unpick that last bit of stitching and we'll go back over it together?"

Mrs. Brady disappeared into the hallway and Izzy could hear her dialing her father's office, the low murmur of her voice. Izzy stared out of the window at the gray skies, her finger tracing the rivulets that zigzagged down the pane, squinting at a horizon that was no longer visible.

Well, your father thinks we should stay put. He says we might call Carrie Anderson in Old Louisville and see if she and her family want to rest here a day or two just in case. Lord knows what we'll do with all those little dogs of hers, though. I don't think we could cope with the—Izzy? . . . *Izzy?*" Mrs. Brady spun around in the empty parlor. "Izzy? Are you upstairs?"

She walked down the hall and through the kitchen, where the maid turned from her dough-rolling, nonplussed, and shook her head. And then Mrs. Brady saw the back door, the inside slick with raindrops. Her daughter's leg brace lay on the tiled floor, and her riding boots were gone.

Margery and Beth trotted hard down Main Street, a blur of hoofs and spraying water. Around them the unfinished road sent water sweeping down the hill and over their feet, while gutters gurgled, protesting against the weight of it. They rode with their heads low and their collars up, and when they got to the verges they cantered, the horses' feet sinking into the boggy grass. At the lower reaches of Spring Creek, they split to each side of the road and dismounted, running to each front door and hammering on it with wet fists.

"*Water's rising*," they yelled, as the horses pulled back on their reins. "*Get to higher ground.*"

Behind them, a straggle of occupants began to move, faces peering around doors, out of windows, trying to work out how seriously to take this instruction. By the time they were a quarter-mile down the road some behind them had begun hoisting furniture to the top floors of those houses that were double-storied, the rest loading wagons or trucks with what might be protected. Tarpaulins were thrown over the backs of open vehicles, small, querulous children wedged between gray-faced adults. People in Baileyville had had enough experience of floods to know that they were a threat to be taken seriously.

Margery hammered on the last door of Spring Creek, water plastering her hair to her face. "*Mrs. Cornish? . . . Mrs. Cornish?*"

A woman in a wet headscarf appeared at the door, waves of agitation rising off her. "Oh, thank goodness. Margery dear, I can't get my mule." She turned and ran, motioning to them to follow.

The mule was at the bottom of his paddock, which backed onto the creek. The lowest slopes, boggy on the driest of days, were now a thick slick of toffee-colored mud and the little brown and white mule stood immobile, apparently resigned, up to his chest in it.

"He can't seem to budge. Please help him."

Margery pulled at his halter. Then, when that made no difference, she placed her weight against him, trying to tug at a lone foreleg. The mule lifted his muzzle, but no other part of him moved.

"You see?" Mrs. Cornish's gnarly old hands wrung together. "He's stuck fast."

Beth ran to the other side and tried her best too, slapping on his rear end, yelling, and placing her shoulder against him, to no effect. Margery stepped back and looked over at Beth, who gave a small shake of her head.

She tried again with her shoulder against him but, apart from his ears flicking, not a part of the mule moved. Margery stopped, thinking.

"I can't leave him."

"We're not going to leave him, Mrs. Cornish. You got your harness? And some rope? Beth? Beth? C'mere. Mrs. Cornish, hold Charley for me, will you?"

As the rain beat down, the two younger women ran for the harness, then waded back to the mule. The water had risen even since they had arrived, creeping upward across the grass. Where for months it had been a sweet-sounding trickle, a sunlit brook, now it rushed in a wide, unforgiving yellow torrent. Margery slid the harness over the mule's head and fastened the buckles, her fingers slipping on the wet straps. The rain roared in their ears, so that they had to yell at each other and point to be understood, but months of working alongside each other had granted them a shorthand. Beth did the same on the other side, until both shouted: *"Done!"* They buckled the traces to the surcingle, then looped the rope through the brass hook at his shoulder.

Not many mules would tolerate a strap from their girth running through their legs but Charley was smart, and needed to be reassured just once. Beth attached her traces to her horse Scooter's breastplate, and, in unison, each began to urge their animal forward along the less waterlogged ground. *"Go on! Go on, Charley, now! Go on, Scooter!"*

The animals' ears flicked, Charley's eyes widening uncharacteristically as he felt the unfamiliar dead weight behind him. Beth urged him and Scooter forward while Margery tugged at the rope, yelling encouragement at the little mule, which flailed, his head bobbing as he felt himself being pulled forward.

"That's it, fella, you can do it."

Mrs. Cornish crouched on the other side of him, two broad planks laid on the mud in front of his chest, ready to give him something to brace against.

"Come up, boys!"

Margery turned, saw Charley and Scooter straining, their flanks shivering with effort as they dug into the ground in front, stumbling, mud clods flying up around them, and realized with dismay that the mule really was stuck fast. If Charley and Scooter kept digging down with their hoofs like that they would be stuck soon too.

Beth looked at her, her own mind already there. She grimaced. "We gotta leave him, Marge. Water's coming up real fast."

Margery placed a hand on the little mule's cheek. "We can't leave him."

They turned toward a shout. Two farmers were running toward them from the houses further back. Solid, middle-aged men Margery knew only by sight from the corn market, in overalls and oilcloths. They didn't say a word, just slid down beside the mule and began hauling at the harness along with Charley and Scooter, boots braced against the earth, their bodies at a forty-five-degree angle.

"*Go on! Go on, boys!*"

Margery joined them, put her head down, placing her whole weight against the rope. An inch. Another inch. A terrible sucking sound, and then the little mule's near front leg was freed. His head lifted in surprise, and the two men hauled again in unison, grunting with the effort, their muscles bulging against the rope. Charley and Scooter staggered in front of them, heads low, hind legs quivering with the effort, and suddenly, with a lurch, the mule was up, flipped on his side and pulled along the muddy grass a couple of feet before Charley and Scooter knew to stop. His eyes were wide with surprise and his nostrils flared before he stumbled to his feet, so that the men had to leap backward out of his way.

Margery barely had time to thank them. The briefest of nods, a tip to a wet hat brim, and they were gone, running back through the deluge to their own homes to retrieve what they could. Margery experienced a brief moment of pure love for the people she had grown up alongside, those who would not see a man—or a mule—struggle alone.

"Is he okay?" she yelled at Mrs. Cornish, who was running her weathered hands down the mule's mud-covered legs.

"He's good," she shouted back.

"You need to get to higher ground."

"I can take it from here, girls. You git on now!"

Margery winced suddenly at a complaint from some previously unknown muscle in her belly. She hesitated, doubled over, then stumbled toward Charley, as Beth unhooked the traces.

"Where next?" Beth yelled, hoisting herself aboard the skittering Scooter, and Margery, winded from the effort of climbing back aboard Charley, had to bend over a minute and catch her breath before she answered.

"Sophia," she said, suddenly. "I'm going to check on Sophia. If this place is flooding, then Sophia and William's will be, too. You head for the houses across the creek."

Beth nodded, wheeled her horse around, and was gone.

Kathleen and Alice loaded the wheelbarrow with books, covering them with sacking so that Fred could push it up the soaking path toward his home. They had only one barrow, and the women would load it as swiftly as they could, carrying the books in stacks toward the back door, then following him laden with as many other books as they could fit into four saddlebags, knees buckling under the weight, heads bowed against the weather. They had cleared maybe a third of the library in the past hour but since then the water had risen to the second step and Alice was afraid they wouldn't manage much more before it rose right over.

"You okay?" Fred passed Alice on the track back down. He was wrapped in oilcloth, and a trail of water ran from the side of his hat.

"I think Kathleen should leave. She shouldn't be away from her children."

Fred looked up at the skies, then down the road, where the mountains disappeared in a blur of gray. "Tell her to go," he said.

"But what will you do?" said Kathleen, minutes later. "You can't move all these, just the two of you."

"We'll save what we can. You need to go home."

When she hesitated again, Fred put his hand on her upper arm. "They're just books, Kathleen."

She didn't protest a second time. She just nodded, mounted Garrett's horse and swung round, cantering back up the road so that sprays of water shot out behind her.

They rested a moment and stood briefly in the dry of the cabin, watching her go, their chests heaving with the effort. Water dripped off their oilcloth coats into pools on the wooden floor.

"You sure you're okay, Alice? It's heavy work."

"I'm stronger than I look."

"Well, that's the truth."

They exchanged a small smile. Almost without thinking, Fred lifted a hand and slowly wiped a droplet of rain from under her eye with his thumb. Alice was briefly stilled by the electric shock of his skin on hers, by the unexpected intensity of his pale gray eyes, his lashes soaked into shining black points. She had the strangest urge to take his thumb into her mouth and bite it. Their eyes locked and she felt her breath pushed from her lungs, her face coloring, as if he could read her mind.

"Can I help?"

They sprang apart at the sight of Izzy in the doorway, her mother's car parked haphazardly up against the rail, her riding boots in her hand. The roaring of the rain on the tin roof had muffled the sound of her arrival.

"Izzy!" Alice's voice emerged in an embarrassed rush, too high, too shrill. She stepped forward impulsively and embraced her. "Oh, how we've missed you! Look, Fred, it's Izzy!"

"Came to see if I could help," said Izzy, blushing.

"That's—that's good news." Fred was about to speak then looked down and realized she was not wearing her leg brace. "You ain't going to be able to walk the track, are you?"

"Not very fast," she said.

"Okay. Let me think. You drove that thing here?" he said, incredulous.

Izzy nodded. "Not too good on the clutch with my left leg but if I lean on it with my stick I'm fine."

Fred's eyebrows shot up, but he swiftly lowered them. "Margery and Beth have taken the routes nearer the south side of town. Take the car as far up to the school as you can and tell them on the other side of the creek that they need to get to higher ground. But go across the footbridge. Don't try to drive that thing across the water, okay?"

Izzy ran for the car, her arms sheltering her head, and climbed in, trying to make sense of what she had just seen: Fred, cradling Alice's face tenderly in his hand, the two of them just inches apart. She felt, suddenly, like she had done at school, never quite party to whatever was going on, and pushed the thought away, trying to smother it in the memory of Alice's delight at seeing her. *Izzy, we've missed you!*

For the first time in a month, Izzy Brady felt something like herself again. She rammed her stick down onto the clutch, hauled the car into reverse, spun it round and set off for the far end of town, a determined jut to her chin, a woman once again with a mission.

Monarch Creek was already under a foot of water by the time they reached it. This was one of the lowest points of the county. There was a reason that this land had mostly been left to colored folk—it was lush, yes, but prone to flooding; mosquitoes and no-see-ums were thick in the air through the months of summer. Now, as Charley clattered down the hill through the sheeting rain, Margery could just make out Sophia, a wooden box atop her head, wading through the waters, her dress floating around her. A pile of her and William's belongings sat on the slopes of the patch of woodland above. From the doorway William looked out, his face anxious, his wooden crutch wedged under his armpit.

"Oh, thank the Lord!" Sophia yelled, as Margery approached. "We need to save our things."

Margery jumped off the mule and ran toward the house, heading into the water. Sophia had rigged up a rope between the porch and a telegraph pole by the road, and Margery now used this to make her way across the creek. The water was icy and the current ominously strong, although it only came to her knees. Inside the house Sophia's cherished furniture had toppled over; the smaller items bobbing in the water. Margery found herself momentarily paralyzed: what to save? She grabbed for photographs on the wall, for books and ornaments, wedging them into her coat and reaching out for a side table, which she hauled to the doorway and out onto the grass. Her belly ached, the pain low in her pelvis, and she found herself wincing.

"You can't save no more," she yelled at Sophia. "Water's coming up too fast."

"That's everything we own in there." Sophia's voice was despairing.

Margery bit her lip. "One more trip, then."

William was moving around the flooded room, using his arms to support himself on the wall, trying to corral essentials—a pan, a chopping board, two bowls—clasping them in his huge hands. "That rain easing off any?" he said, but his face suggested he already knew the answer.

"It's time to get out, William," she said.

"Let me just fetch a couple more."

How do you tell a proud amputee he can be of no help? How do you tell him the mere fact of him being in there is not just a hindrance but likely to put them all at risk? Margery bit back her words and reached for Sophia's embroidery box, wedging it under her arm and wading outside, where she grabbed a wooden chair from the porch with her other, hauling them up to dry land, grunting with the effort. Then the pile of blankets, ported high above her head. Lord knew how they were going to dry those out. She looked down, feeling the sharp protest again from her womb. The water was now up to her crotch, her long coat swirling around her thighs. Three inches higher in the last ten minutes?

"*We got to go!*" she yelled, as Sophia, her head down, made her way back in. "*No time.*"

Sophia nodded, her face pained. Margery made it out of the water, feeling it drag at her, shifting and insistent. Up on the bank Charley shifted nervously, his reins taut against the pole, signaling his own desire to be far from there. He didn't like water, never had, and she took a second to soothe him. "I know, fella. You're doing so good."

Margery placed the last of Sophia's items on the pile, pulling the tarpaulin over them, and wondering whether she could move any of it further up the hill. Something fluttered deep inside and she was startled until she realized what it was. She stopped and placed her hand upon her belly, feeling it again, flooded with an emotion she couldn't identify.

"*Margery!*"

She spun round to see Sophia clutching at William's sleeve. There appeared to have been some kind of surge and she was now up to her waist. The water, Margery saw, had turned black. "Oh, Lord," she murmured. "*Stay there!*"

Sophia and William had stepped down gingerly onto the underwater steps, one hand each gripping the rope, Sophia's free arm tight around her brother's waist. The inky water rushed past them, its force sending a strange energy into the air. William's eyes were down, his knuckles taut as he tried to steer his crutch forward through the swollen river.

Margery half ran, half stumbled down the hill, her eyes on them as they made their way toward her.

"Keep coming! You can make it!" she yelled, skidding to a stop at the edge. And then—*snap!*—the rope gave way, sending both Sophia and William off their feet and flinging them downstream. Sophia shrieked. She was thrown forward, her arms out, disappeared for a moment and then, emerging, managed to grab hold of a bush, her hands closing tight around its branches. Margery ran alongside her, her heart in her throat. She threw herself down on her belly and grabbed hold of Sophia's wet wrist. Sophia switched her grip to Margery's other wrist and, after a second, Margery had hauled her up the bank, where she collapsed backward and Sophia crouched on her muddied hands and knees, her clothes black and sodden, panting with the effort.

"William!"

Margery turned at Sophia's voice to see William half submerged, his face screwed up with effort as he tried to haul himself back along the rope. His crutch had disappeared and the water was around his waist.

"I can't get through!" he yelled.

"Can he swim?"

"No!" wailed Sophia.

Margery ran for Charley, her wet clothes dragging at every step. Somewhere she had lost her hat and the water sent her hair cascading over her face, so that she had to keep pushing it back to see.

"Okay, boy," she murmured, unhooking Charley's reins from the pole. "I need you to help me now."

She pulled him down the bank and to the water where she waded in, her free hand out to the side to steady her, her boots testing the ground for obstacles. He stalled at first, his ears flat back and his eyes white, but at her urging he took a tentative step and then another and, huge ears flicking forward and back at the sound of her voice, he was splashing his way through, beside Margery, pushing against the torrent. William was gasping by the time they reached him, both hands on the rope as he scrabbled for purchase. He grabbed blindly at Margery, his face a mask of panic, and she yelled to be heard above the sound of the water. *Just hold him round his neck, William, okay? Wrap your arms around his neck.*

William held on to the mule, his great body pressed against Charley's, and, groaning with the effort, Margery turned the two of them in the depths of the floodwater, back toward the bank, the mule protesting mutely at every step. The black water was up to her chest now and Charley, frightened, lifted his muzzle and tried to half leap forward. Another surge of water hit them, and as everything rushed around her she felt his legs lift and was filled with sudden terror, as if the ground would surely slip away from them all for good, but just as she thought they, too, would be carried away, she felt her feet touch the ground again, knew Charley's had done the same, and she felt him take another tentative step forward.

"*You okay, William?*"

"*I'm here.*"

"*Good boy, Charley. Come on, boy.*"

Time slowed. They seemed to move forward in inches. She had no idea what was underneath. A solitary wooden drawer of neatly folded clothing floated by in front of them, followed by another, and then a small dead dog. She noted them only with some distant part of her brain. The black water had become a living, breathing thing. It snatched and pulled at her coat, blocking progress, demanding submission. It was relentless, deafening, and made fear rise, like iron, in her throat. Margery was now blue with cold, her skin pressed against Charley's chestnut neck, her head bumping against William's great arms, all consciousness reduced to one thing.

Just get me home, boy, please.

One step.

Two.

"*You okay there, Margery?*"

She felt William's great hand on her arm, gripping her, and was unsure whether it was for his security or her own. The world had receded until it was just her and William and the mule, the roar in her ears, William's voice murmuring a prayer she couldn't make out, Charley straining valiantly against the water, his body buffeted by a force he didn't understand, the ground slipping and sliding away from him every few steps, then again. A log whooshed past them, too big, too fast. Her eyes stung, filled with grit and water. She was dimly aware of Sophia reaching forward from the bank, her hand outstretched, as if she could haul the three of them up by force. Voices joined hers from the bank. A man. More men. She could no longer see through the water in her eyes. She could think about nothing, her fingers, now numb, wound into Charley's short mane, her other hand on his bridle. *Six more steps. Four more steps. A yard.*

Please.

Please.

Please.

And then the mule lurched forward and upward and she could feel strong hands reaching for her, pulling at her shoulders, her sleeves, her body a landed fish, William's shaking voice, *"Thank you, Lord! Thank you!"* Margery, feeling the river reluctantly relinquish its grip, uttered the same words silently through frozen lips. Her clenched fist, Charley's hair still woven through her fingers, moved unthinkingly to her belly.

And then everything went black.

SEVENTEEN

★

Beth heard the girls before she saw them, their voices high above the roar of the water, childish and shrill. They clung to the front of a ramshackle cabin, their feet ankle deep in water, and yelling at her, "*Miss! Miss!*" She tried to recall the family name—McCarthy? McCallister?—and urged her horse across the water, but Scooter, already spooked by the strange electric atmosphere of the air and the dense, punishing rain, had made it partway across the swollen creek, then half reared and spun away so that she almost fell off. She righted herself but he would not be moved, snorting and running backward until his brain was so addled she feared he would do himself an injury.

Cursing, Beth had dismounted, thrown his reins over a pole and waded across the water toward them. They were young, the youngest maybe two at most, and clad in thin cotton dresses that clung to their pale skin. As she approached, they clamored for her, six little anemone arms, reaching, waving. She got to them just before the surge. A rush of black water, so fast and hard that she had to grab the baby around her middle to stop her being carried away. And then there she was, three small children huddled around her, gripping her coat, her voice making reassuring noises even as her brain raced to work out how in hell she was going to make her way out of this one.

"*Is anyone in the house?*" she yelled at the eldest, trying to be heard above the torrent. The child shook her head. *Well, that's something,* she thought, pushing away visions of bedbound grandmothers. Beth's bad arm ached already, holding the baby tight to her chest. She could see Scooter on the other side, jittering around the pole, no doubt ready to snap his reins and bolt. She had liked the fact that he was part Thoroughbred when Fred offered him to her; he was fast and showy and didn't need to be pushed to go forward. Now she cursed his tendency to panic, his pea-sized brain. How was she going to get three babies onto him? She looked down as the water lapped around her boots, seeping into her stockings, and her heart sank.

"Miss, are we stuck?"

"No, we ain't stuck."

And then she heard it, the whine of a car headed down the road toward her. Mrs. Brady? She squinted to see. The car slowed, stopped, and then, lo and behold, if Izzy Brady didn't climb out, her hand sheltering her eyes as she tried to work out what she was seeing across the water.

"Izzy? That you? I need help!"

They shouted instructions to each other across the creek, but were unable to hear each other properly amid the noise. Finally Izzy waved her hand, as if to wait, crunched the big glossy car into gear and began to creep forward toward them, its engine roaring.

You can't drive the damn car across the water, Beth breathed, shaking her head. *Did the girl have no sense at all?* But Izzy stopped just as the front wheels were almost submerged, then ran lopsidedly to the trunk and hauled it open, pulling out a rope. She ran back to the front of the car, unspooling it, and hurled the end of the rope at Beth, once, twice, and again before Beth was able to catch it. Now Beth understood. At this distance it was just long enough to secure to the post of the porch. Beth put her weight on it and noted with relief that it held firm.

"Your belt," Izzy was yelling, gesticulating. *"Tie your belt around the rope."* She was securing her end of the rope to the car, her hands swift and certain. And then Izzy took hold of the rope and began to make her way toward them, her limp no longer visible as she navigated the water. "You okay?" she said, as she reached them, hauling herself onto

the porch. Her hair was flat and under her felt coat her pale, baby-soft sweater sagged with water.

"Take the baby," Beth answered. She wanted to hug Izzy then, an uncharacteristic feeling, which she smothered in brisk activity. Izzy grasped the child, and gave the little girl a beaming smile, as if they were simply out on a picnic. All the while she was smiling, Izzy pulled her scarf from around her neck and wrapped it around the eldest's waist, tying it to the rope.

"Now, me and Beth, we're going to walk across, holding on, and you're gonna be right between us, tied to the rope. You hear?"

The eldest child, her eyes wide and round, shook her head.

"It'll only take us a minute to get across. And then we'll all be nice and dry on the other side and we can get you back to your mama. C'mon, sweetie."

"I'm scared," the child mouthed.

"I know, but we still have to get across."

The child glanced at the water, then took a step backward, as if to disappear inside the cabin.

Beth and Izzy exchanged a look. The water was rising fast.

"How about we sing a song?" Izzy said. She crouched down to the child's level. "When I'm afeared of anything, I sing me a happy song. Makes me feel better. What songs do you know?"

The child was trembling. But her eyes were on Izzy's.

"How about 'Camptown Races'? You know that one, right, Beth?"

"Oh, my favorite," said Beth, one eye on the water.

"Okay!" said Izzy.

The Camptown ladies sing this song
Doo-da, doo-da.
The Camptown racetrack's five miles long
Oh, de doo-da day.

She smiled, stepping back into the water, which was now at thigh level. She kept her eye on the child, beckoning her forward, her voice high and cheerful, as if she had not a care in the world.

Going to run all night
Going to run all day
I bet my money on a bob-tailed nag
Somebody bet on the bay.

"That's it, sweetheart, you follow me. Hold on tight now."

Beth slid in behind them, the middle child high on her hip. She could feel the force of the current beneath, smell the hint of acrid chemicals infusing it. There was nothing she wanted to do less than forge this water, and she didn't blame the kid for not wanting to, either. She held the toddler close, and the child plugged in her thumb, closing her eyes, as if removing herself from what she saw around her.

"C'mon, Beth," came Izzy's voice from in front, insistent, musical. "You join in too now."

Oh, the long-tailed filly and the big black horse
Doo-da, doo-da
Come to a mud hole and they all cut across,
Oh, de doo-da day.

And there they were, wading across, Beth's voice reedy and her breath somewhere in her chest, nudging the child forward. The little girl sang haltingly, her knuckles white on the rope, her face contorted with fear, yelping as she was occasionally lifted off her feet. Izzy kept glancing back, urging Beth to keep on singing, keep on moving.

The water was building in height and speed. She could hear Izzy in front of her, calm and upbeat. "And there, now, aren't we pretty much through? How about that. '*Going to run all night, going to run all—*'"

Beth looked up as Izzy stopped singing. She thought, distantly, *I'm sure the car wasn't that far in the water.* And then Izzy was hauling at the

eldest girl's waistband, her fingers fumbling as she tried to release the
knot in her scarf, and Beth suddenly understood why she had stopped
singing, her look of panic, and half threw her own charge onto the
bank as she grabbed at her belt and tried to release the buckle.

Hurry up, Beth! Undo it!

Her fingers turned to thumbs. Panic rose in her throat. She felt
Izzy's hands grabbing at the belt, lifting it so that it was clear of water,
felt the ominous pressure building as it tightened around her waist—
and then, just as she felt herself being pulled forward, *click*, the belt was
slipping through her fingers, and Izzy was hauling at her with a
strength she'd had no idea she had and suddenly, *whoosh*, the big green
car was half submerged and moving down the river at an unlikely
speed, away from them, on the end of its rope.

They scrambled to their feet, stumbling up the hill toward the
higher ground, the children's hands tight in their own, their eyes
transfixed by what was unfolding before them. The rope tightened,
the car bobbed, briefly tethered, and then, faced with an unstoppable
weight, and with an audible fraying sound, the rope, defeated by sheer
weight and physics, snapped.

Mrs. Brady's Oldsmobile, custom-painted in racing green, with a
cream-leather interior all the way from Detroit, turned over elegantly,
like a giant seal revealing its belly. As the five of them watched, drip-
ping and shivering, it rode away from them, half submerged, on the
black tide, turned a corner, and the last of its chrome bumper disappeared around the bend.

Nobody spoke. And then the baby held up her arms and Izzy
stooped to pick her up. "Well," she said, after a minute. "I guess that's
me grounded for the next ten years."

And Beth, who was not known for great shows of emotion, but
suddenly propelled by an impulse she barely understood, reached over
and pulled Izzy to her and kissed the side of Izzy's face, a huge, audible
smacker, so that the two of them began the slow walk back to town a
little pink and, to the confusion of the small girls, prone to abrupt and
seemingly inexplicable bursts of laughter.

D*one!*
The last of the books were tipped into Fred's living room. The door was closed and Fred and Alice regarded the mountainous pile that had taken over his once-tidy parlor, then looked up at each other.

"Every single one," Alice marveled. "We saved every single one."

"Yup. We'll be open for business before you know it."

He set the kettle on the stove, and peered into his larder. He reached in, pulled out some eggs and cheese and put them on the counter. "So . . . I was thinking you could rest here awhile. Maybe have some food. Nobody'll be going too far today."

"I guess there's no point heading back out while it's like this." She put her hand to her head, rubbing at her wet hair.

They knew of the dangers, but for that moment, Alice couldn't help but see the water, running past them down the road below, as her secret ally, halting the normal flow of the world. Nobody could judge her for resting at Fred's, could they? She had only been moving books, after all.

"If you want to borrow a dry shirt there's one hanging on the stairs."

She headed upstairs, peeled off her wet sweater, dried herself with a towel and put on the shirt, feeling the soft flannel against her damp skin as she buttoned it down the front. There was something about sliding into a man's shirt—Fred's shirt—that made her breath catch in her throat. She could not rid herself of the feeling of his thumb on her skin, the image of his eyes burning so intently into her own, as if he could see the very core of her. Every movement now seemed loaded with the echo of it, every casual glance or word between them filled with some new intent.

She walked slowly back down the stairs toward the books, feeling the heat rise in her, as it did every time she thought of his skin touching hers. When she looked round for him, he was watching her.

"You look prettier in that shirt than I do."

She felt herself color and glanced away.

"Here." He handed her a mug of hot coffee and she closed her hands around it, allowing the heat to seep in, grateful for something to focus on.

Fred moved around her, shifting books, then reaching into the log basket to load the fire. She watched the muscles of his forearms tighten as he worked, the steel in his thighs as he crouched down, checking the flames. How had nobody else in this town noticed the beautiful economy in the way Frederick Guisler moved, the grace with which he used his limbs, the wiry muscles that shifted underneath his skin?

Let the flickering flame of your soul play all about me
That into my limbs may come the keenness of fire . . .

He straightened up and turned to her and she knew he must see it then, the naked truth of everything she felt, writ large upon her face. Today, she thought suddenly, no rules applied. They were in a vortex, a place of their own, away from water and misery and the travails of the world outside. She took a step toward him as if she were magnetized, stepping over the books without looking down, and placed her mug upon the mantel, her eyes still on his. They were inches from each other now, the heat of the blazing fire against their bodies, their eyes locked. She wanted to speak but she didn't have a clue what to say. She just knew that she wanted him to touch her again, to feel his skin on her lips, under her fingertips. She wanted to know what everyone else seemed to know so casually and easily, secrets whispered in darkened rooms, intimacy that went far beyond words. She felt consumed by it. His eyes searched hers and softened, his breath quickening, and she knew then that she had him. That this time it would be different. He reached down and took her hand and she felt something shoot through her, molten and urgent, and then he raised it, and she heard her breath catch.

And then he said: "I'm going to stop this here, Alice."

It took a second before she registered what he was saying, and the shock was so great it almost winded her.

Alice, you are too impulsive.

"It's not that—"

"I need to leave." She turned, humiliated. *How could she have been so foolish?* Tears brimmed in her eyes and she stumbled over the books and cursed loudly as she almost lost her footing.

"Alice."

Where was her coat? Did he hang it somewhere? "My coat. Where's my coat?"

"Alice."

"Please leave me alone." She felt his hand on her arm and she snatched it away and held it up to her chest, as if she had been burned. "Don't *touch* me."

"Don't leave."

She felt, embarrassingly, as if she might sob. Her face crumpled and she covered it with her hand.

"Alice. Please. Hear me out." He swallowed, compressed his mouth, as if it were hard to speak. "Don't leave. If you had any idea . . . any idea how much I want you here, Alice, that most nights I lie awake half crazy with it . . ." His voice came in low, uncharacteristic bursts. "I love you. Have done since the first day I laid eyes on you. When you're not around me it feels like I'm just wasting time. When you're here it's like . . . the whole world is colored just that little bit brighter. I want to feel your skin against mine. I want to see your smile and hear that laugh of yours when you forget yourself and just let it burst straight out of you . . . I want to make you happy . . . I want to wake up every morning beside you and—and—" he screwed up his face briefly, as if he had gone too far "—and you're *married*. And I'm trying real hard to be a good man. So until I can work a way around that, I can't. I just can't lay a finger on you. Not how I want to." He took a deep breath and let it out in a shaky exhalation. "All I can give you, Alice, is . . . words."

A whirlwind had entered the room and turned the whole thing upside down. Now it settled around Alice, tiny dust motes glittering as they fell.

A few years passed. She waited until she could be sure her voice had returned to normal. "Words."

He nodded.

She considered this, wiped at her eyes with the back of her hand. She held her hand briefly to her chest, waiting for the beating to subside a little, and when he saw it he winced, as if he had caused her pain.

"I suppose I could stay a while longer," she said.

"Coffee," he said, after a moment, and handed it to her. He took care that his fingers didn't brush hers.

"Thank you."

They exchanged a brief look. She let out a long breath, and then, without saying anything more, they stood side by side and began restacking the books.

It had stopped raining. Mr. and Mrs. Brady picked up their daughter in Mr. Brady's large Ford, and accepted without protest the additional passengers, three small girls who would be houseguests at least until morning. Mr. Brady listened to the tale of the children, and the rope and Mrs. Brady's car, and while he said nothing, digesting the loss of the vehicle, his wife swept in and hugged her daughter tightly and uncharacteristically silently for some minutes before releasing her, her eyes brimming. They opened the car doors in silence and began the short drive home, while Beth began to walk the waterlogged upper trail back to her house, her hand raised in good-bye until the car disappeared from view.

Margery woke to feel Sven's warm hand entwined in hers. She tightened her fingers on it reflexively before creeping consciousness told her all the reasons why she might not. She was half buried under blankets and quilts, the weight of them almost too much, pinning her down. Now she moved each toe speculatively, reassured by the obedience with which her body responded.

She opened her eyes, blinking, and took in the dark, the oil lamp beside the bed. Sven's gaze flickered toward her and they locked eyes, just as her thoughts coalesced into something that made sense. Her voice, when it emerged, was hoarse.

"How long have I been out?"

"A little over six hours."

She absorbed this.

"Sophia and William all right?"

"They're downstairs. Sophia's fixing some food."

"The girls?"

"All safely in. Looks like Baileyville lost four houses, and that settlement just below Hoffman was all destroyed, though I'm guessing it could be more by dawn. River's still up but it stopped raining an hour or two back so we got to hope that's the worst of it."

As he spoke, her body recalled the force of the river against her, the swirling forces that dragged at her, and she shivered involuntarily.

"Charley?"

"All good. I rubbed him down and rewarded him for his bravery with a bucket of carrots and apples. He tried to kick me for it."

She raised a small smile. "Never knew a mule like him, Sven. I asked so much of him."

"Word is you helped a lot of people."

"Anyone would have done it."

"But they didn't."

She lay still, bone-tired, acceding to the pressure of the bedcovers, the soporific warmth. Her hand, deep under the covers, slid across to the swelling of her stomach and, after a minute, she felt the answering flutter that made something in her ease.

"So," he said. "Were you going to tell me?"

She looked up at him then, at his kind, serious face.

"Had to get you undressed to get you into bed. Finally worked out why you've been pushing me away all these weeks."

"I'm sorry, Sven. I didn't . . . I couldn't think what to do." She blinked back unexpected tears. "Guess I was afraid. Never wanted

267

babies, you know that. Never been the kind cut out to be a mother."
She sniffed. "Couldn't even protect my own dog, could I?"

"Marge—"

She wiped at her eyes. "Guess I thought if I ignored it, what with my
age and all, it might . . ." she shrugged ". . . go away . . ." He winced then,
a man who couldn't bear to see a farmer drown a kitten. ". . . but . . ."

"But?"

She said nothing for a moment. Then her voice lowered to a whisper:
"I can feel her. Telling me things. And I realized it out there on the
water. It ain't really a question. She's here already. Wants to be here."

"She?"

"I know it."

He smiled, shook his head. Her hand was still smeared with black
and he let his thumb slide over it. Then he rubbed the back of his
head. "So we're going to do this."

"I guess."

They sat for a while in the half-dark, each accommodating the
prospect of a new and unexpected future. Downstairs she could hear
the low murmur of voices, the clatter of pans and plates.

"Sven."

He turned back to her.

"Do you think—all this business with the floods, all the lifting and
pulling and the black water, do you think it will hurt the baby? I had
these pains. And I got awful cold. Still don't feel myself."

"Any now?"

"Nothing since . . . well, I don't remember."

Sven considered his response carefully. "Out of our hands, Marge,"
he said. He enfolded her fingers in his. "But she's part of you. And if
she's part of Margery O'Hare, you can bet she's made of iron filings.
If any baby can make it through a storm like that, it'll be yours."

"Ours," she corrected him. She took his hand then and brought it
under the covers so that he could rest his warm palm across her belly, his
eyes on hers the whole time. She lay perfectly still for a minute, feeling
the deep, deep sense of peace that came with his skin on hers, and then,

obligingly, the baby moved again, just the faintest whisper, and their eyes widened in unison, his searching hers for confirmation of what he had just felt.

She nodded.

And Sven Gustavsson, a man not known for high emotion, pulled his free hand down over his face, and had to turn away so that she wouldn't see the tears in his eyes.

The Bradys were not accustomed to using harsh words; while their union could not be described as the perfect meeting of minds, neither enjoyed conflict within the home, and each held for the other such a healthy respect that they rarely allowed themselves an openly cross exchange, and knew each other's responses well enough after the best part of thirty years to usually avoid it.

So the evening that followed the floods sent something of a seismic shock through the Brady household. Mrs. Brady, having overseen the feeding and watering of the three children in the guest bedroom, seen Izzy off to bed, and having waited till all the servants had retired, had announced her daughter's intention to rejoin the Packhorse Library project, using a tone that suggested she would accept no further discussion on the matter. Mr. Brady, having asked her to repeat those words twice just to ensure he had heard correctly, responded uncharacteristically robustly—his temper might have been frayed by the loss of a car, and the frequent telephone calls he had received, detailing flooding in various business enterprises in Louisville. Mrs. Brady responded with no less emphasis, informing her husband that she knew their daughter like she knew herself and that she was never prouder of her than she had been that day. He could sit back and let her end up a dissatisfied, unconfident stay-at-home like his sister had been—and they all knew how *that* had turned out—or encourage this bold, enterprising and hitherto unseen version of the girl they had known these twenty years and let her do the thing she loved. And, she added, at some pitch, that if he listened to that fool Van Cleve over his own daughter then, why, she was not sure who it was she had been married to all these years.

Those were fighting words. Mr. Brady met them with equal force, and although their house was large, their voices echoed through the wide, wood-paneled corridors and on through the night until dawn broke—unheard by the comatose children, or Izzy, who had fallen abruptly off a cliff of sleep—at which point, having reached an uneasy truce, both exhausted by this unexpected turn in their union, Mr. Brady announced wearily that he needed an hour of shut-eye at least, because there was a big day of cleaning up ahead and Lord only knew how he was supposed to get through it now.

Mrs. Brady, deflated a little in victory, felt a sudden tenderness for her husband and, after a moment, reached out a conciliatory hand. And it was like this, as the light broke, that the maid found them an hour and a half later, still fully dressed, and snoring on the huge mahogany bed, their hands entwined between them.

EIGHTEEN

An enterprising grocer in Oklahoma recently sold two dozen buggy whips in two days. Three customers however said theirs would be used for fishing poles, while one was sold to a mother who wanted to "whale" her son.

· The Furrow, *September–October 1937*

argery was washing her hair on Sunday morning, her head low over a bucket of warm water, sluicing and wringing it into a thick glossy rope, when Alice walked in. Alice muttered an apology, half asleep and a little groggy—*she hadn't realized anyone was in there*—and began to back out of the little kitchen when she caught sight of Margery's belly, briefly visible through her thin cotton nightdress, and did a double-take. Margery looked sideways at her, wrapping a cotton sheet around her head, and caught it. She straightened up, placing her palm over her belly button.

"Yes, it is, yes, I am, just over six months, and I know. Not exactly part of the plan."

Alice's hand flew to her mouth. She recalled suddenly the sight of Margery and Sven at the Nice 'N' Quick the night before, how she had sat on his lap all evening, his hands wrapped protectively around her middle. "But—"

"Guess I didn't pay as much attention to that little blue book as I should have done."

"But—but what are you going to do?" Alice couldn't take her eyes off the roundness of it. It seemed so unlikely. Margery's breasts, she saw now, were almost obscenely full, a hint of blue veins criss-crossing her chest where her robe had slipped to reveal a sliver of pale skin.

"Do? Not much I can do."

"But you're not married!"

"Married! That's what you're fretting about?" Margery let out a hoot. "Alice, you think I give a fig what people around here think of me? Why, Sven and I are good as married. We'll bring the child up and we'll be sweeter to her and to each other than most married people around here. I'll educate her and teach her right from wrong, and as long as she has her ma and pa to love her, I can't see as what I'm wearing on my left hand is anyone else's business."

Alice couldn't get her head around the idea that someone could be six months pregnant and not care that her baby might be a bastard, that it might even go to Hell. And yet faced with Margery's cheerful certainty, her—yes, looking closely at her face, one might even call it radiance—it was hard to maintain that this really was a disaster.

She let out a long breath. "Does . . . anyone . . . know?"

"Aside from Sven?" Margery rubbed at her hair vigorously, then paused to check the dampness of her hair with her fingers. "Well, we haven't exactly hollered about it. But I can't keep it quiet for much longer. Poor old Charley will be buckling at the knees if I get much bigger."

A baby. Alice was filled with a complex mix of emotions—shock, admiration that, yet again, Margery had decided to play life by her own rules—but shot through it all, sadness: that everything had to change, that she might not again have her friend to gallop up mountainsides, to laugh with in the snug confines of the library. Margery would surely stay home now, a mother like everyone else. She wondered what would even happen to the library with Margery gone: she was the heart and backbone of it. And then a more worrying thought occurred. How could she stay here once the baby was born? There would be no room. There was barely enough for the three of them as it was.

"I can pretty much hear you fretting from here, Alice," Margery called, as she walked back through to her bedroom. "And I'm telling you nothing needs to change. We'll worry about the baby when it comes. No point winding yourself into a knot until then."

"I'm fine," Alice said. "Just pleased for you." And wished desperately that it was true.

Margery rode down to Monarch Creek on Saturday, nodding greetings as she passed families busy cleaning up, sweeping wet piles of silt out of their front doors, ferrying ruined furniture into piles only good enough to dry out for firewood. The floods had devastated the lower reaches of the town, home to the poorer families who were less likely to make a noise about it. Or at least have that noise listened to. In the more affluent parts of town, life had already pretty much returned to normal.

She pulled Charley to a halt outside Sophia and William's house, her heart sinking as she surveyed the damage. You could know something to be true, but it was something else having to look it square in the eye. The little house stood—just—but positioned at the lowest part of the road, as it was, it had borne the brunt of the flood. The posts of the neat deck were cracked and broken, while the flowerpots and the rocking chair that had stood on it had been washed away, along with the two front windows.

What had been a neat little vegetable garden was now a sea of black mud, from which random pieces of broken wood emerged in place of plants, and the stench was foul and sulfurous. A thick dark tidemark rode along the upper part of the frames and weatherboarding, and Margery didn't need to go any further to guess what it was like inside. She shivered, recalling the water's cold grip, and placed her palm against Charley's soft neck, feeling a sudden visceral urge to head home to warmth and safety.

She dismounted—it took a little more effort to clear the saddle now—and hooked the reins on a nearby tree. There was nothing for the mule to graze; just dark sludge for some distance up the slopes.

"William?" she called, her boots squelching as she made her way toward the little cabin. "William? It's Margery."

She called a couple more times, waiting until it was clear that nobody was at home, then turned back to the mule, feeling the unfamiliar stretch and weight in her belly, as if the baby had decided she was now free to make her presence felt. She stopped by the tree, and was reaching for the reins when something caught her eye. She tilted her head, studying the tidemark several feet up from the base of the trunk. The whole way down from the library the marks left by the river had been red-brown, varying in color but essentially mud or silt. The marks here were as black as pitch. She recalled how the water had turned dark abruptly, the chemical tang that had stung her eyes and caught the back of her throat.

Van Cleve had not been seen in town for the three days since the flood.

She squatted, running her fingers across the tree bark, then sniffed them. She stayed there, completely still, thinking. Then she wiped her hands on her jacket and, with a grunt, hoisted herself back into the saddle. "C'mon, Charley boy," she said, turning him around. "We're not going home just yet."

Margery rode high up into the narrow pass to the northeast of Baileyville, a route most considered impassable, given the steepness of the terrain and the dense undergrowth. But both she and Charley, having been raised on rough ground, could see a way through as instinctively as a boss could see a dollar sign, and she dropped the buckle of the reins onto his neck and leaned forward, trusting him to pick a path through while she lifted branches clear of her head. The air grew colder the higher they traveled. Margery wedged her hat down on her head and tucked her chin into her collar, watching her breath rise in damp clouds.

The trees grew closer the higher they went, and the ground was so steep and flinty that Charley, sure-footed as he was, began to stumble and hesitate. She climbed down finally by a rocky outcrop, hooked his reins on some saplings, and hiked the rest of the way to the top on foot, puffing a little with the extra weight of her new cargo. Every now and then she would pause, her hand in the small of her back. She had felt uncommonly tired since the flood and pushed away the knowledge of what Sven would say if he knew where she'd gone.

It took the best part of an hour to climb far enough on the ridge that she could finally see the back of Hoffman, the part of its 600-acre site not visible from the mines, and shielded from wider view by the horseshoe of steep, tree-covered slopes that surrounded it. She grabbed on to a trunk to haul herself up the last few feet and then stood a moment, allowing her breath to settle.

And then she looked down and cursed.

Three vast slurry dams stood behind the ridge, accessible only via a gated tunnel through the mountaintop. Two were full of dull, inky water, still swollen by the rains. The third was empty, its muddy base stained black, and its embankment crumbled to nothing where the slurry had burst out and down the other side, leaving a brackish trail along the winding riverbeds toward the lower end of Baileyville.

I f all the days that Annie could pick to suffer with her legs, this was just about the most inconvenient. Van Cleve muttered to himself as he waited in the booth for the girl to bring his food. Across from him Bennett sat in silence, his eyes sliding toward the other customers as if he were even now trying to gauge what people were saying about them. Van Cleve would have preferred a few more days steering clear of the town, but when your maid wasn't there to cook a meal and your daughter-in-law had still not seen sense and returned home, what was a man to do? Short of driving halfway to Lexington, the Nice 'N' Quick was the only place one could get a hot meal.

"Here you are, Mr. Van Cleve," said Molly, placing a plate of fried chicken in front of him. "Extra greens and mashed potato, just like you said. You was lucky you ordered when you did—cook's nearly out today, what with the deliveries not getting through and all."

"Well, aren't we the lucky ones!" he exclaimed. Van Cleve's mood lifted at the golden, crispy-skinned sight of his dinner. He let out a sigh of satisfaction and tucked his napkin into his collar. He was about to suggest Bennett did the same, rather than fold his on his lap like some damned European, when a gobbet of black mud dropped through the air above his plate and landed with an audible *slop* on his portion of chicken. He stared at it, struggling to register what he was seeing. "What the—"

"You missing something, Van Cleve?"

Margery O'Hare stood over his table, her color high and her voice shaking with rage. She held her arm extended, her fist blackened with slurry. "That wasn't floods took out those houses round Monarch Creek. That was your slurry dam and you knew it. You ought to be ashamed of yourself!"

The restaurant fell silent. Behind her a couple of people stood up to see what was going on.

"You dropped *mud* on my *dinner*?" Van Cleve stood, his chair pushing back with a squeal. "You come in here, after all you've done, and drop *dirt* on my food?"

Margery's eyes glittered. "Not dirt. Coal slurry. Poison. *Your* poison. I went up on the ridge and I saw your busted dam. It was you! Not the rains. Not the Ohio. The only houses destroyed were the ones your filthy water ran right over."

A murmur went around the restaurant. Van Cleve wrenched his napkin from his collar. He took a step toward her, his finger raised. "You listen here, O'Hare. You want to be *very* careful before you start throwing accusations around. You've caused enough trouble—"

But Margery squared up to him. "*I've* caused trouble? Says the man who shot my dog? Who knocked two teeth right out of his daughter-in-law's head? Your flood almost drowned me, and Sophia and William! They had near on nothing to start with and now they got less! You would have drowned three little girls if *my* girls hadn't got there to save them! And you swagger around here pretending like it's nothing to do with you? You want arresting!"

Sven appeared behind her and placed a hand on her shoulder but she was in full flow and shook him off. "Men die because you prize dollars over safety! You trick people into signing away their own houses before they understand what they've done! You destroy lives! Your mine is a menace! *You* are a menace!"

"That's enough." Sven now had his forearm around Margery's collarbone and was pulling her backward, even as she pointed at Van Cleve, still yelling. "C'mon. Time to go outside."

"Yes! Thank you, Gustavsson! Take her outside!"

"You act like you're the goddamn Almighty! Like the law doesn't count for you! But I'm watching you, Van Cleve. For as long as I have breath in my lungs, I'll tell the truth about you and—"

"Enough."

The air in the room seemed to have disappeared into a vacuum as Sven steered her, still struggling, out of the restaurant door. Through its glass panel she could be seen hollering at him in the road, her arms flailing as she tried to free herself.

Van Cleve glanced around and sat back down. The other diners were still staring.

"The O'Hares, huh!" he said, too loudly, tucking his napkin back in. "Never know what that family's going to get up to next."

Bennett's eyes flickered from his plate and back down again.

"Gustavsson's sound. He knows. Oh, yes. And that girl out there is the craziest of the lot of them, right? . . . Right?" Van Cleve's smile wavered a little until people started to drift back to their food. He let out a breath and motioned to the waitress. "Molly? Sweetheart? Could you—uh—get me a fresh plate of chicken, please? Thank you kindly."

Molly pulled a face. "I'm so sorry, Mr. Van Cleve. The last of it just went out." She eyed his plate, wincing slightly. "I have some soup and a couple of biscuits I could warm up for you?"

"Here. Have mine." Bennett pushed his untouched meal toward his father.

Van Cleve ripped his napkin out of his collar. "Lost my appetite. I'll get Gustavsson a drink and we'll head home."

He glanced through the door to where the younger man still stood outside with the O'Hare girl. "He'll be in once he's seen her off." He was aware of a vague sense of disappointment that it hadn't been his own son who had stood to push the girl out.

But the strangest thing: as O'Hare continued to yell and gesticulate outside, Gustavsson, rather than dusting off his hands and returning to the restaurant, took a step forward, his forehead lowered toward Margery O'Hare's.

As Van Cleve watched, frowning, Margery's hands briefly covered her face and both of them stood very still. And then, clear as anything in the moonlight, Sven Gustavsson placed a protective hand on the swell of O'Hare's belly, waiting until she looked up at him, and covered it gently with her own, before he kissed her.

Exactly how much trouble do you want to get yourself into?"

Margery pushed at Sven blindly, trying to free herself, but he held tight to her upper arms.

"You didn't see it, Sven! Thousands of gallons of his poison! And him acting like it's just the river, and William and Sophia's house ruined, and all the land and water round Monarch Creek destroyed for I don't know how long."

"I don't doubt it, Marge, but going at him in front of a restaurant full of people isn't going to help anything."

"He should be shamed! He thinks he can get away with anything! And don't you dare pull me out of there like I'm a—a badly trained *dog*!" She pushed hard with both hands, finally breaking his grip, and he lifted his palms.

"I just . . . I just didn't want him to come at you. You saw what he did to Alice."

"I'm not scared of him!"

"Well, maybe you should be. You got to be clever with a man like Van Cleve. He's cunning. You *know* that. C'mon, Margery. Don't let your temper trip you up. We'll go about this the right way. I don't know. Talk to the foreman. The unions. Write to the governor. There are ways."

Margery seemed to subside a little.

"C'mon now." He reached out a hand. "You don't have to fight every damn battle by yourself."

Something gave in her then. She kicked at the dirt, waiting for her breathing to slow. When she looked up, her eyes glittered with tears. "I hate him, Sven. I do. He destroys everything that's beautiful."

Sven pulled her to him. "Not everything." He placed his hand on her belly and left it there until he felt her soften in his arms. "C'mon," he said, and kissed her. "Let's go home."

Small towns being what they were, and Margery being who she was, it wasn't too long before word got out that she was carrying, and for a few days at least, every place where townspeople were prone to meeting—the feed merchant, the churches, the general store—was thick with the news of it. There were those for whom this just confirmed everything they thought of Frank O'Hare's daughter. Another no-good O'Hare child, no doubt destined for disgrace or disaster. There would always be those for whom any baby out of wedlock was a matter for vocal and emphatic disapproval. But there were also those whose minds were still thick with the flood and memories of what she'd said about Van Cleve's part in it. Luckily for her, they seemed to comprise most of the townspeople, who believed that when so much bad had taken place, a new baby, whatever the circumstances, was nothing to get too aerated about.

Apart from Sophia, that was.

"You gonna marry that man now?" she said, when she heard.

"Nope."

"Because you selfish?"

Margery had been writing a letter to the governor. She put down her pen and shot Sophia a look.

"Don't you side-eye me, Margery O'Hare. I know what you think about being joined under the Lord. Believe me, we all know your views. But this ain't just about you any more, is it? You want that baby to get called names in the schoolyard? You want her to grow up second class? You want her to miss out because people won't have one of *them* in the house?"

Margery opened the door so that Fred could drop another load of books back into the library. "Can we at least wait for her to get here before you start scolding me?"

Sophia raised her eyebrows. "I'm just saying. Life's hard enough growing up in this town without you giving the poor child another yoke around its neck. You know darn well how people made judgments about you based on what your parents did, decisions you had no hand in."

"All right, Sophia."

"Well, they did. And it's only because you're so pig-headed that you was able to make the life you wanted. What if she ain't like you?"

"She'll be like me."

"Shows how much you know about children." Sophia snorted. "I'm going to say it once. This ain't just about what you want any more." She slammed her ledger down on her desk. "And you need to think about that."

ven was no better. He sat on the rickety kitchen chair, polishing his boots while she sat on one side of the settle, and although his words were fewer, and his voice calmer, his point was just the same.

"I'm not going to ask you again, Margery. But this changes things. I want to be known as this child's father. I want to do it all properly. I don't want our baby to be brought up a bastard."

He regarded her over the wooden table, and she felt suddenly mulish and defensive, as she had when she was ten years old, so that she picked distractedly at a wool blanket and refused to look at him. "You think we don't have anything more important to talk about just now?"

"That's all I'm going to say."

She pushed her hair away from her face and chewed at her lower lip. He crossed his arms, brow lowered, ready for her to yell that he was driving her crazy, that he had promised not to keep going on, and she had had enough and he could git on back to his own house.

But she surprised him. "Let me think about it," she said.

They sat in silence for a few minutes. Margery drummed her fingers on the table and stretched out a leg, turning her ankle this way and that.

"What?" he said.

She picked at the corner of the blanket again, then straightened it, and then looked sideways at him.

"What?" he said, again.

"You ever going to come and sit by me then, Sven Gustavsson? Or have I lost all appeal to you, now you've got me blown up like a milch-cow?"

Alice let herself in late, thoughts of Fred crowding out everything she had seen that day, the apologies of families whose library books had drowned along with the rest of their belongings, the black slurry that marked the base of trees, the scattered belongings, odd shoes, letters, pieces of furniture, broken or ruined, that lined the paths of the now sedate creeks.

All I can give you, Alice, is words.

As she had every morning and every night since, she felt Fred's fingers tracing her cheek, saw his narrowed, serious eyes, wondered how it would feel to have those strong hands tracing her body in that same gentle, purposeful way. Her imagination filled those gaps in her knowledge. Her memories of his voice, the intensity of his expression left her faintly breathless. She thought about him so much she suspected the others could see right through her, maybe catch snatches of the constant fevered hum in her head as it trickled out through her ears. It was almost a relief to reach Margery's cabin, her collar turned up against the April wind, and know that she would be forced to think about something else for a couple of hours at least—book bindings or slurry or string beans.

Alice walked in, closing the screen door quietly behind her (she'd had a horror of slamming doors since she'd left the Van Cleve house), and removed her coat, hanging it on the hook. The cabin was silent, which usually meant that Margery was out back, attending to Charley or the hens. She walked over to the bread bin and peered inside, pondering how empty the place still felt without Bluey's boisterous presence.

She was about to call out back when she heard a sound that had been absent these last weeks: muffled cries, soft moans of pleasure coming from behind Margery's closed door. She stopped dead in the middle of the floor and, as if in response, the voices suddenly rose and fell in unison, threaded through with terms of endearment and suffused with emotion, springs creaking and the head of the bed banging emphatically against the wooden wall and threatening to build to a crescendo.

"Oh, ruddy marvelous," Alice muttered softly to herself. And she put her coat back on, stuffed a piece of bread between her teeth and went to sit outside on the front porch on the squeaky rocker, eating with one hand, and plugging her good ear with the other.

It was not unusual for the snows to last a whole month longer on the mountaintops. It was as if, determined to ignore whatever was going on down in the town, they refused to relinquish their icy hold until the last possible moment, right up until waxy buds were already poking through the thinning crystalline carpet, and on the upper trails the trees were no longer brown and skeletal but shimmered with a faint hint of green.

So, it was some way into April before the body of Clem McCullough was revealed, his frostbitten nose visible first, as the snows melted high on the uppermost ridge, and then the rest of his face, gnawed in places by some hungry creature and his eyes long missing, found by a hunter from Berea, who had been sent to the hillsides above Red Lick looking for deer, and would have nightmares for months afterward about rotting faces with fathomless holes for eyes.

To find the body of a well-known drunk was not that much of a surprise in a small town, especially in moonshine country, and might normally have guaranteed just a few days' chatter and shaking of heads, as news got around.

But this was different.

Clem McCullough's head, the sheriff announced, not long after he and his men came back down the mountainside, had been stove in on the back of a pointed boulder. And resting on the upper part of his chest, revealed as the last of the snow melted away, was a heavily bloodstained, fabric-bound edition of *Little Women*, marked Baileyville Packhorse Library WPA.

NINETEEN

★

Men expected women to be calm, collected, cooperative,
and chaste. Eccentric conduct was frowned upon, and
any female who got too far out of line could be in
serious trouble.

· Virginia Culin Roberts,
The Women Was Too Tough

Van Cleve, his belly full of pork rinds and a fine film of excitement glistening on his brow, walked into the sheriff's office. He brought with him a wooden box of cigars and a beaming smile, not that he would have admitted any particular reason for either. No, but the discovery of McCullough's body meant that the breached dam and the slurry clean-up were suddenly old news. Van Cleve and his son could walk down the street again and, for the first time in weeks as he emerged from his car, he experienced something like a spring in his step.

"Well, Bob, I can't say I'm surprised. You know she's been causing trouble the whole year, destabilizing our community, spreading wickedness." He leaned forward and lit the sheriff's cigar with a click of his brass lighter.

The sheriff sat back in his chair. "I'm not entirely sure I'm with you, Geoff."

"Well, you'll be arresting the O'Hare girl, won't you?"

"What makes you think it has anything to do with her?"

"Bob . . . Bob . . . We've been friends a long time. You know as well as I do the beef the McCulloughs had with the O'Hares. Goes back as far as any of us can remember. And who else would be riding all the way up there?"

The sheriff said nothing.

"And, more pertinently, a little birdie tells me there was a library book found by the body. Well, that just about settles it, I'd say. Case closed." He took a long drag of his cigar.

"Wish my boys was as efficient at solving crime as you, Geoff." The sheriff's eyes crinkled with amusement.

"Why, you know she was responsible for persuading my Bennett's wife away from him, though we've tried to keep that on the low-down, to save him embarrassment. They were happily married until she came along! No, she puts wicked ideas in girls' heads and causes mayhem wherever she goes. I for one will sleep better knowing she's locked up tonight."

"Is that right?" said the sheriff, who had known about the Van Cleve girl's movements for months. There was little in this county that escaped him.

"That family, Bob." Van Cleve blew smoke to the ceiling. "There's bad blood, shot all the way through the O'Hare line. Why, do you remember her uncle Vincent? Now there was a rogue . . ."

"Can't say as the evidence is conclusive, Geoff. Between us, as it stands, we can't prove beyond doubt she was on that route, and our one witness is now saying she can't be sure whose voice it was she heard."

"Of course it was her! You know darn well that the little polio girl wouldn't do it and nor would our Alice. That leaves the farm girl and the colored. And I'd put money on it she don't ride."

The sheriff turned down the corners of his mouth in a way that suggested he was not convinced.

Van Cleve jabbed a finger on the desk. "She's a malign influence, Bob. Ask Governor Hatch. He knows. The way she was spreading salacious material under the guise of a family library—oh, you didn't know about that? She's been fomenting discord up on North Ridge so they wouldn't allow the mine to go about its legal business. Every bit of trouble around here for the past year you can pretty much trace back to Margery O'Hare. This library has given her ideas above her station. The longer she's locked up the better."

"You know she's with child."

"Well, there you go! No moral compass whatsoever. Is that how a decent woman behaves? Is that really someone you want going into houses where there are young and impressionable people?"

"I guess not."

Van Cleve mapped it out with his fingers in the air, looking at some distant horizon. "She took her route, crossed paths with poor old McCullough on his way home, and when she saw he was drunk, she had an opportunity to avenge her no-good father, and killed him with the nearest thing she had to hand, knowing full well he would be buried under the snow. She probably thought the animals would eat him and nobody would ever find the body. It's only luck and the grace of God Almighty that somebody did. Cold-blooded, that's what she is! Contravening the laws of nature in every possible regard."

He took a deep draw of his cigar and shook his head. "I tell you, Bob, I wouldn't be at all surprised if she did it again." He waited a moment, then added. "That's why I'm glad there's a man like you in charge around here. A man who will stop the spread of lawlessness. A man who is not afraid to make the *law count*."

Van Cleve reached for his cigar box. "Why don't you take a couple of these home for later? Tell you what, take the whole box."

"Most generous of you, Geoff."

The sheriff said nothing more. But he took a long, appreciative drag on his cigar.

Margery O'Hare was arrested at the library on the evening they moved the last of the books back to their shelves. The sheriff arrived with his deputy and at first Fred greeted them warmly, thinking they'd come to examine his newly replaced floorboards and relined shelves, as townspeople had been doing all week; checking on the progress of everyone else's repairs had added a new dimension to the daily passing of time in Baileyville. But the sheriff's face was long and cold as a tombstone. As he planted his boots in the center of the room and gazed around him, something in Margery plummeted, a heavy stone in a bottomless well.

"Which one of youse takes the route up to the mountains above Red Lick?"

Their eyes slid toward each other.

"What's the matter, Sheriff? Someone late returning their books?" said Beth, but nobody laughed.

"The body of Clem McCullough was found on Arnott's Ridge two days ago. Looks like the murder weapon came from your library."

"Murder weapon?" said Beth. "We don't have no murder weapons here. Murder stories, we got those."

Margery's face drained of color. She blinked hard, put out a hand to steady herself. The sheriff caught it.

"She's in the family way," Alice said, taking her arm. "She gets a little light-headed."

"And that's dramatic news for a woman in the family way to have to hear straight out," Izzy added.

But the sheriff was staring at Margery. "You take that route, Miss O'Hare?"

"We share the routes, Sheriff," Kathleen interjected. "It really depends on who's working that day and how each horse is doing. Some ain't so good on those longer, rougher routes."

"You keep records of who goes where?" he said to Sophia, who stood up behind her desk, her knuckles tight on the edge.

"Yes, sir."

"I want to see every route taken by every librarian over the past six months."

"Six months?"

"Mr. McCullough's body is in a state of . . . some decay. It's unclear how long he has lain there. And his family don't seem to have reported him missing, according to our records, so we need all the information we can gather."

"That's—that's a lot of ledgers, sir. And we're still in a little disarray here because of the floods. It may take me a while to locate them among these books." Only Alice was positioned so that she could see Sophia slowly nudge the ledger on the floor firmly under her desk with her foot.

"To be frank, Mr. Sheriff, we lost a good many of them," Alice added. "It's entirely possible the relevant entries have suffered catastrophic water damage. Some were even washed away." She said it in her most clipped English accent, which had been known to sway sterner men than him, but the sheriff didn't appear to have heard her.

He had moved around to Margery and stood in front of her, his head tilted to one side. "The O'Hares had a long feud with the McCulloughs, am I right?"

Margery picked at a scuff on her boot. "I guess."

"My own daddy remembers your daddy coming after Clem McCullough's brother. Tom? Tam? Shot him in the stomach Christmas 1913 . . . 1914, if I remember right. I bet if I asked around there'd be other bad blood could be recalled between your two families."

"Far as I'm concerned, Sheriff, any feud died with the last of my brothers."

"Be the first blood feud around here just melted away with the snows," he said, and put a matchstick between his teeth, which he waggled up and down. "Mighty unusual."

"Well, I've never been what you might call conventional." She appeared to have composed herself.

"So you would know nothing about how Clem McCullough happened to be brought down?"

"No, sir."

"Tricky for you that you're the only living person might have had a grudge against him."

"Ah, come on, Sheriff Archer," Beth protested. "You know well as

I do that family is proper hillbilly trash. They probably got enemies halfway to Nashville, Tennessee."

That was true, they all agreed. Even Sophia felt safe enough to nod.

It was at that point they heard the engine. A car drew up, and the sheriff walked slow and stiff-legged to the door, as if he had all the time in the world. Another deputy appeared, and he murmured something in his ear. The sheriff looked up and behind him at Margery, then leaned in for further information.

The deputy entered the library so that there were three of them. Alice caught Fred's eye, and saw he was as nonplussed as she felt. The sheriff turned and when he spoke again, it was, Alice thought, with a kind of grim satisfaction.

"Officer Dalton here has just been speaking with old Nancy Stone. She says you was making your way to her back in December when she heard a gunshot and some kind of a commotion. Says you never arrived and that, rain or shine, you had never once missed a book delivery before that day. Says you were known for it."

"I recall I couldn't get past the ridge. The snow was too deep." Margery's voice, Alice realized, had taken on a slight tremor.

"Not what Nancy says. She said the snow had eased two days past and that you was by the upper levels of the creek and that she heard you talking right up until minutes before the gun went off. Says she was mighty worried about you for a while."

"Not me." She shook her head.

"No?" He pondered this, his lower lip pushed out in exaggerated thought. "She seems pretty sure there was a packhorse librarian up there. You telling me then it was one of these other ladies that day, Miss O'Hare?"

She gazed around her then, a trapped animal.

"You think maybe I should be talking to one of these girls instead? Think maybe one of them is capable of murder? How about you, Kathleen Bligh? Or maybe this nice English lady? Van Cleve Junior's wife, yes?"

Alice lifted her chin.

"Or you—what's your name, girl?"

"Sophia Kenworth."

"Soph-i-a Ken-worth." He said nothing about the color of her skin, but rolled the syllables around extra slowly so that they felt loaded.

The room had grown very still. Sophia stared at the edge of her desk, her jaw tight, unblinking.

"No," Margery said, into the silence. "I know for a fact it was none of these women. I think maybe it was a robber. Or a 'shiner. You know how it can be up there on the mountains. All sorts going on."

"*All sorts going on.* That's true enough. But, you know, seems mighty odd that in a county stacked full of knives and guns, axes and coshes, that the weapon of choice for your neighborhood hillbilly robber would be . . ." he paused, as if to recall it properly ". . . a fabric-bound first edition of *Little Women.*"

At the dismay that flickered, unchecked, across her face, something in the sheriff relaxed, like a man sighing with pleasure after a big meal. He squared his shoulders, pushed his neck back into his collar. "Margery O'Hare, I am arresting you on suspicion of the murder of Clem McCullough. Men, take her in."

After that, Sophia told William that evening, all hell broke loose. Alice flew at the man like a woman possessed, shouting and hollering, hurling books at him until the officer threatened to arrest her, too, and Frederick Guisler had to wrap both his arms around her to stop her fighting. Beth was yelling at them that they had it all wrong, that they didn't know what they were talking about. Kathleen just looked silent and shocked, shaking her head, and little Izzy burst into tears, kept crying, "But you can't do this! She's having a baby!" Fred had run for his car and driven fast as he could to tell Sven Gustavsson, and Sven had come back white as a sheet, trying to get them to tell him what the heck was going on. And all the while Margery O'Hare had been silent as a ghost, allowing herself to be led past the crowd of onlookers, into the back of the police Buick, her head down and one hand over her belly.

William digested this and shook his head. His overalls were thick with black dirt where he was still trying to clean up the house, and when he ran his hand over the back of his head he left an oily black trace of it on his skin.

"What you think?" he asked his sister. "You think she did murder someone?"

"I don't know," she said, shaking her head. "I know Margery ain't a murderer but . . . there was something off, something she wasn't saying." She looked up at him. "I do know one thing, though. If Van Cleve has any say in this, he's going to make her chances of getting out of it a whole lot smaller."

Even sat that night in Margery's kitchen and told Alice and Fred the whole story. The incident on the mountain ridge, how she had believed McCullough would come after her in revenge, how he had sat out on the porch for two long, cold nights with the rifle across his knees and Bluey at his feet until both were reassured that McCullough had surely slunk back to his falling-down cabin, probably with a sore head and too drunk to remember what the hell he had even done.

"But you have to tell the sheriff!" Alice said. "That means it was self-defense!"

"You think that's going to help her?" said Fred. "The moment she says she slammed that book into him, they'll treat it as a confession. She'll get manslaughter at best. The smartest thing she can do just now is sit tight and hope they don't have enough evidence to keep her in jail."

Bail had been set at $25,000—a sum nobody around there could get close to. "It's the same sum they posted for Henry H. Denhardt, and he point-blank shot his own fiancée."

"Yup, except being a man, he had friends in high places who could post it for him."

Nancy Stone had apparently wept when she heard what the sheriff's men had done with her testimony. She had made her way down the mountain that evening—the first time she had done so in two years—banged on the door of the sheriff's office and demanded that they let her retell her story. "I said it all wrong!" she said, and cursed, through her missing teeth. "I didn't know you was gonna arrest Margery! Why, that girl has done nothing but good for me and my sister—for this town, hang you, and that's how you're going to repay her?"

There had indeed been a murmur of unease around town at the news of the arrest. But murder was murder, and the McCulloughs and the O'Hares had been the death of each other for generations so far back that nobody could even remember how it all started, just like the Cahills and the Rogersons, and the two branches of the Campbell family. No, Margery O'Hare had always been an odd one, contrary since she could walk, and that was just the way these things went sometimes. She could certainly be cold-hearted too—why, didn't she sit stone-faced at her own daddy's funeral without shedding a tear? It didn't take long for the endless seesaw of public opinion to begin to wonder whether maybe there was something of the devil in her after all.

Down in the low-lying little town of Baileyville, deep in the southeastern reaches of Kentucky, the light disappeared slowly behind the hills and not long after, in little houses along Main Street and dotted among the mountains and hollers, the oil lamps flickered and went out, one by one. Dogs called to each other, their howls bouncing off the hillsides, to be scolded by exhausted owners. Babies cried and were, sometimes, comforted. Old people lost themselves in memories of better times and younger ones in the comforts of each other's bodies, hummed along to the wireless or the distant playing of somebody else's fiddle.

Kathleen Bligh, high in her cabin, pulled her sleeping children close, their soft, yeasty heads like bookmarks on each side of her, and thought of a husband with shoulders like a bison and a touch so tender it could make her weep happy tears.

Three miles northwest in a big house on a manicured lawn, Mrs.

Brady tried to read another chapter of her book while her daughter sang muffled scales in her bedroom. She put the book down with a sigh, saddened by the way life never quite turned out how you hoped it would, and wondered how she was going to explain this one to Mrs. Nofcier.

Across from the church, Beth Pinker sat reading an atlas on her family's back porch and smoking her grandmother's pipe, thinking about all the people she would like to hurt, Geoffrey Van Cleve being high on that particular list.

In a cabin that should have had Margery O'Hare in the heart of it, two people sat sleepless on each side of a rough-hewn door, trying to work out a route to a different outcome, their thoughts like a Chinese puzzle, and a solid knot of anxiety too huge and weighty pressing down upon each of them.

And a few miles away, Margery sat on the floor with her back against the wall of the cell and tried to fight the rising panic that kept pushing up from her chest, like a choking tide. Across the hall two men—a drunk from out of state and a habitual thief whose face she could recall but not name—called obscenities at her, and the deputy, a fair man who was troubled that there were no segregated facilities for women (he could barely remember the last time a woman was kept overnight in Baileyville Jail, let alone a pregnant one), had strung up a sheet across half the bars to shield her a little. But she could still hear them, and smell the sour scents of urine and sweat, and all the while they knew she was there, and this lent the confines of the little jail an intimacy that was disturbing and discomfiting to the point where, exhausted as she was, she knew no sleep would come.

She would have been more comfortable on the mattress, especially as the baby was now of a size where it seemed to press down on unexpected parts of her, but the mattress was stained and full of chiggers and she had sat there for a full five minutes before she had started to itch.

You want to peel back that curtain there, girl? I'll show you something that will get you to sleep.

You cut it out, Dwayne Froggatt.

Just having a little fun, Deputy. You know she likes it. Written all over her waistline, ain't it?

McCullough had come for her after all, his loaded weapon his own bloodied body, her library book a written confession on his chest. He had followed her back down that mountain as surely as if he'd done it with a loaded gun in his hand.

She tried to think of what she could say in mitigation; she hadn't known she had hurt him. She had been afraid. She had simply been trying to do her job. She was a woman, just minding her business. But she wasn't stupid. She knew how it looked. Nancy, without knowing it, had sealed her fate by placing her up there, library book in hand.

Margery O'Hare pressed the heels of her hands into her eyes and let out a long, shuddering breath, feeling the panic begin to rise again. Through the bars she could see the blue-mauve of encroaching night, hear the distant birdcall that marked the dying embers of the day. And as the dark fell she felt the walls press in on her, the ceiling lowering, and she screwed her eyes shut.

"I can't stay here. I can't," she said softly. "I can't be in here."

You whispering to me, girl? Want me to sing you a lullaby?

Pull back that curtain. Go on. Just for Daddy.

A burst of drunken laughter.

"I can't stay in here." Her breath bunched and gathered in her chest, her knuckles whitened and the cell began to swim, the floor rising as the panic built.

And then the baby shifted inside her, once, twice, as if telling her that she was not alone, that nothing was to be gained from this, and Margery let out a half-sob, placed her hands on her belly and closed her eyes and let out a long, slow breath, waiting until the terror had passed.

TWENTY

"Did you say the stars were worlds, Tess?"
"Yes."
"All like ours?"
"I don't know, but I think so. They sometimes
seem to be like the apples on our stubbard-tree. Most of
them splendid and sound—a few blighted."
"Which do we live on—a splendid one or a
blighted one?"
"A blighted one."

· THOMAS HARDY, *Tess of the D'Urbervilles*

ord had got round by morning, and a few folk took the trouble to walk down to the library and say how crazy the whole thing was, that they didn't believe ill of Margery and that it was a darn shame the police were treating her so. But a whole lot more didn't, and Alice felt those whispered discussions all the way from their little cabin by Split Creek. She covered her own anxiety with activity. She sent Sven home, promising him she would look after the hens and the mule, and Sven, having enough sensitivity to know that it would not be good for them to be seen sleeping under the same roof, agreed. Though both knew he would probably be back by nightfall, unable to sit alone with his fears.

"I know how everything runs," she said, shoveling an egg and four slices of bacon that would remain untouched onto his plate. "Been here long enough. Margery will be out in a blink. And I'll take her over some fresh clothes to the jailhouse in the meantime."

"That jail's no place for a woman," he said quietly.

"Well, we'll have her out in no time."

She sent the librarians out on their normal routes that morning, checking the ledgers and helping load the saddlebags. Nobody questioned her authority, as if they were just grateful to have someone taking charge. Beth and Kathleen asked her to convey their good wishes. And then she locked the library, climbed onto Spirit, with the bag of Margery's fresh clothes, and rode over to the jail under a clear, brisk sky.

"Good morning," she said to the jailer, a thin man with a weary look, whose huge ring of keys threatened to bring down his trousers. "I've come to bring Margery O'Hare a change of clothes."

He looked her up and down and sniffed, his nose wrinkling. "You got your slip?"

"A slip of what?"

"From the sheriff. Allowing you to see the prisoner."

"I don't have a slip."

"Then you don't get in." He blew his nose noisily into a handkerchief.

Alice stood for a moment, color prickling her cheeks. Then she straightened her shoulders. "Sir. You are holding a woman who is heavy with child in the most unsanitary of circumstances. The very least I would expect you to do is to allow her a change of clothes. What kind of a gentleman are you?"

He had the grace to look a little discomfited.

"What is it? You think I'm going to smuggle her in a metal file? A gun, perhaps? She's a woman *with child*. Here, Officer. Let me show you what I'm planning to hand over to the poor girl. There, a fresh cotton blouse. And here, some wool stockings. You want to go through the bag? You can check, a fresh set of undergarments—"

"All right, all right," said the jailer, holding up a palm. "Put 'em back in the bag. You get ten minutes, okay? And next time I want a slip."

"Of course. Thank you so much, Officer. That's very kind of you."

Alice tried to maintain this air of confidence as she followed him down the steps into the confines of the holding area. The jailer opened a heavy metal gate, his keys rattling, flicked through them until he found another, and opened another gate onto a small corridor, which was lined with four cells. The air was stale and foul down there, and the only light was a sliver from a narrow horizontal window at the top of each cell. As her eyes adjusted to the light she saw shadowy movement in the cells at the left.

"Hers is the one on the right with the sheet on it," he said, and turned to leave, locking the gate and checking it with a rattle, so that her heart rattled with it against her ribs.

"Well, hello, pretty girl," said a male voice from the shadows.

She didn't look at him.

"Margery?" she whispered, walking up to the bars. There was a silence, then she saw the sheet pull back a few inches and Margery stared back from the other side. She was pale, her eyes shadowed. Behind her stood a narrow bunk with a lumpen, stained mattress, and a metal pot in the corner of the room. As Alice stood, something scuttled across the floor.

"Are you . . . all right?" She tried not to let her face reveal her shock.

"I'm fine."

"I brought you some things. Thought you might like a change of clothes. I'll bring you more tomorrow. Here." She began to pull the items from the bag, one by one, feeding them through the bars. "There's a bar of soap, and a toothbrush, and I—well, I brought you my bottle of scent. I thought you might like to feel . . ." She faltered. The idea seemed ridiculous now.

"You got something for me there, pretty girl? I'm real lonesome over here."

She turned her back, away from him. "Anyway." She lowered her voice. "There's some cornbread and an apple in the leg of your drawers. I wasn't sure whether they'd feed you. Everything is fine at home.

I've fed Charley and the hens and you're not to worry about anything. It will all be just as you like when you get home."

"Where's Sven?"

"He had to go to work. But he's coming by later."

"He okay?"

"He's a little shaken up, actually. Everybody is."

"Hey! Hey, come over here! I wanna show you something!"

Alice leaned forward, so that her forehead touched the bars of the cell door. "He told us what happened. With the McCullough man."

Margery closed her eyes for a minute. Her fingers looped around a bar and tightened briefly. "I never set out to hurt no one, Alice." Margery's voice cracked.

"Of course you didn't. You did what anyone would have done." Alice was firm. "Anyone with half a brain. It's called self-defense."

"Hey! Hey! Stop your yammering and come over here, girl. You got something for me, huh? Cos I got something for you."

Alice turned, her face a fury, and placed her hands on her hips. "Oh, *do* shut up! I'm trying to talk to my friend! For *goodness' sake!*"

There was a brief silence, and then, from the other cell, a whinny of laughter. "Yeah, do shut up! She's tryin' to talk to her friend!"

The two men immediately began arguing among themselves, their voices lifting as the air turned blue.

"I can't stay in here," Margery said quietly.

Alice was shaken by how Margery looked after only one night in this place, as if all the fight had seeped out of her. "Well, we're going to work this out. You are not on your own, and we are not going to let anything happen to you."

Margery looked at her with weary eyes. She set her mouth in a thin line, as if she were stopping herself from speaking.

Alice placed her fingers over Margery's, trying to grip her hand. "It *will* all sort itself out. You just try to rest, and eat something, and I'll be back tomorrow."

It seemed to take Margery a minute to register what she was saying. She nodded, shifted her gaze to Alice, and then, with a hand on her belly, she moved back to the floor, where she slid slowly down the wall and sat down.

Alice rapped on the metal lock until she had the guard's attention. He rose heavily from his chair and let her out, closing the gate and eyeing the sheet behind her, from which Margery's shoulder was just visible.

"Now," said Alice. "I will be back tomorrow. I'm not sure if I'll have time to get a slip, but I'm sure there will be no objections to a woman providing basic hygiene and assistance to a mother in waiting. That's just decency. And I may not have been here very long but I do know that Kentucky people are the most decent of people."

The guard looked at her, as if unsure how to respond.

"Anyway," she said, before he could think too hard about it. "I brought you a piece of cornbread to say thank you for being so . . . flexible. It's a rotten situation, which will hopefully be sorted out very soon, and in the meantime I am much obliged for your kindness, Mr. . . . ?"

The guard blinked heavily. "Dulles."

"Officer Dulles. There you go."

"Deputy."

"Deputy Dulles. I do beg your pardon." She handed him the cornbread, wrapped in a napkin. "Oh," she said, as he opened it. "And I'll want that napkin back. If you could just give it to me tomorrow when I bring the next lot, that would be lovely. Just fold it up. Thank you so much." Before he could respond, she turned and walked briskly out of the jailhouse.

Sven hired a lawyer from Louisville, selling his grandfather's silver fob watch to raise the money. The man attempted to demand a more reasonable setting of the bail money, but was refused in the baldest of terms. The girl was a murderer, the answer came, from a known family of murderers, and the state would not be satisfied with knowing she was out and free to do the same again. Even when a small crowd gathered outside the sheriff's office to protest, he was unbending, stating that they could shout all they liked, but it was his job to uphold the law and that was what he was going to do, and if it was their father who had been murdered while going about his lawful business, they might think again.

"Well, the good news is," the lawyer said, as he climbed back into his car, "state of Kentucky hasn't executed a woman since 1868. Let alone a pregnant one." This fact didn't seem to make Sven feel much better.

"What are we going to do now?" he said, as he and Alice walked back from the jailhouse.

"We keep going," said Alice. "We keep everything going as normal and wait for somebody to see sense."

But six weeks passed, and nobody did see sense. Margery remained in the jailhouse even as various other miscreants came and went (and were, in some cases, returned). Attempts to transfer her to a women's prison were rebuffed, and in truth Alice felt that if Margery had to stay locked up it was probably better for her to be where they could stop by and see her than to be somewhere in the city where nobody would know her and where she would be surrounded by the noise and fumes of a world completely alien to her.

So Alice rode to the jailhouse every day with a tin of still-warm cornbread (she had pulled the recipe from one of the library books and could now bake it without even looking) or pie or whatever else she had to hand, and had become something of a favorite with the guards. Now nobody ever mentioned slips but merely handed back the previous day's napkin and motioned her through with barely a word. With Sven, they were a little stickier, because his size tended to make other men nervous. Along with food she would bring a change of undergarments, woolen sweaters, if needed, and a book, although the jail was so dark in the basement that there were only a few hours a day in which Margery could see to read. And nearly every evening when

Alice finished up at the library she would head home to the cabin in the woods, sit at the table with Sven, and they would tell each other that this thing would be sorted out eventually, no doubt, and Margery would resemble herself once she was out in the fresh air again, and neither of them would believe a word the other was saying, until he left, and she would go to bed to lie awake staring at the ceiling until dawn.

That year, it was as if they had missed spring completely. One minute it was frozen, and then it was as if the rains had washed away a whole couple of months because Lee County slammed abruptly into a full-on heatwave. The monarch butterflies returned, the weeds rose on the verges, waist high under blossoming dogwoods, and Alice borrowed one of Margery's wide-brimmed leather hats and wore a handkerchief around her neck to stop herself burning, and slapped at the biting creatures on her horse's neck with the buckle of her reins.

Alice and Fred spent as much time together as they could, but they didn't talk too much about Margery. Once they had done their best to meet her practical needs, nobody knew what to say.

The coroner's inquest had found that Clem McCullough had died from a catastrophic injury to the back of his skull, probably caused by a blow to the back of his head or by falling onto a rock. Unfortunately the decomposition of the body did not allow for a more accurate conclusion. Margery had been due to testify at the coroner's court, but an angry crowd had built up outside it and, given her condition, it was decreed that it would not be wise for her to enter.

The closer she drew to her due date, the more frustrated Sven had become, railing at the jailhouse deputy until he had been barred from visiting for a week—it would have been longer, but Sven was liked in town, and everyone knew nerves were getting to him. Margery had grown milk-pale, and her hair hung down in a dirty plait; she ate the food Alice proffered with a kind of detached observance, as if she would really rather not but she understood that she was obliged to do so. There was not a time that Alice visited her when it didn't seem that having Margery stuck in a cell was a crime against nature: a flat-out reversal of how everything should be. Everything felt wrong while she was locked away, the mountains empty, the library missing some vital piece. Even Charley was listless, pacing backward and forward along the rail, or just standing, his huge ears at half mast, his pale muzzle lowered halfway to the ground.

Sometimes Alice waited until she was alone on the long ride back to the cabin and, shielded by the trees and the silence, cried huge sobs of fear and frustration. Tears she knew Margery would not cry for herself. Nobody spoke of what would happen when the baby came. Nobody spoke of what would happen to Margery afterward. The whole situation was so surreal and the child was still an abstraction, a thing that few of them could imagine into existence.

Alice rose at 4:30 a.m. every day, slung herself across Spirit and disappeared into the densely forested mountainside laden with saddlebags so that she'd done the first mile before she'd had a chance to wake fully. She greeted everyone she passed by name, usually with some piece of information that might be pertinent to them—"Did you get that tractor repair book, Jim? And did your wife like the short stories?"—and would place her horse in front of Van Cleve's car whenever she saw it, so that he was forced to stop, engine idling in the road, while she stared him down. "Sleep well at night, do you?" she would call, her voice piercing the still air. "Feeling pleased with yourself?" His cheeks blown out and purple, he would wrench his car around her.

She was not afraid to be in the cabin alone, but Fred had helped her set more traps to alert her should anyone come close. She was reading one night when she heard the jingle of the bell string they had strung between the trees. With lightning reflexes, she reached back to the fireplace and pulled down the rifle, standing and cocking it on her shoulder in one fluid movement, placing the two barrels against the narrow gap in the door.

She squinted, trying to make out whether there was any movement outside and remained preternaturally still, scanning the darkness a moment or two longer, before she let her shoulders drop.

"Just deer," she muttered to herself and lowered the rifle.

It was only as she left the next morning that she found the note that had been slipped under the door overnight with its heavy black scrawl.

You do not belong here. Go home.

It wasn't the first, and she bit down hard on the feelings the notes provoked. Margery would have laughed at them, so that was what she did. She screwed the paper into a ball, threw it into the fire, and cursed under her breath. And tried not to think about where home might be, these days.

Fred stood beside the barn in the dimming light chopping wood— one of the few tasks that still defeated Alice. She found the weight and heft of the old ax unnerving, and rarely managed to split the logs along the grain, usually leaving the blade wedged at an awkward angle, stuck fast, until Fred returned. He, in contrast, hit each piece with a clean, rhythmic motion, his arms circling in a great sweep, the ax slicing each into halves and then quarters, pausing each three strikes, to hold it loosely in one hand while with the other he tossed the new logs onto the pile. She watched him for a moment, waiting until he stopped again, drew a forearm across his brow, and looked up at where she stood in the doorway, glass in hand.

"That for me?"

She took a few steps forward and handed it to him.

"Thank you. There's more here than I thought."

"Good of you to do it."

He took a long swig of the water and let out a breath before he handed back the glass. "Well. Can't have you getting cold in winter. And they dry out quicker if you cut them smaller. Sure you don't want to have another go?"

Something in her expression seemed to stop him.

"You okay, Alice?"

She smiled and nodded but even as she did so she barely convinced herself. So she told him the thing she had put off telling for a full week. "My parents have written. To say I can come home."

Fred's smile evaporated.

"They're not happy, but they say I can't stay here alone and they're prepared to chalk the marriage up to youthful error. My aunt Jean has invited me to stay with her in Lowestoft. She needs help with her children and everyone agrees that this would be a good way of . . . well . . . getting me back to England without making too much of a scene. Apparently we can address all the legal matters from a suitable distance."

"What's Lowestoft?"

"A little town on the North Sea coast. Not exactly my first choice, but . . . Well, I suppose I'd have some independence at least." *And be away from my parents*, she added silently. She swallowed. "They're forwarding money for my passage. I told them I needed to stay for the end of Margery's trial." She let out a dry laugh. "I'm not sure if my being friends with an accused murderer improved their opinion of me any."

There was a long silence.

"So you're really leaving."

She nodded. She couldn't say any more. It was as if with that letter she had suddenly been reminded that her whole life here up to this point had been a fever dream. She pictured herself back in Mortlake, or in the fake-Tudor house in Lowestoft, her aunt's polite inquiries as to her sleep, whether she was ready for a little breakfast, whether she might like to take a walk to the municipal park that afternoon. She looked down at her chapped hands, at her broken nails, at the sweater she had worn for fourteen days straight over the other layers, with its tiny fragments of hay and grass seed embedded in the yarn. She looked at her boots, with the scuffs that told of remote mountain trails, of splashing through creek beds or dismounting to make her way up narrow passes in mud, fierce sunshine or endless, endless rain. What would it be like to be that other girl again? The one with polished shoes, stockings and a tame, orderly existence? With nails that had been carefully filed, and a shampoo-and-set twice a week? No longer dismounting to relieve herself behind trees, picking apples to eat as she worked, her nostrils full of woodsmoke and damp earth, but instead exchanging a few polite words with the bus conductor about whether he was sure the 238 stopped outside the railway station.

Fred was watching her. There was something so pained and raw in his expression that she felt hollowed out by it. He hid it, reaching for the ax. "Well, I guess I might as well do the rest of these while I'm here."

"Margery will need them. When she comes home."

He nodded, his eyes on the blade. "Yup."

Alice waited a moment. "I'll fix you something to eat . . . If you're still happy to stay."

He nodded, his eyes still downcast. "That would be good."

She waited a moment longer, then turned and walked back into Margery's cabin with the empty glass, and the sound of each whack of the blade splintering the wood behind her made her flinch, as if it were not just the wood being rent in two.

The food was terrible, as food cooked without heart often is, but Fred was too kind to comment on it, and Alice had little to say, so the meal passed in an unusual silence, accompanied only by the rhythmic croaks of the crickets and frogs outside. He thanked her for her efforts and lied that it had been delicious, and she took the dirty plates and watched as he stood, straightening stiffly as if the wood chopping had taken more out of him than he'd let on. He hesitated, then walked out onto the stoop, where she could see his shadow through the mesh of the screen door, looking out at the mountainside.

I'm so sorry, Fred, she told him silently. *I don't want to leave you.*

She turned back to the plates and began scrubbing furiously, biting back tears.

"Alice?" Fred appeared at the door.

"Mm?"

"Come outside," he said.

"I have to do the pl—"

"Come. I want to show you something."

The night was possessed of the thick darkness that comes when clouds swallow the moon and stars whole, and she could only just make him out as he motioned to the swing seat on the porch. They sat a few inches apart, not touching but linked by their thoughts, which, underneath, wound around each other's like ivy.

"What are we looking at?" she said, trying surreptitiously to wipe her eyes.

"Just wait," came Fred's voice, from beside her.

Alice sat in the dark, the seat creaking under their combined weight, her thoughts tumbling as she considered her future. What could she do if she didn't go home? She had little money, certainly not enough to find a house. She was not even sure she would have a job—who was to say that the library would continue without Margery's fierce steerage? More importantly, she could hardly stay forever in this small town, with the looming cloud of Van Cleve, his rage and her ill-fated marriage hanging over her. He had got to Margery, and he would surely get to her too, one way or another.

And yet.

And yet the thought of leaving this place—of no longer riding these mountains, accompanied only by the sound of Spirit's hoofs and the glinting, dappled light of the forest, the thought of no longer laughing with the other librarians, stitching quietly beside Sophia or tapping her foot as Izzy's voice soared into the rafters filled her with a grief that was visceral. She loved it here. She loved the mountains and the people and the never-ending sky. She loved feeling as if she was doing a job that meant something, testing herself each day, changing people's lives word by word. She had earned every one of her bruises and blisters, had built a new Alice over the frame of one with whom she had never felt entirely comfortable. She would simply shrink back if she returned, and she could already taste how easily it would happen. Baileyville would become a little interlude, fade into another episode that her parents, tight-lipped, would prefer not to refer to. She would pine for Kentucky for a while, and pull herself together. Then, after a year or two perhaps, she would be allowed to divorce and she would eventually meet a tolerable man who didn't begrudge her complicated past, and settle down. In some tolerable part of Lowestoft.

And then there was Fred. The thought of being parted from him made her stomach cramp. How was she supposed to bear the prospect of never seeing him again? Never seeing his face light up simply because she had walked into the room? Never catching his eye in a crowd, feeling the subtle heat that came with standing alongside a man she knew wanted her more than any other? She felt that every day they were together now, even when no words were spoken—the unspoken conversation that ran, like an undercurrent, under everything they did. She had never felt so connected, so sure of somebody, had never wanted somebody else's happiness so keenly. How was she supposed to give that up?

"Alice."

"Sorry?"

"Look up."

Alice's breath stopped in her throat. The mountainside opposite was alive with light, a wall of glinting fairy lights, three-dimensional among the trees, winking and twinkling as they shifted, illuminating the shadows of the inky dark. She blinked at it, disbelieving, her mouth open.

"Fireflies," he said.

"Fireflies?"

"Lightning bugs. Whatever you want to call them. They come every year."

Alice couldn't quite take in what she was seeing. The clouds parted and the fireflies glinted, mingled, traversed upward from the illuminated shadows of the trees, and their million luminous white bodies melded seamlessly with the starry night sky above, so that it seemed for that moment that the whole world was carpeted with tiny golden lights. It was such a ridiculous, unlikely, insanely beautiful sight that Alice found herself laughing out loud, both hands pressed to her face.

"Do they do this often?" she said. She could just make out his smile.

"Nope. A week, maybe, every year. Two at most. Never seen them quite this beautiful, though."

A huge sob rose from Alice's chest, something to do with overwhelming emotion and, perhaps, impending loss. The absence at the heart of the cabin, and the man beside her whom she couldn't have. Before she could think what she was doing, she reached across in the dark and found Fred's hand. His fingers closed around hers, warm, strong, entwining, as if they were molded to each other. They sat like that for some time, gazing at the glittering spectacle.

"I . . . I know why you need to go." Fred's voice broke into the silence, halting, his words careful. "I just need you to know that it will be awful hard when you do."

"I'm in a bit of a bind, Fred."

"I know that."

She took a deep, shaking breath. "It's all a bit of a mess, isn't it?"

There was a long pause. Somewhere in the distance an owl hooted. Fred squeezed her hand and they sat for a while, feeling the soft night breezes around them.

"You know what's really wonderful about those fireflies?" he said, finally, as if they had been having a whole other conversation. "Sure, they live for just a few weeks. Not much at all in the grand scheme of things. But while they're there, the beauty of them, well, it takes your breath away." He ran a thumb over the ridge of her knuckles. "You get to see the world in a whole new way. And then you have that beautiful picture burned onto the inside of your head. To carry it wherever you go. And never forget it."

Before he had even said the next words Alice felt the tear begin to slide down her cheek.

"I worked it out sitting here. Maybe that's the thing we need to understand, Alice. That some things are a gift, even if you don't get to keep them."

There was a silence before he spoke again.

"Maybe just to know that something this beautiful exists is all we can really ask for."

She wrote to her parents confirming her return to England, and Fred drove the letter to the post office, on the way to delivering a young colt to Booneville. She saw the stiffening of his jaw as he registered the address and hated herself for it. She stood, arms folded in her white linen shirtsleeves, as he climbed into the back of his dusty pickup truck, the rattling trailer attached to the back and the horse kicking impatiently to be gone. She watched them head the whole way up Split Creek until the truck was out of view.

Alice squinted at the empty road for a while, at the mountains that rose on each side of it, disappearing into the haze of summer, at the buzzards that wheeled lazily and impossibly high above them, her hand shielding her brow. She let out a long, shaky breath. Finally she dusted her hands on her breeches and turned to walk back into the library.

TWENTY-ONE

T he call came at a quarter to three in the morning, on a night so warm that Alice had barely slept, but instead wrestled, sweaty and fitful, with a sheet through the small hours. She heard the rapid banging on the door and sat immediately upright, her blood chilled, ears straining for clues. Her bare feet met the floorboards silently and she shrugged on her cotton robe, grabbed the gun she kept by the side of the bed and tiptoed toward the door. She waited, her breath tight in her chest, until the noise came again.

"Who's there? I'll shoot!"

"Mrs. Van Cleve? That you?"

She blinked and peered out of the window. Deputy Dulles was standing there in full uniform, one hand rubbing anxiously at the back of his neck. She moved to the door and unlocked it. "Deputy?"

"It's Miss O'Hare. I think it's her time. I can't raise Dr. Garnett and I don't feel happy with her laboring down there alone."

It took Alice a matter of minutes to haul her clothes on. She saddled a sleepy Spirit and followed the treads of Deputy Dulles's tire marks, her determination overriding any natural hesitation Spirit might have had about negotiating the deep woods in the black of night. The little horse trotted out into the darkness, ears pricked, wary but willing, and Alice wanted to kiss her for it. When she got to the mossy track by the creek bed she was able to break into a gallop, and she pushed the mare as hard as she could, grateful for the moonlight that illuminated the path.

When she reached the road she did not head straight for the jail, but turned, urging Spirit down toward William and Sophia's house at Monarch Creek. She had changed in her time in Kentucky, yes, and, true, she wasn't afraid of much. But even Alice knew when she was out of her depth.

By the time Sophia reached the jailhouse, Margery, slick with sweat, was pushing against Alice like someone in a rugby scrum, doubled over and moaning with pain. Alice could only have been there for twenty minutes but felt as if it had already been hours. She heard her own voice as if from a long distance—praising Margery for her bravery, insisting that she was doing so well, that the baby would be here before she knew it, even as she knew that only one of those things might possibly be true. The deputy had lent them an oil lamp and the light flickered, sending uncertain shadows up the cell walls. The scents of blood, urine and something raw and unmentionable filled the thick, stale air. Alice hadn't realized birth would be so *messy*.

Sophia had run all the way, her mother's old midwife's bag under her arm, and Deputy Dulles, softened by two months of baked gifts, and confident that the librarians essentially meant well, pulled back the cell door with a clatter and allowed Sophia in.

"Oh, thank goodness," said Alice, into the dim light, as he locked it again behind them with a crash of keys. "I was so afraid you wouldn't get here in time."

"How far along is she?"

Alice shrugged, and Sophia ran her hand over Margery's forehead. Margery's eyes were clamped shut, her mind somewhere far from them, while another wave of pain crashed over her.

Sophia waited, her eyes alert and watchful, until it passed. "Margery? Margery, girl? How far apart are your pains?"

"Don't know," Margery murmured through dry lips. "Where's Sven? Please. I need Sven."

"You got to pull yourself together now, stay focused. Alice, you got your wristwatch there? You start counting when I say, okay?"

Sophia's mother had been the midwife for all the colored folk in Baileyville. When she had been a child, Sophia had accompanied her on visits, carrying her mother's big leather bag, handing her the instruments and herbs as they were needed, helping her sterilize and repack them ready for the next woman. She wasn't fully trained, she said, but she was probably the best Margery was going to get.

"You girls okay in there?" Deputy Dulles stood respectfully behind the sheet as Margery began to wail again, her voice lowing, then building to a crescendo. He had made sure he was well away when his own wife had borne their children, and the indelicate sounds and scents of it made him a little queasy.

"Sir? Could we possibly have some hot water?" Sophia motioned to Alice to open the bag, gesturing at a clean fold of cotton.

"I'll ask Frank, see if he can boil some. He's usually up at this hour. Be right back."

"*I can't do it.*" Margery's eyes opened, fixed on something neither of them could see.

"Sure you can," said Sophia, firmly. "That's just nature's way of telling us you're nearly there."

"I can't." Margery sounded breathless, exhausted. "I'm so tired . . ." Alice took a handkerchief and wiped her face. Margery looked so pale, so drawn, despite her swollen belly. Without the daily rigors of her life outside, her limbs had lost their muscle, grown soft and white. It made Alice feel uncomfortable to see her, her cotton dress tight around her, the way it stuck to her damp skin.

"A minute and a half," she said, as Margery began to moan again.

"Yup. Baby's coming all right. Okay, Margery. I'm going to lean you back here for a moment while I put a sheet down on this old mattress. Okay? You just hang on to Alice."

"*Sven . . .*" Alice saw Margery's lips shape his name as her knuckles grew yellow-white on Alice's sleeve, her fingers a vice. She heard Sophia's voice murmuring reassurances as she moved, sure-footed, in the near dark. The cells opposite were uncharacteristically silent.

"Okay, sweetie. Now that baby's coming, we need to get you into a position where she can make her way out. You hear me?" Sophia motioned to Alice, helping her turn Margery, who barely seemed to register. "You keep listening to me, you hear?"

"I'm afraid, Sophia."

"No, you ain't, not really. That's just the laboring talking."

"I don't want her born here." Margery opened her eyes and looked imploringly at Sophia. "Not here. Please . . ."

Sophia put her hand on the back of Margery's damp head and placed her cheek against hers. "I know, baby, but that's what's gonna happen. So we're just gonna make it as easy as we can for the two of you. Okay? Now you turn over onto all fours. Yes, all fours—and just grab a hold of that bunk. Alice, you get yourself in front of her and hold tight on to her, okay? It's going to get a little rough shortly and she's going to need you to hang onto. That's it, you give her your lap to rest on."

Alice didn't have time to feel fear. Almost as soon as she said it, Margery's hands were gripping her, her face pressed into Alice's thighs as she wailed, trying to bury the sound in Alice's breeches. Her grip was so strong, as if she were possessed by forces beyond herself. Alice watched the tremors pass through her and winced, trying to ignore her own discomfort, hearing the unconscious words of encouragement stream from her mouth, even as she was swept along in the slipstream. Behind her Sophia had lifted Margery's cotton dress, and positioned the oil lamp so that she could look at the most intimate parts of her, but Margery didn't seem to care. She just kept moaning, her body rocking from side to side, as if she could shake off the pain, her hands grasping stickily for Alice's own.

"I got your water," came Deputy Dulles's voice. And when Margery began to yell, he said, "I'm going to unlock the door and just push the jug inside. Okay? I've sent for the doctor, just in case. *Oh, dear*

JOJO MOYES

Lord, what in God's— You know what? I'm just— I'll leave it outside.
I— *Oh, dear God—*"

"Can we have some fresh water in here too, please, sir? Drinking
water?"

"I—I'll leave it outside the door. Going to trust you girls not to go
anywhere."

"You got nothing to concern yourself with, sir, believe me."

Sophia was a whirlwind, laying out her mama's steel instruments,
placing them carefully on the clean folded cotton square. She kept one
hand on Margery at all times, as one might a horse, reassuring, cooing,
encouraging. She peered underneath her, positioned herself.

"Okay, I think she's coming. Alice, you hold on now."

After that everything became a blur. As the sun rose, forcing fingers of blue light through the narrow bars, Alice remembered the
events as if on a ship in high seas: the rocking of the floor beneath
them, Margery's body, thrown one way and then another by the force
of her labors, the scents of blood and sweat and bodies pressed together, *the noise, the noise, the noise.* Margery hanging on to her, her
face pleading, afraid, begging them to *help me, help me,* her own rising
panic. And underneath it all Sophia, calm and reassuring one moment,
bullying and fierce the next. *Yes, you can, Margery. C'mon, girl. You got
to push now! Push harder!*

Alice had feared for a dreadful moment that here, in the heat and
the dark and the animal sounds, with this sense that they were on their
own, locked into this journey, the three of them, she might faint. She
was frightened of the uncharted depths of Margery's pain, afraid to see
this woman who had always been so strong, so capable, reduced to a
crying, wounded animal. Women died doing this, didn't they? How
could Margery not, in such agony? But just as the room swam, she
caught Sophia's fierce expression, saw Margery's furrowed brow, her
eyes swimming with tears of despair—*I can't!*—and she gritted her
teeth and leaned forward so that Margery's forehead was pressed against
her own.

314

"Yes, you can, Marge. You're so close now. You listen to Sophia. You can do this."

And then suddenly as Margery's wail reached an unbearable pitch—a sound that was like the end of the world and all its agonies compressed, thin, drawn out, unendurable—there was a shout and a noise like a fish landing on a slab and Sophia was suddenly gripping this wet, purple creature in her arms, her face illuminated and her apron bloodied as the baby's hands lifted blindly, grappling with the air for something to hold on to.

"She's here!"

And Margery turned her head, the tendrils of hair stuck to her cheeks, the survivor of some terrible, solitary battle, and on her face was an expression Alice had never seen before, and her voice was a soft keening, like cattle in a shed, nuzzling a calf, "Oh, baby, oh, my baby!" And as the tiny girl let out a thin, lusty cry, the world shifted, and they were suddenly laughing and crying and clutching at each other, and the men in the cells, whom Alice had not known were there, were exclaiming in heartfelt tones, "Thank the Lord! Praise Jesus!" And in the darkness and the filth and the blood and mess, as Sophia wiped the baby, wrapped her in the clean cotton sheet and handed her to the trembling Margery, Alice sat back and wiped her eyes with her sweating, bloodied hands and thought she had never been anywhere so glorious in all her born days.

She was, Sven said that evening, as they toasted him in the library, the most beautiful child who had ever been born. Her eyes the darkest, her hair the thickest, her tiny nose and perfect limbs unparalleled in history. Nobody felt inclined to disagree. Fred had brought a Mason jar of moonshine and a crate of beers, and the librarians wetted the baby's head and thanked the Lord's mercy, deciding for that evening at least not to look further than the joy of that safe delivery, that Margery was even now cradling the tiny child with a mother's fierce pride, enraptured by her perfect face, her tiny seashell fingernails, briefly oblivious to her own pain and circumstances, while even Deputy Dulles and the other jailers passed by to admire her and offer their congratulations.

No man had ever been prouder than Sven. He could not stop talking—of how brave and clever Margery was to produce such a creature, of how alert the child was, the way she had held his finger in a fierce grip. "She's an O'Hare all right," he said, and they all cheered.

For Alice and Sophia the night's events had started to catch up with them. Alice was exhausted, her eyelids drooping, her gaze flickering to Sophia's, which was tired but relieved. Alice felt as if she had emerged from a tunnel, as if she had lost some layer of innocence she had barely been aware of.

"I've sewn her a layette," Sophia told Sven. "If you could take it to Margery tomorrow the child will have something decent to wear. A blanket, some booties, a little hat and a sweater in light cotton."

"That's mighty kind of you, Sophia," said Sven. He was unshaven and his eyes kept filling with tears.

"And I have some things from my babies she can have," said Kathleen. "Spare undershirts and cotton squares and suchlike. It's not like I'm going to need them again."

"You never know," said Beth.

But Kathleen shook her head firmly. "Oh, I know." She stooped to pick at something on her breeches. "There was only one man for me."

At this Fred caught Alice's eye and, after the euphoria of earlier in the day, she felt suddenly sad, and weary. She hid it under a toast. "To Marge," she said, holding up her enamel mug.

"To Margery."

"And Virginia," said Sven, and, as they all looked at him: "After Margery's sister." He swallowed. "That's what she wants. Virginia Alice O'Hare."

"Well, that's just a beautiful name," said Sophia, nodding her approval.

"Virginia Alice," they echoed, lifting their mugs. And then Izzy abruptly got up and announced that she was sure there was a book of names somewhere and she would very much like to know where it came from. And everyone else, swallowing just as hard and more than grateful for the distraction, agreed, so that nobody had to look at Alice, who was now sobbing, silently, in the corner.

TWENTY-TWO

★

An unbelievably filthy institution in which are confined men and women serving sentence for misdemeanors and crimes, and men and women not under sentence who are simply awaiting trial. . . . *Usually swarming with bedbugs, roaches, lice, and other vermin; has an odor of disinfectant and filth.*

· JOSEPH F. FISHMAN, *Crucibles of Crime*, 1923

The jailhouses of Kentucky, like those across much of America, were run on an ad-hoc basis and their rules, and laxity, varied considerably depending on the rigidity of the sheriff, and in the case of Baileyville, his deputy's fondness for baked goods. As such, Margery and Virginia were able to receive a stream of visitors and, despite the unpleasant confines of the cell, Virginia spent her first weeks in much the same way that all beloved babies spend them—in clean, soft clothes, admired by visitors, celebrated with small toys, and spending a good part of her day nestled against her mother's bosom. She was a remarkably alert baby, her dark eyes scanning the cell for movement, her tiny starfish fingers stroking the air or making little fists of contentment as she fed.

Margery, meanwhile, was a woman transformed, her face softened, her whole focus on the tiny child, carrying her around as easily as if she had done it for years. Despite her previous reservations, she seemed to take to motherhood instinctively. Even when Alice scooped up the baby so that Margery could eat, or change her clothes, Margery had one eye on her, a hand reaching out to touch Virginia, as if she could not bear to be separated from her even for a moment.

Alice noted with relief that she appeared less depressed than before, as though the baby had given her something to fix on other than what she had lost beyond the walls. Margery ate better ("Sophia says I gotta eat to keep the milk coming"), smiled frequently, even if her smiles were directed chiefly at the child, and moved around the cell, bouncing on her heels to soothe the baby, whereas before she had seemed chiefly pinned to the floor. Deputy Dulles had lent them a bucket and a mop, to make it all a little more sanitary, and when the girls had brought her a fresh bed roll, complaining that it wasn't right to make a baby sleep on a dirty old pad with chiggers in it, he had agreed without complaint. They had burned the old one in the yard, wincing at its myriad stains.

Mrs. Brady visited Margery on the sixth day after she'd given birth, bringing with her a doctor from out of town to check that she was healing properly and that the baby had everything she needed. When Deputy Dulles had attempted to protest, given the absence of slips or indeed any prior warning, Mrs. Brady had cut him down with a look that could have frozen hot soup and announced imperiously that should she be impeded in *any way* while tending a nursing mother Sheriff Archer would be the first to hear about it, and Governor Hatch the second, and Deputy Dulles should be in no doubt about it. The doctor examined mother and baby while Mrs. Brady stood in the corner of the cell—she had squinted at her surroundings in the half-dark and decided not to sit—and while conditions were far from ideal, the doctor had announced both to be in good health and in as good spirits as could be expected. The men in the nearby cells had a few words to say about the stink of the baby's soiled diapers, but Mrs. Brady told them to hush their mouths and announced that the occasional brush with soap and water wouldn't hurt them none either, frankly, so maybe they should put their own house in order before complaining.

The librarians only discovered this visit after the event, when Mrs. Brady turned up at the library and declared that, having discussed matters at length with Miss O'Hare, they had agreed that she would step in and take over the day-to-day running of the library, and that she hoped very much this wouldn't inconvenience Mrs. Van Cleve, knowing, as she did, how hard she had worked to keep things going while Margery was *incapacitated*.

Alice, while a little taken aback, was not inconvenienced at all. She had been running on empty these last weeks, trying to visit Margery every day, keep the cabin in good order, and run the library, all while dealing with her own complex and overwhelming feelings. The idea that someone else would take over even one of those things came as a relief. Especially, she thought privately, as she would be leaving Kentucky before long anyway. Not that she had told any of the others; they all had enough to deal with just now.

Mrs. Brady removed her coat and asked to see all the ledgers. She sat at Sophia's desk and went through the payroll records, blacksmith's bills, cross-checked the wage slips and petty cash, pronouncing herself satisfied. She returned after supper and spent an hour with Sophia that evening checking up on the whereabouts of missing and damaged books, and berated Mr. Gill as he passed the door as to the late return of a book on raising goats. Within a few hours her being there felt unremarkable. It was as if a grown-up were in charge again.

In this way, summer inched forward under a blanket of heavy heat and flying bugs, of humidity and sweaty, fly-bothered horses, and Alice tried to live day to day, dealing with the minor discomforts, and without thinking of the many more substantial and infinitely more unpleasant discomforts that were lining up, like skittles, in her future.

Sven resigned from his job: with his shifts he could not make it over to see Margery and the baby during the week, and half his heart, he told Alice, was always there in that damned cell anyway. Hoffman's firemen lined up with their pickaxes against their shoulders and their helmets pressed against their chests when he told them of his departure, much to the fury of the foreman, who took Sven's departure somewhat personally.

Van Cleve, who was still smarting from the discovery of Sven's long-standing relationship with Margery O'Hare, said it was good riddance, that he had been a spy and a traitor, despite there being no evidence for either, and warned that if that snake Gustavsson was seen heading inside the Hoffman gates again he would be shot without warning, just like his godless hussy.

Sven would have liked to move into Margery's cabin, Alice knew, to be in some way closer to her, but instead, ever the gentleman, he refused her offer so that Alice could escape the censure of those in the town who would have seen something suspect in a man and a woman resting under the same roof, even if it was clear to all that both loved the same woman, albeit in very different ways.

Besides, Alice was no longer afraid to stay alone in the little cabin. She slept early and deeply, rose at 4:30 a.m. with the sun, splashed herself with icy water from the spring, fed the animals, climbed into whatever clothes she had laid out to dry and cooked herself a breakfast of eggs and bread, scattering the remaining crumbs to the hens and the red cardinals that gathered on the windowsill. She ate while reading one of Margery's books, and every other morning she baked a pan of fresh cornbread to take to the jailhouse. Around her the early-morning mountain rang with birdsong, the leaves of the trees glowing orange, then blue, then emerald green, the long grass mottled with lilies and sage grass, and as the screen door closed, huge wild turkeys rose up in an ungainly flap, or small deer skittered back into the woods, as if it were she who was the intruder.

She turned Charley out from the barn into the small paddock that backed the cabin, and checked the chicken coop for eggs. If she had time she would prepare food for the evening, knowing she would be tired when she returned home. Then she saddled Spirit, packed whatever she needed that day into the saddlebags, slammed the broadbrimmed hat onto her head, and rode down the mountain to the library. As she passed along the dirt track, she let the reins hang loose on Spirit's neck, and used both hands to tie a cotton handkerchief around her collar. She barely used the reins any more; Spirit would gauge where they were going as soon as she started each route, and stride out, ears pricked, just another creature who knew—and loved—her job.

Most evenings Alice would stay an hour later at the library alongside Sophia, just for the company, and occasionally Fred would join them, bringing food from the house. Twice she had walked up the track and eaten at Fred's, suspecting she was old news, and that few people were likely to see her make that short journey anyhow. She loved Fred's house, with its scent of beeswax, and its well-worn comforts, less rough and ready than Margery's, and with rugs and furniture that told of family money that went back more than one generation.

There was a reassuring lack of ornaments.

They would eat Fred's food and talk of everything and nothing, breaking off to smile at each other like fools. Some nights Alice would ride the track back to Margery's and have no idea what they had even said to each other, the hum of want and need in her ears drumming out whatever conversation had occurred. Sometimes she wanted him so badly she would have to pinch her hand under the table to stop herself reaching out for him. And then she would arrive back at the empty cabin and lie under the covers, her mind trying to conjure what might happen if once, just once, she invited him to come in with her.

. . .

Sven's lawyer visited every fortnight, and Sven asked if the meetings could take place at Fred's house, and whether she and Fred would sit alongside him. Alice understood that it was because Sven became so anxious, his leg jiggling with uncharacteristic nerves, his fingers tapping on the table, that afterward he would invariably have forgotten half of what he'd been told. The lawyer tended to speak in the least straightforward way possible, his language ornate and tortured, taking routes around and under what he meant to say rather than just state it outright.

He observed that, despite the unexpected disappearance of the relevant ledger (he left a meaningful pause at this point), the Commonwealth was confident of the evidence against Margery O'Hare. In her initial interview the old woman had placed Miss O'Hare at the scene, no matter what she claimed afterward. The library book, spattered with blood, appeared to be the only possible murder weapon, given there were no gunshot or stabbing injuries. No other of the packhorse librarians rode as far as Miss O'Hare, judging by the other ledgers, so the chances of anyone else using a library book as a weapon at that spot were limited. And then there was the difficult matter of Margery's character, the many people who would happily speak up about the long-standing feud between her family and the McCulloughs, and Margery's habit of saying the least palatable things without considering the impact her words might have on those around her.

"She will need to be mindful of these things when we come to trial," he said, gathering his papers. "It's important that the jury find her a . . . sympathetic defendant."

Sven shook his head mutely.

"You won't get Marge to be anyone other than who she is," said Fred.

"I'm not saying she has to be someone else. But if she cannot win the sympathy of the judge and the jury, her chances of freedom are severely diminished."

The lawyer sat back in his chair and put both hands on the table. "This is not just about truth, Mr. Gustavsson. It's about strategy. And no matter what the truth of this matter is, you can bet that the other side is working hardest on theirs."

Y ou like it, then."

"Like what?" Margery looked up.

"Being a mother."

"Got myself so swimming in feelings I don't know which way is up half the time," Margery said softly, adjusting the cotton vest at Virginia's neck. "Boy, it's even warm up here. Wish we could catch a breeze."

Since Virginia's birth Deputy Dulles had allowed the visits to take place in the empty holding cell upstairs. It was lighter and cleaner than those in the basement—and, they suspected, more acceptable to the redoubtable Mrs. Brady—but on a day like today, when the air hung warm and heavy with moisture, there was little relief.

Alice thought suddenly how awful the jailhouse would be in winter, with its exposed windows and cold cement floor. How much worse would the state penitentiary be? *She will be free by then*, she told herself firmly. *No thinking ahead. No thinking beyond today, this next hour.*

"Didn't think I could love another creature like this," Margery continued. "Feels like she's taken a layer of skin off me, you know?"

"Sven is truly besotted."

"Ain't he just?" Margery smiled to herself at some memory. "He's going to be the greatest daddy to you, tiny girl." Her face shadowed, as if there were something she didn't want to acknowledge. And then it was gone, and she was holding the baby up, gesturing to her head, smiling again. "You think her hair's going to be dark like mine? She's got a little Cherokee in her, after all. Or you think she'll lighten up, more like her daddy? You know when Sven was a baby his hair was white as chalk."

Margery wouldn't discuss the trial. She would shake her head twice, tiny movements, as if suggesting there was no point in it. And despite this new softness, there was something steely enough in that movement for Alice not to try to contradict it. She had done the same to Beth and to Mrs. Brady when they visited, and Mrs. Brady had arrived back at the library quite pink with frustration.

"I was talking to my husband about the trial, and what happens afterward . . . if things do not go the way we hope. He has some friends in the legal world and apparently across state lines there are some places that allow the children to stay with the mother, and matrons to attend properly to the women. Some have quite good facilities all told."   ·

Margery had acted like she hadn't heard a word.

"We're all praying for you in church. You and Virginia. Isn't she the dearest thing? I just wondered whether you would like us to try to—"

"Appreciate your thoughts, Mrs. Brady, but we'll be fine."

And that was it, Mrs. Brady said, throwing her hands into the air. "It's as if she's burying her head in the sand. Honestly, I don't think she can simply rely on the idea of getting out. She needs to plan."

But Alice didn't feel that optimism was at the heart of Margery's behavior. It was one of the many reasons she felt increasingly anxious with every day that the trial grew closer.

Exactly one week before the trial was due to start newspapers began to speculate on its suspect. One had got hold of the picture of the women from the Nice 'N' Quick, and cropped it so that only Margery's face was visible. The headline read:

THE LIBRARIAN KILLER:
DID SHE MURDER INNOCENT MAN?

The nearest hotel, in Danvers Creek, swiftly found itself with every room booked, and there was talk that some neighbors had tidied up back rooms and put beds in them to house the reporters who were also coming to town. It seemed that Margery and McCullough were all anybody talked about, except within the confines of the library, where nobody talked about them at all.

Sven headed to the jail in the height of the afternoon. It was an excessively warm day and he walked slowly, using his hat to fan himself, and raising a hand in greeting to those he passed, his outward demeanor revealing nothing of what he felt inside. He handed the tin of Alice's cornbread to Deputy Dulles, and checked his pockets for the clean vest and bib that Alice had folded neatly for him to bring. Margery was in the holding cell upstairs, feeding the baby, seated cross-legged on the bunk, and he waited to kiss her, knowing as he did how easily distracted the baby was. Usually she would raise a cheek for him but this time she kept gazing down at the child, so after a moment he sat down on the stool nearby.

"She still feeding all night?"

"Much as she can get."

"Mrs. Brady said she might be one of those babies needs solid food early. I got a book about it from the girls, just to read up a little."

"Since when have you been chatting with Mrs. Brady about babies?"

He looked at his boots. "Since I quit my job."

When she stared at him, he added: "Don't worry. I've not been out of work since I was fourteen years old. And Fred is letting me stay in his spare room so I'm good. We'll be good."

Margery didn't speak. Some days she was like this now. Would barely say a word the whole time he was there. Those days had grown fewer since Virginia arrived—it was as if she couldn't help but talk to the child, even if she was feeling down, but Sven still hated to see them. He rubbed at his head. "Alice said to tell you the chickens are doing fine. Winnie laid a double-yolker. Charley's getting fat. Quite enjoying the rest, far as I can see it. We've got him turned out this week with Fred's young ones and he's showing them who's boss."

She looked down at Virginia, checking that she had finished, then adjusted her dress and placed the baby against her shoulder for burping.

"You know, I was thinking . . ." Sven continued. "Maybe when you come home we could get another dog. There's a farmer over at Shelbyville got a hunting bitch I've fancied for a long time that he wants to put to pup. She's got a sweet nature. It's good for a child to grow up around a dog. If we get a puppy, he and Virginia could grow up together. What do you say?"

"Sven . . ."

"I mean, we don't have to get a dog. Could wait till she's a little older. I just thought . . ."

"You remember I once told you I would never tell you to leave me?" Still she kept her eyes on the child.

"I do indeed. Almost made you write it on a piece of paper for proof." He raised a wry smile.

"Well . . . I made a mistake. I need you to go."

He leaned forward, his head cocked. "I'm sorry—what?"

"And I need you to take Virginia." When she finally looked up at him her eyes were wide and serious. "I was arrogant, Sven. I thought I could live as I wanted, long as I didn't hurt nobody. But I've had time to think in here—and I worked it out. You don't get to do that in Lee County, maybe not in the whole of Kentucky. Not if you're a woman. You play by their rules or they . . . well, they squash you like a bug."

Her voice was calm and even, as if she had rehearsed the words in her many silent hours. "I need you to take her far away, to New York State or Chicago, maybe even the West Coast, if there's work. Take her somewhere beautiful, somewhere she can have opportunities and a good education and not have to worry about whatever shitty scars her family left on her future before she was even born. Take her from people who will judge her for her name long before she can even spell it."

He was nonplussed. "You're talking crazy, Marge. I'm not leaving you."

"For twenty years? You know that's what they're going to give me even if I get manslaughter. And it'll be worse if it's murder."

"But you didn't do nothing wrong!"

"You think they care a whit about that? You know how this town works. You know they're gunning for me."

He looked at her as if she were mad. "I'm not going. So you can forget it."

"Well, I'm not going to see you any more. So, you don't get a say."

"What? What are you talking about now?"

"This is the last time I'm going to see you. It's one of the few rights I get in here, the right not to see visitors. Sven, I know you're a good man, and you'll do anything to help me. And, by God, I love you for it. But this is about Virginia now. So I need you to promise me you'll do as I ask, and never bring our daughter back to this place." She leaned back against the wall.

"But . . . what about the trial?"

"I don't want you there."

Sven stood up. "This is crazy talk. I'm not listening to this. I—"

Margery's voice lifted. She lurched forward and gripped his hand, stopping him. "Sven, I have nothing left. I have no freedom, no dignity, no future. The only damn thing I have is hope that for this girl, my *heart*, the thing I love most in the whole world, it might work out different. So if you love me, like you say you do, give me what I'm asking. I don't want my baby's childhood marked out in visits to the jail. I will not have you both watch me waste away week by week, year by year in the state prison, with lice in my hair and the stink of the slop buckets, beat down by the bigots that run this town and going slowly stir crazy. I will not have her seeing it. You'll make her happy, I know you can, and when you talk of me, you tell her not of this, but of me riding out on Charley, in the mountains, doing what I loved to do."

His hand closed around hers. His voice broke, and he kept shaking his head, in a way that suggested he wasn't even sure he was doing it. "I can't leave you, Marge."

She withdrew her hand. She took the sleeping baby and placed her gently in his arms. Then Margery leaned forward, and placed a kiss on the baby's head. She kept her lips there for a moment, her eyes closed tight. She opened them, drinking her in as if she were imprinting some part of her deep within. "Bye-bye, sweetheart. Mama loves you very much."

She touched the back of his knuckles lightly with her fingertips, an instruction. And then, as Sven sat in shock, Margery O'Hare stood upright, her hand braced on the table, and shouted for the jailer to walk her to her cell.

She didn't look back.

True to her word, he was the last visitor she saw. Alice arrived that afternoon with a pound cake and Deputy Dulles said regretfully (for he did love Alice's cakes) that he was real sorry but Miss O'Hare was adamant she didn't want to see anyone that day.

"Is there a problem with the baby?"

"Baby ain't there no more. She left with her daddy this morning."

He was real sorry but rules was rules and he couldn't force Miss O'Hare to see Alice. He did, however, agree to take the cake with the promise he'd carry it down to her later. When Kathleen Bligh went two days later she would receive the same response, and Sophia and Mrs. Brady after her.

Alice rode home, her mind spinning, and found Sven on the porch with the baby resting on his shoulder, her button eyes wide at the unfamiliar sunlight and the moving shadows of the trees. "Sven?"

Alice dismounted, hooked Spirit's reins over the post. "Sven? What on earth is going on?"

He couldn't look at her. His eyes were red-rimmed, and he kept his face turned away.

"Sven?"

"She's the stubbornest damn woman in Kentucky."

On cue the baby started to cry, the raw, ragged cries of a child who has had to cope with too many changes in a single day and is suddenly, catastrophically, overwhelmed. Sven patted her back ineffectually and, after a moment, Alice stepped forward and took the baby from him.

His face sank into his broad, scarred hands. The baby nuzzled into Alice's shoulder, then pulled her head back, her tiny mouth an O of dismay, as if appalled by the discovery that this was not her mother.

"We'll fix it, Sven. We'll make her see sense."

He shook his head. "Why would we?" His voice emerged muffled through his rough hands. "She's right. That's the worst of it, Alice. She's right."

Through Kathleen, who knew everything and everyone, Alice found a woman in the next town who would wet-nurse the baby, her own having recently weaned, for a small sum. Every morning Sven would drive the baby over to the white clapboard farmhouse and little Virginia would be handed over for food and care. It made all of them a little uneasy to see it—the child belonged with her mother—and Virginia herself had swiftly become withdrawn, her eyes watchful, her thumb plugged warily into her mouth, as if she no longer trusted the world to be a benign and reliable place. But what else could they do? The child was fed; Sven was free to find work. Alice and the girls were able to get by as best they could, and if their hearts were sick and their stomachs tight with nerves, well, that was the way it was.

TWENTY-THREE

✦

*I don't ask you to love me always like this, but I ask
you to remember. Somewhere inside me there'll always
be the person I am to-night.*

· F. Scott Fitzgerald, *Tender Is the Night*

A near circus atmosphere descended on Baileyville, the kind of commotion that made Tex Lafayette's appearance look like a Sunday School reunion. As news of the start date had broken across the town the mood seemed to shift, and not necessarily in Margery's favor. The extended McCullough clan began to arrive from out of town—distant cousins from Tennessee, from Michigan and North Carolina, some of whom had barely seen McCullough in decades but who now found themselves highly invested in the idea of retribution for their beloved relative, and swiftly took to congregating outside either the jailhouse or the library, to shout abuse and threaten vengeance.

Fred had come down twice from his house to try to calm things, and when that failed, to reveal his gun and announce that the women must be allowed to get on with their work. The town seemed split in two with their arrival, dividing between those who were disposed to see all the wrong in Margery's family as evidence of her own bad blood, and those who preferred to go on their own experience, and thanked her for bringing books and a little pleasantry into their lives.

Twice Beth got into fist-fights on the back of Margery's reputation, once in the store and once on the steps outside the library, and had taken to walking around with her hands bunched, as if permanently braced to throw a punch. Izzy wept frequently and silently, and would shake her head mutely if anyone spoke to her of it, as if the act of talking were too much. Kathleen and Sophia said little, but their somber faces told of which way they thought this would go. Alice could no longer visit the jail, in accordance with Margery's wishes, but felt her presence in the little concrete building as if they were connected by threads. She was eating a little, Deputy Dulles said, when she stopped by. Didn't speak much, though. Seemed to spend a lot of time sleeping.

Sven left town. He bought a small wagon and a young horse, packed up what remained of his belongings and moved out of Fred's to a one-room cabin a short distance from the wet-nurse on the eastern side of the Cumberland Gap. He could not stay in Baileyville, not with people saying what they were. Not with the prospect of seeing the woman he loved brought even lower, and the crying baby in earshot of her mother. His eyes were red with exhaustion, and new deep grooves ran down each side of his mouth that had nothing to do with the baby. Fred promised him at the first word of anything he would drive right over.

"I'll tell her—I'll tell her . . ." Fred began, then realized he had no idea what he would tell Margery. They exchanged a look, then slapped each other on the shoulder, in the way near silent men have of conveying emotion, and Sven drove off with his hat pulled low over his brow and his mouth set in a grim line.

Alice also began to pack up. In the quiet of the little cabin she began to separate her clothes into those she might find some use for in England, in her future life, and those she could not imagine wearing again. She would hold up the fine silk blouses, the elegantly cut skirts, gossamer slips and nightwear and frown. Had she ever been this person? In the emerald floral tea-dresses and lace collars? Had she really required all these hair rollers, setting lotions and pearl brooches? She felt as if such ephemera belonged to someone she no longer knew.

She waited until she had completed this task before she told the girls. By this stage they had all, by some unspoken agreement, taken to staying at the library together until way beyond their finishing time. It was as if this was the only place they could bear to be. Two nights before the trial was due to start she waited until Kathleen began gathering her bags, then said, "So—I have some news. I'm leaving. If anyone wants any of my things I'll be leaving a trunk of clothes in the library for you all to go through. You're welcome to any of it."

"Leaving where?"

"Here." She swallowed. "I have to go back to England."

There was a heavy silence. Izzy's hands flew to her mouth. "You can't leave!"

"Well, I can't stay, unless I go back to Bennett. Van Cleve will come after me once he's got Margery safely locked up."

"Don't say that," said Beth.

There was a lengthy silence. Alice tried to ignore the looks passing between the other women.

"Is Bennett so bad?" said Izzy. "I mean, if you could persuade him to move out from his daddy's shadow, maybe you two would have a chance. Then you could stay."

How could she explain now how impossible it would be to return to Bennett, feeling as she did about Fred? She would rather be a million miles from Fred than have to walk past him every day and know she had to go back to another man. Fred had barely touched her yet she felt they understood each other better than she and Bennett ever had.

"I can't. And you know Van Cleve won't rest until he's got rid of the Packhorse Library, too. Which will put us all out of a job. Fred saw him with the sheriff and Kathleen saw him twice last week with the governor. He's working away to undermine us."

"But if we don't have Margery and we don't have you . . ." Izzy's voice trailed away.

"Does Fred know?" said Sophia.

Alice nodded.

Sophia's eyes held hers, as if confirming something.

"When are you going?" said Izzy.

"Soon as the trial is done." Fred had barely spoken the whole drive home. She had wanted to reach out, to touch his hand and tell him she was sorry, that this was so far from what she wanted, but she was so frozen with grief at her possession of the paper ticket that she couldn't move.

Izzy rubbed at her eyes and sniffed. "Feels like everything's falling apart. Everything we worked for. Our friendship. This place. Everything is just falling apart."

Normally when one of the women expressed such dramatic sentiments the others would leap on her, telling her to stop being ridiculous, that she was crazy, that she simply needed a good night's sleep, or some food, or to get a hold of herself; it was her monthlies talking. It was a measure of how low they all felt that this time nobody said a word.

Sophia broke the silence. She took an audible breath and placed both hands palm down on the table. "Well, for now we keep going. Beth, I don't believe you've entered your books from this afternoon. If you'd be kind enough to bring them over here, I'll do them for you. And, Alice, if you can give me the exact day you're planning on leaving, I'll adjust the payroll."

Overnight two trailer homes arrived on the road by the courthouse. Extra state policemen were visible around town, and a crowd began to build outside the jailhouse by teatime on Monday, fueled by a newspaper report in the *Lexington Courier* headlined: Moonshiner's Daughter Killed Man With Library Book In Blood Feud.

"This is trash," Kathleen said, when Mrs. Beidecker handed her a copy at the school. But that didn't stop the people gathering, a few starting to catcall out back so that the sound would reach through the open window of Margery's cell. Deputy Dulles came out twice, his palms up, trying to calm them, but a tall mustachioed man in an ill-fitting suit, whom nobody had seen before and claimed to be Clem McCullough's cousin, said they were just exercising their God-given right to free speech. And if he wanted to talk about what a murdering bitch that O'Hare girl was then it was nobody else's damn business. They jostled each other, fueling their bold claims with alcohol, and by dusk the yard outside the jailhouse was thick with people, some drunk, some shouting insults at Margery, others yelling back at them that they were not from round here and why didn't they keep their troublemaking ways to themselves? The older ladies of the town withdrew behind their doors, muttering, and some of the younger men, emboldened by the chaos, started a bonfire by the garage. It felt, briefly, as if the orderly little town had become a place where almost anything could happen. And none of it good.

Word got to the librarians as they returned from their routes, and each put away her horse and sat in silence with the door open for a while, listening to the distant sounds of protest.

Murdering bitch!

You gonna get yours, you whore!

Now, now, gentlemen. There are ladies in this crowd. Let's keep things reasonable.

"I swear I'm glad Sven isn't here to see it," said Beth. "You know he wouldn't stand to hear Marge talked about that way."

"I can't bear it," said Izzy, who was watching through the door. "Imagine how she must be feeling having to listen to all that."

"She'll be so sad without the baby too."

It was all Alice could think about. To be the recipient of such hate, without the prospect of a word of comfort from those who loved you. The way Margery had isolated herself made Alice want to weep. It was like an animal that deliberately takes itself off somewhere solitary before it dies.

"Lord help our girl," Sophia said quietly.

And then Mrs. Brady walked through the door, glancing behind her, her cheeks ruddy and her hair electric with fury. "I swear I thought this town knew better. I am ashamed of my neighbors, I really am. I can only imagine what Mrs. Nofcier would say if she happened to catch wind of this."

"Fred reckons they'll be out there all night."

"I simply do not know what this town is coming to. Why Sheriff Archer doesn't take a bullwhip to them I have no idea. I swear we're becoming worse than Harlan."

It was then that they heard Van Cleve's voice rising above the swell of the crowd: "You can't say I didn't warn you, people! She's a danger to men and to this town. The court is going to hear what kind of malign influence the O'Hare girl is. Only one place for her!"

"Oh, hell, now *he's* fixing to stir things up," said Beth.

"Folks, you will hear how much of an abomination the girl is. Against the laws of nature! Nothing she says can be trusted!"

"That does it," said Izzy, her jaw clenched.

Mrs. Brady turned to look at her daughter, as Izzy climbed to her feet. She grabbed her stick and walked to the door. "Mother? Will you come with me?"

They moved as one, pulling on boots and hats in silence. And then, without discussion, they stood together at the top of the steps: Kathleen and Beth, Izzy and Mrs. Brady and, after a moment's hesitation, Sophia, who rose from behind her desk, her face tense but determined, reaching for her purse. The others stopped to look at her. Then Alice, her heart in her throat, held out her arm and Sophia slid her own through it. And the six women walked out of the library and, in a tight group, along the shimmering road toward the jailhouse in silence, their faces set and their pace determined.

The crowd broke as they arrived, partly through the sheer force of Mrs. Brady, whose elbows were out and whose expression was thunderous, but partly in shock at the colored woman who stood between them, her arms linked with those of Bennett Van Cleve's wife and the Bligh widow.

Mrs. Brady reached the front of the crowd and pushed her way through so that she was standing with her back to the jail and turned to face them. "Are you not ashamed of yourselves?" she bellowed at them. "What kind of men are you?"

"She's a murderer!"

"In this country we believe in the presumption of innocence unless proven otherwise. So you can take your disgusting words and your slogans and you can darn well leave that girl alone until the law says you have good reason!"

She pointed at the mustachioed man. "What business do you have in our town anyway? I swear some of you are here just to cause trouble. Because you're sure as anything not from Baileyville."

"I'm Clem's second cousin. Got a right to be here as much as anyone. I cared about my cousin."

"Caring cousin my backside," said Mrs. Brady. "Where were you when his daughters were starving, their hair full of cooties? When they were stealing food from people's gardens because he was too drunk to bother feeding them? Where were you then, huh? You have no genuine feeling for that family."

"You're just sticking up for your own. We all know what them librarians have been up to."

"You know nothing!" retorted Mrs. Brady. "And you, Henry Porteous, why, I thought you were old enough to know better. As for this fool—" she pointed at Van Cleve "—I honestly believed our neighbors would have more sense than to trust a man who has built an entire fortune on the back of misery and destruction, mostly at this town's cost. How many of you lost your homes to his slurry dam, huh? How many of you were given warning to save yourselves by Miss O'Hare there? And yet, given baseless rumor and gossip, you would rather castigate a woman than look at the true criminal around here."

"Those are slanderous words, Patricia!"

"So sue me, Geoffrey."

Van Cleve's skin flushed florid purple. "I've warned y'all! She's a malign influence!"

"You're the only malign influence around here! Why do you think your daughter-in-law would rather live in a cowshed than share one more night in your house? What kind of man beats up on his son's wife? And you stand there presenting yourself as some kind of moral arbiter. Why, the way we judge the behavior of men against women in this town is genuinely shocking."

The crowd began to murmur.

"What kind of woman kills a decent man with no provocation?"

"This has nothing to do with McCullough and you know it. This is about getting back at a woman who showed you up for what you are!"

"See, ladies and gentlemen? This is the true face of that so-called library. A coarsening of female discourse, behavior contrary to what's proper. Why, do you think it's right that Mrs. Brady should speak in such a way?"

The crowd surged forward, and was stopped abruptly by two gunshots in the air. There was a scream. People ducked, glancing around nervously. Sheriff Archer appeared in the back doorway to the jailhouse. He surveyed the crowd. "Now. I've been a patient man, but I do not want to hear one more word out here. The court will decide this case from tomorrow and due process will be followed. And if one more of you steps out of line you'll be finding yourself in the jailhouse alongside Miss O'Hare. That goes for you too, Geoffrey, and you, Patricia. I'll put any one of youse away. You hear me?"

"We got a right to free speech!" a man shouted.

"You do. And I got a right to make sure you're speaking it from one of my cells down there."

The crowd began to yell again, the words ugly, the voices harsh and clamorous. Alice looked around her and began to tremble, chilled by the venom, the hate etched on faces she had previously waved a cheery good morning to. How could they turn on Margery like this? She felt something fearful and panicky rise in her chest, the energy of the crowd charging the air around her. And then she felt Kathleen nudge her, and saw that Izzy had stepped forward. As the protesters railed and chanted around her, pushing and jostling, she limped her way out in front of them, a little unsteady and resting on her stick, until she was underneath the cell window. And as everyone watched, Izzy Brady, who struggled to stand in front of an audience of five, turned to face the shifting crowd, looked around her, and took a deep breath.

And she began to sing.

Abide with me; fast falls the eventide;
The darkness deepens; Lord, with me abide.

She paused, took a breath, her eyes flickering around her.

When other helpers fail and comforts flee,
Help of the helpless, oh, abide with me.

The crowd quieted, unsure at first what was going on, those at the back straining on tiptoe to see. A man catcalled and someone cursed him. Izzy stood, her hands clasped in front of her, shaking slightly, and sang out, her voice growing in strength and intensity.

Swift to its close ebbs out life's little day;
Earth's joys grow dim; its glories pass away;
Change and decay in all around I see;
O Thou who changest not, abide with me.

Mrs. Brady, her back straightening, took two, three strides, pushed through the crowd and placed herself beside her daughter, her back against the outside of the jailhouse wall, and her chin lifted. As they sang together, Kathleen, then Beth and, finally, Sophia and Alice, their arms still linked, moved to stand beside them and lifted their voices, too, their heads up and their gaze steady, facing down the crowd. As the men shouted insults, their six voices grew in volume, drowning them out, determined and unafraid.

Come not in terrors, as the King of kings,
But kind and good, with healing in Thy wings,
Tears for all woes, a heart for every plea—
Come, Friend of sinners, and thus abide with me.

They sang until the crowd was silent, watched by Sheriff Archer. They sang, pressed shoulder to shoulder, hands reaching blindly for hands, their hearts beating fast but their voices steady. A handful of townspeople stepped forward and joined them—Mrs. Beidecker, the gentleman from the feed shop, Jim Horner and his girls, their hands clasped together and their voices lifting, drowning the sounds of hate, feeling the resonance of each word, sending comfort, while trying to offer a little of that elusive substance to themselves.

A few inches away, on the other side of the wall, Margery O'Hare lay motionless on the bunk, her hair stuck to her face in damp tendrils, her skin pale and hot. She had lain there for almost four days now, her breasts aching, her arms empty in a way that made her feel as if someone had reached inside her and simply ripped out whatever kept her upright. What was there to stand up for now? To hope for, even? She was unnaturally still, her eyes closed, the rough hessian against her skin, listening only dimly to the crowd hurling abuse outside. Someone had managed to throw a stone through the window earlier and it had caught her leg, where a long scratch remained, livid with blood.

Hold Thou Thy cross before my closing eyes,
Shine through the gloom and point me to the skies.

She opened her eyes at a sound that was both familiar and strange, blinking as she focused, and it gradually registered that the sound was Izzy, her unforgettable sweet voice rising into the air outside the high window, so close she could almost touch it. It told of a world far beyond this cell, of goodness, and kindness, of a wide, unending sky into which a voice could soar. She pushed herself up onto her elbow, listening. And then another voice joined hers, deeper and more resonant, and then, as she straightened, there they were, separate voices she could just distinguish from the others: Kathleen, Sophia, Beth, Alice.

Heaven's morning breaks and earth's vain shadows flee.
In life, in death, O Lord, abide with me.

She heard them and realized then that it was to her they were singing, heard Alice's shout as the hymn drew to a close, her voice still clear as crystal.

"You stay strong, Margery! We're with you! We're right here with you!"

Margery O'Hare lowered her head to her knees, her hands covering her face and, at last, she sobbed.

TWENTY-FOUR

★

I loved something I made up, something that's just as dead as Melly is. I made a pretty suit of clothes and fell in love with it. And when Ashley came riding along, so handsome, so different, I put that suit on him and made him wear it whether it fitted him or not. And I wouldn't see what he really was. I kept on loving the pretty clothes—and not him at all.

· Margaret Mitchell, *Gone with the Wind*

By common agreement, on the opening day of the trial the WPA Packhorse Library of Baileyville, Kentucky, remained closed. As did the post office, the Pentecostal, Episcopalian, First Presbyterian and Baptist churches, and the general store, which opened only for an hour at 7 a.m. and then again for the lunch hour to cater to the influx of strangers who had arrived in Baileyville. Unfamiliar cars parked at haphazard angles all along the roadside from the courthouse, mobile homes dotted the nearby fields, and men with sharp suits and trilby hats walked the streets with notebooks in the dawn light, asking for background information, photographs, anything you like, on the murdering librarian Margery O'Hare.

When they reached the library, Mrs. Brady waved a broom at them, told them she would take the head off any one of them who ventured into her building without an invitation, and they could put that in their darned paper and print it. She didn't seem to care too much what Mrs. Nofcier might think of *that*.

State policemen stood talking in pairs on the corners of the streets, and refreshment stands had been set up around the courthouse, while a snake-charmer invited the crowds to test their nerve and come closer, and the honky-tonks offered special deals on two-for-one keg beers at the end of every court day.

Mrs. Brady decided there was little point in the girls trying to make their rounds today. The roads were clogged, their minds were all over the place, and each of them wanted to be in court for Margery. And, anyway, long before seven that morning there was a queue of people trying to get into the public gallery. Alice stood at the head of it. As she waited, joined by Kathleen and the others, the queue built swiftly behind them: neighbors with lunch pails, somber recipients of library books, people she didn't recognize, who seemed to think of this as fun, chatting merrily, joking and nudging each other. She wanted to scream at them, *This is not some nice day out! Margery's innocent! She shouldn't even be here!*

Van Cleve arrived, pulling his car into the sheriff's parking slot, as if to let them all know just how close to the proceedings he was. He didn't acknowledge her, but marched straight into court, jaw jutting, confident his own place had already been reserved. She didn't see Bennett; perhaps he was minding business at Hoffman. He had never been much of a gossip, unlike his father.

Alice waited silently, her mouth dry and her stomach tight, as if it were she, not Margery, who was on trial. She guessed the others felt the same. They barely exchanged a word, just a nod of greeting, and a brief, tight clasp of hands.

At half past eight the doors opened, and the crowd flooded in. Sophia took a seat at the back with the other colored folk. Alice nodded at her. It felt wrong that she wasn't sitting with them, another example of a world out of kilter.

Alice took her seat near the front of the public gallery on the wooden bench, flanked by her remaining friends, and wondered how they were meant to endure this for days.

The jury was called—all men, mostly tobacco farmers judging by their clothes, Alice thought, and none likely to be sympathetic to a sharp-talking unmarried woman with a bad name. Women, the clerk announced, would be allowed to leave several minutes before the men at lunchtime and at the end of the day in order to prepare meals, a fact which caused Beth to roll her eyes. And then Margery was led into the dock with cuffs around her wrists, as if she were a danger to those present, her appearance in court accompanied by low murmurs and exclamations from the gallery. She sat pale and silent, apparently un-interested in her surroundings, and barely met Alice's eye. Her hair hung lank and unwashed and she looked impossibly weary, deep gray shadows under her eyes. Her arms lay in an unconscious loop, in a way that might have supported a baby, had Virginia still been there. She looked unkempt and uncaring.

She looked, Alice thought, with dismay, like a *criminal*.

Fred had said he would sit a row behind Alice, for appearances' sake, and she turned to him, anguished. His mouth tightened, as if to say he understood, *but what could you do?*

And then Judge Arthur D. Arthurs arrived, chewing ruminatively on a wad of tobacco, and they all were standing on the instructions of the clerk. He sat, and Margery was asked to confirm that she was, in-deed, Margery O'Hare, of the Old Cabin, Thompson's Pass, and the clerk read out the charge against her. How did she plead?

Margery seemed to sway a little, and her eyes slid toward the public gallery.

"Not guilty," she answered quietly, and there was a loud scoffing sound from the right-hand side of the court, followed by the loud banging of the judge's gavel. *He would not, repeat not, have an unruly court and nobody here was to so much as sniff without his permission. Did he make himself understood?*

The crowd settled, albeit with an air of vaguely suppressed mutiny. Margery looked up at the judge and, after a moment, he nodded at her to sit down again, and that would be the extent of her animation until she was allowed to leave the courtroom.

The morning crept forward in legal increments, women fanning themselves and small children fidgeting in their seats, as the prosecuting counsel outlined the case against Margery O'Hare. It would be clear to all, he announced, in a somewhat nasal, showman's voice, that before them was a woman brought up without morals, without concern for the decent, rightful way of doing things, without *faith*. Even her most visible enterprise—the so-called Packhorse Library—had proven to be a front for less savory preoccupations, and the state would show evidence of these through evidence from witnesses shaken by examples of her moral laxity. These deficiencies in both character and behavior had found their apotheosis one afternoon up on Arnott's Ridge when the accused had come across the sworn enemy of her late father, and taken advantage of the isolated position and inebriation of Mr. Clem McCullough to finish what their feuding descendants had started.

While this went on—and it did go on, for the prosecuting counsel loved the sound of his own voice—the reporters from Lexington and Louisville scribbled furiously in small lined notebooks, shielding their work from each other and looking up intently at every new piece of information. When he came to the bit about "moral laxity," Beth called out *"Bullcrap!"* earning herself a cuff from her father, who sat behind her, and a stern rebuke from the judge, who announced that one more word from her and she would be sitting outside in the dust for the rest of the trial. She listened to the remainder of the statement with her arms folded and the kind of expression that made Alice fear for the prosecution lawyer's tires.

"You watch. Those reporters will write that these mountains run red with blood feuds and such nonsense," muttered Mrs. Brady, from behind her. "They always do. Makes us sound like a bunch of savages. You won't read a word about all the good this library—or Margery— has done."

Kathleen sat silently on one side of Alice, Izzy the other. They listened carefully, their faces serious and still, and when he finished they exchanged looks that said they now understood what Margery was up against. Blood feuds aside, the Margery the court had described was so duplicitous, so monstrous, that if they had not known her they might have been afraid to sit just a few feet away from her too.

Margery seemed to know it. She looked deadened, as if the very thing that made her Margery had been squeezed out of her, leaving only an empty shell.

Alice wished for the hundredth time that Sven had not absented himself. Surely, no matter what she'd told him, Margery would have taken some comfort from having him there. Alice kept imagining what it must be like to be sitting in the dock, facing the end of everything she loved and held dear. It hit her then that Margery, who loved nothing better than solitude, to be left alone, unexamined, and who belonged outside, like a mule or a tree or a buzzard, was going to be in one of those tiny dark cells for ten, twenty years, if not the rest of her life.

And then she had to stand and push her way out of the gallery because she knew she was going to throw up from fear.

Y ou okay?" Kathleen arrived behind her as she spat into the dust.

"Sorry," Alice said, straightening. "I don't know what came over me."

Kathleen passed her a handkerchief and she wiped her mouth.

"Izzy's holding our seats. But we'd best not be too long. People are already eyeing 'em."

"I just . . . can't bear it, Kathleen. Seeing her like that. Seeing the town like this. It's like they just want the slightest excuse to think badly of her. It should be the evidence on trial, but it feels like it's the fact that she doesn't behave like they think she should."

"It's ugly, that's for sure."

Alice stopped for a minute. "What did you just say?"

Kathleen frowned.

"I said it's ugly. Seeing the town close against her like this." Kathleen looked at her. "What? . . . What did I say?"

Ugly. Alice kicked at a stone on the ground, digging her toe in until it dislodged. *There is always a way out of a situation. Might be ugly. Might leave you feeling like the earth has gone and shifted under your feet.* When she looked up her face had cleared. "Nothing. Just something Marge once said to me. Just . . ." She shook her head. "Nothing."

Kathleen held out her arm and they walked back in.

There were lengthy lawyers' arguments behind the scenes and these blurred into a break at lunchtime, and when the women left the courtroom they didn't know quite what to do with themselves so ended up walking slowly back toward the library in a clump, followed by Fred and Mrs. Brady, deep in conversation.

"You don't have to go back in this afternoon, you know," said Izzy, who was still a little appalled by the idea of Alice throwing up in public. "If it's too much for you."

"It was just nerves getting the better of me," said Alice. "I was the same when I was a little girl. Should have made myself eat some breakfast."

They walked on in silence.

"It'll probably be better once our side gets to speak," Izzy said.

"Yeah. Sven's fancy lawyer will put them straight," said Beth.

"Of course he will," said Alice.

But none of them sounded convinced.

Day Two, it turned out, was not much better. The prosecution team outlined the autopsy report on Clem McCullough. The victim, a fifty-seven-year-old man, had died from a traumatic head injury consistent with a blunt instrument to the back of the head. He also had suffered facial bruising.

"Such as, for example, could be caused by a heavy hard-backed book?"

"That could be the case, yes," said the physician who had conducted the autopsy.

"Or a bar fight?" suggested Mr. Turner, the defense lawyer. The physician thought for a moment. "Well, yes, that too. But he was some way from a bar."

The area around the body had not been carefully examined, given the remoteness of the trail. Two of the sheriff's men had carried it down the mountain track, a journey that had taken several hours, and a late snowfall had covered the ground where it had lain, but there was photographic evidence of blood, and possibly hoof-prints.

Mr. McCullough had not owned a horse or mule.

The prosecution counsel then interviewed their witnesses. There was old Nancy, who was pushed again and again to confirm that her first statement had stated clearly that she had heard Margery up on the ridge, followed by the sound of an altercation.

"But I didn't say it like you've made it sound," she protested, her hand reaching for her hair. She turned to look at the judge. "They twisted my words all this way and that. I know Margery. I know she would no more murder a man in cold blood than she would . . . I don't know . . . bake a cake."

This prompted laughter in the courtroom and a furious outburst from the judge, and Nancy put both hands to her face, guessing, probably correctly, that even that simile would add to the idea that Margery was somehow transgressive, that in her non-baking habits she went against the laws of nature.

The prosecution counsel got her to talk some more, about how isolated the route was (very), how often she saw anyone up there (rarely) and how many people regularly made the trip. (Only Margery, or the odd hunter.)

"No further questions, Your Honor."

"Well, I would like to add one thing," Nancy announced, as the court clerk made to lead her out of the witness box. She turned to point at the dock. "That there is a good, kindly girl. She's brought us reading books through rain and shine, both for me and my sister who ain't left her bed since 1933, and you so-called Christian folk judging her might want to think hard about how much you do for your fellow man. Because you're none of you so high and mighty that you're beyond judgment. She's a good girl, and this is a terrible wrong you're doing her! Oh, and, Mr. Judge? My sister has a message for you too."

"That would be Phyllis Stone, older sister of the witness. She is apparently bedridden and could not make it down the mountain," murmured the clerk to the judge.

Judge Arthurs leaned back. There may have been a faint roll of his eyes.

"Go ahead, Mrs. Stone."

"She wanted me to tell you . . . 'Y'all can go to Hell, because who's going to bring us our Mack Maguire books now?'" she said loudly. Then she nodded. "Yup, y'all can go to Hell. That was it."

And as the judge began to bang his gavel again, Beth and Kathleen, on each side of Alice, couldn't help but let out a small burst of laughter.

Despite that moment of cheer, the librarians left the building that evening in muted mood, their faces drawn, as if the verdict could only be a formality. Alice and Fred walked together at the rear, their elbows bumping occasionally, both deep in thought.

"It might improve once Mr. Turner gets his say," said Fred, as they reached the library building.

"Perhaps."

He stopped as the others went inside. "Would you like something to eat before you head off?"

Alice glanced behind her at the people still spilling out of the upper level of the courthouse and felt suddenly mutinous. Why shouldn't she eat where she wanted? How much of a sin could it be, given everything else that was going on? "That would be lovely, Fred. Thank you."

She walked up to Fred's house alongside him, her back straight, daring anybody to comment, and they moved around each other in the kitchen, preparing a meal, in some strange facsimile of domesticity, one that neither of them felt able to remark upon.

They didn't talk of Margery, or Sven, or the baby, even though those three souls were lodged almost permanently in their thoughts. They didn't talk of how Alice had divested herself of almost all the belongings she had acquired since arriving in Kentucky, and that just one small trunk now sat in Margery's cabin, neatly labeled and awaiting her passage home. They remarked on the good taste of the food, the surprising harvest of apples that year, the erratic behavior of one of his new horses and a book Fred had read called *Of Mice and Men*, which he wished he hadn't, despite the quality of the writing, as it was too darn depressing just now. And two hours later, Alice set off for the cabin and, while she smiled at Fred as she left (because it was almost impossible for her not to smile at Fred), within minutes of her departure she found that, behind her benign exterior, she was filled with a now semi-permanent rage: at a world where she could sit alongside the man she loved for only a matter of days more, and at a small town where three lives were about to be ruined for ever because of a crime a woman had not committed.

The week slid forward in fury-inducing fits and starts. Every day the librarians took their seats at the front of the public gallery, and every day they listened to various expert witnesses expounding and dissecting the facts of the case—that the blood on the edition of *Little Women* matched that of Clem McCullough, that the bruising to the front of his face and forehead was consistent with a blow from the same. As the week drew on, the court heard from the so-called character witnesses: the purse-mouthed wife who announced that Margery O'Hare had pressed upon her a book she and her husband could only describe as "obscene." The fact that Margery had just had a baby out of wedlock, and with no visible shame whatsoever. There were the various older men—Henry Porteous for one—who felt able to testify to the length of the O'Hares' feud with the McCulloughs, and the capacity for meanness and vengeance in both families. The defense counsel tried to pick apart these testimonies in the interests of balance: "Sheriff, isn't it true that Miss O'Hare has never been arrested once in her thirty-eight years for any crime whatsoever?"

"It is," the sheriff conceded. "Mind you, plenty of moonshiners around here ain't never seen the inside of a cell either."

"Objection!"

"I'm just saying, Your Honor. Just because a person ain't been arrested don't mean they behave like an angel. You know how things work around these parts."

The judge ordered the statement expunged from the record. But it had done what the sheriff had known it would, and stained Margery's name in some vague, unformed way, and Alice watched the jurors frowning and making little notes on their pads and saw Van Cleve's slow, satisfied smile along the bench. Fred had noted that the sheriff now smoked the same brand of fancy cigar as Van Cleve, imported all the way from France.

How was that for a coincidence?

By Friday evening the librarians were despondent. Lurid headline had followed lurid headline, the crowds, while having thinned a little, at least to the point where baskets of food and drink were no longer having to be raised and lowered from the second floor, were still transfixed by the *Bloodthirsty Girl Librarian From The Hills*, and when Fred had driven over to see Sven on Friday afternoon after the court had gone into recess for the weekend to give him a report from inside the court, Sven had put his head in his hands and not spoken for a full five minutes.

That day the women walked down to the library and sat in silence, not having anything to say, but none of them wanting to leave for home either. Finally Alice, who had begun to find the silence oppressive, announced that she was going to head to the store to get some drinks. "I reckon we've earned them."

"You don't mind being seen buying alcohol?" said Beth. "'Cause I can go get some 'shine from my daddy's cousin Bert, if you'd prefer. I know it's hard for you with—"

But Alice was already at the door. "To Hell with them. I'll most likely be gone within the week," she said. "They can gossip about me all they like by then."

She walked down the dusty street, weaving in and out of the strangers who, having exhausted the day's entertainments at the courthouse, were now zigzagging to the honky-tonks or the Nice 'N' Quick, all of which were struggling to feel too bad for Margery O'Hare, given the roaring trade. She walked briskly, her head down and her elbows slightly out, not wanting to exchange small talk or even acknowledge any of those neighbors to whom she and Margery had brought books over the past year, and who now appeared traitorous enough to be enjoying the week's events. They could go to Hell, too.

She pushed her way into the store, stopping in her tracks and sighing inwardly as she realized there would be at least fifteen people in the queue before her, and glanced behind her, wondering if it was worth heading to one of the bars to see if they would sell her something instead. What kind of a crowd would be in there? She was so full of anger, these days, that she felt like a tinder box, as if it would take only one wrong comment from one of these fools for her to—

She felt a tap on her shoulder.

"Alice?"

She turned. And there, by the preserves and canned goods, dressed in his shirtsleeves and his good blue trousers, without a speck of coal dust on him, stood Bennett. He had probably just finished work, but looked, as ever, as fresh as if he'd stepped out of the pages of a Sears catalog.

"Bennett," she said, blinked and looked away. It wasn't as if she was physically moved by him any more, she realized, searching for the reason for her sudden discomfort. There was only the vaguest hint of residual affection. What she felt was mostly disbelief that this man, standing here, was someone she had wrapped herself around, skin to skin, kissed and pleaded for physical contact with. This strange, unbalanced intimacy made her feel vaguely ashamed now.

"I . . . I heard you were leaving town."

She picked up a can of tomatoes, just for something to do with her hands. "Yup. Trial looks to end on Tuesday. I'll be headed out on Wednesday. You and your father won't have to worry about me hanging around."

Bennett glanced behind him, perhaps conscious that people might be watching, but all the customers were out-of-towners, and nobody saw anything gossip-worthy in a man and a woman exchanging a few words in the corner of the store.

"Alice—"

"You don't have to say anything, Bennett. I think we've said enough. My parents have engaged a lawyer and—"

He touched her sleeve. "Pa says nobody managed to speak to his daughters."

She pulled back her hand. "I'm sorry? What?"

Bennett looked behind him, his voice low. "Pa said the sheriff never spoke to McCullough's daughters. They wouldn't open the door. They shouted to his men they had nothing to say on the matter and they wouldn't be talking to nobody. He says they're both crazy, like the rest of the family. Says the state's case is strong enough not to need them anyway." He looked at her intently.

"Why are you telling me this?"

He chewed at his lip. "Figured . . . I figured . . . it might help you."

She stared at him then, at his handsome, slightly unformed face, and his baby-soft hands, his anxious eyes. And briefly she felt her own face fall a little.

"I'm sorry," he said quietly.

"I'm sorry too, Bennett."

He took a step back, ran a hand down his face.

They stood for a moment longer, shifting a little on their feet.

"Well," he said eventually. "If I don't see you before you leave . . . safe travels."

She nodded. He headed for the door. As he reached it he turned, his voice lifting a little to be heard. "Oh. Thought you'd like to know I'm fixing to get the slurry dams made up. With proper housing and a cement base. So they can't burst again."

"Your father agreed to that?"

"He will." The smallest smile, a flash of someone she had once known.

"That's good news, Bennett. Really good news."

"Yeah. Well." He looked down. "It's a start."

With that her husband tipped his hat, opened the door, and was swallowed by the crowds still milling around outside.

The sheriff didn't speak to his daughters? Why not?" Sophia shook her head. "It doesn't make no sense to me."

"Makes perfect sense to me," said Kathleen, from the corner, where she was stitching a broken stirrup leather, grimacing as she forced the huge needle through the leather. "They got all the way up to Arnott's Ridge, to a family they was expecting trouble from. They figure the girls wouldn't know nothing about their daddy's movements, given he was a known drunk who used to disappear for days on end. So they knock a few times, get told to git, then give up and come back down, and it takes them half a day each way to do it."

"McCullough was a sundowner and a mean one at that," said Beth. "Might be the sheriff didn't want to push them too hard in case they told him something he didn't want to hear. They need him to sound like a good man to make Marge seem bad."

"But surely our lawyer should have gone asking questions?"

"Mr. Fancy Pants out of Lexington? You think he's going to ride a mule half a day up to Arnott's Ridge to speak with a bunch of angry hillbillies?"

"I don't see how this is going to help us none," said Beth. "If they won't talk to the sheriff's men they ain't hardly going to talk to us."

"That may be exactly why they would talk to us," said Kathleen.

Izzy pointed at the wall. "Margery put the McCullough house on the list of places not to go to. *On no account.* Look, it says so right here."

"Well, maybe she was just doing what everyone's done to her," said Alice. "Going on gossip without actually looking at the facts."

"Those girls haven't been seen in town for nigh on ten years," Kathleen murmured. "Word is their daddy wouldn't let them leave the house after their mama disappeared. One of those families that just stays in the shadows."

Alice thought of Margery's words, words that had rung through her head for days: *There is always a way out of a situation. Might be ugly. Might leave you feeling like the earth has gone and shifted under your feet. But there is always a way around.*

"I'm going to ride up there," said Alice. "I can't see what we have to lose."

"Your head?" said Sophia.

"Right now, the way my head is, it wouldn't make that much difference."

"You know the stories come out of that family? And you know how much they hate us right now? You just fixing to get yourself killed?"

"You want to tell me what other chance Margery has right now?" Alice said. Sophia gave Alice a hard look but didn't answer. "Right. Does anyone have the map for that route?" For a moment Sophia didn't move. Then she opened the drawer wordlessly and flicked through the assembled papers until she found it and handed it over.

"Thank you, Sophia."

"I'm coming with you," said Beth.

"Then I'm coming, too," said Izzy.

Kathleen reached for her hat. "Looks like we got us an outing. Here, eight tomorrow?"

"Let's make it seven," said Beth.

For the first time in days Alice found she was smiling.

"Lord help the lot of you," said Sophia, shaking her head.

TWENTY-FIVE

★

It was clear within a couple of hours of setting out why only Margery and Charley ever undertook the route to Arnott's Ridge. Even in the benign conditions of early September, the route was remote and arduous, taking in steep crevasses, narrow ledges and a variety of obstacles to scrabble down or over, from ditches to fences to fallen trees. Alice had brought Charley, confident he would understand where he was going, and so it proved. He strode out willingly, his huge ears flicking backward and forward, following his own well-worn tracks along the creek bed and up the side of the ridge, the horses following on behind. There were no notches on trees here, no red ribbons; Margery had plainly never expected anyone but herself to take such a route, and Alice glanced behind her intermittently at the other women, hoping she could trust Charley as a guide.

Around them the air hung thick and moist and the newly amber forests lay dense with fallen leaves, muffling sound as they made their way along the hidden trails. They rode in silence, focused on the unfamiliar terrain, only breaking off to praise their horses quietly or warn of some approaching obstacle.

It occurred to Alice as they headed along the track into the upper reaches of the mountains that they had never ridden together, not all of them, like this. And then that it was entirely possible this would be the last time she rode into the mountains.

In a week or so she would be making her way by train toward New York and the huge ocean liner that would take her to England, and a very different kind of existence. She turned in her saddle and looked at the group of women behind her and realized she loved them all, that leaving each of them, not just Fred, would be a wrench almost greater than anything she had endured up to now. She couldn't imagine meeting women with whom she would feel so in tune, so close to in her next life, over polite chit-chat and cups of tea.

The other librarians would slowly forget her, their lives busy with work and families, and the ever-changing challenges of the seasons. Oh, they would promise to write, of course, but it wouldn't be the same. There would be no more shared experiences, the cold wind on their faces, the warnings of snakes on tracks, or commiserations when one of them took a fall. She would gradually become a postscript to a story: *Do you remember that English girl who rode with us for a while? Bennett Van Cleve's wife?*

"Think we're getting close?" Kathleen broke into her thoughts, riding up alongside.

Alice pulled Charley to a halt, unfolding the map from her pocket. "Uh . . . according to this, it's not far over that ridge," she said, squinting at the hand-drawn images. "She said the sisters live four miles that way, and Nancy would always walk the last part because of the hanging bridge, so I make the McCullough house . . . somewhere over there."

Beth scoffed. "You reading that map upside down? I know for a fact the damn bridge is that way."

Alice's belly was tight with nerves. "If you know better, you want to head off on your own and let us know when you're there?"

"No need to get ornery. You're not from here is all. I just thought I—"

"Oh, and don't I know it. Like the whole town hasn't spent the last year reminding me."

"No need to take it like that, Alice. Shoot. I just meant some of us might have more knowledge of the mountains than—"

"Shut up, Beth." Even Izzy was irritated. "We wouldn't even have got this far if it wasn't for Alice."

"Hold up," said Kathleen. "Look."

It was the smoke that alerted them, a thin apologetic whisper of gray that they might not have spotted had the trees nearby not lost their leaves from the crown, so that the wavering plume was briefly visible against the leaden sky. The women stopped in the clearing, just able to make out the shack squatting on the ridge, its shingle roof missing a couple of tiles, its yard unkempt. It was the only house for miles and everything about it spoke of neglect and an antipathy toward casual visitors. A mean-looking dog tethered to a chain set up a fierce, staccato bark, already aware of their presence through the trees.

"Think they'll shoot at us?" said Beth, and spat noisily.

Fred had instructed Alice to bring his gun and it was slung over her shoulder by its strap. She couldn't work out whether it was a good or a bad thing for the McCullough family to see she had it in her possession.

"Wonder how many of them are in there. Someone told my eldest brother that none of the out-of-town McCulloughs even came up this far."

"Yeah. Like Mrs. Brady said, they most likely just came for the circus," said Kathleen, squinting as she tried to see better.

"Ain't like they were coming for the McCullough riches, is it? What did your mama say about you coming up here, anyway?" said Beth to Izzy. "I'm surprised she let you."

Izzy pushed Patch forward over a small ditch, clearing it with a grunt.

"Izzy?"

"She doesn't exactly know."

"Izzy!" Alice turned in her saddle.

"Oh, hush, Alice. You know as well as I do that she would never have let me." Izzy rubbed at her boot.

They all faced the house. Alice shivered.

"If anything happens to you, your mother is going to have me in that dock alongside Margery. Oh, Izzy. This is not safe. I would never have let you come had you told me." Alice shook her head.

"So why did you come, Izzy?" said Beth.

"Because we are a team. And a team sticks together." Izzy lifted her chin. "We are the Baileyville packhorse librarians and we stick together."

Beth punched her lightly on the arm as her horse moved forward. "Well, goddamn to that."

"Ugh. Will you *ever* stop cursing, Beth Pinker?"

And Izzy punched her back and squealed as the horses collided.

In the end it was Alice who went first. They walked up as far as the snarling dog on the chain would allow, and Alice dismounted, handing her reins to Kathleen. She took a few steps toward the door, staying wide of the dog, its teeth bared and its hackles lifted in little spikes. She eyed the chain nervously, hoping that the other end was pinned securely.

"Hello?"

Two windows at the front, thick with dirt, stared back blankly at them. If it hadn't been for the trickle of smoke she might have been certain that nobody was home.

Alice took a step closer, her voice lifting. "Miss McCullough? You don't know me, but I work at the Packhorse Library down in town. I know you didn't want to talk to the sheriff's men but I would very much appreciate it if you could help us at all."

Her voice bounced off the mountainside. There was no movement from within the house.

Alice turned and looked at the others uncertainly. The horses stamped their feet impatiently, their nostrils flaring as they eyed the growling dog.

"It would really only take a minute!"

The dog turned its head and quieted briefly. For a moment the mountain was possessed of a dead silence. Nothing stirred, not the horses, the birds in the trees. Alice felt her skin prickle, as if this presaged something terrible. She thought of the description of McCullough's body, his eyes pecked clean out of his head. Lying not too far from here, for months.

I don't want to be here, she thought, and felt something visceral and fearful trickle down her spine. She looked up and saw Beth, who nodded at her, as if to say, *Go on—try again.*

"Hello? Miss McCullough? Anybody?"

Nothing stirred.

"Hello?"

A voice broke into the silence: "*You all can git and leave us alone!*"

Alice turned on her heel to find two barrels of a gun visible through the gap in the door.

She swallowed and was about to speak again, when Kathleen appeared on foot beside her. She put a hand on Alice's arm. "Verna? Is that you? I don't know if you remember me but it's Kathleen Hannigan, now Bligh. I used to play with your sister down at Split Creek? We made corn dollies with my ma one harvest time and I think she made one for you. With a spotted ribbon? Would you remember that?"

The dog was eyeing Kathleen now, its lips pulled back over its teeth.

"We're not here to cause no trouble," she said, her palms up. "We're just in something of a fix with our good friend and we'd be real grateful for the chance to speak with you for a moment or two about it."

"*We got nothing to say to any of youse!*"

Nobody moved. The dog stopped growling briefly, its nose pointing toward the door. The two barrels didn't budge.

"I ain't coming to town," said the voice from inside. "I . . . I'm not coming. I told the sheriff what day our pa disappeared and that's that. You ain't getting nothing else."

Kathleen took a step closer. "We understand, Verna. We would just really welcome a couple minutes of your time to talk. Just to help our friend. Please?"

There was a long silence.

"What happened to her?"

They looked at each other.

"You don't know?" said Kathleen.

"Sheriff just said they found my pa's body. And the murderer to go with it."

Alice spoke up. "That's pretty much it. Except, Miss Verna, it's our friend who is standing trial and we would swear on the Bible that she is not a murderer."

"Miss Verna, you may know of Margery O'Hare. You know her daddy's name travels before her." Kathleen's voice had lowered, as if they were in some casual conversation. "But she's a good woman, a little . . . unconventional, but not a cold-blooded killer. And her baby faces growing up without a mother because of gossip and rumor."

"Margery O'Hare had a baby?" The gun lowered an inch. "Who'd she marry?"

They exchanged awkward glances.

"Well, she ain't exactly married."

"But that doesn't mean nothing," Izzy called hurriedly. "Doesn't mean she isn't a good person."

Beth brought her horse a few steps closer toward the house, and held up a saddlebag. "You want some books, Miss McCullough? For you or your sister? We got recipe books, storybooks, all kinds of books. Lots of families up in the mountains happy to take them. You don't have to pay, and we'll bring you new ones when you like."

Kathleen shook her head at Beth and mouthed, *I don't think she can read.*

Alice, anxious, tried to talk over them: "Miss McCullough, we're truly, truly sorry about your father. You must have loved him very much. And we're really sorry to trouble you with this matter. We wouldn't be here unless we were desperate to help our friend—"

"I ain't sorry," the girl said.

Alice swallowed the rest of her sentence. Her shoulders slumped a little. Beth's mouth closed in dismay.

"Well, I appreciate it's natural you would harbor ill-feelings toward Margery but I would beg you just to hear—"

"Not her." Verna's voice hardened. "I ain't sorry about what happened to my pa."

The women looked at each other, confused. The gun lowered slowly another inch, and then disappeared.

"You the Kathleen used to have braids pinned upside your head?"

"That's me."

"You rode all the way up here from Baileyville?"

"Yes, ma'am," said Kathleen.

There was a brief pause.

"Then you'd best come in."

As the librarians watched, the rough wooden door slid open a fraction, and then, after a moment, opened a little wider, creaking on its hinges. And there, for the first time, in the gloom, they saw the twenty-year-old figure of Verna McCullough, dressed in a faded blue dress with patches on the pockets and a headscarf knotted over her hair, her sister moving in the shadows behind her.

There was a short silence while they all took in what was in front of them.

"Well, *shit*," said Izzy, under her breath.

TWENTY-SIX

★

Alice was first in the queue for the courthouse on Monday morning. She had barely slept and her eyes were sore and gritty. She had brought fresh-baked cornbread to the jail earlier in the morning, but Officer Dulles glanced down at the tin and observed apologetically that Margery wasn't eating. "Barely touched a thing over the weekend." He looked genuinely concerned.

"You take it anyway. Just in case you can get her to eat something later."

"You didn't come yesterday."

"I was busy."

He frowned at the abruptness of her answer, but plainly decided that things were off-kilter enough in the town that week without him questioning it further, and headed back down to his cells.

Alice took her place at the front of the public gallery and regarded the crowd. No Kathleen, no Fred. Izzy slid in beside her, then Beth, smoking the tail end of a cigarette that she stubbed out under her feet.

"Heard anything?"

"Not yet," said Alice.

And then she startled. There, two rows back, sat Sven, his face somber, and his eyes shadowed, as if he hadn't slept for weeks. He kept his eyes to the front and his hands on his knees. There was something in the rigidity of his bearing that suggested a man working hard to keep himself contained, and the sight of him made her swallow painfully. She flinched as Izzy's hand reached across and squeezed her own, and she returned the pressure, trying to keep her breath steady in her chest.

A minute later Margery was led in, her head down, and her gait slow. She stood, her expression unreadable, no longer even bothering to meet anybody else's eye. "C'mon, Marge," she heard Beth mutter beside her.

And then Judge Arthurs entered the courtroom and everybody rose.

Miss Margery O'Hare here is a victim of unhappy circumstance. She was, if you like, in the wrong place at the wrong time. Now only God will ever know the truth of what happened on the top of that mountain, but we do know that it is only the flimsiest of evidence that takes a library book, one which by all accounts may have traveled halfway across Lee County, and places it near a body that may have come to rest some six months earlier." The defense counsel looked up as the doors at the back opened and everyone swiveled in their seats to see Kathleen Bligh march in, sweaty and a little breathless.

"Excuse me. I'm very sorry. Excuse me." She ran to the front of the court where she stooped to speak to Mr. Turner. He glanced behind him and then stood, one hand on his tie, as the people in the court murmured their surprise.

"Your Honor? We have a witness who would very much like to say something before the court."

"Can it wait?"

"Your Honor, this has a material bearing on the case."

The judge sighed. "Approach the bench please, Counsels."

The two men stood at the front. Neither attempted to lower their voices much, one from urgency and the other from frustration, so the court got to hear pretty much everything that was said.

"It's the daughter," said Mr. Turner.

"What daughter?" said the judge.

"McCullough's daughter. Verna."

The prosecution counsel glanced behind him and shook his head. "Your Honor, we have had no prior notice of such a witness and I object in the strongest terms to the introduction of such at so late—"

The judge chewed ruminatively. "Did the sheriff's men not go up to Arnott's Ridge to try to talk to the girl?"

The prosecution counsel stammered, "Well, y-yes. But she wouldn't come down. She hasn't left that house in several years, according to those familiar with the family."

The judge leaned back in his chair. "Then I would say if this is the victim's daughter, possibly the last witness to see him alive, and she is now content to make her way down into the town to answer questions about his last day, then she may well have information pertinent to the case, wouldn't you agree, Mr. Howard?"

The prosecution counsel glanced behind him again. Van Cleve was straining forward in his seat, his mouth compressed with displeasure.

"Yes, Your Honor."

"Good. I will hear the witness." He waved a finger.

Kathleen and the lawyer spoke for a minute in hushed voices, and then she ran to the back of the court.

"When you're ready, Mr. Turner."

"Your Honor, the defense calls Miss Verna McCullough, daughter of Clem McCullough. Miss McCullough? If you could make your way to the witness box? I would be much obliged."

There was a hum of interest. People strained in their seats. The door opened at the back of the court, revealing Kathleen, her arm through that of a younger woman, who walked a little behind her. And as the court watched in silence, Verna McCullough made her way slowly and deliberately to the front of the courtroom, every stride an apparent effort. Her hand rested on the small of her back and her belly sat low and huge in front of her.

A murmur of shock, and a second wave of exclamation as the same thought occurred to each person, went up around the room.

Y ou live at Arnott's Ridge?"

Verna had held her hair back with a bobby pin and now fiddled with it, as if it were out of place. Her voice emerged as a hoarse whisper. "Yes, sir. With my sister. And before that our father."

"Can you speak up, please?" said the judge.

The lawyer continued. "And it's just the three of you?"

She held on to the lip of the witness box and gazed around her, as if she had only just noticed how many people were in the room. Her voice faltered for a moment.

"Miss McCullough?"

"Uh . . . Yes. Our mama went when I was eight and it's been us three since then."

"Your mama died?"

"I don't know, sir. We woke up one morning and my daddy said she was gone. And that was it."

"I see. So you are unsure as to her fate?"

"Oh, I believe her to be dead. Because she always said my daddy would kill her one day."

"Objection!" said the state prosecutor.

"Strike that from the record, please. We will leave it on file that Miss McCullough's mother's whereabouts are unknown."

"Thank you, Miss McCullough. And when did you last see your father?"

"That would be five days before Christmas."

"And have you seen him since?"

"No, sir."

"Did you look for him?"

"No, sir."

"You . . . weren't troubled? When he didn't come home for Christmas?"

"It was not . . . unusual behavior for our daddy. I think it may be no secret that he liked a drink. I believe he is—was—known to the sheriff." The sheriff nodded, almost reluctantly.

"Sir, would it be possible for me to sit down? I'm feeling a little faint."

The judge motioned to the clerk to bring her a chair and the court waited while it was positioned and she was able to sit. Someone brought her a glass of water. Her face was only just visible above the witness box and most in the public gallery leaned forward to try to see her better.

"So when he didn't come home on the . . . twentieth of December, Miss McCullough, you didn't see anything particularly untoward in that behavior?"

"No, sir."

"And when he left, did he tell you where he was going? To a bar?"

For the first time, Verna hesitated a good while before she spoke. She glanced at Margery, who was looking at the floor.

"No, sir. He said . . ." She swallowed, and then turned toward the judge. "He said he was going to return his library book."

There was an outburst from the public gallery, a sound that might have been shock or a burst of laughter, or a mixture of both; it was hard to tell. Margery, in the dock, lifted her head for the first time. Alice looked down to find that Izzy was gripping her hand, her knuckles white.

The defense lawyer turned to face the jury. "Can I check that I heard that correctly, Miss McCullough? You said your father set out to return a *library book*?"

"Yes, sir. He had recently been receiving books from the WPA Packhorse Library and he believed it was a great thing. He had just read a fine book and said it was his civic duty to return it as soon as possible so that some other person could have the benefit of reading it."

The heads of Mr. Howard, the state prosecutor and his second were pressed together in urgent conversation. He raised his hand but the judge dismissed him with a wave. "Go on, Miss McCullough."

"Me and my sister, well, we did warn him in the strongest terms not to set out because the conditions were bad, what with the snow and ice and all, and that he might slip and fall, but he had taken a fair bit to drink and he would not be told. He was insistent that he didn't want to be late back with his library book."

Her gaze flickered around the courtroom as she spoke, her voice now level and certain.

"So Mr. McCullough set out by himself, on foot, into the snow."

"He did, sir. Taking the library book."

"To walk to Baileyville."

"Yes, sir. We warned him it was a foolish enterprise."

"And you never saw or heard from him again?"

"No, sir."

"And . . . you didn't think to look for him?"

"Me and my sister, we don't leave our home, sir. After our mama went our daddy never liked for us to come to town, and we didn't like to disobey him, what with his temper and all. We went around the yard before nightfall and shouted for him, just in case he had taken a fall, but most times he would just come back when it pleased him."

"So you just waited for him to return."

"Yes, sir. He had threatened to leave us before now, so I guess when he didn't return some part of us thought maybe he had finally done so. And then back in April the sheriff came up to tell us he was . . . dead."

"And . . . Miss McCullough. May I ask one more question? You have been most courageous making this trip down the mountain and completing this difficult testimony, and I am much obliged to you. One final question: do you remember what book it was that your father enjoyed so much, and felt such an obligation to return?"

"Why, yes, I do, sir. Most clearly."

And here Verna McCullough turned her pale blue eyes on those of Margery O'Hare, and to those nearest it was possible that the faintest smile played around her lips. "It was a book by the name of *Little Women*."

The court exploded into a wall of noise, so that the judge was forced to bang his gavel six, eight times before enough people noticed—or could hear enough—to quiet it. There was laughter, disbelief, and shouted fury from different parts of the court, and the judge, his brows an overhanging ledge, grew puce with anger.

"Silence! I will not have this court held in disrespect, do you hear me? The next person to make a sound will be in contempt of court! Silence in the court!"

The room quieted. The judge waited a moment to be sure that everyone had got the message.

"Now, Counsels, will you approach the bench?"

There was some muttered conversation, this time inaudible in the court, under which a low hum of whispers had begun to escalate dangerously. Across the courtroom, Mr. Van Cleve looked like he was about to combust. Alice saw him get up once, twice, but the sheriff turned and physically forced him to sit down. She could see Van Cleve pointing, his mouth working, as if he couldn't believe he, too, didn't have the right to go up and debate with the judge. Margery sat very still, disbelieving.

"Go on," muttered Beth, her knuckles white where she gripped the bench. "Go on. Go on."

And then, after an age, the two lawyers made their way back to their seats and the judge banged his gavel again.

"Can we call the physician back, please?"

There was a low murmur as the physician was recalled to the witness box. The public gallery was full of people shifting in their seats, pulling faces at each other.

The defense counsel rose.

"Dr. Tasker. One further question: in your professional opinion, would it be possible that the bruising to the victim's face might have been caused by the weight of a large hard-backed book falling onto it? For example, if he had slipped and fallen backward." He motioned to the clerk and held up the copy of *Little Women*. "One the size of this edition, for example? Here—I'll let you feel the weight of it."

The physician weighed the book in his hands and considered this for a moment. "Why, yes. I would imagine that would be a reasonable explanation."

"No further questions, Your Honor."

It took the judge two more minutes of legal conversation to conclude. He banged his gavel to quiet the court. Then, abruptly, he rested his head in his hands, and stayed like that for a full minute. When he raised it, he eyed the court with what seemed to be an impossibly weary expression.

"It seems to me in the light of this new evidence I am minded to agree with the defense counsel that this can no longer be positioned with any certainty as a murder trial. All solid evidence seems to suggest this was . . . an unfortunate accident. A good man set out to do a good deed, and due to the, uh, prevailing conditions—shall we say?—suffered an untimely end."

He took a deep breath and placed his hands together.

"Given the Commonwealth evidence in this case is largely circumstantial, and heavily dependent on this one book, and given the witness's clear and unwavering testimony as to its prior whereabouts, I am moved to strike this trial and instead record a verdict of accidental death. Miss McCullough, I thank you for your efforts in doing your . . . civic duty, and I wish to convey my public and heartfelt condolences, once again, for your loss. Miss O'Hare, you are hereby free to leave the court. Clerks, if you could release the prisoner."

This time the court did erupt. Alice found herself suddenly enveloped by the other women, who were jumping up and down, yelling, tears streaming from their eyes, arms and elbows and chests pressed together in a giant hug. Sven vaulted over the barrier of the public gallery and was there as the jailer undid Margery's handcuffs, his arms closing around Margery just as she began to sink to the floor in shock. He half walked, half carried her swiftly out of the back exit, Deputy Dulles shielding them before anyone could really work out what was happening. Through it all, Van Cleve could be heard yelling that this was a *travesty*! An absolute *travesty of justice*! And those with particularly good hearing could just make out Mrs. Brady retorting, "Shut your fat mouth for once in your life, you old goat."

In all the hubbub nobody noticed Sophia quietly leave the colored section of the public gallery, her bag tucked neatly under her arm, disappearing through the door and briskly making the short walk to the library, picking up speed as she went.

And only those with the very keenest hearing would have heard Verna McCullough, as she was steered out past the librarians, her hand still on the small of her back and her face grimly determined as she muttered under her breath: "Good riddance."

Nobody felt Margery should be left alone, so they brought her to the library and locked both doors, mindful that Kentucky's most widely circulated newspapers, as well as half of the town, suddenly wanted to talk to her. She said barely a word during the short walk there, her movements slow and oddly frail, as if she had been ill, though she did eat half a bowl of bean soup that Fred brought down from the house, her eyes fixed on it as she ate, as if it were the only thing of any certainty around her. The women exclaimed among themselves about the shock of the verdict, Van Cleve's impotent fury, the fact that young Verna had indeed done as she had promised.

She had spent the previous night at Kathleen's cabin, having been walked down on Patch, and even then she had been so nervous at the prospect of facing all those townspeople that Kathleen had been afraid she would find her gone when she awoke. It was only when Fred arrived in the morning with his truck to bring them to court that Kathleen believed they might be in with a chance, and even then the girl was so odd and unpredictable that they had no idea what she was going to say.

Margery listened to all this as if from a distance, her expression oddly blank, and distracted, as if she found the noise and commotion too much after the months of near-silence.

Alice wanted to hug her and yet something about Margery's demeanor forbade it. None of them knew what to say to her and found themselves talking as if to a near stranger—did she want some more water? Was there anything they could get for her? Really, Margery should only say.

And then, almost an hour after they arrived, there was a short rap at the door and Fred, hearing a familiar low voice, moved to unlock it. He opened it a fraction, then his eyes fixed on something unseen and his smile widened. He stepped back, and up the two short steps walked Sven, holding the baby, who was wearing a pale yellow dress and bloomers, her eyes button bright and her hands gripping his sleeve tightly in her tiny fist.

Margery's head lifted and her hands moved slowly to her mouth as she saw her. Her eyes filled with tears and she rose slowly to her feet. "Virginia?" she said, her voice cracking as if she could barely trust what she was seeing. Sven moved to her, and handed the baby to her mother, and Margery and the child gazed into each other's eyes, the child scanning her mother's as if to reassure herself of something. And then, as they watched, the tiny girl took a moment, then let her head come to rest in the space under her mother's chin, her thumb plugged into her mouth, and as she did Margery closed her eyes and began to sob, silently, her chest heaving violently as if some terrible pain was exorcising itself, her face contorted. Sven stepped forward and placed his arms around the two of them, holding them close to him, his head lowered, and mindful that they were now privy to something that felt beyond the realms of what was decent, Fred and the librarians tiptoed out of the library and made their way silently up the path to Fred's house.

The Baileyville WPA packhorse librarians were a team, yes, and a team stuck together. But there were some times when it was only right to be alone.

It would be several days before the other librarians noticed the ledger the sheriff had believed missing, disappeared in the Great Floods, stacked neatly with the others in the shelf to the left of the door. Under the date of December 15, 1937, it showed a loan to *Mr. C. McCullough, Arnott's Ridge,* of *one hardback edition of* Little Women, *by Louisa May Alcott (one page ripped, back cover slightly damaged).* Only someone who looked terribly hard might have noticed how the entry sat between two lines, its ink a very faintly different shade from those around it. And only if you were very cynical indeed might you wonder why there was a one-word entry beside it, written in that same ink: *unreturned*.

TWENTY-SEVEN

★

Up in this high air you breathed easily, drawing in a
vital assurance and lightness of heart. In the highlands
you woke up in the morning and thought: Here I am,
where I ought to be.

· KAREN BLIXEN, *Out of Africa*

Much to the disappointment of the traders and bartenders, it took less than a day for Baileyville to empty. After the "NOT GUILTY—SHOCK VERDICT" headlines had been reduced to firelighters and draft-proofing, and the last of the mobile homes had rattled their way back across county lines, and the prosecution lawyer with the three inexplicably slashed tires had managed to get a spare set sent over from Lexington, Baileyville swiftly returned to normal, leaving nothing but muddy tracks and empty food wrappers dotted along the verges to show that a trial had ever taken place.

Kathleen, Beth and Izzy escorted Verna back to her cabin, taking turns to walk while Verna rode the sturdy Patch. The journey took the best part of a day, and they parted with promises that Neeta, Verna's sister, would come and find them if she needed help with her laboring. Nobody ever spoke of the paternity of the child, and Verna had once again grown silent by the time they reached the door, as if exhausted by all the unfamiliar contact.

They did not expect to hear from her again.

. . .

That first night Margery O'Hare lay in her own bed facing Sven Gustavsson in the near dark. Her hair was soft and clean from her bath and her belly was full, and out of the open window she could hear the owls and the crickets calling into the darkness of the mountainside, a sound that made the blood slow in her veins, and her heart beat with an easy rhythm. They watched the tiny girl who lay between them, her arms thrown back in sleep, her mouth making soft shapes as she dreamed. Sven's hand rested on the swell of Margery's hip and Margery relished the weight of it, the prospect of the nights to come.

"We can still leave, you know," he said quietly.

She lifted the child's cotton blanket, tucking it under her chin. "Leave where?"

"Here. I mean, what you said about your mother's warning, and getting a fresh start. I've been reading up on places in northern California where they're seeking farmers and homesteaders. Think you'd like it up there. We could make a good life."

When she said nothing he added: "Doesn't have to be in a city. It's a big old state. People go to California from all over so nobody looks twice at someone from elsewhere. I got a friend with a cantaloupe farm says he'll give me work while we find our feet."

Margery pushed her hair back from her face. "I don't think so."

"Well, we could look at Montana, if you prefer the sound of it."

"Sven, I want to stay. Here."

Sven propped himself up on his elbow. He studied her expression as best he could in the dim light. "You said you wanted Virginia to have freedom. To live however she wanted."

"I know I did," said Margery. "And I do. But it turns out we have real friends here, Sven. People who have our backs. I've thought about it, and as long as she's got those, she'll be okay. We'll be okay."

When he didn't speak, she added, "Would that . . . be agreeable to you? If we just . . . stayed?"

"Any place that has you and Virginia is agreeable to me."

There was a long silence.

"I love you, Sven Gustavsson," she said.

He turned toward her in the dark. "You're not getting sentimental on me, are you, Marge?"

"Didn't say I was going to say it twice."

He smiled and lay back against the bolster. After a moment he reached his hand across and she took it and held it tight in her own, and that was how they slept, for a couple of hours at least, until the baby woke again.

It had been shocking to Alice how quickly her feelings of delight and elation at Margery's return home had turned to cold stone as she grasped that this meant there was no longer a single obstacle left to her own immediate departure. That was it. The trial was over, and so was her time in Kentucky.

She had stood among the librarians and watched Sven drive Margery and Virginia up the road toward the Old Cabin and felt herself begin to calcify by inches as she realized what it meant. She managed to maintain her smile as they all drifted away, exclaiming to each other, hugging and kissing, had promised she might see them at the Nice 'N' Quick later for a celebration. But the effort was too great, and even as Beth kicked her cigarette butt into the road and gave a cheery wave, she could feel something hard settling in her chest. Only Fred caught it, something in his expression mirroring her own.

"Would you care for a bourbon?" said Fred, as they locked the library door and walked slowly up to his house. Alice nodded. She had just a matter of hours left in the town.

He poured two tumblers and handed her one and she sat down on his good settle with the buttoned cushions and the patchwork quilt over the back, the one his mother had made. It had grown dark outside and the balmy weather had given way to a brisk wind and fine, spitting rain, and Alice was already dreading heading out in it again.

Fred reheated the rest of the soup, but she had no appetite, and, she realized, nothing to say. Alice tried not to look at his hands, both of them conscious of the clock ticking on the mantel and what it meant. They talked of the trial, but even though they painted it in bright colors, Alice knew that Van Cleve would be even more furious now, would no doubt redouble his efforts to ruin the library, or make sure her life was as uncomfortable as it could be. Besides, no matter what Margery had said, she couldn't stay in the cabin any longer. They all knew that Sven and Margery would need time alone and it was telling that when she told them she had been invited to stay at Izzy's that evening their protests had been half-hearted.

"So what time is your train?" said Fred.

"A quarter past ten."

"You want me to drive you to the station?"

"That would be kind, Fred. If it's no trouble."

He nodded awkwardly and tried to raise a smile, which slid away as quickly as it arrived. She felt the same residual pain she always did at his discomfort, knowing that she was the cause of it. What right had she had to make any claim on this man anyway, knowing it was impossible? She had been selfish to allow his feelings to come anywhere near her own. Sunk in misery that neither of them felt able to articulate, their conversation had swiftly become strained. Alice, sipping a drink she could barely taste, wondered briefly if it had been a good idea coming here at all. Perhaps she should have gone straight to Izzy's. What was the point in prolonging all this heartbreak?

"Oh. Got another letter this morning at the library. In all the commotion I forgot to give it to you." Fred pulled the envelope from his pocket and handed it to her. She recognized the writing immediately and let it fall to the table.

"You not going to read it?"

"It'll just be about me coming back. Plans and suchlike."

"You read it. It's fine."

While he cleared the plates she opened the envelope, feeling his eyes on her. She scanned it swiftly and shoved it back inside.

"What?"

She looked up.

"Why'd you wince like that?"

She sighed. "Just . . . my mother's manner of talking."

He walked back around the table and sat down, taking the letter from the envelope.

"Don't—"

He pushed her hand away. "Let me."

She turned away as he read it, frowning.

"What's this? *We will endeavor to forget your latest efforts to embarrass our family.* What is that supposed to mean?"

"It's just how she is."

"Did you tell them Van Cleve beat you?"

"No." She rubbed at her face. "They would probably have assumed it was my own fault."

"How could it be your fault? A grown man and a bunch of dolls. Jeez. Never heard anything like it."

"It wasn't just the dolls."

Fred looked up.

"He thought—he thought I had tried to corrupt his son."

"He thought . . . *what*?"

She was already regretting having spoken.

"C'mon, Alice. We can tell each other anything."

"I can't." She felt her cheeks color. "I can't tell you." She took another sip, feeling his gaze rest on her, as if to work something out. Oh, what was the point of hiding it? After today she would never see him again. Finally she blurted out: "I brought home a book that Margery gave me. About married love."

Fred clenched his jaw a little, as if he didn't want to think about Alice and Bennett and any kind of intimacy. It took a moment before he spoke. "What would he have to mind about that?"

"He—they both—thought I shouldn't be reading it."

"Well, maybe he felt that as you were in your honeymoon period you—"

"But that's the thing. There was no honeymoon period. I wanted to see if—"

"If?"

"To see . . ." she swallowed ". . . if we had . . ."

"You had what?"

"Done it," she whispered.

"To see if you had done what?"

She threw her hands up to her face and wailed, "Oh, why are you making me say this?"

"Just trying to understand the facts of it, Alice."

"If we had done it. Married love."

Fred put down his glass. A long, painful moment passed before he spoke. "You don't . . . *know?*"

"No," she said miserably.

"Whoa. Whoa. Hold on. You don't know if you and Bennett . . . consummated your marriage?"

"No. And he wouldn't talk about it. So I have no way of knowing. And the book told me some things but, to be honest, I still couldn't be sure. There was a lot of stuff about wafting and rapture. And then it all blew up anyway, and it's not as if we ever discussed it so I'm still not sure."

Fred ran his hand over the back of his head. "Well, Alice, I mean— it's—uh—pretty hard to miss."

"What is?"

"The— Oh, forget it." He leaned forward. "You really think you might not have?"

She felt anguished, already regretting that this would be the last thing he remembered of her. "I don't think so . . . Oh, Lord, you think I'm ridiculous, don't you? I can't believe I'm telling you this. You must think—"

Fred stood up from the table abruptly. "No—no, Alice. This is great news!"

She stared at him. "What?"

"This is wonderful!" He grabbed her hand, began to waltz her around the room.

"Fred? What? What are you doing?"

"Get your coat. We're going to the library."

Five minutes later they were in the little cabin, two oil lamps burning as Fred scanned the shelves. He quickly found what he was looking for and asked her to hold the lamp while he flicked through the heavy leather-bound book. "See?" he said, jabbing at the page. "If you haven't consummated your marriage, then you're not married in the eyes of God."

"Meaning?"

"Meaning you can have the marriage annulled. And marry who the hell you like. And there's nothing Van Cleve can do about it."

She stared at the book, read the words that his finger underlined. She looked up at him, disbelieving. "Really? It doesn't count?"

"Yes! Hang on—we'll find another of those legal books, and double-check. That'll show you. Look! Look, here it is. You're free to stay, Alice! See? You don't have to go anywhere! Look! Oh, that poor damn fool Bennett—I could kiss him."

Alice put down the book and looked at him steadily. "I'd rather you kissed me."

And so he did.

Forty minutes later they lay on the floor of the library on Fred's jacket, both of them breathing hard and a little in shock at what had just transpired. He turned to her, his eyes searching her face, then took her hand and raised it to his lips.

"Fred?"

"Sweetheart?"

Alice smiled, the slowest, sweetest smile, and when she spoke it was as if her voice dripped honey and was shot through with happiness. "I have *definitely* never done that."

TWENTY-EIGHT

From the body of the loved one's simple, sweetly colored flesh, which our animal instincts urge us to desire, there springs not only the wonder of a new bodily life, but also the enlargement of the horizon of human sympathy and the glow of spiritual understanding which one could never have attained alone.

· DR. MARIE STOPES, *Married Love*

Sven and Margery were married in late October, on a clear, crisp day where the mists had lifted from the hollers by dawn and the birds sang loudly about the importance of a blue sky and squabbled noisily on branches. Margery had told him she would agree under sufferance because she didn't want Sophia yammering on at her till the end of time, and only if they told nobody and Sven "didn't make a thing of it."

Sven, who was agreeable in almost all things where Margery was concerned, greeted this invitation with a hard no. "If we marry, we do it in public, with the town, our child and all our friends in attendance," he said, his arms folded. "That's what I want. Or we don't marry at all."

And so they were wed in the small Episcopalian church up at Salt Lick, whose minister was a little less picky than some about children borne out of wedlock, and in attendance were all the librarians, Mr. and Mrs. Brady, Fred and a fair number of the families they had brought books to. Afterward they held a reception at Fred's house, and Mrs. Brady presented the couple with a wedding quilt that her quilting circle had embroidered, and a smaller one for Virginia's cot to match it, and Margery, despite looking somewhat awkward in her oyster-colored dress (borrowed from Alice, the seams let out by Sophia), wore an expression of embarrassed pride and managed not to change back into her breeches until the following day, even though it clearly pained her. They ate food brought by neighbors (Margery hadn't intended so many people to come, and had been a little taken aback by the endless stream of guests), someone started up a hog roast outside and Sven wore a look of intense happiness, showing off Virginia to everyone, and there was fiddling and some fine dancing. At six, just as dusk was falling, it was Alice who left the wedding party and finally located the bride sitting alone on the path to the library steps, gazing up at the darkening mountain.

"Are you all right?" Alice said, sitting down beside her.

Margery didn't turn her head. She stared up at the tips of the trees, sniffed loudly, then let her gaze slide sideways toward Alice. "Feels kind of weird to be this happy," she said, and it was the most unsettled Alice had ever seen her.

Alice considered this, then nodded. "I understand," she said. And she gave her friend a nudge. "You'll get used to it."

Two months later, after the Gustavssons had acquired a dog (a wall-eyed runt of a puppy, unwanted, some way from the quality hound Sven had suggested—he was, of course, crazy about it), Margery went back to work at the library. Virginia was minded four days a week by Verna McCullough, along with her own baby, a rather frail, freckled child by the name of Peter. Sven and Fred, aided by Jim Horner and a couple of the others, raised a small cabin a short walk from Margery's, with two separate rooms, a chimney and a working WC outside, and the McCullough sisters moved into it willingly. They returned to their old home only to bring back a jute bag of clothing, two pans and the mean dog. "The rest of it stunk of our daddy," Verna said, and never spoke of it again.

Verna had begun to make the walk down into town once a week, mostly just to buy provisions with her wages, but also to have a look around, and people generally tipped their hat or left her alone, and her presence swiftly became unremarkable. Neeta, her sister, was still not much inclined to leave the house, but they both doted on the babies and seemed to enjoy a little socializing, and over time passersby (who were not many in number) would remark that the dilapidated cabin up on Arnott's Ridge had began to collapse, roof shingles first, then the chimney, and then, as the high wind caught the loose weatherboarding, the house itself, broken window by broken window, until it was half reclaimed by nature, shoots and brambles clawing it back to the earth, as they had so nearly done with its owner.

Frederick Guisler and Alice were married a month after Margery and Sven, and if anybody noticed how much time they seemed to spend alone in Fred's house before they were legally tied, nobody seemed much inclined to comment on it. Alice's first marriage had been annulled quietly, and with little fuss, once Fred had explained the bones of it to Mr. Van Cleve who, for once, did not seem to feel the need to shout, but engaged a lawyer who was able to facilitate such things swiftly and with, perhaps, a little greasing of the wheels to ensure confidentiality. The prospect of his son's name being associated publicly with the word "annulment" seemed to stay his habitual temper, and after that meeting he barely mentioned the library publicly again.

Under the agreement they let Bennett marry again first. The librarians felt they owed the younger Van Cleve for the help he had given them, and Izzy even attended the day with her parents and said it was lovely, all things considered, and that Peggy made a beautiful and very contented bride.

Alice barely noticed. She was so ridiculously happy that most days she didn't know how to contain it. Every morning before dawn she would unwrap her long limbs reluctantly from those of her husband, drink the coffee he insisted on making for her, then walk down to open the library and get the stove going, ready for the others to arrive. Despite the cold and the brutal hour, she was almost always to be found smiling. If Peggy Van Cleve's friends chose to remark that Alice Guisler had let herself go something awful since she'd started up at that library, what with her un-set hair and her mannish outfits (and to think her so refined and well-dressed when she came, and all!), then Fred couldn't have noticed less. He was married to the most beautiful woman in the world, and every night after they had each finished work, and put away the dishes side by side, he made sure to pay homage. In the still air of Split Creek it was not unusual for those who were walking past in the darkness to shake an amused head at the breathless and joyous sounds emanating from the house behind the library. In Baileyville, in winter, there was not much to do after the sun went down, after all.

Sophia and William moved back to Louisville. She did not want to leave the library, she told the other women, but she had been offered a job back at the Louisville Free Public Library (Colored Branch) and, given their cabin hadn't been the same since the floods, and William's chances of work were limited, they figured they would do better in the city, especially a city where there were large populations of people like themselves. Professional people. Izzy cried, and the others didn't feel much better about it, but there was no arguing with good sense—and not much arguing with Sophia. Some time later, when they started to receive the letters she forwarded from the city, and the photograph of her promotion, they framed it, and put it up on the wall, next to the one of them all together, and felt a little better about it. Though it had to be said, the shelves were never quite as well organized again.

Kathleen, true to her word, did not remarry, although there was no shortage of men who stopped by asking to court her once a decent amount of time had passed. She had no time for all that, she told the other librarians, what with the washing and the cleaning and looking after her children on top of her work. Besides, there was not a man who could measure up to Garrett Bligh in the whole state. Though she would admit, when pushed, that she had been a little taken aback at how Jim Horner had scrubbed up at Alice's wedding, having received the attention of a professional barber and put on his good suit. His face was quite pleasing, liberated from all that hair, and his general appearance was much improved out of his dirty overalls. She would not marry again, oh, no, she was adamant, but within a few months it was not unusual for the two of them to be seen taking a stroll around the town with their children and maybe attending a local fair together in the spring. It was good for his girls to have a feminine influence after all, and if there were some sly looks and raised eyebrows, well, that was their business. And Beth could stop looking at her like that, *thank you very much.*

Beth's life remained largely unchanged immediately following the trial. She remained at home with her father and brothers, complained bitterly about them at every turn, smoked in private, drank in public, then surprised everybody six months later by announcing that she had saved every penny she had ever earned and was about to leave on an ocean liner to see the continent of India. They laughed at this at first—Beth was possessed, after all, of the strangest sense of humor—but she pulled the ticket from her saddlebag to show them. "How on earth did you raise all that money?" said Izzy, confused. "You told me your daddy took half of it toward running the house."

Beth grew uncharacteristically tongue-tied and stammered out some response to do with extra work and savings that were her own and not knowing why everyone in this darn town needed to know each other's business anyway. And when, a month after she had departed, the sheriff uncovered an abandoned still over by Johnsons' fallen-down cow barn, the ground around it littered with cigarette butts, it was decreed that the two things could not possibly be related. Or, at least, that was how they put it to her father.

Her first letter came from a place called Surat and had the fanciest postmark you ever saw and contained a picture of her wearing a brightly colored embroidered robe called a sari and holding a peacock under her arm. Kathleen exclaimed that it wouldn't shock her a whit if Beth ended up marrying the King of India because that girl was plumb full of surprises. To which Margery responded drily that that would certainly surprise them all.

Izzy cut a record, with her father's permission. Within two years she had become one of Kentucky's most popular singers, known for the purity of her voice and her penchant for performing in floor-length flowing dresses. She recorded a song about a murder in the hills that was popular across three states and performed an onstage duet with Tex Lafayette at a music hall in Knoxville that left her quite overcome for the best part of a week afterward, not least because he held her hand during the high notes. Mrs. Brady said that when it reached number four in the gramophone charts, it was the proudest moment in her life. Second only, she admitted privately, to the letter she had received from Mrs. Lena C. Nofcier some two months after the close of the trial, thanking her for her extraordinary efforts in keeping the WPA Packhorse Library, Baileyville, running in a time of crisis.

We women face many unexpected challenges when we choose to step outside what are considered our habitual boundaries. And you, dear Mrs. Brady, have proven yourself more than a match to any such challenge that has arisen. I look forward to discussing this and many other pertinent issues in person with you one day.

Mrs. Nofcier had not yet made it as far as Baileyville but Mrs. Brady was pretty sure it was going to happen.

The library opened five days a week, its management split between Alice and Margery, and during that time the women continued to lend every possible kind of novel, manual, recipe book and magazine. Memories of the trial faded quickly, especially among those who realized they might like to continue to borrow books after all, and life in Baileyville returned to its normal rhythms. Only the Van Cleve men seemed at pains to avoid the library, driving their cars at speed up and down Split Creek, and mostly taking a route some way around town to avoid that building altogether.

So when, several months into 1939, Peggy Van Cleve stopped by, it came as something of a surprise. Margery watched her spend some moments loitering outside as if searching for something vitally important in her purse, then peering through the window to check if Margery was on her own. She wasn't known to be the most voracious of readers, after all.

Margery O'Hare was a busy woman, what with Virginia, the dog and her husband, and all the many distractions her home seemed to hold, these days. But that evening she would break off what she was doing and smile to herself, wondering whether to tell Alice Guisler how the new Mrs. Van Cleve had stepped inside, lowered her voice, and after some prevarication and a lot of theatrical scanning of random titles on the shelves, asked whether there was truth in the rumor that there was a book here that advised ladies regarding certain *sensitive matters relating to the bedroom*. Or how Margery had kept a straight face and said, why, yes, of course. It was just the facts, after all.

She would still be thinking about it—and still trying not to smile— when they all arrived back at the library the following day.

POSTSCRIPT

The WPA's Packhorse Librarians of Kentucky program ran from 1935 to 1943. At its height it brought books to more than a hundred thousand rural inhabitants. No program like it has ever been set up since.

Eastern Kentucky remains one of the poorest—and most beautiful—places in the United States.

Acknowledgments

T his book, more than anything I've ever written, was a labor of love. I fell in love with a place and its people, and then the story as it came, and that made writing an unusual joy. To that end I want to thank Barbara Napier and everyone at Snug Hollow in Irvine, Kentucky, especially Olivia Knuckles, without whose voices I wouldn't have found those of my heroines. Your spirit and that of the holler runs through this book and I am so happy to call you friends.

Thank you to everyone at Whisper Valley Trails in the Cumberland Mountains, who enabled me to ride the kind of routes that the women would have done, and to everyone I stopped and quizzed and harangued and chatted to during my travels.

Closer to home, I'd like to thank my editors Louise Moore and Maxine Hitchcock of Penguin Michael Joseph in the UK, Pam Dorman of Pamela Dorman Books, Penguin Random House in the US, and Katharina Dornhoefer of Rowohlt in Germany, none of whom flinched when I told them that my next book would be about a group of horseback librarians in rural America during the Depression. Even though I suspect they might have wanted to. Thank you all also for continuing to help me better my books—all stories are a collaborative endeavor—and for your continuing faith in them and in me. Thanks to Clare Parker and Louise Braverman, Liz Smith, Claire Bush, Kate Stark and Lydia Hirt and all the teams at each publishing house for your awesome skills in helping me get these stories in front of people. On a wider scale, thanks to Tom Weldon and Brian Tart and in Germany to Anoukh Foerg.

Thanks as ever to Sheila Crowley at Curtis Brown for being cheerleader, sales guru, fierce negotiator and emotional support in one. And to Claire Nozieres, Katie McGowan and Enrichetta Frezzato for keeping it global on a fairly spectacular scale. Thank you also to Bob Bookman of Bob Bookman Management, Jonny Geller and Nick Marston for the task of keeping this machine running across all sorts of media. You all rock.

A big thanks to Alison Owen of Monumental Pictures for "seeing" this story when it was just an elevator pitch, and for your ongoing enthusiasm, and to Ol Parker for the same, and for helping me shape key scenes and making it fun. I can't wait to see what you do with it.

Heartfelt thanks to Cathy Runciman for driving duties across Kentucky and Tennessee and making me laugh so much we nearly ran off the road more than once. Our friendship is embedded in these pages too.

Thanks also to Maddy Wickham, Damian Barr, Alex Heminsley, Monica Lewinsky, Thea Sharrock, Sarah Phelps and Caitlin Moran. You all know what for.

Gratitude as ever to Jackie Tearne, Claire Roweth and Leon Kirk for all the logistical and practical backup without which I couldn't get through each week, let alone life. It is so very much appreciated.

I'm indebted to the Kentucky Tourist Board for its advice, and thank you to everyone who helped me in Lee and Estill Counties. And Green Park, for being an unlikely source of inspiration.

And last but very much not least thanks as ever to my family: to Jim Moyes, Lizzie Sanders and Brian Sanders. And most of all to Charles, Saskia, Harry and Lockie.